GOBBELINO LONDON & A MENACE OF MERMAIDS

GOBBELINO LONDON, PI
BOOK SIX

KIM M. WATT

For further information contact www.kmwatt.com

Cover design: Monika McFarland, www.ampersandbookcovers.com

Editor: Lynda Dietz, www.easyreaderediting.com

ISBN ePub: 978-1-7385854-1-0

ISBN Ingrams paperback: 978-1-7385854-3-4

ISBN KDP paperback: 978-1-7385854-2-7

First Edition May 2023

10 9 8 7 6 5 4 3 2 1

CONTENTS

*To everyone
who ever wanted to run away to sea
and become a pirate.
(It's not too late.)*

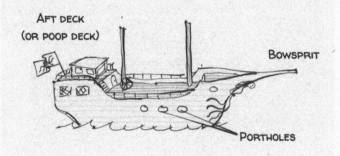

AFT DECK
(OR POOP DECK)

BOWSPRIT

PORTHOLES

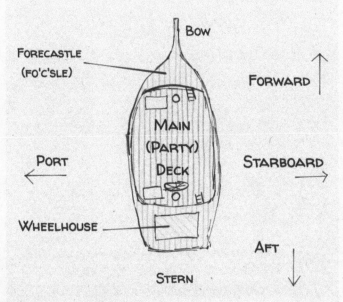

BOW

FORECASTLE
(FO'C'SLE)

FORWARD

MAIN
(PARTY)
DECK

PORT

STARBOARD

WHEELHOUSE

AFT

STERN

ALL YOU CAN DRINK RUM PUNCH!
*safety not guaranteed.
*please mind the mermaids.

THE SAVAGE SQUID
WHITBY PIRATE CRUISES

PIRATE DICTIONARY

Aft: indicating direction toward the back of the boat (he's gone aft; or it's aft of the cabin). Opposite to *forward*.

Avast that: pirate speak for *stop that*.

Belay that: also pirate speak for *stop that*, although to belay something is also to make it fast. Pirates were kind of keen on people not doing things, apparently.

Bilge: the mucky spaces at the bottom of the hull, on the inside (under the floorboards for the most part, except usually around the engine, where they're often open). Guaranteed, any tool or part dropped while working on the engine ends up lost in the bilge, often under an appetising mix of sea water and oil. Also used to indicate someone's talking rubbish.

Bow: the pointy bit at the front. The *bowsprit* sticks out from it.

Forecastle: pronounced (and sometimes written) *fo'c'sle*. The forward cabin of the boat.

Forward: indicating direction toward, well, the front bit of the boat. Often pronounced as *for'ard*, and the opposite to *aft*.

Galley: what a boat kitchen is called. (Also a type of old-school boat, but that's not really relevant right here.)

Gunwales: pronounced *gunnels*. The top bit of a boat's sides.

Head: what a boat toilet is called – can be just the toilet itself, or often the whole bathroom setup.

Hornswoggle: *arr.* To swindle someone.

Keelhaul: a really nasty punishment, where someone is thrown overboard and lines (ropes) are used to drag them under the boat and back up the other side. Not only are they trapped by the lines, but where a boat has lots of barnacles after a long slow passage, ow.

Midships: the, um, middle part of the boat.

Painter: someone who paints. No, in the nautical sense it's a line (which is a piece of rope but if you call it rope someone's going to whisper *landlubber* behind you) on the bow of a dinghy, used to tie it up.

Poop deck: no snickering. The raised aft deck of an old sailing ship, which usually has the captain's cabin under it.

Port: the left side of the boat as you face the bow. Opposite to *starboard*. These don't change – port is always port, so if you face aft, the port side will now be on your right.

Port (2): another name for a harbour. Or a fortified wine. You know, there are a few uses of port, now I think about it.

Ports/portholes: little, often round windows in the hull of the boat. Sometimes they open, sometimes they don't. Cannons also have ports to fire through, but they don't have glass in them. Obviously.

Rudder: the paddle bit in the water at the back (stern), which is moved by turning the wheel or moving the tiller, and so directs the boat.

Scupper that: to scupper something is to sink it, so this is an exclamation suggesting someone should give up on an idea if they know what's good for them.

Standing rigging: rigging that isn't walking. No, sorry. Standing rigging is a term that covers the bits of line and wire that hold the masts in place. They don't move. *Running rigging*, on the other hand, are the bits of line that do move, such as to raise sails, but the poor old *Squid* is rather lacking on that front.

Starboard: the right-hand side of the boat as you face the bow. Opposite to *port*.

Stern: the back of the boat. Or, if you've been paying attention, the *aft end*.

Swab: a bit of a derogatory term for a low-ranking sailor, whose chores often included *swabbing*, or mopping the decks.

Tiller: a stick-like bit attached directly to the rudder that smaller boats use to steer rather than a wheel (smaller outboard motors also use tillers).

There are many more that I've missed, but that should be enough to be going on with. I will offer the disclaimer that this book is not *entirely* factual (I know! Shocking, right?), so I'm not being too picky on my maritime terms.

1

IT'S THE PIRATE LIFE FOR US

THE EARLY AFTERNOON LIGHT WAS THIN AND RELUCTANT, trapped between a lowering bank of heavy dark clouds and the slow roll of the cold green sea that spread out from the shore to chase the horizon. Raw cliffs heaved themselves out of reaching waves like monsters intent on escape, and houses tumbled down scarred folds in the land to meet the enclosed curve of the harbour. Everywhere was the heavy scent of salt and cold wind and restless movement, underscored by the cries of gulls. The ship rolled with the swells, humming with the throb of the engine, and behind us the decks heaved to the stomping feet of a pirate horde.

A parrot screamed from the rigging, using language that would likely be described as authentic, and someone shrieked a reply, waving a cutlass above their head with inadvisable enthusiasm and sending a feathered hat flying into the sea.

"Rum! More rum, me hearties!" someone bellowed.

This was greeted with a cheer and a general exhortation that someone needed to walk the plank, although the who was a little vague. The North Sea in February wasn't exactly encouraging anyone to volunteer, and our pirate captain – who, as it happened, was the one shouting for more rum – didn't seem inclined to nominate anyone. Probably be a nightmare for health and safety, although I was unconvinced as to just how much attention was paid to such things around here.

I adjusted my position against the heavy wooden railings that surrounded the decks. After the first couple of sorties I'd kept my tail out of the way of the horde. It turned out that drunken pirates either got alarmingly grabby when confronted with a good-looking black cat (my scars just give me more character and add a touch of realism to the whole pirate boat scene), or careless as to where they put their boots, and neither scenario exactly filled me with joy. So I was currently tucked into a nook where the rigging ran down to meet the deck, the jumble of unused ropes and pulleys and mysterious bits and bobs attached to the planking and railing giving me a good vantage point of the piracy while I could remain mostly unseen.

"*More rum, you scurvy dog!*" the captain shouted again, leaning out of the wheelhouse. "Don't make me keelhaul you like the last deckie!" She shook a wooden stick in my general direction before vanishing back inside.

Next to me, Callum adjusted the red bandanna on his head and said, "I'm never sure how serious she is about that."

"Well, we never met the previous deckhand," I said. "Take from that what you will."

Callum sighed. "The pirate with the big hat pinched my bum when I took the last round of drinks out. She asked me if I was an obliging cabin boy."

I squinted at the sea. "Tell Green Snake to pinch her back."

The snake in question lifted his head out of Callum's coat pocket and looked at me inquiringly.

"You could do to make yourself useful," I told him. "*We've* both got jobs."

"Yes, you're working so hard at keeping the ship rat-free," Callum said.

"It's a delicate process."

He looked back at the captain, who gesticulated in a way that suggested she was saying more than *scurvy dog*. "This isn't."

"We must be almost done for the day. It's looking really nasty out there." I lifted my snout at the clouds that were building up in woolly layers across the sky, stealing the pale winter light.

"Says the experienced ship's cat."

"*I* don't get seasick."

"That was *once*." Callum pushed off the wooden rail with a sigh. "I almost miss our flat."

"Oddly, I'm not that homesick for a flat that tried to eat me."

"Eh. Fair point."

"*Callum!*" the captain hissed, then hurriedly added an *arr* to the end. She'd emerged from the wheelhouse that perched above the main deck where we stood, and she leaned over the poop deck rails to glare down at us with her one good eye and one false one. It was unnerving, that eye, particularly as she changed it regularly. Today's was a warm brown that wouldn't have looked out of place on a teddy bear, but looked very out of place on a human. "They're going to raid the bloody bar in a minute – get serving! And bring me a top-up."

"Okay—"

"No," she started, and Callum waved apologetically.

"I mean, aye, aye, Cap." He flipped his eyepatch back down and scowled at me. "I don't mean I actually want to go back to our flat. And the boat's not so bad. But *this* I am not enjoying."

"I would help, but no thumbs," I said, raising one paw to demonstrate.

"Convenient." He mustered a grin from somewhere then turned and edged into the crowd, trying to avoid the grabby pirate in the big hat, and vanished into the forward cabin. He emerged a moment later to a chorus of cheers, carting two big jugs of rum punch.

"More grog!" he shouted, and the captain popped out of the wheelhouse again to yell, "*Arr!*" while glaring at him furiously.

"*Arr*," Callum agreed, with rather less enthusiasm, as the overexcited pirates swamped him and he concentrated on topping up the plastic glasses being waved in his general direction. We went through copious quantities of said grog on every trip, and I had a suspicion that the bit on the dock sign that read ALL YOU CAN DRINK RUM PUNCH INCLUDED!!! was the main reason we were still busy in the depths of a North Yorkshire winter.

I also had suspicions that *rum punch* was overstating things somewhat, as when Hilda, our one-eyed, white-haired, parrot-owning captain had shown Callum how to make it, it had mostly consisted of half a bottle of dubious spirits with a blurry, misprinted label that *might* have said something about rum, but also might have said *rubbing alcohol*; a carton of nearly out of date tropical juice that promised it was made from 100 percent fruit flavourings; and a can of fruit salad with a torn label and a dented side.

Not that our current pirate party were too worried. It was someone's birthday, or wedding, or who knew what, and they'd evidently been celebrating fairly enthusiastically before they even got on board. And, to be fair, no one ever seemed to complain after the first couple of drinks. Callum had had to half-carry two very drunken sailors ashore last week, and they'd been so delighted they'd promised to give us five stars on TripAdvisor.

A *sploosh* pricked my ears, pulling my attention back to the muscular sea. We'd only been working on board for a few weeks, ever since the landlord at the boarding house had slapped Hilda's business card in front of us and grunted, "Job."

We'd rocked up to the dock expecting another day of cleaning things, which was how we'd been paying our rent since we'd arrived in Whitby. But Hilda had offered us an *actual* job, accommodation included, and we'd taken it. I mean, *job* was pushing things a little, as she had yet to actually pay us, but we got a share of tips (more rum punch equalled more tips, we'd discovered, so it paid to be generous), a steady supply of tea, leftover party food, and even the odd tin of tuna, plus a bed somewhere that didn't have the boiled meat whiff of the boarding house. Although there was a persistent funk of pipe smoke and seaweed, which I wasn't sure was better.

Anyhow, we hadn't been here that long, but a few weeks was enough for me to know what were usual boat noises and what weren't. That *sploosh* wasn't usual. I peered over the high, dark-painted wooden sides, down to the water, and met the gaze of a man looking back at me. I blinked at him. He was in a small wooden dinghy that had seen better days, water washing around his ankles, and there was just one oar hanging out the back like a tail. *The Savage Squid* was not built for speed, but she was still faster than the man should have been able to row, no matter how many oars he had.

Well, *man*. Male-looking, but likely not human, which probably pointed to unusual rowing methods. He had sharp, bright edges that marked him as Folk, and he spoke directly to me in a way humans rarely do.

"Permission to come aboard?" he asked. His voice was all easy curves, like sun on a windless sea, and he gave the same impression. Hard muscle under the softness of good insulation.

"Why?" I asked.

"Because there's weather coming in, and I've only got a little dinghy." He indicated it. It seemed to have taken on more water just in the few moments since I'd seen him, and there was sand in the bottom. Also a starfish that was trying to climb his leg. He ignored it, standing straddling the midships seat and clinging to one of the ports as he looked up at me with big dark eyes.

"Should've gone out in something bigger, then, shouldn't you?" I said.

He grinned, a flash of white teeth in the dim day rendered strange by the wash of multicoloured lights coming from the strings that hung over the deck. "If I had something bigger, I would've."

We looked at each other for a moment, then I caught the scuff of worn trainers on the deck, and Callum leaned on the rail next to me, flipping up his eyepatch. "I swear Hilda drinks more of that punch than they do— Hello."

"Hello," the man in the dinghy said. "Permission to come aboard?"

"Um—"

"We can't give permission," I said, the hair along my spine starting to creep up. I wasn't sure if it was those wide liquid eyes, or the shiny white teeth, or the fact that I just couldn't smell him right. He was all muddled up with the diesel fumes of the engine, and the flat salt of the sea, and a fishy whiff that both made my mouth water and made me wish we were back in Leeds, miles from the bloody seaside.

"Of course you can," he said. "Help a guy out, can't you? That weather's looking nasty, and all I've got is a little dinghy. I won't make it into the harbour in time if I have to row."

"Well," Callum started, and I interrupted him.

"We're just crew. The captain has to give permission."

A shadow of irritation passed over the man's face, and he glanced behind him at a sudden swirl in the water, accompanied by a deep, hungry *splosh*. When he looked back at us, the irritation had given way to something with raw, fearful edges. "Please?" he whispered. "I really won't make it in."

Callum extended his hand. "Throw me a line."

The man didn't. He just grasped Callum's hand with his own, his grin widening, and there were *far* too many teeth in it. Sharp ones. And his eyes were too big and round and dark, the whites non-existent, and *he* was too big, bigger than Callum. He pulled, and Callum slipped, his own eyes widening in alarm. He tried to brace himself against the rail.

"Hang about, I can't—"

The man reached up with his other hand, grabbing for Callum's shoulder as if he'd topple him into the water, an offering to whatever was *splosh*ing about down there. He was still grinning, and Callum tried to pull away, but the angle was bad and muscle rolled on the man's shoulders, raw and powerful.

"Say permission to board," the man said.

"What're you *doing?*" Callum twisted, fighting the man's grip, but he just pulled harder, and quite suddenly Callum's toes were barely touching the deck. "*Hey!*"

"*Say it.*"

Well, there went the pleasantries. I leaped for the rail, touched it as I went over and launched myself at our would-be boarder, baring my teeth in a poor imitation of his own. He gave a startled yelp and shielded his face with one hand, but still clung to Callum with the other. I latched onto his forearm with a growl, biting down hard and tasting the salt on his clammy skin.

"Gobs!" Callum hissed. "Gobs, stop that!"

"*Me?*" I demanded, spitting out my mouthful of weird seaman, and at that moment the dinghy surged, as if buffeted by an unexpected swell. The man staggered, and only his grip on Callum stopped him falling. I dug my claws in harder, suddenly not wanting to be any closer to the opaque surface of the cold green sea.

"Please let me up," the man said, and he looked suddenly no more toothy than anyone else. "Please!"

"Give me Gobs," Callum said, nodding at me. The man lifted me up, and I scrambled back onto the boat, eyes on the water. *There*. Another swell, at odds to the first, but whatever caused it was too quick or too hidden. I couldn't see what might be under the surface, but the hair on my tail took exception and puffed up in alarm.

"Now, please." The man looked up at Callum pleadingly. "*Please*. They're almost here."

Callum didn't bother to ask what. I guess he could see those weird movements below the dinghy as well, and he never could resist a good rescue. "Come on," he said, bracing himself. "Permission to board."

The man threw himself at the boat, stretching to reach the rail and using his grip on Callum to help lever himself higher. The dinghy bobbed heavily as his weight left it, bouncing once against the hull then spinning away as we kept powering back toward the harbour. The man got one arm over the railing, released Callum so he could use both hands, and muscled himself up until his waist was resting on the heavy wood of the rail. He paused there for a moment, breathing hard, and I had an idea it was less from effort than relief.

"Thank you," he managed. "Really, thank you so much—"

"*No!*" Hilda grabbed Callum, hauled him backward, and swung a knobbly walking stick straight at the man's face. He yelped, dropping down off the rail until he was clinging on by his fingertips.

"What're you doing?" Callum demanded, trying to put himself between Hilda and our new arrival.

She poked Callum with her stick. "Me? What're *you* doing? Did you invite him aboard?"

"Yes! He's in trouble."

"He *is* bloody trouble. They all are." She poked Callum again, hard enough to force him back, then swung around and slammed her stick down on the man's fingers. "*Permission revoked!*"

The man howled and let go with one hand, dangling precariously from the other as he swung away from the hull. He tried to swing back in, scrabbling for another grip, but before he could find one Hilda dealt the same unforgiving shot to his other hand.

"Oh, you savage old—" The rest was lost as the man hit the water, and Callum and I hung over the side, staring into our wake. The man didn't surface.

Callum stared at Hilda. "What did you *do?*"

"You don't invite them on board! You never invite them on board!" Hilda leaned her walking stick against the rail and dug a flask out of her faded waterproof coat, taking a generous swig. "Never! No mermaids on board!"

"*What?*" Callum and I asked together, because if that had been a mermaid then some old sailors had some serious explaining to do.

"Polly says no mermaids," the parrot shrieked, swooping

down to land on Hilda's shoulder in a flurry of green and gold.

The crowd cheered, and someone shouted, "Does Polly want a cracker?"

"No, Polly want a bloody holiday and some decent single malt," the parrot said, but kept his voice low.

"Don't we all," Hilda said, and stomped back off to the wheelhouse, lurching slightly. I wasn't entirely sure if she had a peg leg or not, since she always wore long black trousers that were in even worse repair than Callum's jeans, and old blue wellies with gaffer tape holding the soles on, but given the limp, I felt the odds were good.

The pirate party was shouting for more rum again, and demanding to know if Polly did any tricks, but Callum and I ignored them, leaning back over the side. There was that *sploosh* again, and the man – mermaid, whatever – surfaced, keeping pace with us as we pottered back toward harbour. His eyes were even wider than before, and he stuck as close to the hull as he could, moving with it like a dolphin.

"Please help," he hissed.

"We really can't," Callum said. "We'll get fired."

"Gods forbid," I muttered, although it wasn't like we had any better options at the moment.

"*They're going to kill me*," the mermaid said, and there was a tremor on the edge of his voice.

Callum looked at me.

"No," I said.

"They're going to kill him."

"Maybe he deserves it. We don't know him. We don't even know who *they* are."

Splash **splash**. Harder and sharper this time, and the mermaid cursed in a way that suggested sailors might have picked up a lot of their vocabulary from unexpected sources. Pressure waves ran though the water, suggesting big, fast shapes powering under the surface, bigger than the mermaid. He moaned in fright, scrabbling at the hull, and Callum said to me, "Keep an eye out for Hilda."

"Sure," I said. "Great. I'm sure she doesn't know at all what she's talking about when she told us that mermaids can't come aboard. I'm sure it's just a harmless prejudice. I—" I stopped, because Callum had run back down the deck and out of earshot, to where the rubber-tubed dinghy was tied at the stern. We didn't technically need the dinghy, since we never put ashore anywhere but the town dock, but Hilda always kept it handy. It seemed that a fair proportion of evening cruises ended up with someone in the water by accident or design, and hefting them into the dinghy was easier than persuading drunk people to climb rope ladders. Which illustrated the health and safety standards aboard *The Savage Squid* pretty well.

I checked the wheelhouse, but Hilda was arguing with the parrot about something and wasn't paying any attention to anyone else, and the partiers had discovered the last couple of jugs of rum punch and were helping themselves. I ran after Callum instead, in time to see the dinghy's outboard start up with a cough of oily smoke. Before I could reach the stern he'd already unclipped the painter line and jammed the engine into gear, roaring up alongside the boat. The mermaid abandoned the shelter of the hull and shot across to him, vanishing under the surface then surfacing in a leap that landed him straight in the dinghy. I had the confused impression of a seal-like, grey body, then he was human shaped again, shouting, "Go, *go*, hurry!"

Twin swells shot toward the dinghy, like torpedoes racing for a target, and Callum opened the throttle up. The dinghy wasn't big, and the engine wasn't either, but the mermaid threw his bulk forward and the little vessel lifted as it sped up, until it was skipping across the water, tearing toward the pincer-like opening of the harbour. Hilda stuck her head out of the wheelhouse and bellowed, *"You son of a sea biscuit!"* at the dinghy as it vanished ahead of us.

I ran for the bow, trying to get a better view, and poked my head under the rail in time to see two giant fins surface, speeding after the dinghy. Someone was clinging to one of them, and I had that same confused sense of a human/not human shape, this one crowned with kelp-green hair. Dinghy-mermaid obviously spotted them too, because he started shouting and waving, and Callum glanced back. He tried a bit of evasive action, spinning the dinghy in one direction then the other, but all that did was slow the little boat down, and the fins followed effortlessly. Sleek dark backs emerged as the creatures surfaced in tandem, puffing air, then slipped back down, their fins slicing the water as slickly as claws through custard. Kelpy kept pace effortlessly, one moment as indistinct and water-bound as a seal, the next raising smooth bare arms over their head as they dived, hitching a ride on a fin then rolling free on the pressure wave of the creatures' passage.

Water swirled as the trio closed on the dinghy, then suddenly the surface was empty. I couldn't see where they were, which was even worse than watching two angry fish-monsters bearing down on Callum. The harbour loomed just ahead of the dinghy, tucked behind the protection of piers, and the lights of the beacons blipped green and red in the dull grey afternoon. Callum and the mermaid were both leaning forward in the little boat, and the engine screamed as they pelted toward shelter, and for a moment I thought they might make it.

Then the fins broke the surface again, bulleting toward them, far faster than the dinghy could hope to outrun.

"Aw, sink me," I hissed.

I raced back to the wheelhouse, dodging a couple of

shouts of "puss puss!" and some cheers, skidded through the open door and gave Hilda my best big eyes.

"Help them!"

"I told him," she said, not taking her gaze off the dinghy scudding ahead of us. "I *said* mermaids are bad news."

"You can't just let those bloody great fish eat him," I insisted. "You *can't!*"

She shot me a glare from her mismatched eyes that would've had all the hair on my back standing up if the mermaid hadn't already seen to that. "I bloody can," she said, and I was about to see if I could make her eyes match when she glanced at the parrot, sitting on a perch by the door. "But best not. There'll be questions."

"*Arr*," the parrot said. "Polly doesn't like questions."

"No," Hilda agreed, and snatched something off one of the shelves that ran around the top of the wheelhouse, above the windows. She gave it to Polly, who grabbed it in one claw and launched himself out over the boat.

"Polly want a sodding raise and some mangoes, though," he shouted as he surged forward with heavy wingbeats, closing the distance to the dinghy rapidly. The fins were criss-crossing its wake, and as we watched one slipped underneath the little boat and rose up again, giving us a glimpse of a powerful piebald body as it lifted the dinghy clear of the sea. Callum and the mermaid were both shouting, the words indistinguishable from here, and the engine screamed as it lost its grip on the water. The little boat hesitated, looking for a moment as if it might flip, then slid off the creature's smooth back, bouncing violently in the churned-up sea.

"How is the bloody *parrot* helping?" I demanded, but Hilda didn't reply. I sprinted back along the deck to the bow, jumping to a vantage point in time to see the dinghy spinning helplessly in a circle, the water boiling as powerful tails worked beneath it. Kelpy was keeping their distance, just visible as a sleek green-brown head and a pair of hands applauding cheerily.

Callum was about to become fish food.

And there was absolutely nothing I could do about it.

2

IT'S NOT JUST THE SMELL THAT'S FISHY

POLLY SWUNG DOWN TOWARD THE WATER AS THE DINGHY'S stern popped suddenly up into the air, the engine giving its panicked screech. The bow dug down hard, pulled by something unseen, while Callum and the mermaid clung on desperately. I still didn't know what the parrot was carrying, and I couldn't see it from this distance, but he dropped it between the swimming mermaid and the dinghy. It barely even made a splash.

I turned to glare at the wheelhouse, wanting to ask Hilda if she had any better plans, and there was a dull, muted, *doof*. I felt it more than heard it, a pressure wave against my ears, and I spun back to see a fat column of water exploding upward toward the parrot. The dinghy crashed back down and shot forward as if someone had given it a slap on the bum, and both Callum and the mermaid ducked into the bottom. The fins surged into sight in an explosion of bubbles and turbulence. One rolled over, the creature flashing a white belly to the sky, bobbed for a moment, then recovered and fled for deeper water. The other turned in three circles, the giant fin leaning under its own momentum, then followed its buddy. The kelp-haired mermaid had both hands pressed to their ears, and they turned to stare at *The Savage Squid*. I could see the flash of white teeth from here, bared and furious. In the dinghy, our rescued mermaid sat up and clapped appreciatively, then waved at the parrot.

The parrot swept back to the boat, and as he went over me he called, "Polly want more than a pat on the head and a shortbread biscuit for this bollocks. Polly got their feet wet."

Callum and the mermaid got the dinghy underway again, heading for the wharf with both of them spending more time looking over their shoulders than at where they were going. *The Savage Squid* bore down on the kelp-haired mermaid as they watched the dinghy go, still with their hands over their ears. For one moment I thought Kelpy was going to be tragically run down by a pirate ship, then the creature looked around at us, flashed a white-toothed, furious snarl, and slipped beneath the surface. They left a swirl of disturbed water in their wake, and I checked on the dinghy again, wondering if we had to keep the rescued mermaid now, and what we were meant to do with it if so. It was enough that we'd acquired a Green Snake. A mermaid seemed excessive.

We docked up without any more strange fins getting in the way, and, as far as I could tell, without running over Kelpy. There was no unexpected bump in our passage, and no one bobbing in our wake, at least, although I wasn't sure if that was a good thing or not. Callum had already tied the dinghy up, and he jumped to *The Savage Squid* from the wharf as Hilda kissed the big boat softly alongside. He grabbed the mooring lines and threw them up to the mermaid, who trussed the boat up with a couple of easy turns around the big metal bollards on the dock, making it look effortless. I suppose he was used to tying up sailors with seaweed, or whatever mermaids get up to.

The pirate party were ushered off, mostly by Hilda standing on the deck and bellowing that if every single scallywag didn't walk the plank in the next five minutes they'd be fish chum. The party cheered good-naturedly and tottered off the gangway without anyone ending up in the harbour, and after a few minutes of Callum trying not to get his bum pinched again they finally accepted he wasn't coming with them. I padded up the gangway and jumped to the top of the nearest bollard to watch Callum putting his dimples to good use as he waved them off, which resulted in quite a few ten-pound notes being tucked into his pockets with varying degrees of affection. The parrot sat on the crosstrees of one of the sail-less masts and every now and then squawked in a bored tone, "*Arr*, pieces of eight, me hearties."

Hilda stumped about checking the mooring lines with her collar turned up and a pipe stuck unlit in the corner of her mouth – she *had* to have a peg leg, I was sure of it – and *arr*-ed a bit as well, throwing in the odd "yo ho ho" for good measure, until finally the boat was empty but for a load of discarded plastic cups and bits of sausage roll and fish fingers trodden into the deck. Callum looked at it and sighed, then dug his tips out of his pockets and handed them to Hilda.

"*Arr*," she said absently, shuffling through the notes. "Should bloody well keep the lot. You invited a *mermaid* on board. Bloody pests, they are."

"We are not," the mermaid said from the dock. "And you'll notice I'm not *on* your boat."

"Not for want of trying," Hilda said, popping her false eye out and shoving another one in its place. It was an angry green, and she used it to glare at the mermaid.

"Polly want some pineapple," the parrot said.

"There's some fruit left in the jugs still," Hilda said, waving vaguely.

"Polly doesn't want *canned* fruit."

"Polly will eat what they're given or it'll be roast bird for Sunday dinner," Hilda replied, tapping her pipe out on the rail.

"Polly want a new human."

"We've all been there," I said to the parrot, who looked at the sky.

"Thanks for the ... whatever you did," Callum said. "Those things were close."

"Just a bit of light explosives," Hilda said. "Not allowed to use it for fishing anymore, but I've still got some lying around."

"That's reassuring," I said, more to myself than anyone else.

"Right, well. Thanks anyway," Callum said, fishing his cigarettes out of his coat pocket.

"Eh. You'd be a decent deckhand if you stopped trying to drag mermaids on board."

"It was the first time," he protested.

"He was following the code of the sea," the mermaid put in. "Helping out a fellow seaman in peril."

"You're a *mermaid*, and I'm certain the peril was entirely your own making," Hilda said, scowling.

"What was chasing you?" Callum asked. "Those fins?"

"Orcas," the mermaid said. "Some mermaids use them for a bit of speed."

"You mean the law keepers use them," Hilda said. "What've you been up to, then? Thieving? Smuggling? Murdering?"

"*Harsh.* Also pot, kettle, and all that."

Hilda crossed her arms. "I'm a legitimate businesswoman."

"You're a *pirate*."

"It's all just a bloody gimmick," she snapped. "Anyway, no one's setting orcas on *me*."

The mermaid shrugged. "It's not my fault some people in power have taken a dislike to me." He hesitated. "Although there may have been a *teeny* bit of redistribution of wealth. But that's just because *some people* like to hoard it." He raised his eyebrows at Hilda, who *hmph*-ed and inspected her pipe.

"Cool," I said. "So we just helped an outlaw mermaid? Does that mean we're in the mermaid bad books now? Banned from the sea?" That wouldn't be so terrible. I'd been happy to be out of the boarding house, but the boat was already starting to wear thin. My fur carried a permanent whiff of seaweed, and Callum was adding a layer of engine oil and dead fish to his usual scents of old cigarettes and strange losses.

"I doubt it," the mermaid said. "They were after me. You'd have just been collateral."

Callum lit his cigarette and offered the pack to the mermaid, who made a face. Callum tucked them away again and said, "You can't complain, Gobs. You're very familiar with people taking a dislike to you."

"*Unfair*," I said. "And I didn't try to pull anyone overboard." I glared at the mermaid, and he shrugged.

"I was panicking. I wasn't *really* trying to pull you in."

Callum nodded as if it didn't matter one way or the other. He really had to learn how to carry a better grudge, simply as a matter of survival. "What's your name?" he asked instead.

"Murchadh," the mermaid said. "But Murty's fine."

Callum offered his hand and they shook, although I'd think that having outrun the mermaid authorities and their hungry panda fish together, they could probably skip the formal introductions.

"You're not permitted on board," Hilda said, pointing her

pipe stem at Murty. "You keep your slimy little flippers on land."

"Sure, sure." He leaned against the back of one of the sheds that lined the wharf. "I'm not interested in your petty wee boat. It doesn't even have sails."

"And what good would they do where you'd take her, anyway?"

"It's a question of appearances."

Hilda *arr*-ed again, and held a handful of notes out to Callum. I was fairly sure it was less than half what we'd taken, but at least it was something. "Make sure you don't let him on board. And you"—she jabbed her pipe at me—"catch some damn rats, can't you?"

"Sure," I said. "They're a bit sneaky is all. Ship's rats, you know. Clever."

"I know they're clever. They won't eat the damn poison or get in the traps. But I can't be having them aboard. That's why you're here."

"I mean, I get that it's probably a bad look for the tourists, but is the odd rat so awful?" I asked.

"These ones are," Hilda said, fixing her false eye on me fiercely. "So you catch them, or there'll be no more kibble."

"Oh, woe," I said, and Callum poked me. I gave him a dirty look. The one thing Whitby had going for it was how easy it was to cadge fish off the locals. That, and the fact that it had turned out to be a good place to be unnoticed. No one noticed weird in Whitby.

Hilda looked from me to Callum. "You just stay in town, right? No matter what bloody mermaids tell you."

"Of course," Callum said, and we watched Hilda lurch away, the parrot fluttering after her and announcing, "Polly want a go on the fruit machines."

"Polly can bugger off and all," Hilda said, vanishing into the patchy mid-afternoon crowds drifting up and down the wharf. The amusement arcades dinged and sang, and the scent of vinegar and hot oil drifted from the fish'n'chip shops, and across the water, on the other side of the harbour, pubs and houses glowed with golden light, forcing back the winter dimness.

"O Captain, my captain," Murty said and grinned.

"She's pretty decent, really," Callum said.

"Oh, I know. The eye's a nice touch."

"Yeah." Callum looked at the rubbish-strewn deck and sighed. "I best get on."

"I can help," the mermaid offered.

"And I suppose we'd have to invite you on board for that?" I said.

Murty snorted. "I could just carry your bin bags or something. It wasn't a ploy."

"It's not just your smell that's fishy," I said, arching my whiskers at him, and he pressed a hand to his chest in mock horror.

"Gobs," Callum said, and I lifted my lip to show him a tooth. He looked at Murty. "Best not, though."

Murty shrugged. "Fair enough." He got up and stretched, and I had that disconcerting impression again, that he was just a well-built man with his shoulders stretching at the seams of his grey top, and that at the same time I was looking at the rippling pelt of a beast built for cold, deep seas. He winked at me, his eyes too big and black, and said to Callum, "I owe you a favour, though."

"It's fine," Callum said. "Are you alright now? Will they be waiting for you?"

"Maybe. But I can stay ashore for a bit. Move down the coast before I go back to sea. I need to see a dwarf about a chicken, anyway."

Callum nodded. "Alright, then."

Murty nodded back and said, "I'll repay that favour," then

ambled off, his hands in the pockets of his grey trousers – and that seemed wrong, too, as if his hands were simply tucked into the folds of his own serene, curving body – and Callum went to dig the bin bags out from behind the bar. I followed, mostly to see if there were any sausage rolls left.

THERE *HAD* BEEN sausage rolls left, but now there were just three satisfied-looking rats. I was starting to see Hilda's point.

"Oh, it's the mighty hunter," one said. "Quick, run!" They all snickered, and I looked at Green Snake, who had escaped Callum's pocket while we were on the dock and had got himself into a mostly empty rum punch jug. He'd discovered a glacé cherry, and was flicking his tongue at it in a lazy sort of manner. He snatched it up quick enough when Callum lifted him out, though.

"Stop eating the fruit," Callum said to Green Snake. "It's not good for you."

Green Snake just swallowed the cherry, looking at Callum with unblinking eyes as the bulge of it made its way down his throat. Or body. It's hard to tell where one ends and one begins with a snake.

Callum sighed, and binned the rest of the leftovers before we could have a drunken snake on our paws.

"Terrible behaviour," I said to Green Snake, who just tilted his head at me. I turned my attention to the rats instead. "You couldn't leave me a sausage roll?"

"'S'not good for you, is it?" the biggest one said. "Not cat food."

"It's not *rat* food, either," I said, and investigated the rest of the platters, but there was nothing left. I opened my mouth to tell Callum I was hungry, but closed it again. He was shoving broken cups and discarded napkins into the bin bag with a weary sort of resignation, an unlit cigarette hanging out of the corner of his mouth, waiting until he was outside again to light it.

This was how we lived now. We'd walked out of Leeds – or driven, rather – with nothing but what had been in the car at the time. Our flat was too dangerous to go back to, and the city too risky to stay in. Things were catching up. North things for Callum, Watch things for me, although I still couldn't say what or why.

Our friend Gerry, the troll mayor of the pocket town of Dimly, had been the one to tell us we had to make ourselves scarce, but we hadn't heard much from him since, other than a terse text telling us to stay in Whitby. We hadn't heard much from *anyone*. We'd rocked up at an address Gerry had given us to find it was the sort of boarding house hotel inspectors would have nightmares about, if they ever knew it existed. Three skinny floors of individual rooms, with a shared bathroom and toilet on the middle floor, all of it smelling faintly of old onions, boiled meat, and damp.

With some grumbling, our heavily bearded landlord, Bob, had put us in the attic, where Callum could only stand straight if he was right in the middle of the room, and where the wind off the sea came in under the eaves like a thief. A really cold, persistent thief. We could never get into the bathroom because someone with a bright-sounding voice always sang out that they'd be done in *just a minute, dears*, no matter if we tried at midnight or six a.m. or half past two in the afternoon. I now suspected it was actually rented out to a retired mermaid, since we seemed to have a pod of them about the place.

Despite the conditions, the boarding house was full. Every door had strange smells seeping from beyond it, rose potpourri or paint thinners or two-minute noodles or hair spray, or other things that made my paws a bit twitchy. We only ever saw Bob and the fake medium, though, plus a strange, hunched form who scuttled around the corridors in the night. *That* made my tail bush out.

Bob lived on the bottom floor, and served us cold toast and slabs of perfectly cooked bacon and lightly poached eggs for breakfast. Well, served Callum. I lived mostly on the fish I begged off the wharf, which was ridiculously easy pickings. I just wandered past the fishers down on the dock every now and then and looked cute, and they'd throw me some herring that were too damaged to keep. I had to fight the gulls for it, but I'd found that fresh herring is good motivation. Although it was getting to the point where I was starting to crave a good tin of off-brand, processed-beyond-recognition meat. There's such a thing as too much fresh fish, it seems.

Anyhow, the fake medium joined us for breakfast the first day, but she shrieked as soon as she saw me and shut herself in the pantry, and wouldn't come out until I left the room. I watched her through the gap at the kitchen door, because people who hate cats are fascinating, and she kept crossing herself and beseeching the Great Flowering Spirit of Yorkshire to protect her. Then she read Callum's tea leaves and declared there was death in our future (no surprise there), and wanted twenty quid to tell us how to avoid it.

Bob had just grunted, distracted her with a Danish pastry, and shoved us a note with an address on it. We'd spent the rest of the day weeding some little old lady's garden.

Well, Callum had. I'd spent the day in more of a public relations role, being fed chicken scraps and so much cream that, in the aftermath, even I had to admit it wasn't good for me. The following days had been more of the same, Callum putting up shelves or cutting grass or scrubbing patios while I supervised or entertained our clients. It was boring and exhausting, but no one tried to blow us up, eat us, or throw us into the void, so that made for a nice change.

Even so, it had been kind of a relief when Hilda offered us somewhere else to live and a chance to earn some actual money. Bob had been taking all the proceeds of our odd jobs as rent, and told us that if we needed extra cash we could clean the boarding house's backyard. I was fairly certain that was basically danger pay, as the yard was so overgrown there could be a city of feral imps in there and we'd never know until we dug them out. Mermaids and orcas aside, the boat seemed a better option.

But it wasn't home. Everything felt like it was on pause, and as much as I could still feel reality fracturing as whatever had been lying in wait at the flat tried to rip me out of this world and into the void, as much as I wanted to not be looking over my shoulder for weres or dodgy magicians or necromancers, this wasn't the answer. And Callum knew it too.

At some point we were going to have to face whatever was following us. And in the meantime, here we were, cleaning up drunk people's rubbish. That had not been in our job descriptions as the best PI firm in Leeds. Well, best *magical* PI firm. Only one, really, but that made us doubly best.

So I decided it'd be strategic to keep my hungry stomach to myself, and looked at the rats instead. "Neecy," I said, to the sleek, dark-furred rodent just outside the door, who was checking the contents of a paper bag before Callum could collect it, "Do us a favour. Make yourselves scarce for a few days? I'll get Callum to pick up some cheese for you."

She eyed me. "You're a really weird ship's cat."

"I prefer to think of myself as openminded. Tolerant. That sort of thing."

"Hilda's not going to be super-tolerant when she finds you're not chasing us off."

I tipped my head. "Are you trying to persuade me to chase you or something?"

"Nah. Just find cats not being cats kind of strange. End of world strange, y'know?"

"I can throw in a bit of a spirited race around the decks if you pick me up some squid rings on your next shore excursion."

Neecy snorted. "Don't mention squid rings around here."

"Why? Because it's *The Savage Squid?*"

"No. We're *here* because it's *The Savage Squid.*" She nodded across the deck at a couple of other rats foraging for leftovers. One of them had milky eyes and twisted paws, and was staring at the sky blankly.

"What's up with Merv? He always freaks me out a bit."

"Merv ate the poison," Neecy said "Not here, on a different boat. Now he sees things. Knows things. He chose this boat for us, and it's the safest we've been."

"He survived poison?" I'd seen rats that had eaten poison. It was a horrible way to go.

"He says the kraken saved him."

"The *kraken?*"

"Yeah, it's a whole thing." She shrugged. "But he was right when he said we had to move to the *Squid*, and he's been right about lots of things. The poison unlocked something in him. He's no regular rat."

I looked at Merv again. He'd turned to stare straight at me with those milky eyes, and I shivered. "Yeah, no baby goats."

"What?"

"Never mind. Just stay out of Hilda's sight for a bit, alright?"

She eyed me. "Decent cheddar? I like a good mature cheddar. With the salty bits in."

"I'll get one with all the salty bits. Just so Hilda thinks I'm doing my job. Don't fancy getting fired over not eating you."

She considered it. "Proper mature cheddar with the salty bits, plus some seedless red grapes, and we'll lay low for a week. You can tell her you saw us all off, and if she sees signs we could be entirely new rats."

"Deal." We touched noses, while I tried not to look at her tail. Rats are, in general, decent sorts, but the naked tails make my paws twitch. Plus they reminded me of a certain hairless cat who also had a naked tail, and who I hadn't seen since our unceremonious departure from Leeds. I just hoped our vanishing act hadn't put her or her large, mostly silent buddy Tam in any trouble. I was fairly certain that whoever was after us was no more bothered by the idea of collateral damage than mermaids apparently were.

Callum stopped to scritch the back of my neck as he picked up the bag Neecy had abandoned. "Hungry?" he asked.

"Obviously."

"Won't take long. We'll get some fish'n'chips."

"I hate to say it, but I might almost be sick of fish'n'chips."

"Things really are getting to you," he said, and went out onto the deck with his bag, grabbing up the debris of the party. I followed him, the fading afternoon wind-torn and filled with the calls of gulls, endlessly circling the lighthouses and hunting the tourists. The Abbey wasn't visible from this angle, but I could feel it looming over the town, half protector, half beacon to the weird. It was that sort of place. Men talking to cats and woman talking to parrots weren't even worth noticing. The cobbled streets rang with the boots of people dressed as vampires or Vikings or some sort of steampunk time travellers, and the shops that weren't selling fish'n'chips and Whitby jet jewellery were selling Dracula memorabilia instead. There were more metres of lace and bouquets of corsets and sets of goggles and fake fangs in the tiny town centre than there were fish still left in the North Sea, as far as I could tell. No one noticed one skinny, needlessly tall man in a scruffy coat, even one accompanied by a small yet well-formed black cat.

Which was why we were here, of course.

3

A NO-VOMIT DAY IS A GOOD DAY

CALLUM SWEPT THE DECKS OF THE DEBRIS OF THE PIRATE party, tipping broken cups and dropped sandwiches and paper eye patches into a bin bag while I batted plastic cups toward him with one paw and told him about the battle I'd had with a seagull that morning while he'd been setting up for the day.

"And then it came diving in at me, and it was screaming, and that beak, you know? It could've split me in two!"

"Could it?"

"It was at least three times my size. Maybe four."

"The beak?"

"No, you bilge-licker. The seagull."

"There's actually no such thing as a *sea*gull. There are gulls of all different—"

"This was a giant one, then, okay? A great, giant, vicious-beaked gull."

He snorted, and stooped to stub his cigarette out in a squished sausage roll before sticking the lot into the bag.

"And this great, giant, vicious-beaked gull—"

"It might've just been hungry, you know. Probably wondering why this scrawny cat's stealing its lunch."

"I am perfectly formed, thank you very much. Take a look at yourself if you want scrawny."

Callum straightened up and examined the deck critically. "Think that's it. Not so bad today."

"No, no vomit. Always a good day when there's no vomit."

"Got to be an improvement on it being a good day when no one tries to kill us."

"Someone did," I pointed out, as he tied off the bag. "You, at least."

"Well, they weren't after *me*. Just the mermaid." He frowned. "Merman?"

"Hilda called him a mermaid."

"I'm not sure that clarifies much."

"Probably not," I agreed. "And that might be worse, you know. We get away from people trying to kill us specifically, and end up killed by someone accidentally."

He smiled and carried the bag over to dump it by the gangway. "Speaking of people trying to kill us, have you heard anything from Ms Jones yet?"

"No," I said flatly, and Green Snake lifted his head out of Callum's pocket to look at me. I ignored him, trying not to think of the sorcerer with her long dark hair and amused eyes, and her fingers digging into my fur, gentle yet strong enough to rip me out of the world. Out of *myself*. "Nothing since we got here."

Green Snake tipped his head to one side. I stared back at him, his glossy eyes giving away nothing, and my stomach gave a slow, sick roll that threatened to ruin our no-vomit day. For a moment my ears were full of a high, whistling scream, and the world darkened at the edges. Somewhere, someone was calling my name. Not calling it, *shouting* it, with an imperiousness that made my paws twitch. The world pulsed, a ripple passing over it, and then the moment was gone, leaving me with a racing heart and Callum with a puzzled look on his face.

"Gobs? What is it?"

"Nothing," I managed, licking my chops.

"Are you sure you haven't heard from Ms Jones?"

"No," I said, not looking at him. "Just bloody cold, is all."

Green Snake looked at the sky, then vanished back into Callum's pocket.

"Are you *sure*? That looked like—"

"It didn't look like anything," I said sharply. "She hasn't been in contact." And she hadn't. Because anyone can call, but it doesn't mean you have to answer. She was looking for me, though. I could feel it, feel the raw, ancient strength of her, lying in wait with a deadly patience. And whenever I thought of her that presence turned toward me, as if my attention called out to hers. So I tried not to think of her at all.

It wasn't just the whole yanking me out of my body thing that made me reluctant to be in touch, although that was bad enough. It was the fact that she seemed to think I should *know* something, remember something about my past lives and my connection to the Watch, the cat council that keeps the worlds of magical Folk and humans apart. And I didn't, other than the bit where the Watch fed me to the beasts of the Inbetween. Which is something I'd really rather forget, but it had kind of stuck with me.

And being as that fun fact was as much as I remembered, there was no point in Ms Jones asking about anything else. And I had no desire to relive such a spectacularly horrible death, so I did my best not to think about anything related to it. It was exhausting, all the not-thinking.

"It's strange she hasn't been in touch," Callum said, scrubbing his hands off under a tap on the deck and shivering at the cold water.

"Not really," I said. "We found her dentist for her. She might be happily shacked up with him back in Leeds by now."

"I mean, yes, we found Malcolm, and we know he's safe—"

"That's all she wanted from us." It was hard to talk about this and still not think of her, skinny jeans and Doc Martens and the musky scent of eternity on her skin. "We were meant to make sure he was safe, and he is, even if he's hanging out with weres." Finding him had meant *us* spending far too much time with weres, too, and also discovering that Callum's magician bestie was very fond of magical firebombs that had almost killed us twice. Hence the *any day no one tries to kill us is a good day* thing.

And that wasn't even why we were hiding out in Whitby – or not entirely. We were here because the Watch were getting a little too interested in me. Again. They'd ended every one of my previous three lives, and I really had no idea why they had it in for me so much, but I had every intention of not being killed by them this time around. Plus, Callum's past was catching up with *him*, which was proving dicey. My scruffy partner and his homicidal sister had turned out to be the last of the Norths, a human family that had run the actual north with the use of both hired muscle and strategic Folk skills for generations, and it seemed that no matter how much he felt he was done with it, it wasn't done with him.

So things in Leeds and its pocket town of Dimly had been getting a bit dodgy for us, even before someone – or something – tried to grab me out of my own flat and heft me into the void. And somehow all these things were linked, as well as potentially being linked to necromancers, who weren't even meant to exist anymore. All of which sounds very confusing, but trust me – it felt even more so, and meant that I was almost happy to only have to deal with seagulls and drunk pirates.

Callum fished his cigarettes out of his pocket. "I just thought we might have heard if Ms Jones was okay. We never did figure out where she was, or why she couldn't find Malcolm herself. And we haven't heard from Claudia, either. It just seems weird *no one's* been in touch but Gerry."

Claudia of the Watch. Claudia of the lovely mismatched eyes and sucker scars that mirrored mine, from a brief encounter with an Inbetween beast. She was the one Watch cat I trusted, and had last been seen with our friendly local sorcerer. They'd vanished around the same time we'd discovered that necromancers appeared to have risen from the dead, and were quite keen on getting back to their own personal dead-raising.

"I mean, that was kind of the plan," I pointed out. "Us hiding out, you know. Even Tam and Pru haven't been in touch, and they'd find us easier than anyone. They know our scent." Cats can shift through the Inbetween, the space that runs between all things, stepping out of the world and reappearing somewhere else entirely – or they can if the beasts don't have their scent, which is why shifting was out for me. But other cats can track people across the void. It's a bit of a fickle art, though, and we don't talk about it much. It's a bit dog-like, all that scent stuff, and no one wants those sorts of comparisons.

Callum blew smoke over his lip and looked at the rumpled water of the harbour, the channel slipping past the wharf and deep into the land. "I wonder if they can. I think Whitby's a bit of a pocket itself, you know."

"How? Humans bloody love the place." Pocket towns are just what they sound like – little pockets of Folk-friendly towns and villages, left over from the days when magic was as commonplace as chip butties, and humans and Folk had coexisted, if not peacefully, at least no less peacefully than humans did with each other. After the wars of the necromancers, when the power-hungry dead-lovers had tried to enslave both humanity and most of the Folk, the communities had split. Folk hid, became legend, and humans forgot, for the most part, and the Watch now police the division with the sort of mercurial bite only cats are capable of.

But in pocket towns, Folk don't have to hide. Pocket towns protect them, hide them from humans, and different rules apply. Shift locks enclose pockets, stopping cats from appearing and disappearing at will, and charms protect their borders, rendering them elusive. Pockets protect both the guilty and the innocent, from friends and enemies alike. But mostly they keep humans out, because humans only see what they believe to be real, and tend to get a bit punchy when presented with anything else. Which means that any human encountering a pocket town finds themselves inexplicably turning down a different road, avoiding certain parts of town with no way to articulate why, just knowing that it's not a place for them.

Which meant that Whitby couldn't be a pocket town, since humans love the whole seaside carry-on, and around here they were *really* into the Abbey and vampires and all that. No pocket could be that poorly disguised.

"Ever heard of hiding in plain sight?" Callum asked. "The boarding house. Hilda. All those weird cats in town making a point of ignoring each other. There's plenty of Folk and just ... *odd* stuff here, and humans seem to accept it. And *see* us. Haven't you felt it?"

I blinked at him. He was right. Callum was ... Callum. A North. I still hadn't worked him out. He was at least mostly human, although he was entwined in the world of Folk in the way so many people who don't fit into the human world are.

And it rendered him faint, given the same protection that Folk are. People just didn't notice him. And no one notices cats. Wherever we are, humans just assume we're meant to be there, and *we* certainly mean to be there, so it all works.

But here ... here was different. People *looked* at us. Not everyone, of course, but more than was comfortable outside a pocket. And I could feel *something*, had felt it when we drove into town. A faint frisson of charms that I'd dismissed as just some hedge witch's garden spells, but maybe it was something more. Protection of some sort, perhaps. Not as strong as Dimly, but something old and deep-set into the land itself.

And then there were the cats. I'm not a fan of strange cats – not every cat's Watch, but every cat *can* be Watch – so I don't go out of my way to mix with them. But there's also no avoiding them. I've never encountered a place that *didn't* have cats, other than some pocket towns. Cats don't like being told they can't come and go at will, and the shift locks on pockets feel a bit rude, if I'm honest. Whitby didn't have shift locks that I'd come across, and there were certainly cats about.

But the thing was, Whitby's cats were a bit weird even by my standards. I'd come around a corner in the old, slick-cobbled streets of town and almost run straight into a ginger tom about twice my size. He'd just about back-flipped away from me.

"Didn't see you," he'd yelped, already taking off down the street. "Sorry, dude!"

"My fault," I'd said, watching him go. He'd vanished at full sprint, and Callum and I had stared at each other, then taken a different route to the cafe that did cream teas and didn't mind cats on their chairs. We'd seen about a dozen other cats since, and they all ignored both me and each other with great determination. Which was good, but also ... strange.

"Well, if it is a bit of a pocket, that's good," I said to Callum now. "It means your dodgy magician bestie and your even dodgier sister shouldn't be able to track us down."

"It means no one can track us down," he said. "Not Claudia, not Pru, and not Ms Jones if she needs us."

The world dimmed at the edges again, as if the storm had pounced closer – or, worse, as if the sorcerer had. I hunkered down, tail twitching, and said, "We're meant to be lying low, right? That's what we're doing."

He lifted Green Snake out of his pocket and looked from him to me. "For how long, though?"

Neither of us had an answer to that.

AFTER THAT, it seemed like fish'n'chips were necessary, so we locked *The Savage Squid* and headed onto the dock. A storm-edged Wednesday in February isn't exactly high season for a North Yorkshire seaside town, even one like Whitby – by which I mean one that attracts the sort of people who favour dramatic cliff walks in greatcoats over deckchairs and donkey rides. The old clifftop church and the ruins of the Abbey behind it loomed above town on the opposite side of the river to where we were docked, the houses below rubbing shoulders as they clustered over the water, lining the harbour where it pressed deep into the land. A second pier jutted from the headland on that side, a little lower than the one that our dock ran toward, capped with its own light-house, and each pier had a beacon on the end for good measure. It was only mid-afternoon, but with the heavy clouds coming in from the sea, the beacons were already visible, a steadily pulsing red light on the far side to match the green on ours.

The piers curved toward each other like the pincers, their

bases solid under the surface of the churning green sea and offering shelter to the little fishing boats that shot between them with their own red and green lights glittering in the afternoon light. The fat bellies of fishing baskets crowded their decks, and long outrigger poles dipped toward the sea from their midships. Crew in heavy red and yellow waterproofs moved across their narrow side decks and fat sterns, leaning with the movement of the boats in seeming defiance of gravity, and gulls trailed them like airborne escorts.

I padded on the damp, puddled pavement next to Callum as we ambled past the desperately cheerful lights of the amusement arcades and the more softly lit entrances to fish restaurants on our left, and the dock on our right. The streets weren't crowded, but there were dribs and drabs of people wandering around in walking gear, their hoods pulled up against the wind and the chill, and others running into the shelter of pubs with their shoulders hunched and their hands in their pockets.

Along the wharf, the twin masts of one of our competitors poked at the grey sky. There was a pirate mannequin in the crows' nest and the rope of the rigging was stained black, but in a deliberate manner rather than our mouldy way. A large sign proudly proclaimed trips would leave every two hours, on the hour, but I'd only seen it go out a few times, rolling alarmingly as it left the harbour mouth. Evidently sober volunteers for seasickness were in short supply at this time of year, and we'd cornered the market on the less sober ones.

I jumped at Callum and scrambled up to his shoulder as we passed the concrete blocks of the fish market, the snippet of a song painted on the walls.

You shall have a haddock,
You shall have a fin,
You shall have a fishy,

When the boats come in.

"I'm kind of over fishies," I hissed at Callum. "Can we have some chicken?"

He turned his head slightly and blew cigarette smoke at me, and I coughed in his ear.

"Want your fortune read?" someone asked, and I peered around to see a woman in a generous swaddling of lace and multicoloured wool smiling at us. The whiff of incense and talcum powder drifted from the little cabin behind her, where a neon sign proclaimed her as *The infallible Madame Zelda! Know your future! Realise your dreams! Frightfully accurate!* "Oh. It's you." She gave me a suspicious look.

"Hi, June," Callum said, and I twitched my ears at her. Madame Zelda, known when off-duty as June, and not a cat person.

"Eh." She looked along the near-empty road, and sighed. "Well, I'll do your fortune anyway. Just cross my palm with paper. Ten'll do."

"We've moved on from silver, then," I muttered to Callum.

"No thanks," he said.

"Good luck charm? Love spell?" She examined him and apparently reconsidered, going back to, "Good luck charm?"

"We're alright," Callum said.

"Are you sure?" she asked. "You look like you could use some luck."

"*Rude,*" I said. "We're not the ones still living in England's last boarding hovel."

June ignored me, covering her eyes with one hand and extending the other toward Callum, silver bracelets clattering on her wrists. "I see ... I see conflict in your future."

"I thought it was death," I said, and Callum bopped me on the head. "*Ow.*"

"But there is a way to avoid it! I can guide you through this low, tragic stage of your journey and into the glorious freedom that awaits." She opened her eyes and gave Callum a beaming smile. "You are lost. You are bereft. I will be your light on the path to happiness."

"I mean, thanks, but—"

"Ten's half price," she said. "Mate's rates, you know."

"No, we're good." He started to skirt her, and she grabbed his arm, then yelped and jerked back. Callum stopped, frowning, and I slipped across his shoulder so I could stare down at the fake medium.

"Oh, that's unpleasant," she said, shaking her hand out, and stared at Callum. "You really do need some help, you know."

"I think that could be said of anyone who ends up in that boarding house," I said.

"And working on a pirate ship is that much better?" she demanded, and I lifted my lip to show her one tooth.

"Sorry," Callum said.

She examined him, flicked a little, wary glance up and down the dock, then said, "I can help you."

"Got a good recipe for boiled meat?" I asked her, and she gave me a blank look. "The smell? In the boarding house?"

"I hadn't noticed it."

"Yeah, you're really sensitive."

"I *am*," she said, and looked at Callum again. "I know why you can't leave town."

"Well, we weren't planning to," Callum started, and she shook her head.

"No, you *can't*. And I know why."

I peered at Callum. He was frowning. "What d'you mean, we can't?"

"Everyone tells you, don't they? *Stay in town*." She smiled, and straightened the front of her flower-bedecked shirt. "I know why."

"Because of the whole work-for-board thing?" I suggested. "No one wants to lose their free labour."

June shook her head, and peeked each way along the dock again. I found myself doing the same, as if town border guards in Dracula capes were about to appear and order us to stay put. "It's not that. But I can tell you what it is." She held her hand out. "Cross my palm with paper, go on."

I snorted, but Callum just looked at her, and I wondered if I was going to have to intervene before he gave our limited funds to some cut-rate fortune teller. Then June's gaze shifted suddenly, and she gave a little shriek.

"Death follows you! *Death!*" She dived into her cabin and slammed the door behind her, hard enough that the plastic brochure holder screwed to the door juddered in her wake, and a clump of browned holly tucked into it fell to the ground.

"Interesting sales technique," Callum said, while I looked around to make sure I hadn't got it right about the Dracula guards. All I could see was a man walking two chubby chihuahuas, all three of them in matching jackets, which was pretty horrifying but hardly deadly.

"She's got an unhealthy fixation on the death thing," I started, and Callum's mobile rang. We both jumped. Well, Callum jumped, and what with me being on his shoulder I caught it off him. He fished the phone out of his pocket.

"It's Gerry," he said, tipping the phone toward me.

"There we go," I said. "Maybe this is our *everything's fine, come home* call."

"Maybe." Callum hit answer and I leaned close to his ear so I could hear as well. "Gerry? How're things?"

"Oh, you know." Dimly's troll mayor sounded strained. "Just wanted to see where you were at the moment."

"Where we are?" Callum asked. "Working, mostly."

"Yes, but where?"

Callum craned his neck so he could look at me. I bared my teeth. Gerry knew exactly where we were. He'd *sent* us here.

"Callum? Cal— I think you've dropped out. Terrible line."

"Yeah. Yeah, this part of Cornwall gets pretty bad reception."

Hardly smooth, but it was a decent effort. And Cornwall was about as far from Whitby as you could get and still be in England.

"Cornwall? Right, lovely, lovely. And where—"

I hissed into the phone, getting my teeth right up to it, and heard Gerry yelp. Someone else as well, which was handy but worrying.

"Sorry!" Callum shouted over my hissing. "Bad static! Talk later!" He mashed disconnect, and we were both silent for a moment.

"Well," I said finally. "Looks like *someone's* trying to get in touch, anyway."

"But who?" Callum asked. "And why would Gerry phone us with someone there? He could've just sent a message to warn us."

We were both silent. I didn't want to think about who could force a troll to make a phone call – or to do anything at all, really. And I *definitely* didn't want to think about the how of it.

Despite the lack of vomit, it wasn't feeling like such a good day after all.

4

A DEAD LOSS

SOMEHOW THAT PUT US RIGHT OFF OUR FISH'N'CHIPS. CALLUM changed direction, heading into town rather than along the pier, and went into a corner shop for milk and more cigarettes. The young woman behind the counter looked at me, then at Callum, shook her head slightly, and took our money. Like I say, Whitby's weird tolerance is pretty high.

I stayed on Callum's shoulder, and we talked in low voices as we headed back to *The Savage Squid*, feeling oddly exposed on the streets where only half an hour ago we'd been congratulating ourselves on being somewhere we could hide from the sight of planes.

"Any other messages from Gerry?" I asked.

"Nothing for about a week. He usually texts to tell me how William and Poppy are doing."

"He what?" William and Poppy were Gerry's young troll charges, whom he was teaching to be modern trolls. This involved proper elocution and developing interests outside the usual troll fields of smashing people's heads together and breaking things. Poppy had set up some sort of weird animal rescue, and William was running a fancy tea shop, but there had been the inevitable pushback. Some people just want trolls to be trolls, and don't hold much with them having their own ideas of how they want to live. Still, updates on that didn't really seem worth risking contact for.

"It's code, Gobs. If they're all good, nothing's changed. If Poppy has some escapees, people are sniffing around, asking about us. If William burns a batch of scones, there's someone getting a bit too close – not necessarily figured out where we are, but making some good guesses."

"How many of those codes have you had?" I demanded. "And why didn't you tell me?"

"You almost fell off the pier when that woman in a witch costume tried to pet you last week. I didn't want to add to your stress load."

"*I am not stressed*," I hissed, then realised my claws were dug so far into the shoulder of his coat they'd run against the resistance of his skin. "Sorry."

"Do you even sleep?"

"Do you?" I shot back. Sleep made me uneasy these days. It wasn't just the sorcerer trying to tug me out of my body, after all. Someone in our old flat had tried to shove me into the void, and Callum had been the only thing that stopped me.

"Not much," Callum admitted, and scrolled through his phone, stopping on Ifan's number. His dodgy magician bestie.

"*Don't*," I said. "We don't want that scurvy bilge-licker knowing where we are."

"You've taken to this nautical thing disturbingly well," Callum said, and tapped the message icon instead. "Ifan might know more about what's going on in Dimly."

"Ifan tried to firebomb us, stuck a were in wolf form permanently, and has been known to mess around with necromancers. I trust him about as much as I do that parrot."

"The helpful parrot who dropped explosives in the harbour this afternoon?"

"He listens to us. I think he's a spy."

"For who, Hilda?" Callum started typing.

"Maybe."

"Do you think you might be suffering a little from the lack of sleep?" he suggested, and I peered over his shoulder. He'd simply put, *What's up?* Above that succinct message was one from Ifan, which seemed to be a long and involved anecdote involving a wizard, a juggling goblin, and a duck.

"You've been talking to him all the time," I said accusingly. "*He* probably knows where we are!"

"I've not talked to him that much," Callum said. "And I certainly haven't told him where we are. But he's been keeping me updated. As long as he thinks we're still friends, he'll tell me things. And we've got no one else who might know what the hell's going on in Dimly and Leeds other than Gerry, who can't risk being in contact more than he is already. We need to know what's happening, Gobs. There's no other way to figure out what to do next."

"How do you know he's not lying to you? Making stuff up to get you to come back so he can shove an ancient god in you again?"

"That was his dad, and I don't. But I do know him." He scritched the top of my head. "He'll tell me as much truth as he thinks will work."

"Such a good friend to have," I said. "Told you to stick with cats."

"Oh, because you're in such close contact with other cats?"

"Fine, *one* cat, then."

He snorted and pocketed his phone as we reached the gangway. I could smell sleeplessness and long, slow grief on him in equal measure, the pale taste of restless nights and distrust. "It's not like I have any choice on that one."

"True," I agreed. "Now what was that thing about the wizard?"

"Yeah, I'm not explaining that to you."

"Why not?"

"Human stuff," he said, stepping over the very effective rope gate and heading onto the deck.

"There was a goblin in it! And a duck. How can—"

"Hello?"

I froze mid-word, even though most humans are so conditioned to believe cats don't talk that all they'd hear is *meow*. But Whitby, like I say, is not a place for *most humans*. Callum turned back to the gangway, his messy hair glinting with hints of copper in the fading afternoon light.

"Callum? Gobbelino?" the newcomer said, her tones almost bewildered.

"Emma?" Callum asked, and we both stared at the woman on the wharf. She looked from one of us to the other, a gently curved woman with soft hair and, currently, deep lines drawing at the corners of her mouth. I could smell her from here, even over the ever-present salt of the sea, cupcakes and something floral underlying a quiet, resilient optimism, and dead things. "What are you doing here?" Callum asked.

"Mini-break," she said, with no enthusiasm.

"That's ... nice?"

"Yes," she said, and sniffled, and I realised she was trying not to cry.

"Has something happened?" Callum asked, which just proves that humans are clueless. Even *I* could see that something had happened. Emma wasn't the sort of person who wandered around the streets crying on mini-breaks, even if it was Whitby.

"It's Gertrude," Emma said. "She's missing."

"*Gertrude?*" Callum and I said together, and Emma nodded, not looking at us.

"Oh, candied jellyfish with barnacles on," I said.

Because Gertrude was a reaper. A proper one, with a tenuous relationship to our dimensions and a scythe sharp enough to cleave souls from the world, as well as a passion for baking and lacy doilies.

How does a reaper go missing?

CALLUM DID what humans always do in times of crisis. He invited Emma on board, and offered her a drink. We had to hand a wide variety of bottles that resembled rum of different guises, left behind from assorted boat parties. They'd evidently proved too off-brand for even Hilda's flask, so offering them to Emma probably bordered on assault by alcohol, but I suppose it's the thought that counts. Humans deal with crises in a wide variety of ways, but it's amazing how many of them seem to involve drinking *something*. In Callum's case, a cup of tea, as he'd discovered somewhere around the time we'd met that anything stronger tended to make the crisis worse. He had tested the hypothesis thoroughly before settling on caffeine and nicotine as coping strategies, though.

Emma looked at the bottles dubiously, then opted for tea as well and stared around the wood-panelled forward cabin that held the bar, the last of the afternoon light filtering in through metal-rimmed portholes. *The Savage Squid*, also known as Whitby's most authentic pirate ship adventure (as opposed to the other boat tours in the area, which advertised dolphin tours and good safety records), was built to resemble an old-fashioned galleon in the sense that someone had seen a child's drawing of one once and had taken it for actual plans. She had a high stern and an even higher bow with a bowsprit poking out over the water, which I quite liked sitting on when we weren't moving too much. There was a figurehead under the bowsprit, a squid with a woman's torso and head on it, but whoever had made it had been better at doing tentacles than they had been at carving the woman's features. She looked like she'd been left out in the rain for a few days while the paint was still wet.

The Savage Squid wasn't that long, but she sat high in the water even at the lowest point of her midships, which were so rounded they really looked like they should have cannon ports in the sides. Two stumpy masts poked above the decks, one with a crow's nest for the parrot to abuse passers-by from, and the other adorned with an array of tatty flags. Neither of them had anything approaching a sail, but it wasn't that sort of boat. The main attraction was the broad party deck sandwiched between the captain's cabin at the stern with its green-glassed ports looking over the sea, and the forecastle cabin, which held the bar and a toilet and had almost enough room in it for the regulation fifteen guests to cram into if it rained (as far as I could tell, the regulations had been adhered to on one trip so far). A raised wheelhouse was perched on top of the captain's cabin, so Hilda could see over the pirate parties to the bow.

On the party deck itself upright barrels were fixed in place to use as tables, while wooden seating was built into the insides of the solid wood walls of the hull. The hull walls rose to about waist-height on most of the guests before being capped with some wooden railings for good measure. A couple of big deck lockers offered additional seating, and were filled with plastic swords, cardboard pirate hats, and those rain ponchos that come in a little plastic bag. All for sale, obviously. Hilda didn't give anything away. Under them somewhere were presumably life jackets, going by the stickers on the sides of the lockers, but I'd never seen them. Maybe they were paid extras too.

There wasn't a lot below decks, and all of it other than the captain's cabin was reached through the forecastle cabin. A door marked *Crew Only* led out of it and into a little kitchen – sorry, *galley*, as Hilda insisted we call it – with a two-burner gas stove on which one burner worked half the time, and beyond that was our minuscule cabin and a bathroom – sorry again, *head* – that consisted of a toilet with a shower hanging over it. Further on, in the depths of the hull, was the cramped engine room with its hot, greasy stink, and a cabin given over to spare crates of booze with foreign labels, and mysterious label-less cans of fruit salad or sardines or chick-peas (one never knew which until it was open), and bits of salvage such as old oars and fishing buoys and bits of broken netting.

And that was the entirety of *The Savage Squid*'s crew accommodation. The captain's cabin was big and roomy and bright, and full of books and charts and weird old instruments that had probably gone around the world before even Hilda was born, but it was off limits. She didn't live in it, but we weren't allowed to either. The rats had shown me how to sneak in, though, so I'd had a few midnight forays in search of treasure maps. No luck so far, and still no proof regarding the peg leg, but I was working on it.

Callum vanished to get the stove going and fetch his biscuit stash, which was hidden from Hilda and the parrot. It's impossible to hide much from rats, but I'd struck a deal with them. I looked at Emma, who was standing in the middle of the bar looking around in something like bewil-derment, her fingers twisting through the hem of her water-proof coat. It was bright blue, the sort of thing cheap outdoors shops in tourist spots always have on sale for when people forget their own.

"You can sit down," I said, padding over to one corner, where the cushioned benches built into the wall formed an L-shape. There were a few boxes of juice stacked up in the curve to create a makeshift table, and it was where we spent most of our time. Our cabin had one tiny round porthole that didn't open, and was just big enough for two single bunks, one above the other. It wasn't conducive to lounging.

"Thanks," Emma said, and followed me over, sitting next to me on the bench. She started petting me automatically, and I didn't even complain. The tension thrummed off her, something that twisted the stomach and hurt the heart.

"Whitby, huh?" I said, trying for cheerful. "The seaside in winter. Lovely."

"It's nice. Less busy. And longer nights mean Gertrude can get out more."

Of course. The reaper didn't exactly scream and melt at the touch of sunlight, but I'd seen her precautions. Huge sunhats, specially-made robes, and long gloves, as well as sunblock slathered over her face. And still she tended to burn, apparently.

"When did you arrive?" I asked, wishing Callum would hurry up. Cats aren't built for small talk.

"Um. A couple of nights ago." She looked at the door, apparently wishing the same thing.

"And you've lost her already? Bit careless."

Emma stopped petting me and covered her mouth with one hand, her eyes squeezing shut.

"I didn't mean it," I said. "It was a joke. A really bad joke. Sorry. *Callum!*"

He appeared through the door with two mugs of tea in one hand and a packet of biscuits in the other. "Don't shout."

He sat down on the other side of me, sorting out the drinks. "Alright, Emma?"

"No," she said, her voice small. "Gobs is right. I *was* careless. And it's my fault she's gone."

Callum nodded and offered her the biscuits. "I doubt it. She's a reaper. She's very capable of looking after herself."

"But what if she's done something silly? Something ... I don't know. She's out in the *day*. What if she burned up?"

"I can't see that," Callum said, fishing Green Snake out of his pocket and setting him on the table before going to hang his coat up. "Besides, Gertrude's very sensible."

I thought of the cafe that Gertrude and Emma ran in Leeds, the one where they had actual baby ghouls roaming about the place for the customers to pet. In the low light and with humans being so disinclined to see Folk, the assumption tended to be that they were just very strange dogs, but it still seemed like a sign of questionable judgement to me. Ghoulets were *hungry*.

Emma took a biscuit and nibbled a corner of it, looking as if she wasn't really tasting it at all. Probably for the best. We'd bought them at the same place as we got the juice, and now had twelve packs of *Chokkie Diggles*, which were almost entirely unlike chocolate digestives, as far as I could tell.

"So," Callum said, dunking a Diggle in his tea and eating it quickly, before it could splatter all over his newly cleaned floor. "Tell us what happened."

It was almost like being back home, a new client walking in and us sitting there and sifting through the facts, trying to work out how much was truth, how much was conjecture, and how much we could charge. Except this time we wouldn't be charging, it being Emma. Not that taking cases for bones was unusual for us, even when we didn't know the client. Callum has the worst sort of bleeding heart imaginable, which is why we keep ending up existing on Chokkie

Diggles and the sort of cat food that's probably never even seen a fish before. Although that sounded pretty appealing after all this time in Whitby, to be honest.

"So we live at night when we're away," Emma was saying. "Gertrude doesn't sleep, obviously, being ..." she waved vaguely.

"A reaper," Callum said.

"Dead," I said.

"*Technically* dead," Emma corrected me, and eyed Green Snake. He was investigating the biscuits without much enthusiasm. "At home, I'm up in the day for the cafe, but when we take breaks I try to spend at least part of the night up with her, since she can't go out and about while it's light. I just take a little bit of time for doing my own thing. Walking and so on." She indicated her walking gear and boots. It all looked pretty new, and I guessed walking was more an aspiration than a hobby.

"Anyhow." She took a breath. "I was going to walk to Robin Hood's Bay, along the clifftops, you know?"

We both made noises that indicated we knew, although we hadn't been there. We hadn't left Whitby since we'd arrived.

"But then it started raining, and I just thought, oh, this is no fun. I'd rather go and get a couple of nice big scones with cream, and share them with Gertrude. Well, *share*. I'd eat them while we chatted or whatever."

Reapers also didn't eat or drink, being *technically* dead, which was a double shame when you were a reaper with a sideline in making exceptional cakes.

Emma took a sip of tea and fiddled with the mug's handle. It read *I'd rather be pillaging*, and had a cartoon of a Viking on it that looked quite a lot like Hilda.

"When I got back, Gertrude wasn't there. And it was *daytime*. I tried calling her, but she didn't answer. So I went looking for her. I've been looking all day. *All day.* She's not on the beach. She's not in town. She's not even at the Abbey. I thought she might like the Abbey, but she says that while it's very nice, the churchyard's too close and makes her feel she's stepping on Reaper Scarborough's toes. Reapers don't really take breaks, you know. It's all very unprecedented, and Secretary Reaper covers for us in Leeds, and looks after the ghoulets, but if Grim Yorkshire found out then there might really be trouble, and—"

She stopped as Callum held the biscuits out to her again. She was breathing hard, and she squeezed her eyes shut for a moment. "Sorry. I'm rambling."

"It's okay," Callum said. "It all sounds very tricky even to go away for a bit. And very odd for Gertrude to be out in the day. No wonder you're worried."

"Yes." She took another biscuit. "And, you see, Gertrude *never* just vanishes. If I'm already asleep and she gets a message from DHL – Departed Human Logistics – that a soul's been missed, she leaves me a note. If she goes to the shops and I'm busy, she leaves me a note. Or she texts me. Or she does *something*. She knows I …" Emma hesitated, rolling the biscuit in her fingers. "Once I was with someone who would vanish overnight, or even for days, and when he came back it'd either be with flowers and gifts or … or it'd be bad. *Really* bad. So I always worry when I don't know where someone is. And Gertrude makes sure I never, ever worry." She gave us both a strange, fierce look. "I know people think it's weird, me living with a reaper. But she's so lovely. And I try to be … *better* for her. Alive. For years I didn't feel alive, and now I try to be properly alive, all the time. I try to help *her* remember what it is to be alive."

Callum nodded. "It's not weird. I live with a cat."

"That's pretty normal."

"Have you met him?"

"*Hey*," I said. "Have you met yourself?"

Emma half smiled, and rubbed her face with both hands. "Anyway, that's where I am. I've looked everywhere I can think of, and she's just not anywhere."

"Why did you say it was your fault?" I asked, and Callum poked me. "What? She did say that."

"Tact is not his middle name," he said to Emma.

"I don't have a middle name at all. I have two names already, and that's plenty." Green Snake looked around the biscuits and stuck his tongue out at me, and I said, "What's with you?"

Emma looked from me to Green Snake, then said, "Gobbelino's right. I did say that. And I ... oh, it's so *silly* now." Her voice wobbled, and Callum made a sympathetic sort of noise. I put my paws on her leg and head-bumped her arm.

"You want to know what's silly? Callum almost got eaten by killer panda fish today, and had to be saved by a parrot."

"What?" She looked at me blankly, wiping her eyes with the sleeve of her fleece.

"It was an orca, and it wasn't after me," Callum protested.

Emma gave him a dubious look. "Is that any better?"

"Exactly what I said." I sat down and leaned against her, smelling some softly floral perfume under the tang of her fear. She petted me, and Callum slurped his tea, and Green Snake coiled himself into a luminous puddle in the middle of the table, looking from one of us to the other.

Finally Emma said, "I might have been a bit ... *off* with Gertrude."

"Did you bite her?" I asked.

"What? No, of course not."

"That's what it usually means when I'm off with someone."

"Right, well, I'm not a cat." She took a sip of tea. "Last night I said that I was sick of having to come to Whitby, and couldn't we go somewhere else for a change. So Gertrude suggested Blackpool, and I said that wasn't the sort of somewhere else I was thinking of. I said I wanted to go somewhere that had fruity drinks with little umbrellas in them, not bloody fish'n'chips." She sighed. "When I got up this morning Gertrude had made me this lovely juice with an umbrella in it, and I shouted that it wasn't about the umbrella, and she just didn't understand."

"I'm sure she did," Callum said.

"I don't," I said. "I've never understood the whole drinks and umbrellas situation."

"She doesn't either," Emma said. "I suppose it's a human thing. It's … it stands for something else. For being somewhere exciting and different and really being *on holiday*."

"It's sort of a symbolic umbrella," Callum said.

"You said they were paper last time."

"Sorry," Callum said to Emma.

"It's fine," she said. "This is very like the conversation I had with Gertrude. I'm just shouting less. Anyhow, I stormed off for a walk, and then by the time I'd calmed down and realised how silly I was being … I mean, I *know* she can't go off to the Caribbean or even, I don't know, the south coast. She has to be able to nip back to Leeds if needed, and then there's the whole sun thing …" She shook her head. "Now I don't know what to think. Maybe I really upset her, more than I even realised."

Callum folded his hands on the table. "Could she have gone back to Leeds? For work?"

"The van's still here," Emma said. "And she'd wait until dark, anyway. *And* she'd tell me. She's missing. I know she is."

Callum and I looked at each other.

"Well, shiver me timbers," I said, and he sighed.

5

A ROUGH OLD NIGHT

HUMANS DO INVEST THEMSELVES IN A LOT OF POINTLESS GUILT. You won't find a cat agonising over whether they accidentally offended someone over a paper umbrella misunderstanding. A misunderstanding I was still not very clear on, but we'd evidently moved on and no one seemed inclined to explain it to me. Not that anyone seemed to be feeling any guilt over *that*. Humans.

"When did you last see Gertrude, then?" Callum asked. "What time did you leave this morning?"

"About seven. It was still dark, but I got so upset that I just marched out." Emma took a mouthful of tea, not looking at Callum.

He checked his phone. "It's almost four thirty. So she could've been gone the whole day."

"Almost certainly. Matilda said she saw her leaving not long after me. Which would make sense, that she went out before the sun came up properly."

"Who's Matilda?" Callum asked.

"She's this cat—"

"Cat?" I asked sharply, and Green Snake tilted his head at Emma. "You've been hanging around with a cat?"

"We do every time we come here. Gertrude saved her from some sort of blood sacrifice or demon summoning or something like that on our first visit, and now she comes by whenever we're here." Emma frowned. "Mostly for the smoked salmon, really. Gertrude spoils her. I think she feels guilty that Matilda lost her leg, although I don't think that was Gertrude's fault."

"That's nice," I said. "But is she Watch?"

"I don't know. I'll ask next time I see her. Is it important?"

"Probably not," Callum said. "Unless you mentioned Gobs to her?"

"I didn't even know you were here." Emma locked her fingers around her mug. "Anyway, she told me she'd seen Gertrude going out, and that she was in a hurry. Gertrude, I mean. Wouldn't even stop to give Matilda any salmon, which I think was mostly why Matilda waited around to tell me. But the thing is, she saw Gertrude out yesterday, too. In the *day.* I know it was a bit cloudy, but still. Gertrude never goes out in daylight unless she absolutely has to. It's very uncomfortable for her."

"Where did Matilda see her?" Callum asked.

"Heading toward the beach. I went straight down there as soon as Matilda told me, but I couldn't see her, so I came back and tried town, in case she'd given up on the beach as soon as the sun got stronger, but I still can't find her, and ..." She trailed off and took a steadying breath, then continued a little more calmly. "So I was on my way to try the beach again, in case I missed her, or we passed each other without my seeing her, or *whatever.* But then I saw you, Callum. And I just ... I know you're probably not doing the detective stuff anymore, but I can pay. I can go to the ATM right now and get a deposit, and I promise, *promise* I'll get the rest tomorrow. And, you know, maybe it's not even a problem, maybe she did have to go and do some work, but it's *daylight*, and her scythe's still in the cottage, and her phone's off and ..." She stopped, running down as if the words had simply become too much. "I just want to find her."

"We'll find her," Callum said. "And you don't have to worry about paying. You're our friends."

"And this is why we're currently working on a pirate ship," I said. "Because you won't charge anyone."

Emma looked around, sniffling slightly. "Why *are* you working on a pirate ship? Why are you even in Whitby?"

"It's a long story," Callum said.

"Most everyone in Leeds wants to kill us," I said.

"There's also a short version," he said, looking at me.

"Oh," Emma said, sounding less surprised than seemed polite. "So you came to *Whitby?*"

"It was recommended," Callum said. "A bit out of the way, you know?"

"And the pirate ship?"

"We needed the money."

"Okay," she said, and finished her tea. "I suppose that's why anyone becomes a pirate."

"Mostly I try to stop drunk people falling overboard, and Gobs pretends he's going to catch the ship's rats."

"There's *rats?*" Emma asked.

"Ahoy, matey," a small voice said from near her ankle, and Emma managed to control a small jump rather admirably.

She looked down at Neecy. "Oh. I was thinking pest-type rats, not talking rats."

"All rats talk," Neecy said. "You lot just don't listen well. Got any cheese, by any chance?"

"Not on me," Emma said, clutching her mug a little more tightly, and I had a feeling she was wondering about pest control at the cafe, and if she was trapping talking rats. Not that it was likely she'd actually have to set traps. Not with litters of ravenous ghoulets all over the place.

She looked back at Callum. "So what do we do? How do we start? Do you want to talk to Matilda?"

"No," Callum and I said together, and Emma frowned.

"Why not? She was the last to see Gertrude. Isn't that what you do? Talk to witnesses and stuff?"

"I mean, that's *part* of what we do," I said. "But we've got a professional system, you know."

"Do you?"

"Yes," I said, and Emma looked at me expectantly. I stared back at her.

"We're hiding out," Callum said. "And that includes from unfamiliar cats."

Emma's frown deepened. "You think the people who're after you in Leeds are *cats?*"

"Cats," I said. "Necromancers. Weres. Callum's dodgy sister. Callum's dodgy magician ex-bestie. A sorcerer. All their various sidekicks." I thought about it. "That pretty much covers it, I think."

"Is anyone *not* after you?" Emma asked, and offered her biscuit to Green Snake. He took it delicately.

"There's probably a cat charity that would still take me in," I said.

"Not if they met you," Callum said, and grinned at me. Emma managed a small laugh, so I only growled slightly. Callum looked back at Emma and said, "So. Beach, then."

"That's what I thought. I was just going to start walking toward Sandsend and hope I saw something." She looked at the round window in the closed door that gave onto the deck. "It's almost dark though."

Callum looked at me. "Sandsend?" he suggested. It was the next village north along the coast, visible on a clear day as a cluster of buildings pinned in by a sea wall, huddled just inside the headland that curtailed the long, grey stretches of Whitby sand.

I wrinkled my snout. "What about the whole *stay in town* thing?"

Callum *hmm*-ed. "D'you really think June was onto something?"

"Hilda did say to stay put," I pointed out.

"I thought that was just because she didn't like Murty."

"She had a point with water boy," I said, and we both looked at each other doubtfully.

"I can just go," Emma said. "If you have to work, or whatever." She had the brittle brightness in her voice that goes all jaggy in the ear, the way a fresh frost crumbles under-paw.

"No, we're coming, aren't we?" Callum said.

I sighed. "Well, we're going to have to try leaving sometime."

"What d'you mean, *try*?" Emma asked.

Callum scratched his cheek, stubble rasping under his fingertips. "Yes. So. We sort of …"

"It seems like we're meant to stay in Whitby," I said. "Both the pirate and the fake medium said so, but I think the pirate might have been influenced by the panda fish."

Emma just stared at me blankly for a moment, then looked at Callum and said, "I take it back. Living with him must actually be *more* weird than living with a reaper."

"You have no idea," he said.

EMMA GAVE HALF a Chokkie Diggle to Neecy while Callum tried calling Gertrude on his phone, just in case she was avoiding Emma for some reason – probably the umbrella situation. There was no answer, and Emma gave him a *told you so* look as she brushed crumbs off her fingers.

"These are terrible biscuits," Neecy said. "The captain has much better ones."

"You're not meant to be eating the captain's ones," I said. "That was the deal. I wouldn't actually chase you and you'd make more strategic choices when it comes to scavenging."

"Then you need to up your biscuit game," she said, looking at a chunkier rat who was chewing on a piece of tinned fruit Callum had missed.

He burped and nodded. "Yeah, and there's not much rum in your punch, you know."

"They didn't need much," Callum said. "Neither do you."

"Nothing wrong with a bit of rum," the big rat said. "Keeps out the cold, like."

"Come on, Carlos," Neecy said. "Don't want you falling in the bilges again."

"That was totally deliberate," he said, slightly muffled as he stuffed the rest of the fruit in his mouth. "Acrobatic, that was."

"Falling on your head, more like." She glanced at us, her gaze lingering on Callum. "Watch that mermaid. They're trouble, you know."

"Mermaid?" Emma asked, as Neecy vanished through a skinny gap in the bulkhead. Carlos followed, getting stuck for a moment with his back paws pedalling wildly, then flopping through. "You've seen a *mermaid?*"

"Don't get too excited," I said. "He was kind of big and toothy."

Emma gave me startled look, and Callum snorted. "Well, he wasn't in a shell bikini, anyway." He got up and collected the mugs and biscuits, ducking through to the galley with them, then re-emerged a moment later in his ancient, tatty coat.

"What's *that?*" I demanded. Hilda had taken one look at what Callum had been wearing when we'd stepped on board and made him go and change into clothes of her own choosing. That had included a jacket with *The Savage Squid* printed large on the back, along with the image of a kraken taking down a ship. It seemed to me like a slightly inappropriate logo for advertising boat trips, but it was printed nice and big on the T-shirt Callum was wearing under his logo-ed up fleece, too. It was all second-hand gear, and some of it had mysterious rips and stains on it, but at least it wasn't the usual long, damp coat Callum favoured. Small mercies and all that. But now he'd resurrected the coat from somewhere.

He looked down at himself. "It's comfortable. And it doesn't feel right to work without it."

"It's not even waterproof," I pointed out.

"It's not raining," he said, and looked at Emma. "Let's go, then. Before it gets any darker."

Emma nodded, getting up and shrugging back into her own jacket. "I just don't understand what she was doing out in the *day*. Even with her hat on, she still gets burnt, you know. She was all pink last night, and she said she'd caught it through the windows." She frowned. "She *lied* to me! And now she's going to be even *more* burnt!" She sounded as if she wasn't sure which to be more upset by.

"Today's been pretty cloudy," I pointed out, in case that helped.

"Even so." Emma followed Callum out onto the deck and looked up at the darkening clouds, forming bulky layers across the sky. "And if she went out just after I left, she was waiting for me to not be around."

"Maybe she was getting you a birthday present," I suggested.

"It's not my birthday."

"Valentine's, then. That's around now, right?"

Emma sighed. "I don't think Gertrude quite grasps Valentine's."

"Yeah, me either." I followed them up the gangway, and Callum looked at Emma as he hooked the bit of rope that constituted *The Savage Squid's* security measures back in place.

"It'll be something like that, though," he said. "She's a reaper. Nothing too bad can have happened."

"*Hmm,*" Emma said, and we turned toward the pier, where the lighthouse was already painting beams across the low, heavy clouds in the eternal signal.

Danger. Danger. Danger.

WE HEADED STRAIGHT DOWN the wharf toward the pier and the beach that ran north from it, the mingled scents of the fish'n'chip shops and the pubs and the fishing boats being whisked away by a strengthening breeze that smelled of distant storms. My whiskers twitched with the weight of the changing weather as I padded next to Callum, and my ears were full of the cries of the gulls. He fished his cigarettes out and lit one, the flare of the lighter flushing his face in soft orange for an instant. Emma waved the packet away when he offered it to her. A small dog of the bug-eyed variety yapped hysterically at me until its owner picked it up, at which point it bit him. He dropped the dog and swore loudly, and his wife started shouting at him to be more careful and not upset Slocomb. The dog – presumably Slocomb – went back to yapping at me and rolling its bug eyes in horror, twig-like legs trembling.

"Man's best friend," I observed. "Bet you're happy you domesticated them."

"They have the advantage of not talking," Callum said, looking up and down the dockside road as if expecting

Gertrude to pop out of the Dracula attraction and nod gravely at us. "I see the appeal."

"I can shout incoherently and poop on the street if it helps."

"Don't you do that anyway?"

Emma snorted with laughter and I showed her a tooth, but that just made her laugh more. I dodged when she tried to scritch me and scrambled up to Callum's shoulder instead.

"You can walk, you know," he said.

"Puddles," I said. "And dogs."

We walked down the pier first, rather than straight onto the beach. The light was dull and heavy, the beach wide and shadowed, and other than the constant crash of grey waves onto the sand, there was little movement that I could see. Spray hung heavy in the air, stealing details and turning the coast indistinct, but I could make out the faded green roof and red brick of the pavilion just to this side of the beach huts that climbed up the cliff in bright primary hues. Railed concrete walkways ran down to the huts, and there was a shop/cafe type thing dug back into the land among them, shuttered and dark. Sandsend was lost in the fading light, and the wind was picking up, really getting into throwing the sea around.

"See anyone?" I asked. I'd jumped to the ground when we stopped by the fat brick base of the West Pier lighthouse, where the stone wharf ended and wooden slats took over on a newer extension that ran all the way to the beacon at the end. The gaps between the boards looked down to the solid concrete base of the pier, and stairs let fishers go down to set up their bait boxes and nets and deck chairs on quiet days. The sea was building, but there were a last few grimly determined lingerers down there still, the scent of bait buckets and the soft clatter of reels drifting up to us.

Emma held her hair back with both hands, examining the

pier before she turned to look at the beach. "It's getting so dark already. Can you see her, Callum?"

Callum leaned on the railing, squinting along the shoreline as the slowly rising wind tugged at his coat. "There's a couple of dog walkers, but I don't see anyone on their own."

"Who've you lost?" someone asked, and we turned to look at a woman with a bait bucket in one hand and a fishing pole in the other. She had a heavy yellow waterproof coat zipped up to her chin, and her dark hair lashed her reddened face. She smiled at me. "Hello, little one."

I looked back at her blankly, but also with what I hoped was a pleading tilt to my head. She'd donated me more than one decent herring, but I couldn't exactly ask for an encore. Average humans didn't believe there was magic in the world, so they simply didn't see it. Didn't see the dance of lights that were pixies weaving spells in the moonlight, didn't see the folded, leathery wings of a faery as they ran for the bus, didn't see the bare, shining hooves of a faun as they queued for coffee. It was better for them that they didn't, because humans struggle to understand what is different. Struggle to understand, and are inclined to destroy it simply for the fact that it *is* different. So the magical Folk of the world kept their secrets, and the humans kept their beliefs, and cats held their tongues.

Mostly, anyway.

"You haven't seen a woman out walking, have you?" Callum asked, waving his hand vaguely at about shoulder height. "Sort of this tall?"

The woman frowned. "Dog walker?"

"No, just her."

"What colour jacket?"

"Um." Callum looked at Emma.

"Less a jacket than a robe," Emma said. "Black."

"Oh, aye?" The woman raised her eyebrows slightly, and

looked at me. "Black robes and black cats. Wouldn't be the first I've seen out here."

I purred, and went to rub against her leg, but changed my mind at the last moment. She was wearing blue wellies that still had fish blood and scales stuck to them. So I just gave her my most endearing mew instead. She scritched me between the ears and looked back at Emma.

"Why're you looking for this black-robed woman?"

"She's not answering her phone. It's not like her."

The woman nodded thoughtfully. "We all need a little peace at times."

Emma shook her head, and the corner of her mouth twitched down. "She wouldn't worry me. Not like this."

"And you?" the woman asked, looking at Callum.

"We're just helping." Callum gave her his best harmless human shrug, and smiled. "She's a friend of ours."

"We? As in you and the cat?"

"Sure." He smiled a little wider, evidently hoping the dimples kicked in. Something about the dimples rendered a certain proportion of the population unexpectedly helpful and friendly, but the fisher didn't seem to be moved.

"I'll keep an eye out for a woman in a black robe," she said. "Tell her some guy and a cat are looking for her."

"That would actually be fine," Callum said. "She'll know who it is."

The woman stared at him for a moment, then laughed, lines crinkling at the corners of her eyes and her own dimples emerging. "You're an odd one." She nodded along the beach. "No one like that's headed out while I've been here, but if she was out earlier she could have walked as far as Sandsend and caught the bus back."

"Thank you," Emma said. "We'll look."

"I'd stay off the beach," the woman said, her smile fading. "The tide's on the way up, and it's going to be a rough old night. The dark'll come in quick with that." She gestured out to sea with her rod hand, indicating the clouds pressing lower and lower to the horizon. A couple of fishing boats were sprinting in ahead of it.

"But someone told me she went along the beach," Emma said. "I don't think they'd lie."

"She went on her own?"

"Yes."

The woman stole a glance along the shoreline, fading from sight amid the sea spray and the gathering dark. "Unfortunate," she said, her voice quiet, then looked at Emma again. "Take the clifftop path. You'll see better from there." She picked up her bucket and turned toward town, where more lights were coming on. "Stay off the sand. It's not been safe recently."

We watched her go, and after a moment I looked up at Callum. "Tell me we're not going along the beach."

Emma answered before he could. "Matilda said that's where she saw her."

"*This morning.* If she's still walking, she's in bloody Scotland by now."

"The beach doesn't go that far," Callum said.

"Hilarious. Do we even trust this cat?"

"I do," Emma said. "Why would she lie to me?"

I made a disbelieving noise. "At least let's go along the clifftop. Fishy there had a point about being able to see, right?"

"But you can't smell anything from up there," Callum said. "You might sniff Gertrude out on the beach."

"I'm not a bloody dog. All I can smell is dead fish and bird droppings anyway." And the sea. The dank, endless saltiness of it, redolent of tears and hope and sorrow. Nothing much cut through that, and I could never decide if it wore at me, setting my whiskers on edge with its promise of distant shores and lost treasure and vast depths, or if it filled some aching void I'd never even known I carried. Maybe both.

Callum looked at Emma. "I think Gobs could be right. The clifftop path'll give us a better view."

"Fine," she said. "But if I see her, I'm going down to the beach. I don't care what some fisher person says."

"Fair enough," Callum said. We headed back down the pier toward town while the sea crashed beneath us and the wind ran hard fingers across my fur, and salt coated my paws like the world's tears.

6

BEYOND THE BORDERS

I RAN AHEAD OF CALLUM AND EMMA AS WE TOOK THE PATH
that ran up the inside of the cliff to the tops, leaping from
step to step until the bushes gave way to mown grass
unrolling around a dais. On it the statue of some dude with a
ponytail and a look that said *hello, yes, all your land is now
mine*, stared moodily off to sea, and nearby two arching ribs
of a long-dead whale formed a frame for tourists to snap
shots of the Abbey through. A road on the left cut the clifftop
green off from the houses and an elegantly ageing hotel, all
of which had the high windows and faded, genteel air of old
Victorian seaside retreats. Lights were already on inside
many of them, and two small children rugged up in so many
layers that they couldn't put their arms down ran screaming
along the path toward us.

I ignored them, flattening my ears against the wind and
loping across the green to the drive that came up from the
pavilion. Below me I could see the old building clinging
grimly to the edge of the land, rust softly streaking its domes
while layers of salt caked the windows. The slope from here
to the beach was too steep to call a hill, really, but not quite

sharp enough to be a cliff, and was covered in long thick grass and a tangle of concrete walkways and stairs. I stopped at the edge of the drive, looking back at Callum and Emma as they crested the hill, and Callum nodded at me in a way that suggested he wasn't going to talk and let on how out of breath he was, in case I pointed out how much *less* out of breath he'd be if he gave up the cigarettes.

I squinted against the wind as I waited, listening to it scratching through the long grass that covered the hill-slash-cliff like the pelt of a vast sleeping beast. Further along the coast, the slope made up its mind about being a cliff and became still steeper, all exposed red rock and yellow earth, but here it was a rippling sea of bleached green growth.

Callum and Emma joined me, gravel crunching under Emma's fancy walking shoes and the worn-down boots Callum had swapped for his work trainers, and we followed the drive that skirted the pavilion and its cargo of salt-smeared billboards. Beyond it, the beach huts climbed the cliff in neat rows, painted in alternating colours that would've been blinding on a summer's day, but today looked muted and dull. A few of them had little name boards screwed to them, proclaiming them as *The Lookout* or *The Bird's Nest* or something equally imaginative, but others just had numbers, and there was a large sign suggesting brightly that we might like to rent one for our next holiday.

The drive split into three paths, one branch heading back up the cliff and another down toward the beach, and we followed the wider middle way that led to a large circular concrete platform which pressed out from the shuttered beach shop. There was an ice cream poster stuck to one wall, peeling at the edges, as well as a couple of clean-scrubbed blackboards, and painted signs still advertised bucket and spade and deck chair hire. The outer edge of the platform projected over the beach, giving a view back toward town on the right and as far as visibility allowed to the left. The sand was a scoured sweep of grey, pocked with clumps of seaweed and the odd exposed rock, and there was absolutely no one in sight except for one small figure running after three dogs who were sprinting wildly in pursuit of some seagulls. I hoped they caught them. The gulls, that is.

"See anything?" I asked Callum, taking shelter behind his legs. The wind was picking up the sand on the path and flinging it in my eyes.

"No. But she could have stopped in Sandsend, like the fisher said."

"We need to walk down there," Emma said.

"Is that really going to help?" I asked. "It's not like we're going to catch her if she went out first thing this morning."

"We might meet her on the way back."

"Look, I know reapers are weird, but it's hardly the afternoon for a pleasant stroll on the beach. Only dogs and their humans are that misguided. *And* it's going to be dark soon." *And the fisher said to stay off the beach.* There was something about her that made me want to listen. She wasn't Folk – she didn't have that whiff of strangeness Folk carried – but that didn't mean she wasn't *something*. Like Callum. Some nights I watched while he twitched in restless dreams, waiting for him to reveal himself, but he still smelled of nothing more than stale smoke and old books and an emptiness that had no answer.

"We can't just leave her," Emma said, and we both looked at Callum.

Callum drummed his fingers on the railing, pulling himself forward over it as if it might help him see further along the foam-wreathed coast. He didn't answer.

"What if something's happened?" Emma asked. "Like Gobs said, it's not a day for being out there. She might've fallen on the rocks or something."

"She's a *reaper*," I said. "I don't think a stubbed toe is going to slow her down."

"But if she's been out in the sun all day, who knows what might've happened? What *does* happen to a reaper if they're in the sun too long? She could have sunstroke!"

"*Sunstroke?* It's February in bloody North Yorkshire!"

"Well, I'm going," Emma said, and glared at me. "You do whatever you want, but *I'm* not leaving her out there." And she marched off down the walkway with her back straight and her soft brown hair whipping around her head like a living thing.

"At least let's stay on the clifftop," I yelled after her, but she either ignored me or didn't hear.

Callum watched her go, then looked at me.

"Aw, come on," I said. "It's wet. And windy. And *sandy*. And she's a *reaper*."

"Emma's not. What if it gets dark and she ends up hurt, and then we've got a missing reaper *and* an injured Emma?"

I sighed. "Don't you do the appealing-to-my-nature thing."

"*Better* nature."

"I have a great nature. It's all of the better sort."

"Sure it is." He looked at me, squinting as the wind shoved his hair into his eyes. "And, of course, we'd have an angry reaper if we had an injured Emma. That can't be good."

I wrinkled my snout, the constant thud of the waves on the sand echoing in my ears. "Can we charge them, at least?"

"Obviously not." He started along the path that ran down to the base of the cliffs, following the shape of the beach.

"I don't see what's obvious about it," I complained, loping after him. "We're broke."

"Not really. Piracy pays better than PI-ing."

"It's messier, though."

"Eh. Not always. Besides, I think it might be handy to have a reaper on our side, don't you?"

I grumbled, but didn't argue. He did have a point. Although pirate wages still weren't going to buy us passage to anywhere with paper umbrellas.

WE CAUGHT up to Emma as she strode along the concrete pathway, the drier sand scratching and whipping around us and the long grass that coated the hill whistling and rustling like the approach of a herd of snakes. The visibility was even worse down at beach level, and the wind seemed stronger than it had higher up. The waves rolled across the sand with relentless, endless hunger, reaching a little higher with every stretch, and the lights of Whitby were lost around the headland behind us. Emma gave us a look that was half grateful, half obstinate, then scrambled down the rocks, off the relative safety of the path and onto the beach. Callum followed her, and I voiced some keen observations about humans and their thinking processes, which no one paid any attention to, then followed.

The hard-packed sand was cold beneath my paws, and I stuck close to where the rocks met the beach, keeping a wary eye on the incoming tide. Callum looked at me questioningly, and I gave him a shrug. I was trying to catch any lingering scents of voids and cold steel the reaper might have left behind her, but I couldn't find much of her or anyone else, not in the wind and the beginning edge of a sharp rain in the air. Other than the occasional whiff of dog, there was nothing. Just the muscular scent of the sea swallowing everything.

We kept on anyway, Emma pulling on a woolly hat to hold her hair in place while Callum's whipped around his face like the enthusiastic arms of sea anemones. My snout felt like it was cramping from being continually wrinkled by the combined assault of wind and sand and sea spray, and despite our pace I was starting to shiver. This was pointless. Whatever signs the reaper might have left behind her, she was *gone*. And I still thought we were more likely to get into some sort of mess than she was. After all, she had a scythe that could cleave souls from the world – although Emma had said that was still in their holiday cottage, which seemed odd.

I was momentarily distracted from the misery of wind and sand as I wondered what sort of holiday cottages reapers favoured – something with frills and doilies, at a guess – and I didn't spot the three dogs we'd seen from the path until they were almost on us. I shot behind Callum's legs, claws tearing the sand, but the mutts raced past without noticing me, still chasing the gulls with their tongues out in great dopey grins. Emma turned to watch them go, smiling, and a few moments later a slight woman sprinted along the sand toward us, her hair in a ponytail that streamed like a flag in the wind and her face flushed pink with cold and effort. She slowed as she approached us.

"Tide's coming in," she shouted.

"We're looking for someone," Emma called back. "A woman out walking on her own. Have you seen her?"

The runner shook her head. "No one out here but me. It's getting late. And the tide's coming in," she repeated, nodding back toward town. "I'd head in if I were you. You don't want to get caught out."

"Thanks. We'll just go a bit further. Make sure she's alright."

"Suit yourselves. But don't get stuck. No excuse for it, and no reason to have the lifeboat called out on you." She gave Callum a severe look, as if suspecting he might be a problem. Then she was running again, the wind buffeting her and making her stagger sideways a couple of steps with a yelp of delight. She followed the dogs down the beach, her footprints crossing ours.

"Humans," I said, watching her go.

Callum watched her as well, then looked at me. "Footprints," he said.

"Paws," I said, shaking one out. The sand was caking under my claws.

"No, look – the tide was high early this morning. Gertrude would've had to stay close to the cliffs, and the tide's only coming back in now. So we might still be able to see her footprints."

"Right. Because you know what they look like, do you?"

"I do," Emma said, her voice raised against the wind. There was a touch of excitement to it. "She doesn't wear shoes. There can't be that many people barefoot at this time of year, can there?"

"I wouldn't bet on it," I said, but she had a point.

Callum peered along the beach. "It narrows things down."

"Sure. Why not," I said. "Nothing better to do than be out on a bloody freezing beach in a hurricane, right?" But I was already moving past him, loping across the hard-packed sand and keeping a wary eye out for gulls as we hunted out the footprints that ran like stories along the salt-soaked coast.

There were a few sets of tracks left by running shoes high on the beach, crumbling at the edges and leaving nothing behind them but the faintest whiff of self-punishment. Dog walkers left the steadier prints of waterproof boots, torn in places by paw prints of varying sizes and wet-dog excitement. I imagined on a more reasonable day for outdoor activities there'd be a tangled mess of walking shoes and even bare feet everywhere, but not today, in the foam-filled air and the storm-low clouds.

It was starting to spit sharp points of rain, the darkening sky promising more to come, when we stopped next to a trail of prints formed by skinny, long-toed bare feet. There was the suggestion of something skeletal to them, even though they were clearly a *footprint*, not a bone-print. They headed steadily along the shining grey sand, detouring now and then where the owner had stopped to look at an interesting piece of driftwood, or to stare out to sea, and the prints of dog paws ran toward them then detoured abruptly.

"It's her!" Emma said. Her face with pink with cold. "It has to be!"

I paced around the prints, snuffling at the sand and trying to ignore the odd raindrop whipping into my ears. "I can't smell much other than bloody dead fish." But that wasn't quite true. There was a whiff of something deeper and darker, too, something still and silent and gentle. "But I suppose it could be her."

"It can't be anyone else," Callum said, and looked along the beach in the direction the prints were heading. Somewhere out there Whitby ended, although there was no telling how it was marked, or if we'd even recognise the marks when we saw them.

"Are we going?" Emma demanded, and Callum looked at me.

"'Course we are," I said, and shook a raindrop out of my ear. "Not going would be sensible, and when have we ever been accused of that?"

"Thanks?" Emma said, the corner of her mouth twitching up. At least someone was amused.

"Want a lift?" Callum asked me.

"It's the least you can do," I said, and he picked me up, tucking me inside his coat where it was a little warmer, if a bit whiffy of cigarettes. Green Snake lifted his head out of the inside pocket and stared at me. I bared a tooth at him and said to Callum, "Don't get hypothermia. I'm not doing the Lassie routine for you."

"Good to know," he said, and headed down the beach at a pace that was almost a jog, Emma hurrying next to him as we followed Gertrude's footprints, leading us on into the low dusk of the storm.

GERTRUDE HAD BEEN STRIDING PURPOSEFULLY ALONG the shore, according to her footprints, only stopping occasionally to look out to sea. But the further we went along the beach, the more she paused, and her trail veered closer and closer to the water's edge, sometimes vanishing altogether before reappearing again a few paces later.

Finally Callum stopped, and I peered through the neck of his coat at the damp sand in front of us. The rain was getting heavier. "What?" I asked. "I can't see anything."

"Exactly," he said. "We've lost the prints."

"She must've kept going," Emma said. "She *must* have. She wouldn't have gone into the water."

"Not a swimmer?" I asked.

"No. She paddled a bit, but she didn't like it much."

Callum nodded. "Reapers and water don't really mix. I might've got the tide times a bit wrong – perhaps she had more beach to walk on." He sounded dubious, though. One of his jobs on *The Savage Squid* was to take down the marine forecast from the radio every morning. I'd pointed out to Hilda that there were such things as phones and apps these days, but she'd just asked me if I'd caught any rats yet, as she wanted to see their tails. Which, *ew*. But it also meant I doubted Callum *had* got the tides wrong.

"Well, we've only seen the footprints go one way. We need to keep going to Sandsend," Emma said.

I suddenly thought of the landlord at the boarding house, all heavy red whiskers and faded eyes, sliding the address of the day's work over to us and saying the same thing every day: *Tell Doris* – or Betty, or Judith, or whichever of Whitby's little old ladies Bob had charmed into paying him a direct debit for handyman duties, as it seemed he had most of that particular demographic covered – *tell them you're my cousin. No taking tips. No accepting extra jobs. No leaving town*. I hadn't even noticed it, and even if I had, I'd've thought it was him worried he wasn't going to keep his free labour. But then not-psychic June had come out with that stuff on the dock. And Hilda saying the same thing, which was maybe to do with Murty, but maybe not. And— "Hang about," I said to Callum. "*Gerry* told us not to leave town too, didn't he?"

"He did. But that might've been more so we kept a low profile."

"Sure. Except *everyone* seems kind of keen on us not leaving town. So what's all that about?"

"I don't know." Callum took his cigarettes out, looked at the wind and rain, and put them back again with a sigh.

Emma had taken a few steps along the beach, and now she looked back at us. "I'm going. I *have* to. Are you coming? Because we need to hurry. The tide's getting higher."

"Gobs?" Callum said.

"I'm not getting down," I said. "My paws are already far wetter than I'm comfortable with. You can carry me."

"I expected nothing else." He set off at an actual jog this time, and I rather rapidly decided I'd made a bad decision. He was still holding me inside his jacket with one arm, and the jostling was going to make me seasick, so I struggled out, growling, and jumped to the sand. The light was fading steadily, and the broad expanse of beach had already narrowed to an alarming degree. I glanced up at the cliffs, but there were no houses visible along this stretch of shore, and the concrete path had run out back where we'd met the runner and her dogs. There was no one out here, and no way off the beach. There was just us, and the wheeling gulls, and the grumble of the hungry sea. I ran after Callum, ears back and nose full of the scent of salt, wondering where the border of Whitby was.

We were racing the light as much as the tide, staying just beyond the roll of the waves, eyes on the sand as we ran, still hunting for Gertrude's footprints. Emma pushed on ahead of us, her pace steady and measured. Callum slowed now and then to catch his breath, but his stride was longer than hers, and he caught up again easily. I just kept going at a steady lope. My fur was full of sand and my nose burned with salt, but further along the beach lights were beginning to loop toward the shore as the cliffs dropped lower and the road came out to meet the waterfront. Still further on the tiny village of Sandsend announced itself as a blur of orange and yellow emerging out of the murk.

And two things didn't happen. Gertrude's footprints didn't come ashore, and nothing stopped us. There was no frisson of charms as we passed through Whitby's borders, and I wondered if the sea had swallowed it, or if maybe Sandsend was still part of Whitby, or if the charms had already relinquished what little protection they'd given us. In the wind and the rain and the salt, all I felt was the increasing dampness of my paws and the weight of my coat.

We passed the first of Sandsend's houses, jumping a shallow rivulet that spilled out across the sand, and ran on under the buttress of the high retaining walls that held the road and the town beyond, the sea close enough now that we were sprinting in a channel between the oncoming waves and the sheer rock. The headlights of cars splintered on the spray, and the warm glow of streetlights and houses grew auras in the damp air above us.

Still no footprints. Still no charms.

We dodged leftover wooden posts that had once held a

jetty or a wharf, growing out of the sand like broken teeth in a rotting jaw, the crash of waves on the next headland building like the growl of an approaching beast. The bigger swells turned the sand under-paw soft and sticky, and Callum was panting steadily.

No footprints. No charms.

Callum and Emma hurdled a spreading waterway that was flooding inland with the tide, and I splashed through it without stopping. I was soaked anyway. The buildings and the lights ran out, and suddenly the twilight was both wilder and more insistent. The short day was all but done, and the sand was giving to more and more rock and cast-off seaweed and debris. Callum gave a sudden yelp and swerved toward the shoreline, grabbing me as a rogue wave pounced after us. The headland reared up, cutting off the beach abruptly, pocked with the deeper shadows of caves and topped with weathered, twisted vegetation.

Emma stumbled to a stop, looking from the headland to the sea, then back at the retaining wall, the tops of parked cars just visible over it. There was nowhere left to go but back. Callum put a hand out to support himself against the stone, panting.

"She didn't come ashore," he managed, and Emma shook her head, not speaking. She was taking quick, hitching breaths, but I didn't think it was from the run.

"But she's a *reaper*," I said, and the words tasted flat and slick as the rotting fish on the wind.

7

ADDING SALT TO INJURY

THE SEA WAS RECLAIMING THE BEACH AT AN ALARMING RATE now, and the rain had come in with conviction, so I didn't try to get down as Callum persuaded Emma to head for the steps up to the car park. She'd started talking and couldn't seem to stop, the words tumbling out over themselves.

"But she doesn't *swim*," she kept saying. "And she wouldn't go out in a boat. Would she? Might there have been a boat? Where would she get a boat? *Why* would she get a boat? Did we miss her? Maybe we missed her. Could we have missed her?"

We didn't have any answers. All we had was the tide, coming in steadily, and our narrowing patch of sand. That, and a crawling feeling in my spine, trying to convince my sodden hair to stand up. It wasn't Ms Jones, I didn't think, although we were beyond whatever protection Whitby had offered us here. I hadn't felt it go, but now we'd stopped I could feel the difference, a strange sense of exposure that had nothing to do with the wind and the storm.

But there were other things to worry about than impatient sorcerers keen on yanking me out of my skin, which was a concerning thought. And something around here was tickling my whiskers. I jumped down and padded a few steps back the way we'd come, my ears twitching with the wind. I could hear Callum telling Emma that we couldn't do any good here, that we had to get off the beach and get dry. He was right, and I wanted nothing so much as a warm blanket, a large bowl of highly processed cat food, and, preferably, a good roaring fire, but ... But. I peered down the beach, painted in shades of grey as the night and the storm joined forces to wash the light from the day. I couldn't see anything, but my paws were itching and the skin on my back kept jumping like there was a hand about to grab it.

Every creature remembers, at some level, what it is to be hunted. And I'd had some decent practice at it, as much as I'd have preferred not to. My life choices seemed determined to keep me on the wrong side of the predator-prey equation. I couldn't see anything but rain-smeared lights and the white-foamed sea, couldn't hear anything but the crashing sea, couldn't *smell* anything but the bloody sea, yet my heart was painfully fast and every muscle in my body was coiled in readiness. I turned to look at Callum. He was waiting at the bottom of the steps, watching me.

"We need to go back," I said.

"What?" he asked, then shook his head. "No, Gobs. We can't. The tide—"

"Listen, you algae-ridden bilge-dweller – we're outside Whitby. We have to go back. *Now.*"

"We're going to. Just by land," he said, and started up the steps.

"*Callum!*" I bawled, and he stopped again, scowling. Emma was standing at the top of the steps, ignoring us and looking at the sea as if she might glimpse Gertrude out there if she just stared hard enough. "Listen to me. We have to go."

"Why?"

"I don't know," I admitted. "But I *know*. Cat thing."

"Oh, for ..." He threw one longing look at the yellow lights of Sandsend, then stomped back down the steps, reaching for his cigarettes. "*Fine.* Bloody hell. Don't get us drowned out here, Gobs."

"I'll try to avoid it," I said, and turned to head back along the beach.

"Emma," Callum started, faintly muffled as he tried to create enough shelter to light a cigarette.

"I'm coming," she said, sounding oddly calm. "Maybe we'll see her if we go back." She trotted down the stairs and joined me. "Come on, then. Off we go. Lead on, Gobbelino." I half expected her to clap her hands like a schoolteacher, chivvying us along, but she just gave me a lopsided sort of smile and didn't bother to wipe the water from her face. I had an idea it wasn't all rain.

I narrowed my eyes against the wind, put my nose to Whitby, and led on.

It wasn't long before I was convinced that if anyone – any*thing* – was actually out hunting us in this, they were welcome to catch us if they just promised to put us in a nice dry holding cell with central heating. Of course, they were more likely to tear us limb from limb, if previous experience was anything to go by, so I just kept grimly trudging on ahead of Callum and Emma. Every time I looked back she was staring out at the approaching waves, and Callum looked like he was ready to tackle her if she made a dash for it. I was busier looking at the land, but I still hadn't seen any movement to give me an idea of what was out there. *If* anything was, and I wasn't just jumpy with mermaids and fake medium threats, and the endless watchfulness against sorcerers and the Watch and unknown enemies, and that itch in the back of my mind that felt like it was building to a scream.

The sea kept pushing us further and further toward the cliffs, and at one point I had to sprint for the crumbling edges of the land and scramble into the rocks to avoid getting my paws wet. Well, *wetter*, since the water from above was doing a perfectly good job of things.

"We have to go up," Callum shouted, words torn by the wind. "We're going to run out of beach." He looked as wet as I did, and had only managed about half a cigarette before he'd lost it to the rain. It didn't seem to be improving his disposition, and he waved impatiently at the cliffs.

Emma looked at the foam swirling around her boots and nodded. "But how?" she called. "It's straight up!"

"I'll try it," I said, peering up at the wall of rock and wet earth above me. Even with my eyes, it was too dark and mucky to be able to pick out any sort of path, so I just went for the random attack option. I jumped to the top of a fallen boulder, gathered myself, and leaped for an outcropping further up. My paws slipped on the slick mud covering it, and I jumped again before I could lose my grip entirely, turning my climb into a scramble as I searched for a perch. I made it up a couple of metres further, but the rain had turned the cliff face into a treacherous mix of loose rock and sludgy mud. The earth just kept vanishing beneath my paws, and I squawked as a small slip morphed into a rapid backward slide. I flung myself clear as a clump of soil gripped in the roots of some tussocky grass threatened to roll over me, and landed back on the edge of the beach on all fours, belly dropping low to the sand as my legs took up the shock of the fall.

"Are you alright?" Emma asked.

"It's too loose!" I shouted. "And if I can't climb it, you two've got about as much chance as a haddock in a gull fight."

Callum peered up and down the beach, sheltering his eyes from the salt spray with his hands, then looked at me, and said, "Not saying you're overreacting or anything, but can you actually see anything behind us? It's a lot closer to go back to Sandsend than to try and reach Whitby."

I gave a hiss of impatience and ran at him, intending to scramble to his shoulder for a better vantage point, but he grabbed me up before I could jump, swinging around so that we were both facing back to Sandsend.

For a moment I saw nothing but the lights strung like blossom along the shoreline, edges gently smeared by the thundering spray, and I wondered if I'd been wrong. If the sleepless nights and my restless prowling had me seeing threats where there was nothing but the unknown and indifferent. The sea rolled in endlessly, white-streaked and frothing, and Sandsend turned its back to it, looking inward to warm fires and golden light, leaving everything else shadowed and half-seen. No one was out. Who would be, in this? Just us, running from nothing.

Then Callum said, "Are those seals?" There was an edge of hopefulness in his voice.

"I think … seals don't *run*," Emma said, and I strained to spot what they were looking at.

It was the regular movement that finally caught my eye. Not the repetitive yet erratic wash of the waves, but a rhythmic rising and falling. Four hulking shapes loping along the edge of the water, the sea breaking around them like the headland itself. Where the lights of the town touched them, their backs gleamed darkly.

"Oh, fish biscuits," I said, the skin on my own back crawling. "I could've really done with being wrong."

"Yeah, you had to break that pattern *now*," Callum said.

"Any chance they're just nice pooches who've broken out for a run?"

"About the same chance as them being chihuahuas," I said. "And I don't know what you mean. I'm very often right."

"Depends how you define *right*." He shifted his grip on me and looked at Emma. "We have to get off the beach."

She looked at the beasts, still loping steadily toward us with great hungry strides, and said, "Maybe they're nothing to do with us."

"That basically never happens," I said. "Besides, they look big and bitey, and a lot bloody faster than us. I don't fancy risking it."

Emma rubbed her face with one hand, then gave a surprisingly loud bellow of, "*For God's **sake**, Gertrude!*" Then she spun back toward Whitby and broke into a decent sprint, despite the chunky walking boots. Callum launched himself after her with me still clutched in one arm, dodging rocks and driftwood and seaweed and the advancing tide. The sea pounded the sand furiously, reaching for us with snapping waves and making the sand soft and treacherous, and I tried to peer around Callum to see how close our pursuers were. But with him still holding me against his chest I couldn't get a good look at them, and instead turned my gaze to the cliff, hoping to spot a way up and away from the water. Away from whatever was coming. There was nothing, just those crumbling, mud-drenched edges of the land, threatening to fall under their own weight, let alone ours.

And I'd thought the mermaid was a problem.

CALLUM LOOKED BACK AND SWORE, putting some more effort into his stride, wheezing. "They're gaining," he managed.

I tried to see past him again, but it was impossible with

the movement. I wasn't quite sure if that was a good thing or not. I didn't fancy being sneaked up on, but I also didn't want to watch the beasts bearing down on us.

"Emma!" Callum shouted. "How far to the path? Can you see a way up yet?"

She slowed to let us catch up, shaking her head rather than answering. She pointed toward Sandsend and managed between breaths, "Are you sure they're after us?"

"I'd be surprised if they weren't," I said. "Most things seem to be after us. *Us* as in me and Callum, though. You're probably safe."

"But why?" she asked. "You haven't done anything."

"I keep saying that," I said.

Callum turned, and I got my first good look at the beasts. They were close enough to see clearly now, not rushing, big strides closing the distance effortlessly. Their bulky shoulders rolled with almost mechanical precision, and their heads hung low and broad.

"They don't look like they're coming in for a belly tickle," I said.

Emma looked up at the cliff. "If we can just get off the beach—"

"They'll follow." Callum's voice was flat. "And Gobs is right. I don't think they're here for you."

"Are they ..." I stared at the oncoming beasts, cut out of the night. No variance on their coats, no fluffy ruffs or edged tails. Just smooth, sleek lines, easily loping voids. "They're not weres, are they?"

"No," Callum said.

"Rottweilers, maybe? Overly muscled Dobermans? Dobermen? Doberpeople?"

"I can't tell," Emma said. "They just look like big black dogs."

"Yeah," I said. "That's what I thought. With capitals."

"With teeth, more to the point," Callum said, while Emma gave me a puzzled look. "We're going in the water."

"We're not," Emma and I said together.

"We are." He tightened his grip on me as I started to wriggle down. "Or you and I are, Gobs. And I think you should come with us, Emma. Black Dogs can't cross running water."

"Does the sea even count as running water?" I demanded.

"It's going to work better than a cliff." He kicked his boots off and dropped his phone into one, not that it'd help much – I could see water dripping from it already. "Are you coming?" he asked Emma.

"I can't," she said, her voice strained. The first of the dogs was close enough now that I could see the dark gape of its mouth, a void within a void. "It's rough. I can't ... I can't swim that well."

Callum looked at the dogs. "You could stay. Try getting up the cliff. They really might not be after you." I heard the *but they might* at the end of the sentence, and from the way Emma's hands were twisted into the front of her coat, I think she did, too.

For one moment I thought she was going to risk it, and I didn't know what that meant Callum and I were going to do. Stay in case they *were* after her and we could ... well, likely get our heads chewed off and not slow them down at all? Run and hope one of them stood on a seashell and they gave it up as a bad job? Leave her to it and throw ourselves into the North Sea? None of the options sounded great. The dogs hadn't randomly appeared just for a bit of a jog around Whitby, and *someone* was getting eaten if we all stayed on the beach.

Then Emma grabbed Callum's hand and said, "Don't let me go."

"I won't," he promised, and ran straight into the sea with me still bundled in one arm.

"*I do not like this,*" I shrieked, and Green Snake came slithering frantically out of Callum's coat pocket as the waves crashed around us. I snatched the silly little reptile up in my jaws before he could fall off, and twisted myself out of Callum's grip, leaping for his shoulder. As I did the bottom fell away under us, or a bigger wave swept us up, because suddenly Callum was swimming, and Emma had vanished underwater entirely, just her hair swirling above her. The wave retreated, and Emma spluttered as she re-emerged, kicking and splashing. Callum hauled her upright and fought his way forward as a cresting wave rolled toward us.

"Hold on!" he yelled, and then everything was foam and salt and darkness, and I was torn from his shoulder as effortlessly as shaking a leaf from my whiskers.

I rolled twice, squinting against the wash with Green Snake still clamped in my jaws, then someone snagged me around the belly and hoisted me aloft. The wave moved on, unperturbed, and Callum dumped me on his shoulder.

"I said hold on," he said, then yelled, "*Emma!*" He must have let go of her to turn and grab me, and she was suddenly an awful lot further out than we were. She didn't look around at his shout, just kept up a grim doggy-paddle toward the distant horizon. "Emma, *stop!*"

"*Mmpf,*" I managed around Green Snake, and peered at the shore. Three beasts were standing at the edge of the water, watching us, and the fourth was chewing on one of Callum's boots. They looked just as much like little snippets of escaped void has they had before, and I couldn't quite convince myself that there was still a chance they weren't Black Dogs. But whatever they were, they weren't swimming after us, at least.

Callum struck out after Emma in a clumsy breaststroke

type thing that washed water over me and Green Snake with every surge forward. He kept shouting her name, but she either wasn't listening or couldn't hear. At least her doggy-paddle was even less efficient than Callum-paddle, and we were gaining on her.

It was brutally cold. The water felt *sharp*, like every bit of salt and sand had grown hard edges, and the air was pins and needles that scraped at every inch of me. Another wave rolled toward us, and Callum ducked under it, one hand clamping me to his shoulder. It wasn't as much of a tumble as before, but we still bobbed and swirled in the wake of the wave, everything directionless and muddled for a painful, stretched instant before we surfaced again. We'd been dragged further out, and Emma wasn't far off.

"Emma, stop!" Callum shouted again, and she looked at him.

"I can't!" she shouted back. "It's too cold! If I stop I'll never start again."

"I know," Callum said, looking back at the beach. "We've got to get back to shore."

My grip on Green Snake was faltering as the chill set in deeper, and as if realising, he took the chance between waves to wrap his tail around my shoulders and squeeze. I let him go, spluttering, and he tightened his grip.

"Now what?" I bellowed at Callum, and got a mouthful of sea for my efforts as a smaller wave slapped us. "How do we get past the bloody Dogs?"

Callum grabbed me and hefted me up as another roller washed toward us. He ducked underwater to avoid the worst of it, and for a moment there was no one but Green Snake and myself, clutched in the disembodied grip of his hand as the sea swallowed the world. I looked back at the beach, but I couldn't see past the breakers crashing into the sand. The lights of Whitby were nothing more than smudges, and

Sandsend wasn't much clearer. There was no one out here, because why would there be? It was night, slap in the middle of a February storm. No one with half an ounce of sense was out in this.

Callum surfaced, his hair slicked across his face like seaweed, dumped me back on his shoulder, and grabbed Emma, who'd been washed up to us and was huffing and splashing like a seal. "We're going back," he said.

"So we're going with eaten rather than drowned?" I spluttered again as a wave hit us, and Green Snake squeezed me in alarm. "Right, I see your point."

"If we stay in the shallows they might not reach us," he said, turning for the shore, then swore. "How'd we get out so bloody far?"

I blinked at the cliffs. Between the rolling waves and the dark and all the panicked paddling, it was hard to have any real sense of distance. But the beach seemed more indistinct than ever. Never mind the dogs – I couldn't even see the sand where it met the cliffs. There was just ocean and land, and nothing in between.

The next wave got us from behind when I wasn't looking, sweeping me straight off Callum's shoulder and sending me tumbling over more times than I wanted to count. But it did finally release me, and I breached like a small furry porpoise who hadn't quite got the hang of the breath-holding just yet, Green Snake's grip panic-tight around my ribs.

"Gobs!" Callum was shouting.

"Here," I wheezed, paddling furiously.

"Alright?"

"Just bloody fabulous." I peered around for him, but the waves kept getting in the way. "Where are you?"

"Swim this way!"

"Which way?"

"Here!"

I still couldn't see him, but I followed his shout as well as I could.

"Emma!" he was yelling now. "Emma, head this way!"

"*What way?*" she shouted, from somewhere that seemed to be much further off than she should be.

"*The shore! Swim for the shore!*"

"*I'm trying!*"

"Dammit – *Emma! Gobs!*"

I couldn't spare the breath to answer. I was paddling as hard as my cold, weary limbs could manage, but my back end was sinking and my throat was full of salt.

"*Gobs!*"

A wave that looked impossibly big rolled toward me, reared up, and crashed down again, taking me with it. I tumbled, pressed deep beneath the surface, and the moment stretched out, oddly peaceful. Under the water was quieter and warmer than the wind-torn surface, and there was less panic than when I was up there, struggling to keep my nose clear. Green Snake was still with me, but that was okay. We'd both be better down here.

And then some great shape flicked through the green-shaded depths, coming at me so fast I had no chance of avoiding it. I just had enough time to think *orca*, but not enough to actually get panicked about the whole thing, and then it was on me. There were no teeth, not even any real impact, which seemed considerate, then I shot *through* the surface so fast that I had a confused moment where I really thought I'd learned how to be a porpoise after all, and could go splashing and leaping happily all about the place like the world's first mer-cat. Then I crashed into the water so hard it knocked the sense back into me. The impact forced me under, and I felt Green Snake fall away as I surged back up, head as high as I could hold it, paddling hard. I heard Callum yell, "*Gobs!*" from somewhere to my right, over a couple of waves.

"Snake!" I yelled in return. "Where's the bloody *snake?*"

Callum shouted something I couldn't hear, and a wave snatched me up, tumbling me so hard I couldn't tell what way was up, let alone where Callum or the snake were. My lungs strained with the effort of holding my breath, then suddenly I was clear again, but the wave sucked me along with it as it built up into another towering breaker.

"*Old Ones take you sodding Dogs and pirates and—*" I was underwater again, screaming bubbles, and as soon as my head broke the surface I continued. "*Soggy godsdamn mermaids and bloody weres and sorcerers and magicians and will you stop this you horrible great body of stinking water—*" I was under again for at least the last half, but that didn't stop me shouting. Shouting seemed good. It had been too quiet, too tempting, when I'd been under before, and I knew the sea was lying to me. Knew that as much as fighting hurt, stopping would hurt more. "*Callum!*" I shrieked as I broke the surface again.

He shouted, but it was so far away, further than he had been before, *miles* away, an impossible distance, and where was the snake? We couldn't lose the snake, annoying as he was. Small green snakes didn't stand much chance in all this wild green sea.

Another wave tumbled me, and this time I bumped my head on the sand, which was really just adding salt to injury. Or salt to salt, given the fact that I felt stiff with it. I came up with seaweed tangled around my back legs, and kicked wildly, sure there were tiny crabs crawling all over it. Crawling all over *me*. Before I could even right myself I was rolled again, and this time when I hit the sand I stayed there. I gasped a couple of times, then the water came back and dumped the seaweed on

top of me, so I leaped up with a screech and bolted away from
it. I only made it a few paces before I realised I'd made it back to
the beach, and stumbled to a stop again, staggering around in a
circle. No Black Dogs. No Emma. No Green Snake. No Callum.

"Hairy seaweed balls," I whispered, and promptly hacked
up what felt like half the North Sea.

8

DON'T REAP THE MESSENGER

I DIDN'T WAIT AROUND FOR TOO LONG. AS SOON AS MY LEGS felt like they could be trusted, and the sea had mostly stopped running out of my nose, I started padding down the beach. It was a wobbly sort of progress, and I stuck as close to the base of the cliffs as I could, peering out to sea. The last time Callum had shouted, he'd sounded as if he were back toward Whitby – or I thought he had. The waves had been so confusing that it was hard to tell. But I wasn't going the other way. I had no intention of venturing past the borders again. The Black Dogs didn't seem to have hung around, but it seemed too much of a coincidence for them to have appeared just after we'd left Whitby. The odds were high that someone had set them to keep us in, which was a nasty move. And either way, I didn't feel up to testing the hypothesis.

The sea seemed to have settled a little, sated, perhaps, so I only occasionally had to scramble onto the crumbling bases of the cliffs to avoid the advancing waves. Every now and then I stopped and bellowed, *"Callum!"* into the thundering night, but the wind shoved the word back at me with casual amusement. As much as I strained my ears, I never heard a shout in reply. But he could swim, and with his excessively long limbs he'd touch sand a long time before I did. He must have come ashore further toward Whitby. *Had* to have.

That was assuming the thing, the shadow that had hit me, hadn't grabbed Callum. Maybe it preferred scruffy PIs with nicotine habits to small black cats. I wouldn't have even been a mouthful to it, after all, and the sea was full of hungry things. Funny how good it had been at finding us, though.

Maybe it had been something else. Did Black Dogs have marine counterparts? Black Mer-dogs? Black Seals? After all, where did Whitby's borders end? At the low tide mark? At the end of the pier? Could you put some sort of protective charm on the sea? Or was it fair game as soon as you hit the water?

"Callum!" I yelled again, and spotted something rolling at the edge of the surf. The sea gave one final heave, and flung it to the base of the cliff just ahead of me, and I managed a shuffling run to reach it before the next wave stole it again.

Callum's coat, crumpled like a shed skin. And for one moment I wondered if I could just curl up on it and go to sleep right here. I was exhausted enough for it.

But then I snagged a sleeve in my teeth and started walking, growling a steady stream of curses as I went.

THE TUMBLED ROCKS at the base of the cliff were distinctly unhelpful to small cats dragging human-sized coats behind them, which just infuriated me further. By the time the streetlights of Whitby emerged above me, glowing at the top of the cliff, my jaws were aching, my legs were trembling, and my ears hurt from both the wind that kept sticking its fingers in them and the fact that I couldn't stop flattening them to try and avoid that very thing.

"Hate rocks. Hate the seaside. *Told* him I hate the seaside. But does he listen? Does he, bollocks, the spindly bloody tube worm. Should've taken up with the sorcerer after all. Or Gerry. Be warmer. Drier. Less people might be trying to kill me." I caught one paw on some seaweed and staggered, dropping the coat and hissing at the night in general. My chest was heaving with effort and weariness, and I still hadn't found anyone. No Green Snake. No Callum. No Emma. I peered up at the cliff above me. The beach huts weren't in sight yet, but I could dimly make out the paved path running down to where it met the sea. It wasn't far, but after that I still had to get up the hill. And then what?

And then what. The weight of the thought buffeted me, and I sat down abruptly, squinting at the waves. The wind tugged at my whiskers, and the smell of salt and secrets seemed to have seeped so far under my skin that it had become part of me. The clouds were low and heavy, reaching out to the sea pleadingly, and the steady, long rolls of night-dark water were streaked with foam and topped with broken caps.

And then I had to find him. He couldn't be *gone*. The thought of it made no sense at all. But I couldn't think how to start looking, so I just sat there, blinking at the sea.

I'm not sure how long I might have been fixed to the sand, staring at the waves, if a light hadn't called my attention back in. It was moving steadily along the shore where the last scraps of sand met the sea, swinging gently, and had the low orange glow of a flame rather than a torch. I watched it, wondering what else the night had in store. Nocturnal beachcombers? Smugglers? Luminous bloody gulls?

The light kept coming, the sturdy form of its bearer slowly emerging as it drew closer. I wasn't sure if I should be retreating or not. I seemed to have run out of the energy to be terrified, and some night-time walker seemed rather less worrying than packs of lurking Black Dogs and a sea full of hungry shadows.

So I just watched the light as the person holding it moved steadily up the beach toward me. Between the wind and the sea I couldn't get a whiff of them, and with the light casting forward rather than back they remained nothing but a vaguely human form until they stopped in front of me and crouched down, holding the lantern high. It really did have a flame. It was some old-fashioned metal thing with heavy glass, and a handle looped above it, and I could hear the fuel sloshing inside as its bearer adjusted a little metal sleeve that circled the lamp so that more light fell on us.

Hilda looked down at me with the damp white strands of her hair emerging from under a heavy wool hat with *The Savage Squid* embroidered on the front. Her hands were bare and pinched by the cold, and there were scars on the knuckles of the one she rubbed my head with. She wore two heavy silver rings, twisted and intricate, and without the pipe smoke and alcohol she smelled of salt and distant sun and the sort of sharp fierce winds that set paws dancing.

"There you are," she said, and from somewhere above there was a shriek like a pterodactyl in the night.

"Kitty owes Polly a hot toddy!"

"Do you want a lift?" Hilda asked.

"I can walk," I said, then tried standing up. Everything wobbled, and I sat back down again. "Then again, I should conserve my energy. In case of emergencies."

"Seems fair." She poked the coat lying next to me, with its freight of sand and seaweed and scraps of driftwood. "What's this?"

"Callum's coat."

She frowned at me. "I gave him a work one."

"He was off-duty."

"It's good advertising, this," she said, pointing at her own hat.

I tipped my head to the side and said, "Have you seen him? Does he inspire that much confidence in your seagoing skills?"

She shrugged. "People seem to like him."

"There's that." I gave standing up another try, and this time I stayed up. "Speaking of – *have* you seen him?" I tried to keep the question light, but there was a curling worm of dread gnawing at the ends of the words.

"Not yet." She unzipped her coat and tucked me inside, sand and salt and all, then zipped it up again so that only my head stuck out. "But we'll find him. The sea gives back."

"In one piece, though?"

She made a non-committal noise, picked up Callum's coat in one hand and her lantern in the other, and headed back toward Whitby.

WE HEARD them before we saw them. Not words, at first, just the clamour of raised voices, all trying to reach some sort of rhythm that was evidently a bit tricky for all involved. I narrowed my eyes against the wind. The beach was still dark, the lights of the beach huts and the clifftop road only serving to create deeper shadows. The tide was almost full, and the sea ran to the base of the cliff to play among the stones before retreating. Hilda made her way steadily along the concrete walkway just above the beach, wet with spray and the occasional overenthusiastic wave. But beyond where the path climbed up to head for the pavilion, where the final headland between the beach and Whitby loomed up, there were dancing lights that looked a lot like ... I squinted, eyes watering.

"Are those glow sticks?" I asked.

"Bloody witchy tourists," Hilda muttered.

"What?"

"There's always some. Dancing about the place in sodding robes—"

"Robes?" I scrabbled inside her jacket, trying to get a better look, until she swore and unzipped it, dumping me unceremoniously on the hard ground.

"*You're welcome*," she said, but I ignored her, jumping down through the rocks to the wet sand. It was still hard to make out much, but there were definitely robed figures clustered near the cliff, where a little patch of sand survived just on the edge of the tide's reach, and I trotted stiffly toward them, my eyes stinging with salt. The chanting seemed to have stopped for now, and I caught snatches of conversation over the crash of the sea.

"I'm sure it doesn't matter if we use English," one was saying. "It's the intent, right?"

"It *does* matter, but it's not like it's going to work. It needs to be full moon."

"Full moon's not for a week. I'm not coming back for that. Some of us actually work."

"I work!"

"You make baubles."

"*Arcane jewellery.*"

"Jenny, Jim, stop it," a third figure said. "Can't we have one assembly without you two being at each other?"

"You should just get a room and get it over with," a fourth person commented. They were crouched on the sand, their robes pooling around them.

"You can sod right off, Angie," one of the arguing pair, presumably Jenny, said. "I would *never*."

"Her? She's about as much my type as, as a, as—"

"Yeah, yeah." Angie stood up. "It's no good. The tide's too

high. It keeps washing the sigils away. I thought you said it was low, Saz."

"I thought it was." Saz pushed her hood back, revealing long dark hair pulled into a ponytail.

"You read it wrong again, didn't you?" Jim said. "Just like the moon. I thought we went over this."

"Well, did you bother to check? Did you bother to sort accommodation? Did you decide on the incantations? Did you—"

"Okay, okay. Sorry." He looked around, frowning in a dissatisfied manner, and spotted Hilda. "Hello. Can we help you?"

"No," she said, packing tobacco into her pipe. "Just watching."

"I'm not sure that's allowed. This is a coven meeting. It's not a spectator sport."

"Coven, is it? Thought that was witches."

"It is," Jenny said.

"So you a boy witch, then?" Hilda cupped a hand over the end of her pipe, trying to get the tobacco to catch.

"I'm a *witch*," Jim said. "The gender's unimportant."

Hilda nodded, and sat down on a rock, stretching her legs out in front of her and crossing them at the ankles. "Fair dos."

There was silence for a moment, other than the crumple of waves further out and the deeper *whumpf* as they collapsed on the sand, and the singing of the wind in my ears. Had that bloody Matilda seen one of this lot? Had we been out here on a wild reaper chase the whole time?

"As you were," Hilda added, looking at me. I twitched my ears at her, but I couldn't exactly say, *Ask them if they've seen anyone in **proper** robes about the place*.

"Right," Saz said, turning her back on Hilda. "Look, we're here. We may as well give it a go."

"We don't have a protective circle," Angie said. "That's risky."

"If anything *happens*," Jenny said, mostly under her breath.

The wind really did sound like singing, and I shook my head, wondering how much water was still caught in my ears.

The four members of the coven joined hands and went back to their chanting. Even close up, I couldn't make out what they were saying. There seemed to be quite a lot of difference of opinion occurring around pronunciation, and more than once I was sure I heard Jenny whisper, "Something something." The wind tugged at their robes, alternately swirling the cloth and pressing it against them, and the sea ran up to their feet and away again. They all seemed to be wearing wellies, which was perhaps not sartorial accurate, but certainly looked sensible.

And the singing wouldn't go away. I was starting to worry there was a fish stuck in my ear canal, singing the song of its people, and I sat back on my haunches to have a bit of a scratch. Then Saz looked over her shoulder, out to sea, her eyes wide.

"Aye, aye," Hilda said. "Something's happening."

"*Ooh,*" Jim said, and put a little extra vigour into his chanting.

"We summon you!" Saz cried suddenly, as the wind carried a melody toward us. "We call you, oh spirits of the sea! Come to us!"

Faintly, I heard, "*Sooooon maaay the Wellerman come, to bring us sugar and tea and rum,*" which seemed a little on the nose. Surely sea spirits could come up with something a little more inventive.

"We hear you!" Jim shouted. "We welcome you, oh spirits!"

"I wouldn't do that," Hilda said. "Seems dodgy, like." She

took a nip from her flask, so I took it she wasn't against *all* spirits.

There was a lot of "*da-da-da-da-da*" going on out in the water, so the spirits had apparently forgotten the next line.

"Stand before us!" Saz shouted. "Show yourselves! Share your secrets! We command you to appear to us!"

"*Before the boat had hit the water, the whale's tail came up and caught her—* oops!" The *oops* was a shout, and the coven looked blankly at each other. In the darkness a wave surged, and a half-seen shape rode it toward shore. A whoop of delight rose from the plummeting form, along with a yelp of alarm, and then the wave ploughed the whole thing under. The shouts were cut off abruptly, and I watched with my tail twitching as the water rushed up and around the ankles of the coven. Jenny staggered, and Jim steadied her, and a tangle of limbs was deposited on the edge of the circle. I took a careful step forward as the wave retreated, and Murty sat up.

"Nice," he said, and grinned at the coven.

Saz stared at him. "Are you a spirit?"

"No," he said, and the form next to him pushed itself up onto its elbows, tried to take a breath, and promptly started coughing water everywhere. "Alright, mate?" Murty started pounding his companion on the back, and I shot across the beach, earning a shriek of alarm from Angie.

"Callum?" I stopped short, staring at him, and he waved weakly, wheezing. I took a breath, sat down and said, "Well, if I'd known you were out surfing and sea shanty-ing, I'd've just gone home."

He nodded, coughed again, and said, "Sorry. I'll leave a note next time."

"Do that." I looked up at the coven, who were all staring at me, and said, "Aw, *barnacle sauce.*"

"*Did that cat just speak?*" Jenny asked, her voice suddenly high and very squeaky.

"No," Callum wheezed.

"It did! It spoke!" She waved at me urgently, staring at her companions. "You heard it, right?"

"That were me," Murty said. "You just couldn't see my lips move from there."

"It wasn't you," Jim said, looking as if he wanted to nudge me with his wellie. I bared my teeth.

"But it can't have been *the cat*," Saz said, her eyes huge. "Although – remember that time at the Abbey? When that weird woman broke it all up? Wasn't there a cat ...?"

"We're not even from here," Callum said, trying to stand up. He was having difficulty, and Murty patted his arm.

"Easy, man." The mermaid, unsurprisingly, looked perfectly happy, his dark hair decorated with a crown of seaweed. "Give yourself a moment. Near-drowning's no fun thing."

"Did we summon the cat?" Jim asked suddenly. "Is that cat a spirit?" They all stared at me, and I stopped the teeth-baring and tried to look ethereal. It's hard when you've got so much sand in your fur it won't even lie flat.

"Close the circle!" Saz shouted. "They might *all* be spirits! Stop them getting away!"

The coven hustled to join hands, enclosing Murty, Callum and myself like they were about to play ring-a-rosies around us. Instead they started to chant, hesitantly at first, with Saz leading them, until the others joined in with a few stumbles.

"How'd he find you?" I hissed at Callum, and he shook his head, tried to say something, then coughed and spat water onto the beach.

"*Ooh*." Murty said to the coven. "Careful. You'll raise the dead, like." He winked at Saz, who tried to scowl at him, but her mouth seemed to want to smile instead.

"*Mermaids*," Hilda grumbled. "Are you lot coming? Only

it's damn cold out here, and I can't get my pipe lit." She waved it at us while the chant continued to rise and fall in steady, building rhythm.

"Emma," Callum managed, his voice rough.

"I've not seen her," I said.

He stared at me, then at the mermaid. "Murty, we need—" He leaned on one hand as he tried to get up, but Angie yelped and kicked his arm out from under him, sending him sprawling to the sand.

I hissed at her, and Murty said, "Easy there, witchy."

"They're trying to escape!" Angie shouted. "I *knew* we needed the protective charms!"

"We have to find Emma," Callum said. "Murty, you'll help, right?"

"Aw, dude. I already repaid the favour," the mermaid said, sounding almost regretful.

"Don't break the circle," Saz said, not that the coven seemed in any risk of doing so. They were clinging to each other grimly, while the wind whistled above us, and somewhere gulls screamed in the night, and the sea pounded on, and on, and on.

"Do me another favour," Callum said. "Then I'll owe you one."

Murty grinned, his teeth white and sharp, and I shivered, looking out to sea. Looking for Emma.

"*Nope*," Hilda said, getting up. "Not happening."

"Not your business," Murty said.

"My deckie, my responsibility," she said, raising her voice to be heard over the chanting, which was getting very fevered.

Murty started to say something, then gave a little *huh* of surprise and said, "Hello." He nodded out to sea.

Jenny just about gave herself whiplash trying to look around without breaking the circle, and Angie gave an alarmed little cry. I craned around to see where they were looking, and the fur crawled on my spine. Even Hilda made a sound that might have indicated some level of astonishment.

A shape slouched out of the sea. When the waves rose about it, it might have been a seal's head, if a somewhat skinny one. Then the water sucked away, and skeletal shoulders emerged, glimpses of exposed skin luminously pale in the light creeping off the land. Jenny whimpered, and Saz shouted, "Hold fast! Hold the circle! It can't hurt us!"

"I don't want to do this anymore!" Jim wailed. "I'm not a witch! I'm not!"

"The charm!" Angie shouted. "Say the protective charm! *Hurry!*"

They all started chanting at once, out of sequence and, as far as I could tell, all trying to recite something different, the words tumbling over each other and bouncing about the place as the pale shape kept steadily moving forward, the water falling away from its frame. Bony arms appeared, and hipbones that jutted painfully against what looked an awful lot like pyjama bottoms. Seaweed tangled around skeletal legs, and shadowed eyes turned toward us.

The coven, to give them credit, didn't break and run. They clutched each other's hands so tightly that I could see the white of their knuckles, and they kept chanting their various protective charms. Jim had squeezed his eyes shut, and Jenny was trying so hard to look over her shoulder she seemed in danger of dislocating something, while Saz and Angie glared out at the figure as if they could send it back where it came from by force of will alone.

But still the figure came, until it stood just beyond the circle, water washing around its bare ankles, and raised one bony hand. Green Snake was coiled around it, and he looked at the coven and hissed. The newcomer smiled, probably a very polite smile by some standards, but with her drowned white skin pulled tight over her bones, and her thin, pale hair slicked to her scalp, not even the fact that she was wearing a T-shirt with a cutesy cartoon cat snoozing on it was enough to render her harmless-looking.

Jim broke first. He ripped his hands away from Angie and Jenny and sprinted for the path with a shriek. Jenny hesitated, then as Gertrude – because of course it was our missing reaper, no one else would be paddling about the North Sea in the middle of a storm in kitty pyjamas – started to speak, the wannabe witch just said, *"No,"* and legged it after Jim.

Green Snake looked at me, and we both hissed at Saz and Angie. They stepped back, still holding hands, and Angie made some complicated warding off gesture. Murty pretended to swoon, grinning, and the two women moved slowly backward toward the path, until there was a screech from above.

"Polly want witchy toes for breakfast!"

We all looked up to see the parrot spiralling on the turbulent wind off the cliff, the lights of town gilding his feathers against the dark sky.

"Protective circle," Angie hissed at Saz, and they bolted for the path.

"I think it was something you said," Murty said.

"I didn't say anything," Gertrude replied, handing Green Snake to Callum. I touched my nose to the snake's, smelling deep, silent places on his scales.

"Ah. Maybe *that* was the problem," the mermaid said. "Little small talk goes a long way, you know. Breaks the ice and all."

"Or makes others want to break things," Hilda said conversationally.

Gertrude made a non-committal noise and glared at a

crab clinging to her ankle. She kicked it off with a huff, and said, "I really don't like the seaside."

"With you there," I said, and then we were all silent for a moment.

"What are you doing here?" Gertrude asked, looking from me to Callum. "Has something happened?"

"Um," Callum said, and I sneezed but didn't add anything. Never mind shooting the messenger, the messenger might just get his soul reaped in this case.

9

THE PROBLEM WITH MERMAIDS

THE SILENCE LINGERED A LITTLE LONGER, THEN MURTY SAID, "Well, I personally was returning a small favour—"

"Did he *ask* for a favour?" Hilda demanded. "Or did you just jump in like you usually do?"

"Well, given the choice between drowning and a lift ashore, I'm pretty certain—"

"I know which one *I'd* pick," Hilda said, glaring at him. Her false eye was a milky marble, reflecting the light of her lamp.

"I don't think I'd have made it ashore without him," Callum said, wringing the front of his fleece out. "Sorry you lost the dinghy, though."

"I can get another one," Murty said.

"But why were you in the water?" Gertrude asked. "My understanding of humans is that it's really rather cold and not conducive to bathing at the moment unless you are ..." she paused, apparently trying to recall the correct term. "Complete nutters, I think it was."

"About right," I said. "But it's kind of your fault we're here."

"Why?" The reaper looked from Callum to me, the tight lines of her face somehow drawn even sharper than usual. "Oh no – *Emma*. I didn't mean to be so long." She scanned the shoreline. "Where is she?"

"She thought something had happened to you," I said. "What with being out in the day and all."

Callum nodded. "She asked for help. But we got chased by Black Dogs—"

"Told you not to leave town," Hilda said.

"Could've been more specific," I said. "You know, *don't leave town because Black Dogs will eat you* would be more effective than *stay around, yeah?*"

"Shouldn't need everything spelled out."

"Cats don't do rules."

"Now you know why you should."

"*Emma?*" Gertrude said, and her voice reverberated on the waves. "Where is Emma? Was she with you?"

We all fell silent. I'm certain the edge of the sea crackled with frost where it touched the sand around the reaper's feet.

"She was with us," Callum said quietly. "On the beach. But when we went into the water to get away from the Black Dogs, we got separated." He looked at Murty. "Did you see her?"

"Just you," he said, and I couldn't tell if the answer was too quick or not.

"I have to find her," Gertrude said, turning back to the sea, and Callum and I both shouted, "*No!*"

She stopped, giving us a quizzical look.

"Emma wanted us to find you," Callum said. "You can't just vanish again."

"But I need to look for her."

"The sea's kind of big," I said. "I don't think you're going to find her by just walking in there."

Callum nodded. "And we won't be able to help. Plus I

thought reapers weren't very good with water. Can you even swim?"

"No," Gertrude admitted. "I sink. But I don't need to breathe, so I can just walk."

"You don't breathe?" Hilda asked.

"She's dead," I said.

"*Technically* dead." Gertrude looked at the sea again. "It was strange in there. Confusing. I think ... I think if I hadn't seen your snake I might not have found my way out."

Green Snake gave a self-satisfied little wriggle.

Callum looked at Murty again. "Can you really find Emma? If I promise you a favour?"

"Maybe," he said. "It'd have to be a good one, though. That little disagreement I was running from earlier? It's risky spending too much time in the waters here. Might get my tail nipped."

"What were you doing in there tonight, then?" I asked.

"I owed you a favour," he said, looking at Callum.

"And now you're done," Hilda said. "No one's promising any more favours tonight. Sing up your bloody dinghy and get out of here, Murchadh."

"Not your decision," he said, grinning slightly.

"Want me to make it mine?"

"I have to find Emma," Gertrude said, looking along the beach as if hoping she might just pop up from behind a rock, waving cheerfully.

"If she's ... I mean, it was really rough ..." I wasn't quite sure how to continue, and Gertrude looked at me, a very small smile tugging at her lips.

"My business is souls. Do you think I wouldn't know if hers was gone?"

And I had no answer to that, so we just sat and looked at the sea, while the parrot swung above us and the storm gathered on the horizon, starting to throw lightning about the place.

"I NEED A DRINK," Hilda announced, pulling her hat down more firmly.

"Me too," Murty said immediately.

"You can get yourself back to your cockles and clamshells," Hilda said. "I'm not going anywhere they serve mermaids."

"I just saved your deckie," Murty pointed out.

"We need to find Emma," Callum said.

"We do," Gertrude agreed, squeezing water out of her T-shirt. Her shoulders looked sharp enough to tear through it.

"You need to get warm, Swab," Hilda said to Callum. "I'm not giving you time off for hypothermia."

Callum shivered, as if suddenly reminded he was standing there barefoot and dripping, festooned with sand and seaweed.

"I found your coat," I said. "It's had a wash at least."

"Thanks." He looked down at his feet. "I don't suppose my boots and phone are anywhere?"

"Last seen with a Black Dog chewing on them."

"Awesome." He took his coat from Hilda, then turned and passed it to Gertrude. "Here."

She looked down at herself. The kitten on her T-shirt was on its back with all four paws in the air, and had a *zzzzz* drifting above it. Her pyjama bottoms were pink with black paw prints on them, and she took the coat and pulled it on. "Thank you. This is very unbecoming."

"The coat's not much better, to be fair," I said, and Gertrude nodded. She was shorter than Callum, which wasn't hard with his gangly great form, and the coat reached halfway down her shins, the shoulders hanging off her.

"It is better, though," she said. "One can't be out in pyjamas."

"I suppose one can't," I said.

"Come on," Hilda said, and got up, heading for the path. "It's bloody arctic out here."

Gertrude didn't move, the tatty coat pulled close around her. "But what about Emma?"

"She could be anywhere by now," Murty said. "You wouldn't even know where to start."

"You would," I said to him. "Tell you what, *I'll* owe you a favour if you go take a nosey."

"I don't trade with cats."

"I think Murty's right," Callum said to Gertrude. "We need a plan if we're going to find her."

"It's my fault she was out here," the reaper said. "She was looking for me."

"And it's our fault she was in the water," Callum said, glancing at me.

I bared my teeth. Admitting culpability to a reaper didn't seem likely to extend our life expectancy, but then again, neither did lying to one. "That's true. The Black Dogs might have left her alone if she'd stayed ashore."

"So we're going to find her," Callum added.

"How?" Gertrude asked, looking at the sea. "What sort of plan will help us find her in *this*?" Her wave encompassed the enormity of the churning sea and hungry sky.

Callum looked at me, then at Murty. The mermaid grinned his sharp-toothed grin, turning a pale shell over in his fingers.

"*No*," I said. "Listen to the pirate captain."

"For the Deep Ones' sakes," Hilda shouted from halfway up the path. "Will you *move*? If your Emma is still in one piece, freezing down there's not going to help her. If she's not – well, it's still not going to help her. I need a bloody drink!"

"She has a point," Murty said to Callum. "I'm not doing favours if you're going to drop dead of exposure."

Callum shivered, and looked at Gertrude. "Will you come with us? We'll find her, I promise."

I saw his face twist as he said the word, and knew he was thinking of promising Emma he wouldn't let go. Not that it had been his fault, not in the grip of that hungry sea, but he wouldn't see that. He never could.

The reaper looked at the sea, her mouth a pinched line, then back at us. "She's still out there," she said. "I know she is."

ONE GRUMPY, marble-eyed pirate with a large green parrot on her shoulder; one mermaid with seaweed behind his ear, wearing what looked a lot like velour leisurewear; a barefoot reaper in an oversized coat that gave her the air of a flasher ghoul; one barefoot PI-slash-deckhand in sodden jeans and a fleece that had been lightened about three shades by its freight of sand; one dishevelled, salty black cat and a small green snake. Whitby might have a high weird tolerance, but we weren't getting into any decent pubs.

I expected Hilda would head back to *The Savage Squid*, but instead she led us along the wharf, rowdy groups of pub-crawlers and confused-looking couples in waterproof coats parting around us like waves, and over the swing bridge into the old town. Down a couple of cobbled streets, and we pushed through the squat black door of a pub I hadn't even seen before, the ceiling low enough that Callum and Murty had to duck the heavy, twisting beams that ran across it. It was a rambling sort of place, tables tucked into nooks and crannies made of wooden half-walls and actual white-painted plaster ones, and people huddled alone or in couples and groups over them, humans and dwarfs and fauns, for the most part, although I spotted a couple of goblins in one dark corner. The humans all had Callum's air of *faintness*, of not quite fitting the world, other than a couple who were gulping down smudged glasses of yellow wine rather desperately, evidently regretting their search for local colour. There were a lot of beards and earrings and wind-resistant gear going on, and over the scent of wood smoke was a persistent whiff of fish.

No one looked our way. It was the sort of place where everyone was very clear that they were Minding Their Own Business, and judging by the rough repairs on some of the chair legs there were consequences for not.

"Shep," Hilda said, nodding at a faun behind the bar. He nodded back, and took a tumbler from behind the bar, filling it with a couple of over-large shots of whisky and lining a beer up next to it. He looked at Callum.

"Tea?" Callum asked hopefully.

Shep's eyebrows made an excursion toward his low hair-line, but he pulled a chipped teapot out of a cupboard and looked at Gertrude.

"Hot chocolate, please."

The faun's eyebrows went for an adventure again, but he flicked the kettle on and set two mugs out, glanced at Murty, scowled, then added another whisky tumbler and a beer to the counter. Hilda looked at Callum.

"Your shout," she said. "Least you can do."

"Sure." He dug his sopping wallet out of his jeans and paid the faun in dripping notes. Shep's eyebrows were far less bothered by this – he just clipped the notes to a bit of cord strung above the sink. There were a few drying there already.

Once we had the drinks, plus a bowl of water for me and half an apple for the parrot, Hilda led the way to a table tucked into one of the little nooks, as close to the fire as we could get. Callum stripped off his soaking fleece, but Gertrude kept the coat on. She looked a little uncomfortable.

"I'm dripping on the floor," she said.

"We all are," Murty said, although he seemed to have dried rather rapidly. Either velour was quick-drying, or it was a mermaid thing.

"Should I ask for a mop?" the reaper asked.

"It'll dry," Hilda said, and Gertrude looked at the floor dubiously.

Callum leaned his bare forearms on the table and wrapped his hands around his mug. Green Snake had scooted off to curl himself around the base of the teapot, and now he raised his head and looked expectantly at me. I don't know what he wanted. Cat biscuits were apparently not on the menu here, which seemed a bit rude.

"So what happened?" Callum asked Gertrude. "Why did you go out in the middle of the day? And how did you end up in the water?"

"Isn't it more important that we find Emma?" she asked, leaning over her hot chocolate and taking a deep, longing sniff.

"This is how we start," he said. "She went into the water because *you* went into the water."

Also because we did, but I wasn't about to repeat that. One confession was quite enough. I had a bit of water instead, trying to chase the salt out of my mouth.

Gertrude sighed. "Alright. We've been here a couple of days. It's always a little *odd*, Whitby. So many souls that never came home, torn between the sea and the land."

"The sea is ever hungry," Hilda said, using a folding knife

to carve the apple into more manageable pieces for the parrot.

"Polly want fruit compote."

"Polly can go compote himself." She gave a piece of apple to Green Snake instead.

"*Them*," the parrot said.

"Sorry. Compote *them*self."

Gertrude looked at the parrot blankly, then said, "This time is different, though. A balance is out. When we went down to the sea the first evening, the dead surfaced. A lot of dead. Sometimes one might see the odd soul missed by Marine Division, but this was an awful amount. And they didn't seem *right*, either. They sort of bobbed about, as if they didn't know where they wanted to be. Something's wrong."

"There shouldn't be so many, should there?" Murty asked.

She looked at him, her pale eyes sharp. "What do you know about them?"

"Just that there's too many. And when I asked questions, someone set orcas on me."

I thought of that dark shape beneath the water, and shivered. "Was there an orca around before? I saw something."

"I didn't see one," Murty said, and winked at me. "Saw you, though. So it's a good thing I don't trade favours with cats. Although," he added to Callum. "That kind of means I've over-repaid the favour, doesn't it? Since I saved you *and* your cat."

"Not his cat," I said, at the same time as Callum said, "Not my cat."

Hilda chuckled, then it turned into a coughing fit as she packed her pipe. "Shows how much you know, Murchadh."

The mermaid looked put out, and I said, "Cheers anyway. I'll give you half a herring next time I get one."

"You're alright," he said.

Gertrude had been looking from one of us to the other, and she shook her head slightly. "You're all very distractible."

"Sorry," Callum said. "The souls, then. There's too many? Not reaped, you mean?"

"Exactly. It's all meant to be automated. DHL – Departed Human Logistics – does all the reaping these days. But there's so many dead down there. And ..." She hesitated, then said, "Reaper Scarborough should take any DHL miss on land. And East Yorkshire Marine Division should take the rest. But it was as if *no one* had been around for days. Weeks, really. Where are the reapers? Where's DHL?"

"You think reapers are *missing?*" Callum asked.

"Well, we thought Gertrude was missing," I pointed out.

"*I'm* not. But I think they are."

"I knew it. Dead all over the place," Murty said, throwing back his whisky.

"Yes. Well, after I saw them bobbing around like that ... I mean, I suppose they were trying to reach me. Souls tend to be drawn to reapers, you know. They seek peace. But these were so *confused* ..." she trailed off, frowning, then shook her head. "I tried to go back yesterday for another look, but there was too much sun. So I decided to try again today. I couldn't go at night, of course, in case I ran into Reaper Scarborough. I'm not meant to be here."

"Would it be bad if you were found out?" Callum asked.

"It's rather uncharted territory. Reapers don't take mini-breaks."

"Right."

"We keep to our own areas. Some reapers will meet for *socialising*"—she said it almost distastefully—"but we do not intrude on each others' work."

"Did you find anything, then?" I asked.

"Ye-es. So to speak." She sniffed her hot chocolate again.

Callum and I looked at each other. "Which would be?" he asked.

Gertrude groaned. "I should have known something terrible would happen! What on earth was I doing, taking *mini-breaks*? What a complete mess!"

"What d'you think happened, then?" I asked. "Is this something to do with the whole reaper territories situation?"

Gertrude made an irritated noise. "Not exactly. But I have an idea what's happened."

"That's good, then?" Callum offered.

"Of course it's not *good*," Gertrude snapped. "Honestly, *humans*. That's probably what Emma thought, too. Oh, look at this nice mermaid coming over for a chat. I'm sure that's a *good thing*."

"*Mermaids?*" I said, and looked at Murty, who raised his hands in a *not me* gesture. "You think we have a mermaid problem?"

"Mermaids are always a problem," Gertrude said.

"X marks *that* spot," Hilda said, raising her pint.

"Horrible things. All … nice hair and pretty eyes and … what have you." She glanced at Murty. "Present company excluded, of course."

"I'm not sure if that's more insulting or less," he said. "But I had nothing to do with your Emma, if that's what you're thinking. I'm a little on the outs with … well, everyone, to be honest."

"Oh, good," I said. "You're going to be a great help, then."

"I did just save Callum. *And* you."

"To settle a favour," Hilda said. "Why're you still here?"

"Curious," he said, and grinned at her.

"It's all a front, mermaids," Gertrude said, then added, "No offence, again. But they look all pretty, then they'll steal her off and shove her in a cave and—" Gertrude stopped and took a deep breath. "This is *awful*."

I sat back on my haunches and scratched my shoulder with one back paw, scattering sand and hair over the seat. "I'm not arguing about the whole mermaid thing—"

"I'll just leave you in there next time, then," Murty said, and I ignored him.

"—but what's the deal between the mermaids and the dead?"

"*Mermaids,*" Gertrude said, and sighed. "I mean, I don't know why they want all those souls, but they're up to something."

"You think we're collecting the dead? And *reapers?*" Murty asked. "I mean, I'm the first to say that we're not the most trustworthy, but that's next level, that is."

"I don't know what else it can be. The dead aren't right. There's so many of them, and all in the water. Why haven't they been reaped? Where are the reapers?" She stirred her hot chocolate vigorously. "I just paddled into the shallows for a closer look, and the next thing I knew I was being dragged under."

"By *mermaids?*" Hilda and Murty asked together.

"No." She frowned. "Well, not directly, anyway. It was the dead, but they weren't themselves. The dead might be angry, or sad, or confused, or frightened, but they're not aggressive. Oh, maybe one here and there, but usually they just want to be told things are as they should be, and that they can go. These were ... they were there but not. As if it wasn't *them.* And it didn't seem they had all agreed to work together to get me in. It was more as if they were simply part of one mind. One will."

I licked my chops, tasting salt and fright, then said, "Like Leeds?"

Like Leeds when the dead had risen, hungry and single-minded. Gertrude had helped us put down the start of the zombie apocalypse, as had the sorcerer. I tried to hold back a shiver that was nothing to do with my still-damp fur.

Gertrude looked at me, quiet for a moment. "Those souls were all sticky and awful. These were just *not there.*"

"But could it be *like* Leeds?" I could see the dead in my memory, surging through the market, all grabbing hands and desperate hunger. And plenty of them hadn't even been actually dead. "A different version of it, perhaps? Like that was a trial run?"

"Maybe," she said, and nodded slowly. "Yes, I think maybe. Something else taking over. Something else driving them."

Callum and I looked at each other. We'd figured out that the zombie outbreak had been started more or less accidentally by a hapless undertaker with a syringe full of formula, but we'd never discovered where the formula came from. We did know that there were necromancers out there, though. And they'd always been fond of the dead. Although that wasn't the same as necrophilia, apparently, so Callum said I couldn't call them that. Don't see why not, myself.

"So the dead dragged you into the sea?" Callum asked Gertrude.

"Yes. They kept pulling at me, and then a wave knocked me over." She looked at the table, and in the firelight I thought I saw a little colour rising in her cheeks. "I suppose I'm not terribly good in the water. I got a bit turned around, and then between the dead tugging me this way and that, and the waves and the bad light, I couldn't tell how to get out again until I saw Green Snake."

"And you think the dead are working for the mermaids?" Hilda asked. "I mean, wouldn't put it past them, but surely they'd have just up and grabbed you themselves if they wanted you."

"And why?" Murty asked. "I can't think of any reason to

grab a reaper, unless you had a pocket full of treasure or something."

"Unless they were after my scythe," Gertrude said, giving the mermaid a suspicious look.

He shrugged. "Maybe. Not very treasure-y, though, is it?"

"Well, I don't see who else the dead would answer to in the sea. It has to be them." She frowned at her hot chocolate. "*Mermaids.* They've got such good publicity. And it's all because of, you know." She waved at herself with bony hands.

"They're like reapers?" Callum asked, frowning.

"No!" She waved at herself again. "It's *that.*"

"Coat?" I hazarded. "They go in for tatty coats?"

"Don't be ridiculous. They're *mermaids.*" Gertrude wrinkled her nose. "They all wear bits of rope and limpets and so on. It's not *that.*"

"Not all of us," Murty protested. "That's very stereotypical."

"Only because you nicked someone's clothes off the beach while they were out swimming," Hilda said. "I know you."

"What'm I meant to do? Go to H&M?"

"You could. You just don't want to. Hanging about robbing people instead."

"You can't talk. You're a *pirate.*"

Hilda slammed her pint glass down. "*I run pirate cruises.*"

"Twenty quid to putter around in a circle and go back in? That's a hornswoggle if ever I heard it."

"It's *two hours!* And d'you know the cost of fuel these days? And all the catering?"

I stared at them, then at Gertrude. "I still don't get it."

"Well, it's *that.*" She nodded meaningfully, looking down at herself.

Callum and I looked at each other again. "Kitten T-shirt?"

I tried, and Gertrude made an exasperated noise. "Kitty necklace. Trousers with paw prints on. Um ... dead?"

Gertrude gave me a disapproving look. "*Technically* dead."

"Right. Sorry."

"*Mermaids*," she said. "They don't, um, they dress ... well, they used to lure sailors, and ..." She waved at herself again, looking a lot like she wished she could excuse herself and leave the room.

"They have tails?" I offered. "Not sure how that worked for the sailors, but humans are weird."

"No! I mean, yes, they do, but ..." She raised her hands helplessly. "*You know.*"

"They're topless?" Callum said, sounding like he was trying not to laugh. I glared at him. If he started to laugh, I was going to bite him, agreement or not. Laughing at a reaper seemed like a spectacularly bad idea, even by our standards, and we'd just lost this one's partner, so laughing was *definitely* off the cards.

"Yes," Gertrude said, and coughed. "One never knows where to look."

"I imagine a certain portion of the sailors did," I said, and Callum flicked one of my ears. Fair, really.

10

HOUSE RULES

MURTY HAD LUCKILY MISSED THE WHOLE TOPLESS THING. HE evidently didn't go in for that particular aesthetic, and I wasn't sure if he'd have been offended by more stereotyping on the reaper's part or not. He'd gone to get another round in instead, and came back with more tea for Callum, as well as beer and whisky for himself and Hilda. He also dropped a couple of bags of pork scratchings on the table, which Green Snake, the parrot, and I all lunged at. There was a moment's frenzied scuffle, then the parrot took off across the bar with a shriek of triumph, a pack clutched in his claws, leaving Green Snake and me hissing over the other.

"Great," Murty said, sitting down. "That was exactly why I bought them." He looked at Gertrude. "I didn't get you another, since you've not drunk yours. Do you want something else?"

"I can't drink it," she said. "I still like the smell, though. We didn't have such things back when I was human."

The mermaid nodded, opened the remaining pack of pork scratchings, and gave Green Snake and me a piece each.

"So," he said. "What sort of favour would I earn if I could get your friend back?"

"Oh, here we go," Hilda said, throwing back her whisky.

"I thought you said you were on the out with the mermaids," I said. "That you didn't know anything about what was going on."

He grinned. "Doesn't mean I can't get the job done." He looked at Callum. "I'd need that favour, though. And it has to come from you."

"Don't do it," Hilda said. "Mermaids lie."

"I'll do it," Gertrude said. "I have to get Emma back."

"Not you," Murty said. "Not making deals with reapers. *No offence.*" He winked at Gertrude, then looked back at Callum. "What d'you say? Save your friend? Help the reaper?"

"What's the favour?" Callum asked.

"I don't know yet."

"That's not how favours work," I said.

"Sure it is. I do something for you, you do something for me later."

Callum topped up his mug from the teapot. "But what *sort* of something?"

"You just have to trust me on that one."

"*Don't,*" Hilda said again, and here were hard lines drawn on her face.

"I think we should listen to the pirate captain," I said.

"Save the girl—"

"*Woman,*" Hilda and Gertrude said together.

"—save the day," Murty continued, his sharp-toothed grin lighting his face. "One small favour. Well, one favour, anyway."

"Don't listen to him," Hilda said.

Callum looked at Gertrude.

"No," she said. "You can't do it. You don't know what he'll

ask." Her voice was small, quiet, and she was playing with the kitty necklace.

I could see Callum watching her doing it, and I said, "Callum, don't."

But obviously, he said, "Alright," and held his hand out across the table to the mermaid. "We get Emma back. *Safely.* Then I owe you *one* favour."

"Deal," Murty said, and his eyes were huge and hungry as they shook.

"Great," I said, into a sudden silence around the table. "I don't see how this can go wrong, do you?"

"Well," Gertrude said, then seemed at a loss as to what to say next. Murty had sloped out of the pub shortly after making his agreement with Callum, grinning a little too widely. Hilda had left not long after, muttering about how we'd better be back on board and shipshape in time for an early start. We'd stayed, for no reason other than it was warm in here and we were almost dry.

Now Gertrude pushed her hot chocolate across the table to Callum.

"Are you sure?" he asked.

"Well, I can't drink it, can I?" she said. "Being *technically* dead." She gave me a sideways look.

"I said sorry," I protested.

"Real cats are so rude. I would never have been as fond of them if I knew."

"No one would," Callum said. "I'm going to find a hedgehog next time."

Green Snake lifted his head off the table and gave Callum an indignant look.

"Some good they'll be at getting you out of trouble," I said.

"And who would you turn to for sage life advice and sparkling conversation?"

"The hedgehog would do just fine," Callum said, and I huffed, then turned my attention to Gertrude.

"So, if Emma's ... I mean, you know her soul's still in place, so ... what? Is she like a mermaid princess now or something?" Callum might say I have no tact, but I was actually wondering if Gertrude was mistaken and Emma was mermaid *snacks*, so that just shows I can be sensitive when I want. Given the way Gertrude was looking at me, though, she might have divined the meaning behind *something*.

"I have no idea," Gertrude said. "But she won't have gone with them willingly." She tapped her fingers on the table lightly, then went back to playing with her necklace. "Would she? Did she seem ..." she trailed off, as if unsure what she was trying to ask.

"She said you'd had a bit of an argument," Callum said. "She thought it might be her fault you were out in the day. That she'd upset you."

"Oh, *no*," Gertrude said. "I mean, yes, we did ... well, I don't know that we *argued*, but she was very upset about the paper umbrellas."

"We did hear about the paper umbrellas," Callum said.

"Symbolic *and* paper," I said. "Neither of which seem to be great features for umbrellas."

"*It's not actually about the umbrellas,*" Callum said, squeezing his mug a little too tightly.

Gertrude spread her hands, the skin shining whitely in the warm light. "I just don't understand humans. And it wasn't so long ago that I was one."

"Well. Maybe on the scale of the universe," I said. "It's not yesterday, though, is it?"

She gave me a disapproving look, and I wondered if reapers were as sensitive about their ages as humans were.

Personally, I'd like to get to old age. I was on my fourth life already, and I hadn't made it to the toothless stage once. This life wasn't looking too promising, either. Not that it was my fault. People of various species just kind of had it in for me.

Gertrude looked at her hands, then at us, and said softly, "I do try to understand. And to do as much as I can to make things somewhat normal. Emma always accepts that I can't do some things. But she's not been *able* to do many things before, and I think I might be holding her back a little now that she can. Perhaps this life isn't enough for her."

"That wasn't what she said to us," Callum said. "She just really wanted to find you."

"But what if she isn't happy? And then a mermaid just comes along, and … I mean, she *wouldn't*, would she?" Gertrude gave Callum a pleading look, and he shook his head, although he was hardly the sort of person one goes to for relationship advice.

"Of course not," he said. "And I'm sure if she'd been that unhappy she'd have said something."

"Like, *I'm going to run away to be a mermaid princess?*" I said. "That's quite a conversation."

"She definitely didn't say that," Gertrude said, looking at the hot chocolate as if wishing she hadn't given it up.

"And she wouldn't do that." Callum reached across the table and offered Gertrude his hand. "You're absolutely right. She hasn't just run off. We'll find her."

"*We,*" I said with a sigh. "Do I have to point out again that we're talking *the sea?*"

Both Callum and the reaper ignored me, and she put the little wrapped biscuit that had come with the hot chocolate in his outstretched hand. He blinked at it. "Um … thanks?"

"Quite alright. I can't eat that, either." She sighed, and glanced at the window above our table. The old glass was thick and distorted between uneven wood frames, the paint peeling and blackened with smoke from countless fires. Rain formed slicks on the panes, smearing the streetlights outside still further and rendering the night opaque. "Gobbelino is right, though. It's the *sea*. I don't dare go out too deep again. It's not just the dead, you know. Reapers aren't welcome in the ocean. It'll swallow me whole, and the Sea Witch will claim my scythe for herself, then imprison me in a shipwreck to be eaten by eels for all eternity."

Even I had no answer to that, and we were quiet for a moment. Green Snake slipped across the table and nudged Gertrude's hand a little hesitantly, and she smiled at him, the tight skin of her scalp making it into a grimace. "Of course," she said, "that might just be reaper tales. We're not exactly buoyant, so it might simply be that we sink to the bottom and can't get back up, and the stories are a good way of making sure we don't go for a paddle and never come back. Only Marine Division are meant to be involved with the sea. They swear the Sea Witch exists, but they're very sniffy with their ghost ships and quick-dry robes and so on. They might be making the whole thing up."

"Is there just one Sea Witch?" Callum asked. "Or are there different ones in different areas?"

Gertrude frowned. "I'm not sure I know. I've only heard of *the* Sea Witch, but maybe it's one being with many facets."

Callum opened his mouth to ask something else – probably something to do with the life cycles of Sea Witches and mermaids, knowing him – and I spoke before he could. "So is it just swimming the Sea Witch objects to? Can you go out on a boat?"

Gertrude rubbed the top of Green Snake's head carefully. "Not if we want it to stay safe from rogue waves and whirlpools."

"Definitely don't want to disclose that on the insurance forms," I said.

"Murty's going to help," Callum said. "And we will, too. You shouldn't need to go near the water at all."

"*You* can help," I said to him. "The sea's really wet, if you haven't noticed. And large. And I'm a *cat*."

"All the fish you eat, I'd think you'd be pretty fond of the sea."

"It's a great place for fish. It is not a great place for cats."

"No," Gertrude said. "You shouldn't get any more involved. It's bad enough that we have a mermaid. I never should have let you agree to owe him a favour. They're treacherous things, Sea Witches or not. And if Murty *is* at odds with the other mermaids like he says, you don't want to be seen associating with him. If they get wind of it, you'll never be able to touch the sea again. No, you leave Murty to try alone. I'll think of something."

Callum looked at me, and I huffed. I don't know why I bother arguing for the side of reason anyway. He's like a magnet for lost causes and breaking hearts everywhere.

"Look, land hardly seems safe for us either," he said. "We may as well make it two for two."

"Sure," I said. "Let's have *no* options left."

Gertrude frowned at us. "It's not *land*, though, is it? Just something in Leeds." She waved vaguely. "That strange little man with his potions for the dead."

"He's not been an issue," I said. "On the other hand, we *have* had issues with magicians, unicorns, necromancers who tried to shove an ancient god into Callum, his sister – Callum's, not the ancient god's – weres who might or might not be involved with necromancers but who have definitely got the sorcerer's dentist, someone trying to throw me into a void, the Watch, and can we just circle back to the necromancers, because they're definitely up to something." I thought about it. "Also the sorcerer keeps giving me out-of-body experiences."

Gertrude looked from me to Callum, eyebrows raised.

"He kind of covered it. We're not here on holiday. We're hiding out." He frowned at me. "*Keeps* giving you out-of-body experiences? I thought it was only once."

"Once was enough. It felt like more."

"Ms Jones the sorcerer?" Gertrude asked. "The one who helped with the undead in Leeds?"

"Yes."

"I rather liked her."

"You would," I muttered.

"Why does she keep giving you out-of-body experiences?"

"She's missing," Callum said. "She got in touch with Gobs somehow and told him to make sure her partner Malcolm was safe—"

"The dentist?"

"Yes, him. And we did, but now he's off with weres, looking for her. Or he was – I haven't heard from him since we left Leeds."

Gertrude considered that, her elbows on the table and her fingers steepled together. Reapers are neutral, and tend to have little to do with the living. But, as noted before, Gertrude wasn't exactly a typical reaper. And necromancers do terrible things to souls. Gertrude had been upset enough about the ones bound to the undead, which she said had gone all soggy, and I could imagine her escalating to *rather miffed* if necromancers started randomly shoving broken souls into discarded bodies. It's not like they're careful about it, if the stories are to be believed. Because that's all necromancers are meant to be, of course. They're scary stories to tell small kittens, of ancient beings that were almost gods, and who tried to break the world. The Folk and the humans smashed them apart in one last alliance, then the cats formed the Watch to make sure nothing like it ever happened again. Humans forgot – or were *made* to forget, because cats can do that – and Folk went into hiding. The necromancer blood-line was, in a rather unsettling euphemism, *broken*, and that should have been that.

But magic always finds a way, and the more insidious it is, the more it appeals to the basest desires, the more people covet it. They hide and nurture it, and it grows behind closed doors and under fake names and high pretences. Which anyone with half a brain knew, and the Watch have a lot more than that. So the fact that there really did seem to be necromancer magic loose in the world and the Watch wasn't doing *anything* about it was more than suspicious. It spoke of corruption and treachery on the sort of scale I was trying not to think about. Along with all the other things I was trying not to think about.

None of which I had to say to Gertrude. She might not be old enough to have seen the days of necromancers, but she was old enough to know the ways of the Watch. Now she looked at us over her steepled fingers and said, "This is all most unorthodox. I knew those poor undead souls in Leeds were a bad sign."

"Zombies tend to be," I said.

"And now we have an excess of the dead in the sea, and they're not *right*." She made a thoughtful noise. "I shall have to look into things further. One can't have people running about the place interfering with peaceful souls. And did you mention *possession?*"

"Something like that," Callum said with a shudder.

"Your poor soul," Gertrude said. "It must've been quite bruised. And after the zombie incident, too!"

Callum made an uncertain sound. I think he'd been more bruised by discovering his bestie wasn't dead, just dodgy as a half-price herring. Although being turned into a zombie briefly probably hadn't been great, either.

"Do you think they're connected?" I asked. "The necromancers in Leeds and the dead here? And now Emma going missing?"

Gertrude considered it. "All things are connected at some level."

"Helpful."

She gave me a severe look. "*However*, as I was going to continue, it seems unlikely that undead being created in Leeds and an excess of the dead appearing in Whitby, all arising at the same time as necromancers reappear, would be *un*connected."

"And Emma?"

"I don't know." Her mouth twitched slightly, and she looked back at the table.

"Can you reap these dead?" Callum asked.

"I can reap anything," Gertrude said, and it was a simple statement of fact. "Once, the reapers stood with the Watch against the necromancers. We cut down their armies of the dead, released their poor trapped souls."

"'We'?" I asked, wondering if I'd misjudged the age thing.

"We as in reapers. I'm not quite as old as that."

Callum frowned. "Necromancers would know that. And they might even know you helped in Leeds. So taking Emma, when that might lead you into the sea, where you can't go ..."

"And where a Sea Witch might steal your scythe ..." I added.

"Oh," Gertrude said. "Oh, *Old Ones take you!*" The fire guttered in the hearth, and outside I distinctly heard some gulls screaming in fright. A dwarf on the other side of the fire got up abruptly and hurried deeper into the pub, clutching her beer in both hands. The faun looked up sharply.

"Oi!" he shouted at us. "None of that!"

"None of what?" I demanded.

"Whatever that was." He jabbed a finger at a wooden sign

behind him. Carved into it and stained a deeper brown was: *No spitting. No biting. No fighting. No invoking ancient gods or laying curses. No raising the kraken.* "You'll be out. Bloody tea and hot chocolate. Knew you were trouble."

"Cool it, Mr Tumnus," I said.

"*What?*"

"Thought you'd be good at tea parties."

"*Right,*" he bellowed, slamming the glass he'd been polishing down on the counter as a ripple of muffled laughter ran around the room. "That is *not on! Out!*"

"Nicely done," Callum said to me.

"That wasn't on his list," I pointed out.

"Normally *don't insult the host* is one of those unwritten laws."

"Eh." I jumped to the floor and gave myself a good shake to scatter hair and sand all over the faun's floor on the way out.

THE RAIN WAS HEAVIER NOW, the wind fiercer. It curled and scratched around the buildings, chattering at loose tiles and setting the sign above the pub door swinging and creaking. Callum turned the collar of his fleece up, and Gertrude peeled off his coat and held it out to him.

"You can wear it," he said.

"Our cottage's just around the corner," she said, nodding toward the old town. "And I'm not cold. Just a little embarrassed by the pyjamas."

"I like them," I said. "Cat-themed clothes are the best clothes."

Callum took his coat from Gertrude and said, "Why would the mermaids want your scythe? Or the Sea Witch?"

Gertrude looked up at the dark sky. "A scythe is created

when a reaper is. It is theirs for eternity. There are no spares, or replacements. It's made of the very fabric of the universe, and it can cut through reality itself. Many creatures would want such a thing."

"That sounds like a fun thing for a mermaid to have," I said.

"I'm more worried about the necromancers," Callum said. "If the mermaids have Reaper Scarborough's scythe, and they're working together, that seems like a problem."

No one spoke for a moment, and Gertrude played with her necklace again, twisting the chain through her bony fingers.

"We're going to find Emma," Callum said. "That's first priority. *Then* we'll see about the dead."

"It's too dangerous," Gertrude started, and Callum shook his head.

"No. She's a friend. You're *both* friends, and we're not just going to leave you to it. Especially when it sounds like this is all going to end up connected to our problems in Leeds anyway. And if you can't go on the water, we will. Won't we, Gobs?"

"Can't you just go?" I asked. "I'll supervise from here."

He shrugged. "If you're going to be that much of a pain about it."

"I'm not being a *pain*. I'm just pointing out that water and cats don't mix."

"Tigers like water," Gertrude said. "And the panthers in South America, and many big cats, in fact. Even some domestic cats enjoy water."

"I'm not *domestic*. I'm not a bloody dishwasher."

"I'm merely suggesting that you may be buying into a cultural stereotype." She regarded me calmly.

"Fine. *I* don't like being wet. It takes ages to dry, and I hate water in my ears." I looked at Callum. "But you'll probably end up offering your coat to a mermaid and then we'll have lost both you *and* Emma, so I'll have to come anyway."

"Suit yourself." He found his cigarette packet in the coat pocket and tipped it up, dripping water onto the cobbles. He sighed and tucked it away again. "Let's head back to the beach and see if we can figure anything out."

"It's *dark*," I protested. "I mean, it was already, but it's *really* dark now."

"He's right," Gertrude said. "Don't go out there tonight. The tide's high and the storm's coming in. I'll take a look from the cliff and see if I can spot anything happening, but no one should be on the beach. I'm still not sure you should be doing this at all, but definitely not at night."

"Then we'll come with you," Callum said. He checked Green Snake was in a pocket, and looked at me. "You want a lift?"

"*No*," I said. "If I'm going to get wet, cold, and eaten by sea monsters and cliff ghasts, I'll at least do it with some dignity."

"Are there ghasts?" Gertrude asked with interest. "It's been years since I've seen one."

"Have you seen this place?" I asked. "Of course there'll be ghasts. And probably ogres and trolls and goblins besides."

"Vampires?" Callum suggested.

"Vampires don't exist," I said, but with less conviction than I might once have. After all, I'd said the same thing about zombies.

Gertrude looked in the direction of the Abbey where it loomed above town, unseen on top of the cliffs. "Go home," she said. "Nothing's happening tonight."

"But if you're going out—" Callum started.

"I'm going to change into my spare robes and get my scythe," she said. "And I'll have a look from the cliffs, but then I'm going to check every graveyard I can, just to be sure I'm right about there being no reaper in the area."

"We'll keep watch from the cliffs, then," Callum said. He really can't take an easy way out to save his life. And certainly not when the guilt of letting go of Emma was eating at him like a thousand small, toothy fish. I could smell it on him like the leftover murk of a bad night.

"No. Get some rest. The mermaid's looking for Emma. If nothing else, it might be he brings us some information." She sounded doubtful, and I didn't blame her.

"Well," Callum patted his pockets, then sighed. "I'd say call us, but my phone's still on the beach."

"Probably eaten by Black Dogs," I said.

"I'll see you tomorrow," Gertrude said. "I'll find you." And she turned and slipped away into the shadows, barefoot and silent in her cat-print pyjamas, her thin pale hair plastered to her scalp in the shifting lights of the rain-drenched street.

I squinted up at Callum. "Can we go somewhere with cat biscuits, at least? Mr Tumnus was *not* set up for cat hospitality."

"And you wonder why," he said, turning down the cobbled streets and back toward the wharf. I padded next to him, listening to the waves breaking on the piers like the growls of a great and restless beast.

11

THE KRAKEN COMES

WE WERE SODDEN AGAIN BY THE TIME WE GOT BACK TO *THE Savage Squid,* Callum padding down the gangway in his bare feet and wincing at the non-slip ridges digging into his toes. I trailed after him, so wet that I'd given up on trying to hide from the rain and instead just splashed along pretending to ignore the fact it was running in rivulets down my sides and dripping from my belly and whiskers.

Callum unlocked the forecastle and stumbled in, heading straight for the cabin and the tiny shower, shedding clothes as he went. I followed, and he paused to wrap a towel around me, rubbing me with it lightly while I snuffled and complained. Then he abandoned me to it and vanished into the head. It was more a trickle than a shower, from what I could gather, but we'd never exactly had the sort of accommodation that boasted top notch facilities of any sort. At least he could actually get into the bathroom, unlike at the boarding house.

By the time Callum had emerged, Green Snake and I were both buried under the heavy duvet on the bunk.

"Tell me you're not in there making it soggy," he said, digging in the cabin's little locker for fresh clothes.

"It's possible," I said, not coming out. "But there's two bunks."

He didn't answer, and a moment later I heard him leave, and the gas stove clicking in the galley. I pushed my nose out into the cold air of the cabin, Green Snake wriggling unhappily at being disturbed. I stayed there until I heard the unmistakable sound of a can being opened, then scrambled out and ran to the galley.

"And there he is," Callum said, putting a bowl on our makeshift table in the bar. When we were on the dock there was an extension cord that ran to a shed ashore, which meant the drinks fridges could be cooled right down for the following day and, more importantly, we could run a little fan heater. It was going full tilt in the bar area, and I basked in the heat of it for a moment before jumping up to scoff down some cat food of blissfully dubious but almost certainly fish-less provenance. It might have even met a chicken at some point in its life.

Callum finished making his tea, then went to the door and cracked it open, sitting on the floor just inside with his cigarettes and Chokkie Diggles. I paused to stare at them, licking sticky gravy off my chops. It felt like about a month ago we'd had Emma in here, but I could still catch a whiff of her warm scent when I concentrated.

I examined Callum. He looked almost as pale as the reaper, and he tapped the fingers of his free hand restlessly on his leg, the other pinching the cigarette tight enough that I could see dents in it.

"What?" I demanded. "What is it?"

He shook his head, puffing smoke at the door. Even in the shelter of the harbour the mooring lines creaked and groaned, and the wind whistled in the stubby rigging.

I jumped down from the table and stalked over to him. "It's something. Emma? You getting all twisted up about that? I bet we had no hope of getting her off that beach. Anyone who knows Gertrude knows that taking Emma's their fastest route to getting their fins on a scythe."

He gave me a slight smile. His hair was still wet and hung lankly about his face, making him look half-drowned. "Then we shouldn't have taken her down there."

"Yeah. *We* took *her* down there." I sat down in front of the heater, the blast of it ruffling my fur. "There was no stopping her as soon as that Matilda—" I stopped, and we both stared at each other.

"Set up?" he asked me. "You think Matilda's connected to the necromancers?"

"Maybe. The Watch have been suspiciously paws-off about the whole necromancer situation, so it's possible. Or maybe it's just a mermaid thing and Matilda's really into fish. We still don't know that this is a part of what's happening in Leeds."

Callum nodded, stubbing his cigarette out in an old can. "We don't *know*, but we can guess. Reapers are a threat to the necromancers, because they can reap anything. But if the necromancers can get their scythes off them—"

"Not much to stop the deadheads then," I finished for him. "Plus if scythes can cut through anything, maybe that makes bringing the Old Ones back even easier. Just chop a nice doorway into the orange dimensions."

"Good point. Still doesn't explain the mermaids, though."

"Maybe it really isn't connected to them. Maybe the dead are just in the sea for storage, or something."

"For what?" Callum asked, sipping his tea.

"Storage. I mean, *someone's* going to notice an undead army milling about the place, right? But if you shove it in the North Sea, odds are Betty from down the road isn't going to stumble across them on her morning constitutional."

Callum snorted, then said, "That's weirdly plausible."

"I don't know why you insist on being surprised that I have good ideas."

He rubbed a hand over his stubble and said, "I wish we knew what was going on back in Leeds."

"Hardly matters, does it? We can't leave."

"And isn't that weird? We got in alright."

"Some places are like that," I said, but he was right. It *was* weird, and Black Dogs were a bit of an overkill, even if it had been a pocket town. Which it wasn't. *Couldn't* be.

Green Snake slipped across the floor, lifted his head to examine me, then tried to curl around my paws. I batted him away, and he gave me an affronted look.

"Is that likely?" Callum said. "We get chased out of our flat in Leeds. Dimly's too dodgy for us to go into. Then we come here and find we can't leave, and some places *are just like that?*"

"Look, at this point I'd be more surprised if we went somewhere and things *weren't* weird." I bared my teeth at Green Snake as he came back for another try. "Get off. Callum, haven't you fed him?"

"He just wants to share the heater. I wouldn't mind some heat too, by the way."

"I was here first." But I let Green Snake coil himself next to me when he tried again.

"I'm going to talk to Ifan," Callum said.

"*Don't,*" I said. "Try Gerry again. Or …" I trailed off, trying to think of someone else we could trust. "What about Muscles?"

"I thought you didn't like weres."

"He's only barely a were. And he was a necromancer heavy for a bit. He might know some stuff."

"Not as much as Ifan," Callum pointed out.

"But unlike Ifan, he hasn't tried to kill you. That seems like a positive."

"*Hmm.*" Callum finished his tea and pulled the door shut, turning the lock. "It'll have to wait until morning, anyway. We'll get a phone first thing."

"Good. You can sleep on it and make better decisions."

He just scritched the back of my neck and turned the heater off on his way to the cabin.

It wasn't exactly a restful night after that, but we weren't much accustomed to restful nights. Certainly not peaceful ones. The mooring lines kept up their mournful chorus, and the wind pushed at *The Savage Squid* irritably, as if annoyed it couldn't get enough of a run at her in here, and the sea slapped at the hull with petulant little waves that sneaked through the piers. I curled into the bunk next to Callum, soaking up his warmth, until his constant shifting and muttering got to the point that I batted his ear and jumped to the floor. He swore but didn't emerge from the cocoon of covers, which, as I padded up to the bar, I decided was wise. The storm had come in off cold seas and colder lands, and even inside I could see my own breath misting softly in front of me.

I had an ineffective go at starting the heater up, but the knobs were too tricky for cat paws. I jumped to the seat instead, putting my paws on the bulkhead to peer out the porthole at the harbour. The wind was still up, and the beacons painted the white water of the swells in red and green as they shattered on the harbour wall. The houses and pubs were mostly dark, only illuminated by streetlights and lit signs. I wondered what Gertrude was doing out there, and if Emma was safe beneath the waves. If that was even possible, or if she'd joined the ranks of the dead.

"The ghost ships will be out tonight," a small voice said, almost in my ear, and I squawked and jumped away, turning back to see a brown rat with an oddly hunched posture sitting on the edge of the porthole.

"What?"

"The dead rise with the storms," the rat said, and waved a twisted paw at the harbour.

"What?"

He turned milky eyes on me. "Can you not feel it? The sea is restless. The dead strive to return. Soon will come the kraken, and all will be lost."

I managed not to say *what?* again, and instead went with, "Kraken?"

"It is foretold," the rat said solemnly. "The kraken will sweep the world into the sea and eat the sun." He gave a little rat titter.

"Ah," I said. "Merv?"

"Yes."

"You're the one nibbles on the poison."

"I see such things."

"Yeah, it's called a near-death experience," I said, and gave my back a quick groom. The hair had been starting to stand to attention at all the *dead rise* stuff, but a kraken that eats the sun pushed things into fairy tale territory. The rain had, at least, washed the salt and most of the sand out of my fur, and I'd left the rest in the bunk with Callum.

"Yes, yes. Dismiss it, dismiss it. Weird rat, eats the poison, tells the tales." Merv pressed his snout to the porthole. "Makes up the things, dreams the dreams. Weird. We all need someone to look down on."

"I mean, you *are* pretty weird, dude," I said, and went to see if I could get out on deck. Less to take in what was looking like a very nasty early morning, and more in case Merv went rabid and started chasing me around the cabin.

"And you are so *normal*, with your nightmares and your midnight prowling and your vanishing snake and your human of smoke and sorrow and your lost lives." He didn't say it like a question, more as if he might actually think it *was* normal.

"I'm not comparing weirdness," I said, then wrinkled my snout. "Have you been *spying* on me?"

"Merv sees. Merv knows."

"You've been spying. Great. One more thing to creep me out on this bloody boat."

Merv rubbed his snout with both paws. "I see the pirate. I see the man. I see the whispers and the schemes and the plans."

"Sorry, what?" I turned away from the door. "The pirate and the man? Hilda? And what man?"

Merv shrugged. "Names are so irrelevant."

"The captain? And ..." I thought about it. "The mermaid that was here this afternoon?"

"This afternoon is yet to come. I cannot see that far."

I tried not to show my teeth. "Yesterday afternoon, then."

"Maybe. Time is fluid."

I sighed. "Right. So what did they say?" Not that I could exactly rely on anything the poison-addled rodent came out with, but it seemed careless not to ask.

"They argued about the north. And the man said that danger comes ashore." He nodded wisely. "The kraken, you see."

"The North?" I said. "As in Callum?"

"Perhaps. Or perhaps they mean the north itself. Or maybe they are one and the same."

"Yeah, I don't think they are. Did this man say anything specific?"

Merv shrugged. "The end of the world comes. But we know that." He looked around. "My ear tastes green," he announced, and abruptly leaped off the wall and raced across the floor.

"Hang about," I started, but he'd already vanished through the gap where a locker door hung ajar. I padded across to it and nosed it open, but it was empty other than three caps from rum bottles, lined up neatly, with a gull feather lying over the top of them.

"Hairy squid rings," I muttered, and sat back on the bare wood floor, wrapping my tail over my paws. I wished I knew how much was *weird nonsense* and how much was *weird but true.*

I was mostly hoping the kraken belonged to the former group.

I WASN'T GOING to be sleeping any time soon, not with kraken and ghost ships and plotting pirate captains about the place, so once it seemed Merv wasn't coming back I padded through the galley and into the cluttered belly of the boat. It was dark down there, the only light filtering through from the galley portholes behind me, and the one in our cabin. The other cabin was too full of Hilda's hoard to allow any light in at all, and beyond that the engine room was entirely port-less. But I didn't need light. I was following the faint scent of ship's rats and the even paler whiff of my own paw prints from when I'd crept through here before, exploring the unseen ways of the boat.

I found the opening in the bulkhead that led from the storage cabin to a dead space that ran between the engine room and the deckhead, and wriggled my way through. The gap was tight, and a tangle of wires and cables headed off in meandering directions, some of them looking as if not all of the ships' rats had been confining their diet to sausage rolls. I couldn't stand upright, and had to creep along with my belly brushing the dusty surface beneath me and the deck pressing my ears flat above. But there was space enough. There are advantages to being compactly formed.

It wasn't long until I caught the whisper of fresher air over my whiskers, and I nosed my way over to a spot where a locker didn't quite meet the wall of the captain's cabin. I had no idea if it was shoddy workmanship or the shifting of the boat that created these gaps, but this one was big enough for me to squeeze out, even if it took a bit of wriggling and there were drifts of dark fur decorating the locker by the time I was finished. I shook myself off, gave my shoulders a quick groom, then checked the cabin.

A row of heavy-paned ports overlooked the stern while others looked forward onto the party deck, and the sallow glow of the streetlights bled through both sets, giving everything a grainy sepia tint. It suited the stained, worn wood of the walls, and the ragged old red rug spread on the floor. A double bunk was built against one wall, and there was a desk and seat beneath the ports at the stern, and every flat surface was stacked with rolls of charts and coils of stained rope and boxes of pipe tobacco and collapsed crab pots and even some sails stuffed into faded canvas bags. Not sure what Hilda was holding onto those for, considering *The Savage Squid* had no room on her masts for sails, but given I'd discovered (in my search for treasure maps) that half the charts were for routes around Cape Horn and the rest were for the Caribbean, I thought her stash might be more aspirational than practical.

I nosed about the place, smelling stale smoke and the quiet mustiness of an old boat in winter. I wasn't sure what I thought I might find – a diary detailing Hilda's meetings with mermaids, necromancers, and Black Dogs, perhaps? A signed contract stating that yes, she was trapping us in Whitby, keeping us distracted with pirate tours and engine maintenance, while the Old Ones came to power in Leeds? With the use of stolen reaper scythes, perhaps?

I wanted to believe that all of these things could be unrelated, that the mermaid and reaper issues were entirely independent of the necromancers, that we'd left all our troubles behind in Leeds, and that Merv was spinning tales out of poison dreams, but I couldn't. Things just don't work so tidily in my life. If something looked like it wanted to eat me, the odds were it did.

There was nothing in the cabin that seemed helpful, but I was too restless to go back and try sleeping again, so I headed for the ladder in the corner. The steps were broader than on your average ladder, and had a bit more of a welcoming lean, but none of that qualified them as *stairs*. The varnish was peeling, as were the non-slip strips stuck to the edges, but such things don't bother cats much. I ran up to the top step, shoved my nose into the corner of the wood panel that rested flush with the cabin top directly over the ladder, and forced my way through into the wheelhouse above. The panel was just an old bit of plywood cut to roughly fit, so while I couldn't throw the whole thing back, it was easy enough to push past. There had probably been a nice, custom-made bit of wood there at some point, one that had kept the draughts to a minimum, but this worked much better for marauding cats. And rats, but there was no fresh scent of them in here at the moment.

It was much brighter in the wheelhouse, and I jumped onto the wooden shelving that ran beneath the windows. At the forward end of the little cabin, where the helm was, the shelving curved outward, holding various dials and electronic displays, as well as the comically small wheel and the engine controls. There was a great big wooden wheel on the deck below, but that was strictly for the pirate parties to hang off and take selfies with. This was Hilda's wheel, and I could smell her presence in here like a ghost, all alcohol and crankiness over something deep and sharp and watchful.

The other shelves held books with titles like *North Sea Tidal Streams* and *Bermuda & Other Triangles* and *How to Classify Sea Serpents*, as well as a clutter of pipes and binoculars in various states of disrepair, and bits of interesting driftwood and old shells and smooth rocks. I'd been in here before. There had been nothing to see then, and there was nothing to see now.

"Polly found a thief," a harsh voice said, far too close to my tail, and I shot straight into the air, spinning about as I did so and coming down in a crouch, facing back at the damn parrot.

"You over-salted *pigeon*," I managed. My heart was trying to make its escape from my chest.

"Thieves feed the fishes," the parrot said, tipping his head to one side.

"Yeah, I'm absolutely in here stealing Hilda's pipe collection," I said, sitting up and grooming the hair on my spine back into place. "What're you doing here?"

"Polly watches."

I stopped grooming myself and looked at him. "You can drop the Polly this and Polly that thing, you know."

"Why?"

"There's no one here but us. You don't have to act the parrot."

"Polly doesn't act." He turned his head, so he could look at me from his other eye. They were beady little things, sharp and surrounded by pale skin before the luminous green of his feathers took over.

"Suit yourself," I said. "Polly seen any dastardly doings,

then? Spotted old Hilda making plans to hand my human over to the mermaids or something?"

"Hilda tells your human not to deal with mermaids. She doesn't like mermaids."

"What about necromancers, then? Magicians?"

"Polly doesn't like magicians. They put birds in hats."

"Yeah, I don't like them either." I examined the bird for a long moment, then said, "Is Whitby a pocket?"

"Magicians put birds in pockets, too." He shifted from foot to foot, his head bobbing.

"Sure, but moving on from the magicians—"

"Nasty little magicians with their nasty little handkerchiefs," Polly said, his voice rising. "Handkerchiefs and sticks and clips for the wings!"

"Right," I said, taking a step back. Polly chattered his beak, and while I was pretty sure he wouldn't mistake me for a magician, it was a big beak. I'd seen him crack a crab's leg with it. "Nasty magicians. But—"

"Polly doesn't stand it! They don't!" The parrot opened his wings, beating them against the still air of the cabin and sending gusts to part my fur. "Polly takes his eye!"

"That's great— *what?*"

"Polly's meant to sit in the box then appear in the cage. But Polly doesn't like the cage. Polly shows the magician. Polly *shows* him."

"Dude," I said, then couldn't think of anything else. Polly glared at me. I offered a "Good work?"

He folded his wings and preened himself a little. "Polly's not a dude. Polly's the star of the show."

"Totally." We were both silent for a moment, while I tried to think how to leave without turning my back on the bloodthirsty, fancy-pants chicken.

Then he said, "Someone asks Hilda to keep the human in town."

"Who?" I asked.

The parrot shrugged. "She doesn't tell Polly."

"Did you see them?"

"No. They use the phone."

I sighed, and gave the parrot a sideways look. "What about other magic-workers? Do you—"

"No! They make spells from bird bones! And strip our feathers! And think we're for the sacrificing! *Polly does not like the magic!*"

The volume of his shouting sent my ears back, and I squinted at him. "Got it. No magic on board."

"Polly takes their eyes."

"Right." Well, that kind of suggested that Hilda would be hard-pressed to be working with either Ifan or the necromancers, unless everything was done over the phone. Which I couldn't rule out, but it did mean we likely weren't in any immediate danger of being pounced on – or not by magic-workers, anyway. I wondered if I could risk mentioning pockets again, and decided not. It was far too early in the morning for parrot tantrums. So I went with, "What do you know about Callum, then? Or me? What've people been saying?"

"Hilda says you're a terrible ship's cat. The rats are still here."

"Yeah, yeah. Other than that."

The parrot considered it, and I wondered what went on in that bony head of his. I'd always thought not a lot when it came to birds in general, but I was rethinking, what with the magician stance.

"That maybe even Whitby can't hide you," he said finally. "That the human is hunted, and perhaps there's no hiding anywhere."

"Who said that?" I demanded, and he half-closed his eyes, clattered his beak a couple of times, and didn't reply. "Polly?"

"Polly want an Eccles cake."

"Really?"

"Yep."

I sighed, and looked around the cabin. I wasn't getting any further in here. "Do us a favour, Pol – open the door?" I nodded at the lock, which was too heavy for my paws. I knew, because I'd tried last time I'd been investigating.

Polly eyed me. "Why?"

"I'm bored. I might see if I can find some feline companionship."

The parrot didn't move for a moment, then he said, "Polly doesn't want to hunt you again."

I shivered, even though him hunting us had been what had saved me on the beach. "Got it. I'm not going near the sea."

He watched me a moment longer, and I tried not to shift under his sharp gaze, then he unsnapped his wings and hefted himself aloft, attacking the lock with both claws and beak as he flapped and swung, swearing enthusiastically and sending a few sheets of paper flying across the cabin as his wings beat at the air.

Then the lock clunked open, and the door popped off its latch.

"Cheers, dude," I said, as he fluttered over to perch on the helm. "Leave it open?"

"Not a dude," he said again. "Polly waits."

I slipped out into the thin hours of the early morning, trying to convince myself that was an offer and not a threat.

12

JUST CAT THINGS

So Whitby was no hiding place for us anymore. If it ever had been – after all, a hiding place is only as good as the hider makes it, and we'd both thought it was just temporary. Let things calm down in Dimly and Leeds, and head back. We'd not exactly committed to vanishing. We might not have set up our PI business again in Whitby, and we weren't at the boarding house Gerry had sent us to anymore, but it'd only take one enquiry with the landlord or the other tenants to send any interested parties after us. It should've been enough, though. We were just one cat and one human in a whole mess of them. No one should have been looking for us *that* hard.

We seemed to have misjudged things, though. Gerry was making cryptic phone calls. Ms Jones was still looking for me. Our pirate captain was discussing us with people and conspiring to keep us in town, although I was undecided as to whether that was a problem or not yet. And now we had the dead rising out of the sea. Or hanging out in the sea, anyway. I hadn't seen any actually rising yet. I threw the harbour a suspicious look as I headed up the gangway, just in case they were getting started, but all I could see was dark, choppy water and the broken reflections of the lights from shore spilled across it.

It was still raining as I padded down the deserted wharf, even if it had become more of a sharp drizzle than a downpour. The wind hadn't eased, though, and it ruffled my fur and made my whiskers twitch. But what was making me *really* twitchy was the realisation that, no matter if necromancers were hanging out in the waterfront pubs and weres were supping tea at the Abbey, we couldn't make ourselves more scarce because a) we'd misplaced Emma; and b) there were Black Dogs patrolling the borders, so until we found our missing human and figured out who could call the beasts off, we were stuck.

Stuck, and with Callum guilt-ridden enough about Emma to make deals with mermaids. Plus someone was talking about "losing the North". Merv might've said it was a man, but I didn't have a lot of faith in the rat's tenuous grasp on reality. The odds of it being the same mermaid Callum had just promised a favour to seemed high, no matter how Hilda had fussed about him not being allowed on board. I thought the pirate froths with too much protest, as some dead dude said, and while she'd so far not done anything wrong by us, there was *something* going on there.

But there was no way Callum was going to walk away until Emma was safe, and as skilled a PI as I am, those skills did not extend to water-based activities. Which meant I needed help, and there was only one place I could think of to get it.

I DIDN'T HEAD toward town. Even in this weather, there'd be eyes and ears in the alleys and walls, and for what I was about to do I wanted no witnesses. So, despite what I'd said to Polly (and I did look over my shoulder more than once, just in case the bloodthirsty budgie had followed me), I headed toward the sea.

Not onto the beach, though. I'd been able to hear the crumple of the surf on the sand since I'd stepped out of the wheelhouse, and I had no intentions of repeating my earlier tumble wash. But I trotted down the wharf to where the road switch-backed up to climb the inside of the cliff, passing the amusement arcades and the shuttered food stalls and a couple of sandwich boards that had been toppled by the wind on my way. Right at the end, the pavement left the road and continued straight ahead down the pier, and a slipway to the left led down onto the seaweed-choked sand. White water rushed toward me, smashing against the concrete uprights of the wharf and collapsing on the beach. I could feel the reverberation of it under my paws as a faint yet persistent tremor, as if the town itself were afraid of being stolen by the sea. The air was so thick with salt spray that I could taste it, and however far away the sunrise might actually be, it felt impossibly distant.

I didn't venture onto the pier, but padded onto the patio area in front of the pub that huddled under the cliff just to the left of the slipway. It wasn't a *patio* as in nice tiles and terracotta pots and probably some vines snaking through trellis overhead. We weren't on the Italian riviera. This patio wasn't much more than a bit of sand-crusted concrete between the sea wall and the pub, with a handful of picnic tables for sunnier days and braver souls. It was always busy during opening hours, though, full of groups with pints or families with bundles of fish'n'chips, and there were also, for reasons that escaped me, a handful of kiddies' rides rusting cheerily next to the tables – a half-sized rocket-ship ride that someone had painted to try and resemble a fishing boat, some teacup seats on a spinning wheel, and even something that looked like the little sister of a merry-go-round.

I took shelter in the rocket-fishing boat, jumping down past the seats to the floor, where the nose was covered over at the front and I could avoid the worst of the rain and the wind. And also hopefully go unnoticed by anyone else silly enough to be out in the storm of the season.

The ride smelled of grease and must and ice cream, and I sat there for a bit, my ears twitching. I wasn't procrastinating or anything, I just wanted to make sure the coast was completely clear, no sneaking cats or wandering mermaids or anything like that. But it very quickly became clear that hypothermia was going to be a real issue, even if I was relatively sheltered in here. I grumbled, shifted my paws, shook myself off, then said, "Well? You've been bloody well nagging me enough."

For a moment there was nothing, and I wondered if the deep-set, barely-there charms of Whitby were enough to keep me protected, even when I wasn't concentrating on not thinking about things. Then I felt something change, a thickening of the night or a thinning of the world, and there was a presence close enough to touch. No skinny jeans or daisy-print Doc Martens, though. This presence was what I smelled underneath the superficial humanness of her, the truth beneath the shape she wore. Muscular and fierce and vaguely hairy.

"I can't see you," I said.

I can't see you either.

That was weird. Being wrenched out of my skin was no fun, but I didn't much like this, either. It felt like holding a private conversation by shouting it between two hilltops.

"Can't you do your thing?"

*No, I can't **do my thing**. You're ... obscured.* She sounded both irritated and uncertain, which didn't seem to bode well. *Why haven't you been answering me?*

"I dunno, maybe the whole out-of-body thing wasn't something I wanted to repeat?"

Well, evidently we don't have that problem now. Where's Malcolm?

"With the weres. We told him to come with us, but—"

But he's safer with them. Good.

I decided not to say it hadn't exactly been up to us. "What's going on? We're stuck ... here," I said, not wanting to say where *here* was in case we had eavesdroppers. "And we seem to have a problem with the dead again."

*I can guess where you are. Or what **sort** of place you're in. It's not enough, Gobbelino.*

"What d'you mean? Not enough for what?" The skin on my spine ached with how hard my hair was lifting. The wind whistled outside, and I wondered if I could hear other noises on it. Howls, perhaps.

You won't stay safe for long.

"No baby goats," I said.

What?

"I *know*. We've got ... issues."

There was a pause, and I could feel her scratching at me, trying to get a grip and pull me toward her. I didn't resist it. I *wanted* her to grab me this time. Out-of-body experience or not, we couldn't talk like this. I could almost feel the attention of others turning toward us.

It's no good. You've got to get out of where you are, then we can talk properly.

"I don't know if I can. Where are you, anyway? Can't you come and find us?"

If I could do that, I wouldn't have needed you to find Malcolm, she said, and the words were spiked with yellow irritation.

I growled. "Callum's going to go all bleeding heart and get himself involved in something."

*Then stop him. You **have** to stop him.*

"Oh, sure. Just that easy."

Make it that easy. Get out of ... where you are. Then I can help.

"Can't you just phone him and tell him not to? I mean, we've lost our phone, but we'll have a new one tomorrow."

Phones can be tracked.

I was silent at that, licking my chops. Did she mean our phone, or hers? We'd thought she must be being held somewhere against her will, but I was starting to doubt it. There's not much can hold a sorcerer, after all. They're ancient creatures, and many of them have forgotten entirely what it is to be human. Ms Jones hadn't, and seemed to have held onto weird little human foibles like making bad choices in relationships, if her ex/current partner Malcolm Walker the dentist was anything to go by. And if she had been being held against her will, I didn't think she'd have been spending much time waiting about for me to get in contact. She'd have been fully focused on getting out.

"What's going on?" I asked her. "Where are you? And—"

Stay safe. Keep Callum out of trouble. Get somewhere I can contact you properly. I can't do anything more until then.

And then she was gone, the sound of the surf suddenly loud and hungry in my ears again, and the rain drumming sharply on the body of the rocket above me.

"Cool," I said. "Good chat."

I PADDED BACK to the boat, my ears flattened against the incessant wind, wondering how I was going to persuade Callum to take a trip out of town while Emma was still missing. Reasoning wasn't going to work, especially not while he was still guilt-tripping himself, so out and out nagging would probably be my best bet. It was startlingly effective.

The parrot was dozing in the wheelhouse when I got back, the door closed but not locked. I was able to open it myself – handles with any sort of a lever on them are fine – but getting in was trickier, with the wind trying to blow it shut on my tail. Polly didn't move to help, just watched me with his sharp little eyes, and once I was in he said, "Kitty needs a towel."

"Kitty needs a heated blanket, a roast chicken, and a long nap," I replied. "But Kitty sees none of these things in his future."

"Polly's heart bleeds," the parrot remarked, and closed his eyes.

I wrinkled my snout at him, not quite daring to go with the bared teeth in case he was peeking, and squeezed my way past the panel over the ladder.

I decided that most of my early morning conversations fell into the *mostly unhelpful* category, and that any sharing of them could wait until I'd dried out a bit and had something to eat. Besides, Callum was grumpy enough by the time he finally stopped pushing me off the bunk and went to get my breakfast.

"You'll feel better for getting up," I called, as he clattered around in the galley. I'd parked myself back in front of the heater, working on getting the latest round of salt air and rain out of my coat. "Sleeping late's bad for you."

"Cats are bad for me," he said, over the noise of the kettle coming up to boil.

"Good thing you only hang about with one, then."

He made an unimpressed noise and dumped half a tin of sardines into a bowl. Which wasn't the gravy-laced treat I'd been hoping for, but it also wasn't herring, so I decided it was best not to complain. At least not until he'd had a minimum one cup of tea and two cigarettes.

"What were you *doing* going out again?" he demanded, setting the dish in front of me.

"Cat things," I said.

"In my experience, cat things usually involve staying dry."

"Well, it would be the preferred option."

He shook his head and went to get his tea.

The sun was still a while off rising, and I waited it out huddled in front of the heater. Callum pottered around getting the tidying up from the night before finished, his woolly hat already pulled down over his ears. The heater wasn't doing much to lift the chill in here.

"We need to get out of town," I announced, when he'd sat down next to the door with a cigarette and another cup of tea.

"Oh? And how d'you propose to do that?" he asked. "And where are we going to go?"

"I don't know," I admitted. "But Ms Jones kind of said we had to."

He stared at me. "You said she hadn't been in touch."

"Well, she hadn't, until this morning."

"Had she *tried* to be in touch before?"

I shifted. "Maybe."

"*Gobs.*"

"You try having a sorcerer-based out-of-body experience and see how you like it."

He sighed, took a gulp of tea, and said, "So what did she say?"

"Not much," I admitted. "This time was weird. Weird*er*. We couldn't talk properly – Whitby must block it somehow. But she said we had to get out of town so she could contact us. Maybe she knows something about what's going on in

Leeds. Or with the mermaids. Or anything, really, since we currently know nothing."

"So does that mean she's not back in Leeds?"

"I guess so. She didn't know the dentist was hanging out with the weres still, but she seemed okay with it."

Callum thought about it, rolling the butt of his cigarette between his fingers. He'd grazed his knuckles at some point, and I could see the red rawness where the skin was too damp to heal up properly. He pushed the door open a little further, peering out at the dock. A few people were hurrying along it, bundled in wet weather gear.

"We need a new phone," he said. "Then we can try and figure out what the hell's going on out there."

"Maybe," I said. "But we can't call Ms Jones. Wherever she is, she's worried about her phone being used to track her. What worries a *sorcerer*?"

Callum rubbed his mouth. "Nothing good."

"No fluffy nudibranch legs."

"What?"

"What?" I blinked at him.

"I need to talk to more humans," he muttered, and got up. "Look, Ms Jones or not, we need a phone. We need to be able to call Gertrude and see if she found out anything last night. We need to be in touch with Gerry if he calls again. And—" He hesitated.

I growled softly. "Maybe we're better being uncontactable. That'll break your Ifan habit."

"Information, Gobs. It matters, and sometimes you get it however you can. We're not getting away from what's happening in Leeds just by being here. You know that, right?" He took his *Savage Squid* jacket from its hook on the wall and shrugged into it.

"I hope you're not sending photos," I said, shivering as he

switched the heater off. "Or only for *really* good information."

"*Gobs.*"

"Not judging. Just you can do better than a dodgy magician."

"Good to know." He pulled open the door and we both yelped. Hilda glared at us, the parrot huddled on her shoulder. He appeared to be wearing a patchwork tea cosy, and looked distinctly put out.

"Why isn't the sign up by the gangway?" Hilda demanded.

"Are we going out today?" Callum asked, glancing dubiously out toward the harbour mouth. Not even the most hardcore fishing boat (a small one with a blue hull, crewed by a large woman and an equally large young man who was either her son or much younger brother, because genetics will out) had gone out this morning.

"Doubtful. But we can take bookings. You know about those, don't you?"

"Right. Yes. I can put the sign out. I'm just going to—"

"Start work? That's what you should be doing. I'm paying you, remember?"

"Well, you're not, really," I pointed out.

"Would you like to start paying rent, then?"

"No," Callum said. "And we're very grateful. But we need to get a phone, so we can at least be in touch with Gertrude. I'm worried she's going to try and do something on her own."

"This is the reaper, yes? You think she can't take care of herself?"

"Well, of course she can, but the sea—"

Hilda waved impatiently. There were dark smudges under her eyes, and the heavy white plait that lay over her shoulder looked a little wonky, as if she'd done it in the dark. "Fine, fine. Go and get your phone. But no hanging about."

"Polly's watching," the parrot said, turning a baleful eye on me.

"Polly's looking styling," I said. "Granny chic, is it?"

He chattered his beak at me, and I bared my teeth back, since we had company. The odds were good Callum would intervene before the damn parakeet took my eyes out.

"Polly looks warmer than you do," Callum said to me, and closed the door behind us, heading for the gangway as Hilda stumped off to her wheelhouse, presumably to glare at charts and drink rum until we could go out again. I wasn't quite sure why she lived ashore. She didn't spend much time there.

"Did Hilda seem weird to you?" I asked, once we were hurrying up the road into town, the cold morning peopled with woolly-hatted delivery drivers and be-scarfed workers opening cafe doors and setting up tables and putting black-boards outside early pubs.

"Not really. I thought that was normal morning Hilda."

"I suppose she's always weird."

"Honestly, I can't even tell what's weird or not anymore," he said, turning down an empty side street. We weren't heading to the local Apple Store, even if there was one. We were less in the market for a new phone than just one whose owner wasn't actively looking for it, and there would be a couple of second-hand electronics shops and slightly suspicious phone stores lurking somewhere in the less picturesque corners of town. There always are, in every place with more than one supermarket to its name.

"You think Hilda's on the level?" I asked.

"Why? You still think she's actually a pirate?" He grinned at me.

"Well, she *obviously* is, but that's not what worries me. What if she's working with the mermaids, or the Sea Witch, if that's an actual person?"

"She's been actively trying to stop me getting involved with Murty. And she found you on the beach last night."

"Yeah, and how? How did she know we were out there?"

Callum slowed his pace, frowning. "I thought maybe the parrot ...?"

"Yeah, the parrot. But why was *he* out there?"

"Maybe you're right about the pirate bit. Wreckers used to go out on stormy nights and lure ships onto the rocks with false lights. Maybe Polly was out scouting. Does it matter?" His voice was light, but I could hear the current of unease under it.

"She's keeping an eye on us," I said. "I don't know if we can trust her. And then there's the Black Dogs. She knows about them. What if they're hers?"

Someone turned into the alley ahead of us, trailing a terrier that started snarling at me in a manner that suggested it might actually have a go, rather than the usual dog thing of just shouting about it. Its human looked at me, then at Callum, and didn't make any move to quiet the dog, so I took one flying jump and scrambled up Callum's jacket to his shoulder. I hissed at the mutt from safety, then said quietly, "I mean, I wouldn't put the wrecking thing past her, but it seems like something we'd hear about. Might make the news, like."

"True." He paused outside a shop that was no more than one door and a dirty window with a jumble of decrepit-looking phones sitting in it. "She's not done anything but help us, though."

"Yet," I said.

Callum sighed, and opened the door into the phone shop. I could smell smoke that was quite unlike his cigarettes as a young woman hastily shoved her ashtray under the counter.

WE LEFT with the sort of phone you could drop off a pirate ship mast and it wouldn't even chip its corners when it landed. Callum had inspected it dubiously and said, "Is it any good?"

"For that?" she'd asked, nodding at the crumpled, still slightly damp notes he'd put on the counter. "You're lucky you're getting one that turns on."

"Fair enough," he said with a sigh, and we watched our tips vanish into a box under the counter. We had just enough left for a cheap SIM card from a firm neither of us had heard of, but which gave us enough credit for a bit of internet and some calls.

"Do we call Gertrude now, then?" I asked once we were out in the empty alley again.

"If we get our contacts back," Callum said, poking at the phone. It had dinged once with a sound like a gong in the depths of a well, and now, as I peered down at it from Callum's shoulder, I could see it just had a little hourglass tipping over and over in the centre of the screen. It looked like we'd actually downgraded from our last phone, and that one had been another back alley special. Whether it had actually saved any of our contacts where we could get them back again remained to be seen.

"So what now?" I asked.

Callum took his cigarettes out, checked how many were left, and put them back with a sigh. He looked up and down the alley, the rain speckling his coat.

"We start looking for Emma."

"Or we could find a few things out first," I said, even though the thought of it made my stomach twist. I wasn't sure if it was the Black Dogs or Ms Jones and her body snatching I was most worried about, but neither felt like fun.

"Such as?"

"Such as what Ms Jones wants."

"We could do that," he agreed. "But what about the cat? Matilda? We need to find out what she was doing sending Emma down to the beach, and that seems more urgent, really."

"Is it? We've got the mermaid hunting Emma. Maybe we're best not letting Matilda know we're onto her."

"Except if we know *why* Matilda sent Emma to the beach, we might have a better chance of getting her back."

"Ms Jones might know what's going on, too," I pointed out. "Especially if it is connected to Leeds."

"But then we've got to get past the borders."

I growled. "Those are some bilge-licking choices. Confront sneaky bloody cats that'll probably try to throw me into the Inbetween, or face down Black Dogs trying to eat my soul. You really know how to show a cat a good time."

"I thought so," he said.

"*Gah.* Let's start with the Black Dogs. At least if we get past them we'll have a sorcerer. Then *she* can deal with the cat."

"We'll be *in contact* with a sorcerer," Callum pointed out.

"Don't be realistic at me. It's not the day for it."

"Fair," he said.

13

FAMILY STUFF

"RIGHT," I SAID. "WHAT'S THE PLAN – WE'RE JUST GOING TO walk out of town and hope no one eats us?"

"No. We're going to drive out." Callum headed for the road that would lead us to the boarding house, wedged into the rows of buildings straggling landward from the clifftop above the beach. Whitby wasn't exactly overburdened with parking spaces, but Bob the landlord always seemed to know where there were spots. When we'd been his reluctant tenants he'd given us a grimy parking disc and told us where to leave the car, and we'd never had a problem. I suspected that the discs weren't *quite* regulation issue, and that there was some sort of arrangement going on that bypassed the city council, but that wasn't my concern. And since we'd left the boarding house, he'd rather insistently kept hold of the car. The few times we'd needed transport he'd sent us to different spots to collect the old Rover, so either he kept moving it ahead of the parking inspectors or he was running a nice sideline in renting out decrepit bangers. Either way, it worked for us pretty well.

I stuck to my perch on Callum's shoulder, wondering if

our ancient car could even outrun a pack of regular dogs, let alone Black Dogs. But the excursion was taking us away from the dead in the water, at least, and perhaps if I let Ms Jones do her Old Ones-be-damned body snatching routine again we could get some help. Enough help that Callum wouldn't be dragged to the bottom of the sea and turned into sashimi or whatever fun thing mermaids got up to.

The boarding house was a mid-terrace that looked to be one sagging eave away from being condemned. The tiny front garden was so overgrown with weeds that thorny bushes grabbed at us and snagged Callum's coat as he forced his way through to the cracked stone steps at the front door. The bell sounded like there was a fire station being alerted inside, and next door a woman with massive red-rimmed glasses and her hair in rollers stuck her head out of the nearest window to peer at us.

"Tell that bloody monster to sort his garden out," she shouted. "The postman almost lost an eye the other day, and that was on *my* side of the fence!"

"Will do," Callum said.

"And Mrs Holden on the other side hasn't seen her cat for three days. If it's his greenhouse plants again I *am* calling the council." I popped my head up and she stared at me. "Keep an eye on him and all. They're very *snatchy*, those plants."

"I'll do that," Callum said, ringing the bell again.

"And the recycling was all mixed up on Wednesday. Glass has to be *separate!* You tell him that!"

"Okay," Callum said, trying for a knock.

"And whoever's on the third floor was playing the recorder *far* too late. I've a good mind to report it!"

"To who, the recorder police?" I muttered to Callum, and at that moment the door cracked open. A bright green eye sunk beneath dark eyebrows stared at us from around the same height as the door handle.

"Yes?"

"I'm after my keys," Callum said.

"Is that him?" the woman in the window demanded.

"No," Callum said, and we both stared down at the shape just visible beyond the threshold. It was dark inside, and all I could make out was something small and hunched and rounded, with a suggestion of either a very large fur coat or a non-human level of hairiness.

"What keys?" they asked.

"Rover," Callum said. "Car, I mean."

"*Arf*," the figure said, and giggled. They scuttled away, the motion quick and jerky, and my tail bushed out.

"Who is it?" Next-door demanded. "It is him, isn't it? I want to talk to him!"

"It's not him," Callum assured her, just as there was soft movement behind the door. The green eye reappeared, peeking at the day, then a small, hairy hand emerged, clutching the keys. Callum took them, having to lean down to do so, and the hand patted his arm softly then withdrew. It had nails that were closer to claws, and a silver ring on its thumb.

"Two streets out, past the leisure centre," their owner said. "Drop the keys back before six." The door closed with a quick, gentle *snick*.

Callum straightened up, and the woman next door glared at him. "There's no use him hiding. I'll catch him one of these days."

"I'm sure you will," Callum said, and headed back down the path, ducking to avoid the more aggressive branches.

"*Whitby*," I said.

THE CAR WAS PARKED in a little overgrown lane that cut away from the clifftop road and circled the field beyond the leisure centre, the grass torn in ever-changing patterns by the wind that rushed in off the sea and sent the gulls wheeling inland. Callum kicked a back tyre experimentally, which didn't do anything that I could see, but he grunted and unlocked the driver's door, letting me jump across to the passenger seat before he climbed in. There was a faint whiff of cologne and chocolate inside, and someone had dropped a pink ribbon on the back seat. We both looked at it, then Callum went through the usual performance of flicking things and pumping pedals, a dance to the gods of old engines.

"Any petrol?" I asked him.

"Half a tank."

"Is that more than we had before?"

"Yeah. We have considerate car thieves."

"More like borrowers," I pointed out.

Callum turned the key, and the engine burbled into life so quickly he stalled it. We looked at each other, and he tried again. This time the car gave a hiccough, then rumbled happily, with only a small plume of black exhaust coughing out the back.

"We should let our car get borrowed more often," I said.

"If one could only guarantee the kind of borrowing," Callum said, and puttered down the lane to the clifftop road.

We didn't mess around with trying back roads or farm tracks or strange hours or any of our usual methods for sneaking out of places undetected. Our best bet was broad daylight, straight up the A171 as it plunged away from the coast, crowded with delivery vans and trucks and caravans, spectacularly un-Folk-like, and therefore hopefully unappealing to Black Dogs.

"We'll get beyond the borders, then you see if you can reach Ms Jones," Callum said, as we idled at a set of traffic lights, the Rover for once not sounding like it was about to expire at any moment. The windscreen wipers still screamed like enraged hamsters, though, so no one had fixed those.

"Can't wait," I said. "Really looking forward to being reminded what dying feels like."

Callum checked his phone. "Contacts still haven't updated. But if we don't want to risk the border we could try Matilda instead? Or concentrate on finding Emma for now and worry about the rest later?"

"No. Let's go." I could still smell the musky, deep sea scent of Murty, and see the glitter of his eyes as he said, *a favour*. I didn't know much about mermaids, but I was inclined to believe Hilda in this, dodgy as she might be. Owing one a favour seemed like a bad move, and if Ms Jones could help us get Emma back before Murty worked his fishy magic, then it was worth a little casual disembodiment. Probably.

The lights changed and we wound our way out of town, past houses turned toward the sea and huddled walkers and trees stunted with wind and salt. I couldn't sit still in the seat, but roamed into the back to check we weren't being followed, then returned to the front to put my paws on the door handle and peer out the side window, watching Whitby slip behind us. I couldn't see any sign of pursuit, or charms, or anything else. It was just any old town, crouched in the teeth of a winter wind.

I did feel it when we crossed the border, though. It was soft, a gentle whisper where a real pocket town such as Dimly was the *snap* of something toothed and clawed. But it was unmistakable now that I was looking for it, and I put my paws up on the dashboard so I could see through the windscreen.

"We're out."

Callum slowed as we came up to a roundabout, the green mound of the centre marred with the dark earth of newly dug-over flowerbeds. "Alright. I'll pull over— What the *hell?*" He jammed the brakes on as a white van that had pulled onto the roundabout ahead of us screeched to a halt, bouncing with the abruptness of the stop.

"Oh, sink me," I hissed.

A car behind us laid on the horn, and Callum said, "Yes, that's really going to help." He wound the window down and stuck his head out, trying to see what was going on, and I went from window to window, looking for Black Dogs. I couldn't see any, but this couldn't be unrelated. *Couldn't* be.

The car behind us was going to wear out the battery, the way they were abusing the horn, but it stopped abruptly as the delivery van's door flew open and a bearded man at least as tall as Callum but a few times as wide jumped out, making the van bounce again.

"Everything alright?" Callum called, while I hoped Beardy Man didn't think we were the ones getting enthusiastic on the horn.

"It's like there's been a bloody earthquake, mate," Beardy called back. "Come look." He vanished around the front of his van.

Callum glanced at me, and I shrugged. He swung out of the car into the rain-smeared day and I followed him, trotting up to the van while the driver behind us hit the horn again.

Beardy popped back into sight and bellowed, "Excuse *me,*" which stopped the horn pretty quickly. More cars were getting jammed up behind us, though, and Callum broke into a jog. I overtook him easily, then came to a hard stop in the wet earth at the edge of a chasm.

Well, *chasm.* Callum could have stood at the bottom and touched the top with his fingertips, but it was still a lot larger than you'd want in a road, and it ran straight across both lanes of the one heading out of Whitby. A post van was parked with its nose hanging over the edge on the inbound side, tyres almost touching the gap, and the postie was on her phone, waving fretfully at the cars queued behind her and evidently wishing they'd back up so she could move the van a little.

"You onto the police, mate?" Beardy shouted at the postie, who gave him a thumbs up. Beardy returned the gesture, then looked at Callum. "I've got a fish order to get through."

"Right," Callum said.

Beardy scratched his chin, and looked around as the postie shouted, "Police are on their way."

Another horn blared somewhere further down the queue, which encouraged our horn-blower to have another go. Beardy turned and raised his arms in a questioning manner, then said to Callum, "Reckon you can get around the back of me and across to the next exit?" He pointed over the top of the roundabout, to where another road joined it. The round-about was only a single lane all the way around, but with the postie van stopped before it entered, all we had to do was bounce onto the centre mound, around Beardy's van, and out the next exit.

"Pretty sure," Callum said.

"Right. 'Cause if you do that, see, I can back up and get out the same way. Postie there can deal with the police. I've got fish to deliver."

If I'd been Callum, I'd've said, *sure you do*, but he just nodded and said, "Yeah, we're kind of in a hurry, too."

"We?" Beardy said, and looked at me. I arched my whiskers at him.

"That car behind's going to drive straight up behind you soon as I move, though," Callum pointed out.

"No he won't," Beardy said, and headed that way as a siren started wailing down toward Whitby. We hurried back to the Rover, and I put my paws on the window to watch Beardy leaning down by the driver's side of the car behind us. He was smiling, but he was really very large, and the man in the car had clambered half into the lap of the annoyed-looking woman in the passenger's seat.

Neither of us spoke as Callum backed up as much as he could, then with a bit of back- and forward-ing edged his way out from behind the van, bumped up onto the centre mound of the roundabout, and as soon as he was past the van dropped back onto the tarmac again. The way onto the other road was clear, and a moment later we were rumbling back in the rough direction of Whitby.

"See anything?" Callum asked me.

"No. Didn't smell anything, either. But that hole didn't come out of nowhere."

"No." He thought about it, then said, "I don't think we should try getting out via the Sandsend road or anything. We don't want to cut Whitby off from the rest of Yorkshire entirely."

"Probably fair," I agreed. "What do we do, then?"

"I have an idea," he said. "But it does involve walking."

"Oh, *fun.*"

WE PUT the car back where we'd found it, dropped the keys through the letter box in the boarding house door without getting yelled at by the neighbour, and headed back toward the old town. Callum's stride was long enough that I had to lope to keep up, and I said, "Can you slow down for those of us with normal-size legs?"

"Hilda's going to be wondering where we are," he said, taking his cigarettes from his coat.

"Let her. We're not going out anywhere in this." And the

longer he was away from the boat, the less chance the mermaid had to nab him.

"Yeah, but I don't fancy going back to the boarding house if she fires us, do you?"

"No," I admitted. "Any luck on the contacts yet?"

He lit a cigarette, then took the phone out, squinting against the smoke as he tapped it. "Still going."

He kept tapping though, and I said, "What're you doing?"

"Nothing," he said, and shoved the phone in his pocket when I made the jump to his shoulder. "Bloody hell, Gobs, ask, can't you? You're trashing this jacket."

"Extra ventilation," I said. "Were you texting Ifan? Do you know his number by heart or something?"

Callum blew smoke at me. "Shut up. It's getting busy."

I grumbled, but I did shut up. He was right. As the dull morning wore on to more civilised hours the streets were filling up with walkers in heavy trousers and older women with little tartan shopping trolleys and waterproof hats, and one round-bellied man with shiny shoes and an ill-advised umbrella that turned inside out twice while we followed him along the road that crossed the little swing bridge.

Callum went straight up the main tourist route, with its old stone buildings leaning over the cobbled streets. Sugary scents spilled out of the sweet shops, thick and cloying as summer heat, and jewellery stores promised *genuine Whitby jet*. Pubs and cafes were sparsely populated with weekday, off-season trade, and everywhere were signs for fish'n'chips, with at least three different places promising to be the best in town. A few scattered tourists peered into shop windows at toys and souvenirs and photos of the Abbey printed on canvas, and two women in heavy black skirts swept past us, one of them clutching her top hat in place over a set of brass-framed goggles. The other had a ferret on a leash sitting on her shoulder. It hissed at me, and I hissed back.

The steps to the Abbey were at the top of the street, the old stone worn lower in the centre than at the sides by the feet of generations of church-goers and walkers and tourists and Dracula re-enactors. Houses ranged up the hill to the inland side of them, and on the seaward side the street continued on, toward old fishermen's cottages and a fish smokery and finally to the pier that framed the harbour on this side, smaller than the other but with no less a sense of stolid resilience in the face of the sea. Callum turned up the steps, taking them at a steady pace with his head turned away from the wind. It scratched and tore at his jacket, and threatened to shove me from my perch, until I jumped down in the hope that it would be less intense at a lower altitude.

"What're we doing?" I bawled at him, since no one else was silly enough to be climbing the Abbey steps in this weather.

"The Abbey's sacred ground, right?" he said. "So Black Dogs can't go onto it, but also it's not Whitby – it's its own place."

"You think the Abbey's outside of Whitby's influence?"

He shrugged. "It's worth a try."

"Sure. As long as we don't get blown off the stairs," I pointed out, as a gust sent me staggering sideways.

"Lift?"

"No, I shall face the Black Dogs on all paws, thanks." I ran up the steps ahead of him as the old church and its graveyard of leaning stones came into view on the left, perched on top of the cliff and tucked inside an old stone wall. It stood grey and hunched against the assault of wind and rain, the windows dark and the long grass around the graves dancing. The path pinched between the church wall and a walled field to the other side, giving us some shelter from the wind, and led on to an empty car park. The ruins of the Abbey loomed up to our right, enclosed by stone walls much bigger than the one around the church, but before we reached them we came to an open gateway that gave onto a massive courtyard.

A restored banqueting house, now mostly given over to a museum, stood at the far end of the courtyard, and what looked like it should have been some sort of vast water feature took up most of the space between us and it. There was no water, though, just a lot of jumbled rocks and a statue slap in the middle. I couldn't see anyone about except for a trailer parked just outside the courtyard walls, selling entry tickets to the Abbey. There was one person inside, so bundled up in hat and scarf and gloves and jacket that I couldn't make out anything more than a red nose.

The tickets were only for the Abbey itself, and cost more than we'd made in tips yesterday, so we left the ticket seller and their nose to the elements and headed into the courtyard instead.

"Feel anything?" Callum asked.

"Nothing," I said. "Well, lots, actually, but nothing relevant. This place had a *lot* going on." Old rituals and old beliefs, artifacts sunk deep beneath my paws, encased in stone and dirt, and the memories that had bled down there with them. The Abbey might be the only thing left standing, but there were older things than it that had called this a place of power. As to whether it actually was, any more so than anywhere else? Eh. Cats don't hold to such things so much. But belief is in itself power, and enough belief can seep into the very bones of the world, so it's kind of a chicken and egg scenario. Gods, *chicken.*

"Can we get some chicken?"

"What?" Callum asked.

"I'm really sick of bloody fish. Can we get some chicken?"

"I suppose," he said, frowning at me. "Can you reach Ms Jones or not?"

"Um." I looked around, feeling the old, muscular charms

twined like roots deep in the soil. People had been trying to make this a safe place for centuries, not all of them human. And plenty had known magic. "No. Not a chance."

Callum sighed. "Alright, scratch that. Plan B."

"We have a plan B?"

"This is the walking bit." He nodded toward the clifftop, and a weatherworn wooden sign that pointed along it.

"Right. So if the Black Dogs don't eat us we can just be blown off the top of the cliffs instead?"

"At least we've got options," he said, and gave me a half grin.

"Oh, *funny*." I looked around again, wondering about trying the Abbey grounds themselves, but they weren't going to be any better. The whole place was so full of old belief that the walls were just about dripping with it. "Maybe we should see if Gertrude's back."

"We're here now," he said, and checked the phone. "Damn. No answer yet."

"To who?"

"I memorised Gerry's number. Just in case."

I blinked at him. "How long had you and he been thinking it was going to come to this?"

"Long enough," he said, still looking at the phone.

"Why?"

He poked at the screen. "We've got some contacts back, at least."

"*Why*, Callum? Why would you think it'd come to this? Why's everyone so big on the whole North thing? What is *with* you?"

"It's just family stuff, you know."

"No," I said. "Family stuff is sleeping with your sister's boyfriend while your sister's having twins, then marrying your cousin and getting a tattoo of his face on your bum." I considered it. "The boyfriend, not the cousin. I think. It was a really bad tattoo."

He stared at me for a moment, then said, "Did you discover the Jeremy Kyle show at some point?"

"I don't know. But that was family stuff. It was on the TV when you were doing lawns someplace. The woman with the potted shrimp."

"Yeah," he said. "That's less family stuff than *TV* family stuff."

"Fine, then. What's *your* family stuff? Because if it's going to get us bloody killed by Black Dogs, I'd like to know."

He sighed, tucked the phone away, and said, "Should we just—"

"*No.* I'm cold and wet, and about to get colder and wetter, so bloody well *tell me* what it is with Norths and why everyone's so bothered about you!"

"Then you tell me why the Watch is, so bothered with *you,*" he said, taking his cigarettes out, then swearing as he realised the pack was empty. He shoved it back in his pocket and scowled at me.

"I don't remember," I said, and when he shook his head and started to turn away I said, "I really don't. Everyone thinks I should, somehow, but all I can see when I try to look back is ..." I hesitated, licking my chops. My mouth was suddenly dry. "Well, I can't see anything. I can *feel* it. The Inbetween. The nothing, but a nothing full of *something.* And the hunger. Sea biscuits, they were hungry. So hungry it almost made you forget it was you they were hungry for, because the hurt of it was so *old.* Made you feel sorry for them, just for a bit." I licked my chops again. "Until the pain, anyway. There's nothing like that pain. And I can't see past it. I *can't.*"

Callum watched me for a long moment, then said, "You

went back there, though. You took Ms Jones' book into the Inbetween."

I shrugged, the tension in my limbs making the movement jerky. "Bloody thing was about to eat the world. Eat *us*."

He nodded and rubbed his face, his mouth twisting, then said, "I'm not a sorcerer or a magician, I don't have power. And the Norths ..." He trailed off, looking for words. "Mostly they're what it looks like. Criminal bloody dynasty. I did everything I could to break away from the whole sodding thing, the whole *life,* and to not learn any of it. I always thought the biggest risk would be my family either trying to drag me back in, or trying to get rid of me because I wouldn't *go* back in. All this"—he waved vaguely, taking in Whitby and the gulls and the towering, broken arches of the Abbey—"it's not to do with any of that, and I don't get it. I really don't."

We looked at each other for a while, then I said, "I bloody wish everyone else realised how clueless we were. They might actually leave us alone then."

He started to laugh, then his smile faded as he looked past me, toward the museum.

"What?" I asked, my spine prickling. I didn't want to turn around.

"Well, not Black Dogs, at least," he said.

Which didn't narrow it down much.

14

A BIT OF A CAT FIGHT

I KNOW CALLUM HAD SAID *NOT BLACK DOGS*, BUT I WAS STILL expecting to see them when I turned around. Or perhaps a couple of hungry mermaids, or a squadron of fish-nibbled dead, or ... who knew. Any and all of the above, possibly.

In retrospect, I should have expected who was actually going to be there. We'd done pretty well with staying out of the way of Whitby's cats, and given the one nervy encounter I'd had, I'd started to suspect that all the cats in the place shared my dislike for the Watch. Which had possibly made us a little too casual about things, even given the suspicious Matilda. But now we were collecting Black Dogs and hanging out with mermaids and reapers, and some things just attract attention, particularly when you're new to town. *Not* being checked out by the locals would've been weirder.

And now there were half a dozen cats standing on the edge of the not-a-water-feature, their fur being ruffled and pushed by the wind. A couple of them were big brawlers with heads twice as wide as mine and scars decorating their noses – one had a watery eye suggesting he hadn't moved quite as quick as he might have liked during some long-ago tussle. There was some long-haired white thing looking peeved that her fur was getting messed up, a three-legged black cat with her ears back, and a skinny tabby she-cat with a disgruntled expression. And then there was the bulky grey cat standing in front of them, his gold eyes on mine.

"Morning, Gobbelino," he said.

"Who?" I said.

"Hilarious. As if *I* wouldn't recognise you." He glared at me, and I blinked back at him.

"I have no idea who you are, dude."

"Really."

"Really." I looked at Callum. "I was just telling him what a bad memory I have."

The grey cat looked at Callum, then back at me. "Maybe I should jog your memory." He was there and then not, vanishing where he stood, and I threw myself sideways, not bothering to cry out, just skittering away across the cobbles. Big Grey came out of the Inbetween again almost instantly, but I was already out of reach, my ears back as I hissed at him.

"Sod *that*, you scurvy fish bucket."

He didn't respond, just slipped away again, the fabric of the world swallowing him, and I shot toward the other cats, thinking he wouldn't expect me to go that way. The biggest of the heavies leaped to meet me, his teeth bared, and Callum shouted, "Hang about!"

I spun away from the heavy, barely missing Big Grey as he reappeared, running straight at me. I went sideways again, losing my footing and rolling. Callum shouted something I didn't catch, and I glimpsed Green Snake on the ground, where he was doing a passable cobra imitation, keeping the other heavy and the tabby she-cat occupied. I saw all this, but I barely registered any of it. There was a high, thin whine in my ears, and my heart was skipping with old memories I couldn't quite touch, and I couldn't seem to pull a breath out of the salt-thick air. I came to my feet and bolted for the museum, directly over the jumbled rocks of the not-a-water-feature.

The first cat hit from the side, Heavy One coming out of nothing with no warning, and the mass of him sent me sprawling across the uneven ground. He tried to grab for my throat but the angle was bad and I was faster, twisting away from underneath him and managing a couple of bounds before the fluffy white she-cat appeared and slapped me across the snout. I hit back, snarling, and managed to score a pawful of hair, then Big Grey was there again, coming out of the Inbetween and straight into both of us. I hit the rocks with the big tom on top of me, and just let myself roll with the fall. We tumbled together, his teeth and claws tearing at me as we went, but I didn't try to fight back. I used the momentum instead, keeping the roll going until I was on top and shoved myself away, sprinting for Callum as he ran to meet me.

I leaped for him, and his fingers grazed my coat, but it wasn't close enough. Big Grey hit me in mid-air, and hissed in my ear, "Remember yet?"

The last word was swallowed by silence as the world vanished, and we plunged into a vast and roaring nothing.

IF THE INBETWEEN were simply a *space*, a void between realities, then that would be fine. But it's not. It's *populated*. Things hunt in there. The vast hulks of leviathans, following the distant dance of unknown, crumbling galaxies, endlessly collecting their broken pieces. The quick sharp flutter of insubstantial, inquisitive beings, catching motes of memory and fragments of dreams. And things with teeth and tenta-

cles and rasping tongues, things both swift and patient.
Things that hunger. Things that *remember*.

I felt their attention turn to us as we crashed into the
void. It's not dark in there, not light either – it's *nothing*. All I
knew was the cat's teeth in my scruff, the gouge of his back
claws into my side, and that terrible sense of being *noticed*.
The beasts had torn me apart once. They'd do it again. They
had my scent. They *knew* me. And they had waited. I felt
them at night, when the fabric of the world seemed stretched
and thin, felt their endless patience. And the horror of it all
but froze me. Did, in fact, hanging there helpless as a kitten,
my chest bursting with a yowl that threatened to tear me
apart faster than even the beasts could.

Except then I'd be another life down. I'd have to start
again, *actually* a kitten, and who in all these voids was going
to make sure Callum didn't take up with mermaids then? Or
with his dodgy magician, who was at least as bad? And then
there was Ms Jones and her bloody dentist and bilge-sucking
weres, and I didn't know where Tam and Pru were, or Claudia, or if they were alright, and how was a kitten going to
deal with all that?

Sink this! I bellowed into the nothing, the *everything* of the
Inbetween, and twisted in Big Grey's grip, ignoring the pain
in my scruff as his teeth bit harder. It was nothing compared
to how much it was going to hurt if I didn't get out of there. I
ripped myself free and used the big cat's belly to launch
myself away, punching my hind legs into him like a panicked
rabbit. I spun into emptiness, reaching out as I did so, feeling
the quiet, strange depths of my partner like one of the
beacons calling ships in to the harbour below. I followed it,
ignoring the whisper and snap of something behind me that
almost touched me, ignoring the sudden pain in my tail
where something *did* touch me, and then everything was rain
and wind and snarling cats, and someone shouting.

I came out of the Inbetween so fast that I collided with Callum's chest hard enough to send him stumbling back a couple of paces. He gave an *oof* and grabbed me with both hands, pinning me in place, then Big Grey hit both of us before he could recover. Callum staggered, caught his heel on one of the uneven rocks, and went down with a yelp. Big Grey went for his face. I went for Big Grey. Fluffy White launched herself at my side before I could reach Big Grey, and there was a flash of tabby as one of the heavies piled in from the other side. He reversed direction rapidly with a yowl, and I caught a flash of green from the corner of my eye. Callum was trying to get up, but between Big Grey still on his chest and Heavy Two laying into the top of his head, he had most of his attention focused on not losing an eye. Somewhere above the hissing, spitting, shouting, and swearing the gulls were screeching in excitement, and the wind roared and chased around us, and the rain was getting in on the action too.

I'd like to say we had the upper hand, but I was mostly resisting being dragged back into the Inbetween by just clinging grimly to Callum's jacket, which meant I couldn't help him much. I risked a peek around. Tufts of fur in various hues were decorating the stone where they weren't whipping away in the wind, and the prissy-looking white cat was hurling the sort of language that'd put Hilda to shame, probably related to the fact that Green Snake was hanging off her back leg. Callum had both arms over his face and was trying to roll over so he could get to his feet, but as his belly was currently ground zero for six scrapping cats, it wasn't going well.

Six. I glanced around again, risking a lash out at Heavy Two with a snarl as he took another run at me. Big Grey and Heavy One at Callum's head. Tabby She-cat joining in with them, while Fluffy White was preoccupied with Green

Snake. That left … I looked around again, braced for an attack from the three-legged black cat, and glimpsed her at the gateway. Well, that was one less to worry about anyway. I suppose three legs put you at a disadvantage in a scrap.

Tabby She-cat came at me before I could see if Tripod was up to anything nefarious, and Heavy Two jumped me at the same time, their combined assault tearing me away from Callum and sending all three of us tumbling to the rough ground. I bounced up, intending to bolt back to Callum before anyone could drag me off for void snacks, and a howl cut across the courtyard, freezing us mid-fight. It was the sort of howl that could do that. There was nothing melancholy or wavering about it. There was nothing uncertain. There was no sorrow in it. It was purely the howl of the hunt, the howl of the pack sighting its prey.

"Whoa," Tabby She-cat said, scrambling back to all fours. "I mean, *dude*."

"What the *hell?*" Heavy Two demanded, glaring at me.

"Likewise," I said, staring at the gateway.

Callum shoved Big Grey and Heavy One away and rolled onto his knees. Even Fluffy White had stopped trying to kick Green Snake off, although he was still attached to one of her legs.

"Boris," she said, her voice the sort of cut crystal tones that make you wonder if you should be curtseying (even if she had the vocabulary of a pirate captain). "What in the *realms* have you done?"

"Nothing," Big Grey said. "I don't know what that was."

We were all looking at the gateway. The three-legged cat had vanished. The only person to be seen was the ticket seller, who had emerged from their trailer and walked a few steps toward us. "Are you alright there?" they called.

"Just trying to break up a cat fight," Callum called back.

He'd lost his hat and scratches stood out in bright red lines on his cheeks.

"Right," the ticket seller said, sounding uncertain. "Only—"

The howl came again, and we all shuffled around, instinctively drawing closer to each other and trying to look in every direction at once.

"Is it in the Abbey?" Heavy One asked. "Like, someone's dog or something?"

"Sure," Tabby She-cat said. "That sounds *exactly* like someone's Golden bloody Retriever. Take another knock to the head, why don't you?"

"It might be, though," he insisted.

Big Grey/Boris looked at Callum. "Is it you?" he asked.

"Yeah, I'm a ventriloquist," Callum said, and his eyes never stopping flicking from one point to the next. Gateway. Abbey. Museum. Wall to the field that ran down into town. Gateway— "Dammit," he said.

The ticket seller had retreated back into their trailer, leaving the gateway empty, and into it walked a Black Dog, its ears pointing sharply forward.

"You did *not* mention this," Fluffy White said, glaring at Boris.

"No one mentioned it to me, either," he said, and the Black Dog raised its nose and howled again, sending a collective shiver through us all that resulted in a lot of bushy tails. A second howl came from the Abbey direction, and we all turned that way. A Black Dog stood on the wall, looking down at us. A third howl came from the museum, and we shuffled around to see a Black Dog standing on the roof, framed against the churning grey clouds.

"Nice pose," Heavy Two said. "Effective, like." Tabby She-cat cuffed him. "*Ow.*"

The fourth howl came from the wall above the fields, and

after seeing that yes, there was a beast there too, we all turned as one to look back at the first Black Dog. It was hard to tell, with them all scattered about the place, but it might have been a little bigger, a little broader across the chest, and it padded forward a few paces. I could feel the weight of its gaze, but its eyes were indistinguishable. It was just a sleek, muscled patch of void, given teeth and attention.

Callum got to his feet slowly, his hands held out as if to show he was unarmed. We clustered around his feet, and I bumped Boris away with my shoulder.

"Sod off, you freebooter."

"You *what?*" he demanded, glaring at me.

"Bilge-sucker. Scurvy dog. Slimy swab—" The Black Dog in front of us gave a sudden, imperious huff, and I stopped, staring at it. Perspectives went a bit strange around it. It was as tall as the walls themselves, or pony-sized, or just kind of Doberman-ish. Its feet were sunk *into* the rough rocks, or were somehow drifting above them, and it was only a couple of metres from us, or it was still half the courtyard distant. It had no shadow, or lots of shadows, and I could see the wall through it, or I could see *myself* in it. Nothing about the damn thing made sense.

It growled, and my whole chest reverberated with the sound. The gulls that had been circling overhead, drifting on the gusts, shrieked and spun off in different directions, flapping in jerky, panicked flight.

"Tactical retreat," Boris said abruptly.

"Word," Tabby She-cat said, and vanished. I was close enough to her that I felt the swirl of air filling her absence.

Heavy One and Two went after her, and Fluffy White gave a panicked little mewl, kicking her back leg wildly.

"*Please,*" she said to me.

"I shouldn't," I said, but I batted Green Snake lightly on the head. He gave me a look that I'm sure said many things in snake talk. But he let go, baring his fangs at Fluffy White in the instant before she vanished. Which left just Callum, still watching the Black Dog, and Boris, still watching me.

"I don't remember you," I said flatly. "But I remember what you did."

He lifted his chin at me slightly. His eyes had turned more burnished bronze than gold in the uncertain light of the day. "You'd do better to remember why," he said.

"So tell me."

The Black Dog gave another of those bone-shaking growls, and Green Snake curled himself around my legs, peering at the creature from some semblance of safety. Boris looked at the Dog, then said, "Seems like the Watch aren't the only people you're on the wrong side of. Saves me a job, anyway." And then he was gone, leaving Callum, Green Snake and me facing the Black Dog under the heavy grey sky, the courtyard around us empty but for the last scraps of fur still sticking to the damp ground.

"Is this one of those out of the frying pan while boiling a frog things?" I asked Callum.

"Let's just say yes for the ease of it."

WE DIDN'T MOVE. I was waiting for the Black Dogs to lunge forward and tear us to pieces, or perhaps for some necromancer mastermind to walk in the gateway, probably accompanied by a clap of thunder. Failing that, perhaps Dracula would put in an appearance.

What I was not expecting was for the big boss Black Dog to step away, turning so that they were side on to us, and to look expectantly at the gateway and the street beyond, then back at us.

"Right," Callum said.

"Right what?" I demanded, but it was pretty obvious. Callum started to crouch, and a small growl went up behind us. We both jumped and looked around. The other three Dogs had come down off their various walls, and while they weren't *close*, they were closer than anyone would want a Black Dog to be. The bigger one in front of us huffed softly, and looked at the gateway again.

Callum had halted his crouch at the sound of the growl, raising his hands instinctively, and now he straightened up again and said, "Can you walk?"

"Sure," I said. "Nothing but scratches." It actually didn't feel *entirely* like a lie, but I was aware my heart hadn't slowed down since I'd been dragged into the Inbetween, and there were strange bright edges to everything.

"Can you bring Green Snake?"

I didn't answer, just very slowly dropped my head to pick the silly reptile up in my jaws. He slipped away from my teeth and coiled himself up a foreleg and onto my shoulders without any help. "Got him," I said.

"Alright. Nice and slow." Callum took a step forward, his hands still up in that *look at me I'm harmless* manner, and Biggie took a step back, leaving the way wide open to the gateway.

"So much for your hallowed ground," I muttered, staying as close to Callum's legs as I could without actually tripping him.

"It was a good theory." He kept walking, each stride slow and deliberate, and his eyes never left Biggie.

"How was it a *good* theory if it was entirely wrong?"

"You want to know another theory?"

"Is it a better one?"

"The quieter you are, the more likely we'll get out of this without you accidentally insulting a Black Dog and getting us eaten."

"I'm not sure that's better," I said.

"Shall we test it?"

I didn't answer, because we were passing Biggie. I could feel their regard, but even this close – whatever version of *close* it was, because there was still that sense of being almost able to press my snout to the void of them, and of seeing a gaping wound in the world from half a county away – I still couldn't make out a suggestion of eyes. They didn't move, simply watched us pass, and once we were beyond them Callum picked up the pace a little, checking over his shoulder as he went. I tried to do the same but he stumbled over me, so I just said, "Are we safe? Are we through?"

"Yes to the second, the first is pretty questionable most of the time."

"Fair."

We walked at a carefully measured pace through the gateway, where the rush of wind coming up the cliff was full of the wonderfully cat-free scents of sea and storm and distant thunderstorms. Callum nodded to the ticket seller, who nodded back a little dubiously, then shouted, "Are those dogs yours?"

We both looked back at the Black Dogs, who were following us at the same measured pace. "No," Callum said. "They must've been chasing the cats."

The ticket seller scratched their head through the heavy folds of the hat. "I didn't see where they came from." There was a quiver of uncertainty in their voice, and Callum managed a smile.

"Along the clifftop, probably. Or up the field from town. You were distracted by the cats, right?"

"I mean, yes, but I should have *seen*—"

"So easy to miss on a day like this," Callum said, and gave a quick wave, turning toward the stairs leading back to town.

"But what do I do with them?" the ticket seller shouted after us.

"I'm sure they'll take care of themselves," Callum called back, and hurried down the first lot of stairs, until we were out of sight of the trailer and the courtyard. Then he stopped and dropped into a crouch, unwrapping Green Snake from my shoulders. "How bad?" he asked, as he tried to persuade the snake into his pockets. He didn't seem to want to go.

"Better than your face," I said, but there was shakiness setting into my limbs, and the wind felt even colder than it had earlier.

"Lift?"

"Sure. These stairs aren't cat-size. Bloody uncomfortable, they are." I let him pick me up, and instead of setting me on his shoulder he kept me tucked into one arm as he looked back up the hill.

"Oh," he said.

"Oh? I don't like oh." I craned around his arm, and spotted Biggie on the stairs behind us. From this vantage point I could see one of the other Black Dogs in the churchyard, standing on someone's tomb with their head lifted to the wind howling off the cliff, listening to something I couldn't hear. In the field to the other side of the steps another was drinking from a water trough, which was weirdly *normal* for a creature that could scatter Watch like dandelion fluff. The fourth was rolling in something, which suggested they really did have some dog in there somewhere.

Biggie padded down a few steps. Callum started to retreat down the hill, and the Dog growled. It was only a small sound, but enough to freeze us where we stood. Green Snake had managed to get himself tangled around me again, and now he tried to squeeze his head between me and Callum's chest. Biggie stopped on the step above us and extended their head forward, a stretching movement that spoke of hard ropes of muscle, but there was still no definition at all in the creature's back, even this close. Not even in their head. It was simply a shadow reaching out toward us.

Callum didn't move, and Biggie gave a huff and shook their head. Something flashed in their mouth, and Callum extended a hand hesitantly.

"What are you *doing?*" I squawked, but very quietly.

Biggie dropped something in Callum's hand, then sat back. We both looked down at our new phone, the screen already cracked. Some Black Dog drool, which looked a lot like regular dog drool, decorated the case.

"Thanks," Callum said, and Biggie huffed again. Callum pocketed the phone and started back down the steps, and I clambered stiffly to his shoulder, watching the Dogs until we turned the curve of the stairs and they vanished. Biggie stared back at me the whole time, and just before I lost sight of them their tail gave a soft, cheery wag.

"That was unexpected," I said.

"*Whitby,*" Callum said.

15

THE PIRATE GETS PIRATED

WE MADE IT TO THE BOTTOM OF THE STAIRS BEFORE ANYTHING else happened. I mean, it was a whole five minutes, or something like that. What more could we ask for?

I was fairly sure the Black Dogs weren't going to come tearing down the hill after us, since we weren't currently trying to break out of Whitby. And I was also thinking that I might've been a bit harsh on them, and might even prefer them to cats. Certain cats, anyway. Although there was still the whole chasing us down the beach thing, but I was wondering if we might've got that a bit wrong.

I had let Callum go back to carrying me, since the steps were steep and his shoulder was a bit uncomfortable in all the wind, and I was just about to ask if he thought the creatures had actually been going to eat us last night when Green Snake slipped over me, slithered across Callum's arm, and threw himself into the air.

"Hey—" Callum grabbed for him, but with me in one arm he wasn't quick enough. "Green Snake!"

Green Snake hit the cobbles with a nasty-sounding splat and immediately shot toward a sweet shop.

"Is he after some fudge?" I asked. "I mean, I wouldn't say no, but—"

The snake avoided the door and slithered straight up the wall, diving into a window box thickly planted with winter blooms.

"Frogs?" Callum suggested.

"He can keep those."

There was a distinctly feline squawk from the window box, and the three-legged cat surged out of the flowers, balanced for an instant on the edge of the planter, then jumped to the ground, her ears back.

"Oi!" I shouted, and launched myself out of Callum's grip. "Stop right there, Tripod-face!"

She gave me a disgusted look. "*Tripod*-face? Are you making fun of my disability?"

"Of your face, mostly," I said, limping toward her. My tail was burning, and there didn't seem to be a lot of me that hadn't had a close encounter of the claw or tooth kind. Limping was the best I could do.

Green Snake popped his head out of the flowers with a pleased tilt, and Callum went to extricate him.

"What d'you want?" Tripod asked.

"Are you Matilda?" I demanded. "Emma mentioned something about a three-legged cat."

She wrinkled her snout, and glanced around before she answered. "Yes, I'm Matilda."

"Great. So, want to tell me why you sent Emma out to be dragged into the sea by the dead, and then jumped me with a bunch of Watch heavies?"

Matilda looked from me to Callum, then said, "Not all of us are safe to defy the Watch."

"Yeah, I feel really safe," I snapped. "How long have you been watching me?"

"I haven't. And I'm just—"

"If you say following orders I'll gnaw your other hind leg off."

"Gobs," Callum said, his voice quiet, and we fell silent as two women in matching waterproof jackets paused on their way to the stairs.

"Look at the little cats," one of them said. "Aren't they sweet?"

"Aw," the other said. "Like twins!"

"Are they yours?" the first woman asked Callum.

"Not even one of them," he said, and Green Snake craned his head out of Callum's hands to stick his tongue out at the women.

They looked at each other, then at him, then headed for the steps.

"Odd place, Whitby," one said in a low voice, the wind carrying the words to us.

I looked back at Matilda. "Why would you send Emma out to the beach?"

"The Watch wanted it."

"So you just sent her to be taken by the dead?"

Matilda wrinkled her snout. "I didn't think that would happen. Gertrude was out there—"

"Because you sent her too?"

"No, she just went." She gave me a level look. "*I* told her to leave her scythe behind, because Boris had told me to make sure Gertrude saw the dead."

"Why would you do that?" Callum asked. "It's her best weapon."

"Because if someone's asking about reapers, they don't want *reapers*, do they?" she said. "No one wants a reaper. But lots of people want a scythe. I thought she was safer without it."

"Why?" I asked. "What do the Watch want scythes for?"

She huffed. "I didn't ask. You should know what questioning the Watch gets you."

"Fair," I admitted.

"*Anyway*, I didn't think Emma would actually get in trouble. I thought, right, Gertrude's already on the beach, so she'll see Emma, and she'll get them both out of there." She shifted slightly.

"But?" Callum said.

Matilda bared her teeth at him. "You tell me. All I know is Gertrude was the only one who came home last night. "

"Gertrude wasn't on the beach," I said. "She was in the sea."

"Really?" Matilda wrinkled her snout. "What'd she do that for? And how did Emma end up in there too? Were the Watch really after her?"

Callum and I glanced at each other. The *let's swim from the Black Dogs* plan was looking worse all the time. I looked back at Matilda. "What do you know about the dead, then?"

She shrugged. "It's just the sea. It's full of the dead at the moment. All I know is that Gertrude was in a fuss about it, and Boris wanted to be sure she saw them. Nothing else."

"You're really helpful," I said, and she just looked at me with flat green eyes, her tail twitching. I growled. "Fine. Why call the Watch out on me, then?"

"I didn't. Boris told me he needed an extra set of teeth, is all. But I recognised your scents up there – Gertrude had a whiff of you on her last night, and she said someone was helping her find Emma. Until then I thought you were just any old washed-up cat. We get enough of them here. Ones who want to retire, or hide, or disappear. But if the Watch say help, you help." She sniffed. "I called the bloody Black Dogs for you, though, so *you're welcome.*"

"How did you call them?" Callum asked. "And what're they doing here anyway?"

"I just yelled, *Oi, you lot, someone's trying to eat your herd*, and they came running pretty quick," Matilda said.

"Your *herd?*" I demanded.

"Yeah. They protect things." She gave me a look that suggested I was being a bit slow. "They're *dogs.*"

"They're *Black* Dogs," I pointed out. "They're not known for herding poor wee sheep about the place."

"They're still just dogs. They'll do whatever they've been told to do. And I've seen them shadowing you right through town, so I supposed they were yours."

"Someone's instincts were a little off," Callum said, looking at me. "You missed that."

"I'm not the one who sent us all swimming to avoid *helpful* dogs."

Matilda looked from one of us to the other. "Are we done?"

"No. Why were you hiding in the flowerpots?" I asked.

She sighed. "I wanted to see who came down, just so I knew what way things lay. Plus I don't really want to answer any of Boris' questions regarding where my loyalties lie and all that, so if it was him, then I wanted to be able to make myself scarce. Bloody Watch. Been there, done that, moved to Whitby. Now I do just enough to stop anyone asking awkward questions, and if it requires hiding in flowerpots until the coast is clear, well – they're quite nice flowerpots, as far as that goes."

"So where *do* your loyalties lie?" Callum asked.

"Not close enough to the Watch to let them take you, since you seem to be helping Gertrude and I feel a bit bad about the whole Emma thing. But not close enough to anyone else to get any more involved," she said. "Now, d'you mind? There's a house down Church Street that does a pork roast on Thursdays, and I quite fancy some."

"*Pork,*" I said, looking at Callum.

"Later," he said, still watching Matilda. "Are the Watch going to come back?"

"Of course they are. I'd keep your Black Dogs handy, if I were you." And then she was gone, moving surprisingly quickly with her jerky, lopsided gait.

I looked at Callum. "The Watch want Gertrude and her scythe."

"I somehow doubt it's the Watch itself."

"I know. They'd have no use for it. But that means it really does look like they're working with the necromancers."

He nodded, took his cigarettes from his pocket, sighed at the empty packet and said, "Come on. We need to get back."

"And what? Go back to work as pirate swabs? Serve rum punch and ignore the fact that we now *know* the Watch are after us and are hanging with the necrophiles?"

"Necromancers."

"Same thing."

"It really isn't." He checked his phone. "I was thinking more of working out how to get Emma back. You know, since we lost her. And we're going to need Hilda on side for that, so we probably shouldn't be away too much longer."

"Shall we ask her if she's a wrecker?" I suggested. "Or if she's working with necromancers as well?"

"Probably neither, given the whole wanting to keep her on side thing."

"Clearing the air can be very healing," I pointed out, and Callum just snorted.

"Lift?"

"Very carefully," I said, and he did exactly that, tucking me into his coat for good measure. Everything was aching, and all I could think of was Boris asking me if I remembered him. I didn't, not really, but given the chills chasing through my body, I think some deeper part of me did.

As it turned out, the air was already being cleared when we made it back to the wharf via a shop (cigarettes, a sad-looking sandwich, and a pack of cooked chicken) and the chemist (plasters and hydrogen peroxide, the curer of all ills according to Poppy the troll). The sun was higher than when we'd left but no brighter, and grey light washed the decks of *The Savage Squid* in dingy, tired shades, the tatty flags snapping in the wind like the forgotten ghosts of sails.

Murty was leaning against a lamp-post. He was wearing a different tracksuit today, a deep navy blue that looked as if it should have been cheap cotton, but instead still had that sense of slick velour about it. He had his arms folded over his chest and his legs crossed at the ankles, and the odd fluidity of him meant that at first glance he seemed to have a slightly crumpled blue tail with white stripes running up the sides. The mind couldn't seem to make sense of what it was seeing at all.

His feet were clearly bare, though, and he was scowling at Hilda, who stood at the top of the gangway with a wooden walking stick brandished in one hand like a sword. Gertrude had positioned herself between them, one hand out to each like a matador caught between two bulls. She'd found her spare robes and capped them off with some sort of beekeeper's hat, all heavy pale veils hanging from the wide brim, and she had luminously pink gloves on. Her scythe leaned against her shoulder, the edge glinting in the dull light. A few walkers stood at a safe distance, cameras at the ready and ice creams in hand.

"Polly want a bloody day off!" the parrot screeched from the mast. He still had his cosy on, wings extended through a couple of holes chopped in the sides.

"He is *not* coming on my boat," Hilda said, jabbing the stick at Murty, who rolled his eyes.

"So I'm meant to help from shore? How in the depths am I supposed to do that?"

"You can swim. Help from the water. Mermaids are *not* permitted aboard."

"Ooh," said a young woman who was watching from the road, and nudged her friend. "Did you hear? He's a mermaid."

"Poor casting choice," her friend said. "Very unconvincing."

"Well, he's not in costume, obviously."

"Even so."

Hilda trained her stick and her false eye (today's was a lurid purple) on the women. "Jog on, you lot. This is a private conversation."

"You're on a *dock*," the critic said. "It's a public area."

"What are you meant to be?" the other asked Gertrude. "I like the gloves, but the hat's a bit over the top."

"Polly want to bite someone," the parrot said thoughtfully.

"Hilda, if we could just go aboard," Gertrude started, and Hilda cut her off.

"No! You're bad luck. I'm not having you on, either."

"Well this is going to go well," Murty said. "Why'd you even say you'd help?"

"I'll help on my own terms. You mermaids should know all about that."

"Yeah, they need to recast him," the critic said, and Murty gave her a sideways look. "No offence, but you just don't look the part. I don't buy it. And shouldn't you be a mer*man*?"

"Don't be so rude," her friend said. "I'm sure he'll improve. They're only rehearsing, after all."

"Yeah, but he's ..." the critic trailed off, gesturing a little vaguely. "I mean, a mermaid – or merman – should have a good chest and all that. I'm not so fussed about seeing *his* chest, if I'm honest."

Murty pushed himself off the lamp-post, muscle moving under his tracksuit like the cloth was no more than thick, supple skin, and I caught the glint of sharp teeth as he grinned. Callum set me down hurriedly on a bollard and stepped between the mermaid and the women.

"Right," he said brightly. "It's always really good to hear from the public, and we appreciate your input, even if some of it is a bit *personal*." He gave the women a slightly disapproving look, and the critic flushed.

"Well, I was only being honest," she said. "You can't improve without feedback. I did drama at school, see—"

"We'll take it on board, won't we, team?" Callum gave an urgent little *come on* hand gesture in the general direction of *The Savage Squid*.

"Of course," Gertrude said. "I did wonder about the hat myself."

Hilda grunted, and the parrot said, "Polly still want to bite someone."

"Happy to help," the first woman said, and nudged the critic. "See? I told you it was a rehearsal."

"You've got a lot of work to do," she said, and gave Murty a suspicious look. He slouched back against the post, still grinning at her. There were far too many teeth showing, in my mind, but since no one screamed or pointed I supposed there were wider parameters for such things than I'd thought.

"I guess I need to put a little more work into the character," he said. "Really get under their skin." The *s* in *skin* hissed, sibilant and teasing, and the first woman shivered.

"Come on," she said, and tugged at her friend's arm. "I fancy a cuppa."

They left, the critic keeping her eyes on Murty for a long

time, as if waiting for him to reveal himself to her. I had a feeling he would have, just for the fun of it, if Callum hadn't grabbed his arm and tugged him around, pulling him toward Gertrude and Hilda.

"Can we have a conversation without shouting the whole town down?" Callum asked. "That's not going to help anything."

"Terribly sorry," Gertrude said. "I came down to find you and they were already arguing. Do you have a phone yet?"

"After a fashion," I said, and she looked from Callum to me, then back to him.

"Ah – is that a fashion thing too?"

"What?" Callum asked.

"The scratches." She pointed at her own face, hidden behind the beekeeper's veil. "Are they a choice?"

"No, they're a Watch attack," I said. "And I'm *covered* in them, thanks for asking, plus a void beast bit my tail."

"Oh dear," Gertrude said.

I flicked my tail so she could see the clumsy dressing on the end. "Yes, and we met your Matilda. Turns out she sent Emma down to the sea on the orders of the Watch. Who she then set on us."

"Oh *dear*," Gertrude said, then frowned. "But she told me to leave my scythe behind when I said I was going to check on the dead. And I'm certain the scythe is the whole point, so why would she do that if she's part of this?"

"She didn't really want you to be hurt," Callum said, taking his cigarettes out. "She felt she had no choice, so she sort of followed orders with a bit of a cat interpretation."

"Offence taken," I said. "And also, there's always a choice."

"Except when there isn't," Hilda said, and we all looked at her. "What?"

"Black Dogs?" I asked her. "Was that you? Did you set them on us?"

She took her pipe out and started to fill it. "Not *on* you. You weren't meant to run away from them."

"They're *Black Dogs!*"

"It's just raining cats and dogs," Murty said, mostly to himself, and grinned when Hilda scowled at him.

"Is this relevant right now?" Gertrude asked. "I'm very worried about Emma, and I thought that's what we were doing. Finding her?"

"Useless there was meant to be finding her," Hilda said, pointing her pipe stem at Murty. "How's that gone, fish breath?"

Gertrude tutted and adjusted her gloves. "Insulting each other isn't going to help us find Emma," she said.

"Can we not discuss this on board?" Callum asked again, without sounding very hopeful. He cupped his hands against the wind to try and light his cigarette.

Hilda spat into the water and glared at Murty. "Keep him away from me."

"I'm not going to bite you," Murty said, then grinned. "Unless you ask nicely, of course."

Hilda spluttered something that, had it been comprehensible, would probably have elevated my swearing game to professional grade.

"Polly want a piece of that," the parrot said, swooping down to Hilda's shoulder with a flutter of bright feathers. He glared at Murty, who grinned back, and Callum sighed.

"Really, seriously, is there *any* chance we can just go on board, have a cuppa, and discuss this?"

"*No,*" Hilda and the parrot said together. Murty raised his hands in defeat, grinning.

"Fine." Callum checked the wharf road, which was mostly empty now the drama coaches had moved on, then looked at Gertrude. "Did you find anything last night?"

Gertrude looked around, then leaned in, lifting her

beekeeper's veil so she could whisper in a tone that shivered the bones, "Reaper Scarborough is definitely missing."

"Told you there were too many dead," Murty said, and Gertrude gave him an offended look.

"That was private. I was whispering."

"You need to work on that," Hilda said, and Murty laughed.

"Are you sure they're not just on a mini-break?" I asked Gertrude. "Maybe you've started a trend."

Gertrude shook her head. "I checked all the graveyards and cemeteries I could. There's quite a few missing souls still lingering about the place. I had to reap them myself. One poor soul had been there for *two weeks*." She gave us a wide-eyed look.

"Is that really so bad?" I asked. "I mean, they're dead. They're in no rush."

Gertrude tutted. "Of course it's bad. He was very distressed. No idea where to go or what to do with himself. DHL always miss a few, but the local reaper should pick them up within a couple of nights at the most. Preferably just one. It's no good leaving them moping about the place. That's how you end up with hauntings. Souls slipping through the cracks, then deciding they won't go."

Callum looked out to sea as if expecting a reaper to pop out of the waves. "So you think that's why there's so many dead in the sea? Because Reaper Scarborough's missing?"

"Not entirely," Gertrude said. "Like I say, Marine Division deals with sea deaths. So it shouldn't change anything as far as the dead in the sea. But it seems very strange that there's suddenly a lot of restless dead *and* a missing reaper."

"Polly doesn't believe in coincidences," the parrot said.

"Polly's not wrong," I said, and the parrot dipped his head to me.

"So that means Reaper Scarborough's scythe might be gone," Callum said.

"And maybe Marine Division's," Gertrude said quietly.

"How many scythes is that?"

She gave a small grimace that might've been trying to be a smile, but not a happy one. "At least one. But given all the dead I saw? Maybe more."

"So the mermaids have been taking their treasure again," Hilda said, puffing smoke into the breeze. "And a rough lot it is, too."

We all looked at Murty.

He shrugged. "I've got nothing."

"*Nothing?*" I demanded. "You were our sea contact. Informant. Whatever – you were meant to find what the scaly lot were up to."

He inclined his head slightly. "I mean, *yes*, but I can only do so much. I'm not exactly the most popular mermaid in the North Sea. I didn't find anything about your missing human. And yes, there's too many dead, but no one I spoke to was talking about stealing scythes or anything else. I haven't heard so much as a rumour about that."

"Bilgewater," Hilda said.

"It is not," Murty insisted.

"'Course it is. You've never been popular, but you've *always* known what goes on. So what gives?"

Hilda and Murty stared at each other for a long time, and he was the first one to look away. When he did, it was at *The Savage Squid*.

"Hilds," he said.

"Don't you call me that. You don't get to use nicknames with me."

"You never used to mind," he said, grinning at her, and I was fairly sure he was about to get a walking stick around the ears, but he held up a hand. "Wait, wait – before you hit me with anything, d'you want to tell me if you've got the *Squid* on autopilot or something?"

"What? Of course not—" Hilda turned to look. We all turned to look.

The Savage Squid was slipping away from the dock. Not drifting, either. Her bow had sprung off the wharf and she was swinging around to head for the harbour mouth, with no one visible in the wheelhouse. The mooring lines hung loose from the bollards on the dock, and although her progress was gentle, there was no mistaking the fact she was underway. The lines hadn't suddenly snapped. *The Savage Squid* was under new command.

Hilda swore so creatively that my admiration for her went up several notches, although a woman passing on the dock gasped and covered her son's ears with both hands. Hilda ignored her, hefting the parrot off her shoulder. "Find out who the hell's got my boat," she bawled.

"Polly's not a bloody gopher," the parrot complained, but wheeled away over the water.

Hilda spun on Murty, shoving Callum aside and charging the mermaid with her walking stick raised. "What did you do? *What did you do?*"

"Nothing!" he yelped, fending her off as she swung the stick at his legs. It impacted with a painful sounding *thwack*. "*Ow!*"

Callum grabbed for the stick and got a jab in the ribs for his efforts. "*Hey!* Hilda, *stop*. We'll use the dinghy. We can catch them before they get through the piers. Hurry!"

"Bloody useless stinking mermaids!" Hilda snarled, and belted Murty again. She went in for a third swing, and he dived off the wharf, vanishing into the murky green water.

"*After him!*" Hilda roared, swinging around to take another shot at Callum. "He's taking my ship! *Piracy!*"

"I'm trying!" Callum yelled back, his arms up to cover his

head as he scurried toward where the dinghy was still tied to the wharf. "Just stop hitting me!"

I looked at Gertrude. "I know you're not meant to be on the water, but ..."

"Emma's out there somewhere," she said. "Try and stop me."

16

THE SEA HAS MANY WAYS TO
KILL US

GETTING AN ENRAGED ONE-EYED PIRATE WITH A DODGY LEG, an anxious and heavily be-hatted reaper, plus a gangly great PI into one small rubber-tubed dinghy from a high wharf went about as well as could be expected. Hilda scrambled down the slippery rungs of the metal ladder with her stick gripped in her teeth, muttering balefully around it, and sat herself in the bow. Callum went next, steadying the dinghy as Gertrude picked her way cautiously down.

"*Hurry up!*" Hilda bellowed. "They're taking my boat!"

I'd opted to stay on the wharf until the last moment, in case anyone ended up in the water. Plus, given Gertrude's scythe, there was no guarantee the dinghy was going to stay whole for long. I peered after *The Savage Squid* as I waited. She was still making her way steadily out to the harbour mouth, and I could see Murty's head, sleek as a seal, bobbing around the hull as he followed her. I wasn't sure if he had to be invited on board when the ship wasn't under her own command, but with those high topsides it wasn't looking like he had much chance anyway.

"Am I in?" Gertrude asked, her voice a little higher than

normal. She had both feet in the dinghy, but her pink-gloved hands were still wrapped tightly around the rungs of the ladder.

"Yes, you're fine. Sit down," Callum said.

"Alright. I should just point out, if I go into the water I do sink. Very quickly. And then I'd have to walk ashore, and—"

"*Sit down, for the Deep Ones' sakes!*" Hilda bellowed.

Gertrude sat, choosing to forgo the usual sitting option of the round inflatable tubes that formed the sides of the dinghy, and instead plonking herself down in the bottom and peering about anxiously from behind her veils, clutching the scythe.

"Don't jab the sides with that thing," Hilda said. "Bad enough you being on board at all, but if you jab the tubes we'll all be under before you can say *Davy Jones.*"

"I don't tend to go around jabbing anything with it," Gertrude said, smoothing her robes over her knees with her free hand. "It's not for jabbing."

"Gobs, come on," Callum said, waving at me, and I jumped from the wharf to his shoulder, teetering there for a moment before joining Gertrude. She moved her robes from under my paws with a soft click of her tongue as Callum pulled the starter cord on the outboard. It coughed and died, and he tried again. On the third attempt it roared into rough life, and Hilda waved her stick at the harbour mouth, where *The Savage Squid* was vanishing between the piers. The sea was still churning and rough beyond their protection, and we could see her masts starting to pitch from here.

"*After them!*" the pirate captain roared.

Callum spun the dinghy in a tight circle and got us pointed in the right direction, then opened up the throttle, completely ignoring both the safe speeds signs posted all along the channel and Gertrude's squeak of alarm as her hat was torn away. He snatched at it as it flew past, but it slipped through his fingers.

"No time!" Hilda yelled. "Leave it!"

Gertrude pulled the hood of her robe up and looked at me.

"Hang on," I suggested, as we roared toward the mouth of the harbour and the hungry, wild sea beyond.

CATS DON'T REALLY DO physics. I mean, we *know* about it, as in we know it exists, but mostly we try to ignore it in a sort of *if I can't see you, you can't see me* approach, which generally works. But it doesn't take a BBC boffin to know that if you have a lot of big waves trying to fit into a small gap, things are going to get enthusiastic. Callum was going flat out by the time we reached the first of the swells coming through the harbour mouth, and we rode straight up and over it before slamming down on the other side with a jolt that shook the whole dinghy. Gertrude gave up on her hood and clutched one of the handles fixed to the inflatable tubes instead, still clinging to her scythe with the other hand, and Callum eased off on the throttle.

In the bow, Hilda yelled, *"No! Keep going!"*

Callum hesitated, and we hit the next wave so hard that most of the dinghy was completely airborne for a moment, only the engine keeping the stern pinned to the water. Before the bow could come back down properly it hit another swell and was thrown up again, and at the same time the previous wave slid under our stern and kicked us up from *that* side. We bounced from one wave to the other wildly, Gertrude trying to flatten herself to the bottom of the dinghy while Hilda rode the bow with a whoop that was half fury and half wild joy, her long plait flying. I scooted forward to join her, figuring I'd rather see what was coming, but the next wave sent me fully airborne. I twisted wildly, willing myself to fall fast enough to catch the dinghy, and came down on top of Gertrude. I tumbled off her and slid back to end up at Callum's feet where he knelt at the stern of the dinghy, one hand on the outboard tiller and the other clutching a handle on the tubes.

"Hang on, Gobs," he said, his eyes on the next wave as it rushed toward us.

"How?" I wailed, as the bow launched itself skyward again. It rose higher and higher, and I thought we weren't coming down, that the whole dinghy was going to flip end over end. Callum throttled right back even as Hilda roared at him to keep going, and after one teetering, stomach-swinging moment the bow crashed back down. We all bounced with the impact, and it threw me high enough that I thought I was out of the dinghy again. I came down hard, and threw myself behind one of Callum's legs. We were almost at the mouth of the harbour, *The Savage Squid* visible ahead, powering out to sea, and the waves were breaking as they came through the gap between the piers. White water washed through the heavy legs of the wharves, churning across the concrete fishing platforms, and the wind tore foam from the tops of the waves and flung it at the shore. The beacons strobed above us, painting red and green alarms across the day, and a few hardy walkers who'd ventured onto the main pier trained phones on us as the next wave charged in.

"Weight forward!" Hilda bellowed. "Everyone *forward!*"

Gertrude threw herself toward the bow, the scythe dangerously close to the tubes, and Callum leaned forward as far as he dared, dropping the speed right back as a foaming wave bore down on us. We surged up its face, popping through the top with spray going everywhere, and someone cheered from the shore. There was barely time to recover before the next wave hit us, breaking over the tubes and sending cold water crashing into the bottom of the dinghy, sweeping me out of my nook like I'd been dumped in a washing machine. The impact almost stopped us in our tracks, the surge more powerful than the little engine, then we were off again, driving forward and through the incoming waves. I decided the only thing I could get my claws into was Callum, so I latched myself onto the leg of his jeans as we climbed the next swell.

"Almost out!" Hilda shouted, leaning over the bow as if she could carry us through by will alone. A great green wall rolled toward us, and she added, *"Speed! Get through it, you tea-sotted swab!"*

Callum wrenched the throttle open, and we raced straight at the wave, scampering up its face like some sort of delusional water beetle. It crested as we climbed, and our bow rose higher and higher, our forward movement slowing as the wave opposed us. For one horrifying instant I was sure we were going straight back down with all that foaming water on top of us, then we burst *through* the wave. We were airborne briefly, the engine screaming as the prop lost its grip on the surface, then we slammed back down and skittered away again. We were through. We'd made it past the crush of the sea at the harbour entrance. Hilda whooped and pointed at *The Savage Squid.*

*"I'm coming for you, you scurvy freebooters! And **I give no quarter!**"*

We might've been past the worst in the pinch of the piers, but it wasn't nice out here. We'd swapped the furious power of the breakers squeezing into the harbour for the long, wind-torn swells of the night's storm, gathering mass as they rolled across the North Sea to smash onto the long flat sands and stolid cliffs of the coast. We bounced and crashed and jostled, and there seemed to be almost as much water in the bottom of the dinghy as there was on the outside of it. We were heading into the wind, too, so every time the bow lifted off a wave, the wind dived underneath it, adding its muscle as the sea tried to flip us. At least all the water in the bottom gave a bit of extra weight to help hold us down. I adjusted my grip on Callum, making sure I wasn't going to be washed away.

"Tell me again how bad Dimly was?" I yowled at him.

"You were in the flat. You tell me how bad *that* was," he shouted back, and Hilda glanced around at us.

"Pay attention!" she shouted. "We need to try and come up on the lee side! The sheltered side!"

I peered past her at *The Savage Squid*. I couldn't *see* a sheltered side, although I supposed that technically one side was being marginally less pummelled by the waves than the other. Callum altered course toward it, and as he did something rose out of the water ahead of us.

Hilda yelped, Gertrude muttered, "Oh dear," and Callum said something he must've learned from Hilda as he shoved the tiller across, sending us scooting parallel to the waves rather than into them, the wind more determined than ever to flip us as we rode the edge of the cresting swells.

"What in the mangy rot-ridden seaweed patch was that?" I yelped, and a fin broke the surface, tall and dark, with a notch taken out of it about halfway down. "Oh, herring teeth."

A second fin emerged from the rough water, sliding up through the surface like a much sleeker version of a cartoon periscope, slicing the waves as it angled toward us.

"*What?*" Hilda shouted at them. "We don't have the bloody mermaid!"

Apparently the orcas weren't interested in the mermaid, though, since they crossed paths behind the dinghy, then turned in easy synchrony to cruise after us. Callum opened up the throttle as far as it'd go, scooting us back and forth across the waves, but every time he tried to turn toward the boat the fins slid effortlessly between us and it. They rolled right up to the dinghy, sliding beneath it as they forced us back toward the shore and the unseen beach, while the sound of surf smashing on sand grew louder and louder.

"Dammit!" Hilda jabbed at the nearest orca with her stick, but all that did was add a little more splash to the sea. The orca didn't even seem to notice.

We were approaching the shore at an alarming rate. We could zip back and forth across the waves well enough, but each one carried us closer to land, and the orcas weren't letting us fight away from it. The surf was getting deafening.

Gertrude looked at Callum. "Go toward the boat," she said.

"They won't let me." He was kneeling in the bottom of the dinghy, his hair soaked dark and trying to go in five different directions at once.

"They will." Gertrude shuffled forward on her knees, squeezing into the bow next to Hilda. "Excuse me," she said to her, and leaned against the tube, raising the scythe. "Now, Callum."

Callum swung the tiller across and opened the throttle up, aiming for *The Savage Squid* again. Gertrude braced herself, and as the first orca surged toward us, raising its snout to show us an array of alarmingly sharp teeth, she swung the scythe neatly. The blade scraped across the top of the whale's fin, barely touching it, but the creature just about somersaulted, it dived so hard to get away.

"I'm very sorry," the reaper said, and shifted her grip as the second orca rushed us. "This is most unfair. But necessary." Another sweep, and I swear that over the crash of the waves and the roar of the engine and the constant pummelling of the wind, I heard the thinnest layer of skin being shaved from the orca's fin, a sliver stolen into eternity. There was a thunderous splash as the creature's tail hit the water in alarm, and it vanished below us.

"*Woo-hoo!*" Hilda shouted, and pummelled Gertrude's shoulder. "Now *that's* handy!"

"It's a terrible thing to do," Gertrude said. "Scythes are for souls, not living things."

"Well, you'd have been reaping the lot of us if you hadn't done it," the pirate said cheerfully. "Now come on, Cal! Get after my boat!"

We roared across the rough green sea, the water churned into a chaos of foamy green as the incoming wind-driven swells competed with the surge rebounding off the land. Debris from far-off shores peppered the waves, fishing floats and driftwood and plastic bottles all riding in with the foam and threatening to tangle around the leg of the outboard or jam the prop. I stayed where I was, my claws still hooked into Callum's jeans in case I needed to use him as an anchor or a life raft, and peered around at the surging sea. I couldn't see Murty, but the parrot was dipping and circling over the rolling decks of *The Savage Squid* as we approached her.

Getting on board wasn't going to be easy. The boat was heaving and pitching with the swells, her wooden hull vanishing as she rolled until her rails looked like they might kiss the sea, then surging up into a looming cliff so high I could see the barnacles and weed slicking her bottom. There was no ladder hanging ready over the side to grab onto, and Hilda's shouts to Polly to help out were met with, "Polly doesn't have opposable thumbs!"

"Polly has a *beak*," Hilda roared back, then turned and clambered back to join Callum. "I can't get aboard with my leg. You'll have to jump."

"*What?*" He stared at the violently rolling hull, and I disentangled myself from his jeans hurriedly.

"Go on. You're tall enough. Hurry!" And she all but shoved him away from the outboard, taking over.

Callum scrambled forward, taking Gertrude's place in the bow, and I followed him.

"If you get squished, I'm not staying a ship's cat," I told him. "I'm going shore based."

"If I *don't* get squished, we're both going shore based," he said.

"Deal."

Hilda ran the dinghy's bow straight into the side of *The Savage Squid* as she rolled toward us, the inflatable tube acting as a fender, squealing against the wood as the hull dipped down. Callum took a clumsy leap for the railing as the boat started to roll back in the other direction, and I jumped just ahead of him. I cleared the rail easily and hit the deck, sliding across it with all my claws out, then recovered and sprinted back to the side. The dinghy had pulled back, looking impossibly small amid all that green water, and Callum clung grimly to the railing, kicking at the hull as he tried to find some purchase. The boat rolled back toward him, and the sea surged up around his waist. He yelped as the swell tried to tear him away, but used the lift of it to heft himself higher, and managed to hook his elbows over the railing.

"Get on board!" I said, putting my paws up next to him. "Hurry, before anything tries to eat you!"

"Helpful, Gobs," he gasped, and as the boat rolled toward him again he kicked wildly at the hull, getting the railing to his waist then pitching head first over it to the deck. A cheer went up from the dinghy, and Callum scrambled to his feet. "Let's get— Oh *bollocks*."

I jumped to the railing, balancing there precariously as I spotted the six fins slicing toward the dinghy. "Bollocks is right."

Hilda had spotted them as well. She aimed the dinghy at the boat, and rammed the bow into the hull as *The Savage Squid* rolled toward her again. Callum leaned over the rail, grabbing Gertrude's scythe arm as she latched onto the railing with the other. She was up and over rather more nimbly than he'd been, leaving Hilda in the dinghy as the first orca slipped under it. Hilda gunned the dinghy at *The Savage Squid* again, and hurled the painter line up to Callum as the bow crashed into the hull a third time. He grabbed for the line but the roll was wrong and it fell short. Hilda was still driving the nose of the dinghy into the hull, but an orca's broad back rose up like a surfacing submarine and pushed the little boat back effortlessly. The engine screamed as the dinghy went briefly airborne, Hilda braced in the bottom, then slapped back to the water a few metres away. She grabbed for the engine and tried to rev it up again, but before the dinghy could do anything more than bump forward another orca powered itself fully clear of the water, its body huge and sleek against the clutter of sea and sky.

"*Hilda!*" Callum shouted, and she dived into the turbulent sea, throwing herself clear as the orca came crashing down on top of the dinghy.

Dinghy, Hilda, and orca vanished, leaving a chaos of white water behind, and we froze at the rail, searching for signs of life. The dinghy popped up again, upside down, but otherwise the sea was just a mass of churning green and grey, and the wind howled in the standing rigging like a plea. *The Savage Squid* moved on relentlessly, slow but determined as she held her course.

Then Gertrude said, "*There*," and pointed at a small head bobbing to the surface.

Callum saw it at the same moment, dumped his jacket and a startled Green Snake next to me, and swung himself over the rail.

"What's that going to achieve, you algae-brained mudskipper?" I shouted at him.

He didn't answer, because he wasn't listening. Of course he wasn't. He jumped as the railing rolled closer to the sea, vanishing into the water with a smaller splash than most of the waves were already making. He surfaced in time to see a couple of fins turn toward Hilda, and I spun to look at Gertrude.

"The ladder! Quick, get it over!" I ran to where it was attached to the deck, the bulk of it bundled next to the rail, and Polly swept past, a coiled rope in his claws.

"Polly want shipmates with brains," he announced, and dropped the rope. I was about to yell back that he might have a point, but at least Callum was *doing* something, and how was throwing bits of rope at people going to help, but the bird was already heading back with one end of the rope clutched in his beak. Behind him, Hilda splashed forward and snatched the other end, then grabbed Callum as he reached her.

"Not bad," I admitted.

Polly gave me a side eye and landed next to Gertrude, who had already dropped the ladder over the side. She grabbed the rope and started hauling, moving furiously fast. Hilda and Callum had fallen behind the boat, and watching the reaper pull them in was hideously close to seeing a fishing line being reeled in. The orcas hadn't exactly taken a *fair play, off you go then* stance, either. The fins were still there, closing in but moving almost lazily. And they might as well. As fast as Gertrude was, they were faster.

As Hilda and Callum reached the hull, an orca dipped beneath them. Even in the murky water, I saw the shadow of it surge upward, and a moment later the two swimmers were hefted clear of the surface in the pressure wave of its ascent, both of them yelping in fright. Hilda hit the hull and slipped down it, still clutching the rope as she scrabbled for purchase, while Callum splashed into the water further out, the orcas between him and us.

"*Callum!*" I yelled, and Green Snake gave me a look that clearly said I should be doing something more productive.

Gertrude had pulled the rope taut and hooked it over a cleat, and now she swung over the rail, scrambling down the ladder. She grabbed Hilda's outstretched arm and hauled her in until the pirate could start clambering up. Callum was swimming grimly, but *The Savage Squid* was still underway, and as slow as her progress was, it was too fast for him to keep up. He slipped astern, the orcas circling him casually and the upturned dinghy already blown well out of reach. I ran to the stern, keeping an eye on him, and behind me I heard Hilda bellowing that whoever had charge of her boat better come back around for the man overboard if they knew what was good for them.

But the boat rolled on, and Callum retreated further behind, and there was no way we were going to reach him before the orcas did, even if we turned around right now. A fin vanished, and the next moment Callum was thrown clear of the water, flipping over once before he crashed down again, the foamy green surface closing over him.

He didn't come back up.

17

BIGGER MERMAIDS TO POACH

I WASN'T ABOUT TO JUMP IN AFTER HIM. I MEAN, I'LL JUMP into a lot of situations, but a February North Sea in the tail end of a storm, with *orcas*, is even worse odds than I'm used to. I'm not built for swimming, no matter what the reaper says. And it wasn't like I could do much more than hope I gave one of them a hairball after it swallowed me, after all. So I just ran across the stern, trying to keep my eyes on the spot where Callum had vanished. Everything was a confusion of heaving green swells twined about with tortured foam, the shore a line of hostile cliffs with the beach lost beyond the spray of breakers, and the sky low and grey and turbulent.

"*Callum!*" I yelled again, not that it was going to help matters. I risked a look forward. Hilda was shoulder-barging the wheelhouse door while Polly sat on the roof above her.

"Deep Ones take you, you lily-livered hornswogglers!" the parrot screeched. "We'll measure you for your chains!"

"Let me *in*," Hilda roared, pounding her fist on the wheelhouse door so hard I was surprised the old wood didn't just splinter. But there was no response, and she stepped back, looking for Gertrude. "*Reaper!* Break this door down, can't you?"

Gertrude and Green Snake had joined me, both of them staring anxiously over the water. Now the reaper turned to face the pirate. "I'm not a battering ram."

"Your *scythe*, you technically dead cat-addled skeleton!"

"*Excuse me,*" Gertrude started, then looked at me. I stared up at her, not even needing to put any effort into the big eyes. It was all I could do not to paw her robes like some pathetic begging dog.

"Coming," she said instead, and hurried down the deck while I went back to looking for Callum. A moment later I heard the sound of a door flying open and rebounding on something, and very shortly after that a *lot* of shouting. I hesitated, still staring at my patch of water with my eyes narrowed against the wind. I wasn't at all sure it was the same patch of water now. They all looked the same, and none of them had scruffy heads bobbing about in them.

"*Deep Ones take you!*" Hilda shrieked. "My *boat!*"

The orca fins seemed to have vanished, and the only thing left to see was the dinghy, still upside down, being carried rapidly toward the shore by the wind and swell. No one clinging to it that I could see, but with the waves it was hard to tell. Green Snake nudged me, as if trying to curl around my shoulders again, and I stepped away. My heart was going too fast.

"*Polly! Get the damn things!*" Hilda shouted.

"Polly isn't pest control!"

There was no spotting Callum in this. Even if he'd surfaced again, between the breaking waves and the dull light, and the fact that *The Savage Squid* was still moving, still heading out to open water, there was no way I'd see him. Not from here. I turned around.

"Polly!" I bawled. "You need to look for Callum – I can't see him in this."

"Polly's not a lifeguard."

"Does Polly want to keep his head?" I snarled.

"Polly is *them*, not he," the parrot said, eyeing me fiercely, and I growled.

"Now you tell me. Sorry. Does Polly want to keep *their* head?"

"Oi, ship's cat!" Hilda yelled. "You want to get this boat turned around? Then sort out these bloody rats! They've jammed the steering and the gears."

"*Someone* bloody well watch for Callum, then," I shouted back. "You know, the one who jumped in the shark-infested waters to save you?"

"Orca-infested," Hilda countered, but she was already waving at Polly. "Go on! Look for him, you useless chicken dinner!"

"Polly want to complain to HR," the parrot said, but they took off, winging low over the stern to give me a baleful eye before arching over the waves. I watched them go, then ran to the wheelhouse, Green Snake slithering rapidly after me. The lock had been sheared so neatly that the wood around it hadn't even splintered, although there were a few fine scrapings of sawdust blowing around the wheelhouse. Gertrude was standing outside, her scythe curving over her head and her robes swirling in deep dark shades of royal blues and purples around her skeletal form. Her hood had blown back and she squinted against the dim light, the bones of her skull pressed close to the skin.

"I shouldn't be out here," she whispered.

"I wish none of us were," I said, and padded into the wheelhouse. Hilda was on her knees beside the wheel, and had unscrewed a panel behind it. I could see cables and wiring of various sorts dangling inside, but apparently none of it was what she needed, as she was keeping up a steady stream of creative swearing. "What's happening?" I asked.

"Damn rats," she snarled, sitting back to glare at me. "You were meant to get rid of them."

"Well, I mean, rats are very resilient, and—"

"And you're some bleeding-heart pacifist, are you?"

"Can't say I've been accused of that before."

"They've stolen my boat!"

I stared at her, then at the wires. "Um."

"I *told* you they were trouble! I said! Damn kraken cults."

"Kraken cults?"

She scowled at me. Her false eye had gone a bit wonky at some point, and was pointing off at the corner of the room. Her real one glared at me fiercely. "Every bloody storm. They get all het up about the kraken drowning the world, and try to nick a boat to sacrifice to their damn calamari god. Lost a couple of fishing boats in the harbour that way. *Now* d'you see why I wanted them out?"

"Sorry," I said. "Thought it was more an issue of stolen biscuits."

Hilda made a strangled noise and grabbed for me. Green Snake hissed at her, and I scooted back to the door.

Gertrude peered in at us. "Everything alright?" she asked pleasantly. The scythe fractured the dull light and spilled the scraps into the room rather less pleasantly.

Hilda growled, and pointed at the dangling wires. "Nothing's connected anymore. There were four of the gods-damned rodents in here when I first looked, but by the time we got through the door they were *gone*, and they're controlling everything from the engine, I'm sure of it." She got up, dusting her hands off. "I'm going to have to go in there and hope I can fix it from that end." She stabbed a finger at me. "And you're coming with me."

"Right. Fair enough."

"I expect *corpses*," she snapped, and headed for the door. I started to follow, then hesitated as I caught a hiss from Green Snake. He was pointing his snout at the sky, twisting his head about as if sensing something, and I could smell the rats, their faintly feral, secretive scent under an overlay of sausage rolls and rum-soaked fruit. It wasn't a left-behind scent, either, not entirely. I put my paws up on the edge of the gap behind the panel so I could peer into the shadows beyond.

"Neecy?" I asked. "You about?"

"*Gobbelino!*" Hilda roared from the deck. "Get your scrawny flea-ridden hide out here! If we don't get this boat turned around—"

"*I'm working on it,*" I yelled back. "Let the cat do the cat work, alright?"

Hilda threw her hands up and stomped down the stairs to the party deck, undoubtedly headed to the forward cabin and down into the bowels of the boat.

"Sorry about that," I said to the gap. "Things are getting a little heated. Look, Callum's gone overboard. We've lost the dinghy. There's killer bloody panda fish out there. We *have* to get turned around and go back for him. Can you help a cat out? Get things back online?"

There was silence for a moment, then a quiet voice said from above me, "The kraken comes."

I ducked out from under the wheel and looked up to see a small, milky-eyed head peering down at me from one of the cluttered shelves above the windows. Green Snake was staring at him pointedly, but the damn reptile could've been a *bit* clearer about things.

Merv was ensconced comfortably in a nest of flags, a glacé cherry clutched in his forepaws. He'd apparently been rolling in the engine grease quite liberally, and had given himself camouflage patches. "The kraken comes," he repeated, now he had my attention.

"Right," I said. "The kraken. So can we get Callum before it gets here?"

"The sea is hungry. It takes its offerings."

"No," I said. "Absolutely not."

"It's too late." Merv turned his nose to the door and raised one twisted paw. "*The kraken comes.*"

I stared out at the green sea, half expecting to see a nest of writhing tentacles come swarming up the sides of the boat, or a giant head to surface like an alien egg, but there were just some gulls swinging about the place, and Polly coming in to land on the railing. I gave up on Merv and ran out to meet them.

"Did you see him?"

Polly tipped their head, then said surprisingly quietly, "No. No sign."

I stared at the parrot, then at Gertrude, who was leaning on the railing looking into the water as if she were feeling a bit queasy. "That can't … he can't …"

"The kraken comes!" Merv shrieked from inside, and another rodent voice said, "Easy, Merv."

I spun around and glared at Neecy, who was sitting plump and dark-furred in the doorway to the wheelhouse, keeping one wary eye on Green Snake, who had slithered after me. "Neecy! What the hell are you lot playing at? I mean, I never once even *threatened* to actually catch you, and now this? We've lost Callum! You have to help!"

Green Snake hissed and Neecy looked away from me, suddenly finding something very interesting on the railings. "The sea wants what it wants."

"Oh, that's such—" I was cut off by Hilda shouting as she ran lurchingly across the party deck from the forward cabin to the steps that led up to the wheelhouse and the aft deck. She'd lost her stick in the dinghy, but she'd evidently found another one down below, and she waved it as she ran.

Faintly, in the rhythm of the wind, I thought I could hear someone singing.

"I've got it! We're back on, long as it holds, anyway. I've patched everything together, but the bloody vermin have made a hell of a mess, Sea Witch take their eyes—" She stopped as she arrived at the top of the stairs and saw Neecy. "What the *hell*—"

"It's Callum," Gertrude said suddenly, and now I was certain I could hear singing. "He's there, *quick!*"

Hilda rushed to the rail, while from the wheelhouse Merv shrieked, "*The kraken will not be denied! Rats, take back control of the ship! The kraken comes!*"

"*Shut up!*" Hilda, Polly and I roared at the poison-addled rat in the wheelhouse, and he shrieked back, something wordless and rage-filled. We didn't look away from the sea, suddenly less hostile than it had been a moment ago. Two voices were raised in song, ragged with breathlessness and not particularly tuneful, but the words ran with a liquid, furious energy that shivered the soaking hair on my back.

"What shall we do with a drunken sailor?
What shall we do with a drunken sailor?
What shall we do with a drunken sailor?
Ear-ly in the morning!"

A dinghy heaved into view, breaching the surface as if it had risen from beneath the waves rather than been navigated through them. It was a long wooden thing with graceful lines and a curved belly that looked like it hadn't even seen the sun for about ten years. Barnacles and sprawling tufts of seaweed festooned the gunwales, and as it tipped in a swell I could see that the bottom was full of sand and starfish, and a couple of startled, flopping fish. Callum knelt among them, shoeless, dishevelled, and dripping. Murty was in the bow, and both of them were paddling wildly, if somewhat ineffectively. Callum's oar was barely more than a stick, and Murty's was broken in half so that he had to just about lie over the bow to reach the water. They were also both singing, very badly but with great enthusiasm.

"Way hay and up she rises,

Way hay and up she rises,

Way hay and up she rises,

Ear-ly in the morning!"

"Permission to come aboard!" Murty bellowed, still paddling. Callum kept singing. I had an idea that if he stopped, whatever mermaid magic was keeping the dinghy afloat was going to go belly up, and them with it.

"Sod off and suck barnacles, fish man!" Hilda bawled back, and I yelled over her, so loudly that it tore my throat.

"Permission granted!"

The dinghy angled toward the boat.

"Shave his belly with a rusty razor,

Shave his belly with a rusty razor—"

Hilda glared at me. "You can't give permission. You're the *ship's cat.*"

"Still crew," I said, baring my teeth at her.

"Callum, *paddle!*" Murty shouted.

"What d'you think I'm doing?"

They both went back to singing. *"Shave his belly with a rusty razor, ear-ly in the morning!"*

Something rolled in the water behind them, muscular and half-seen.

"The kraken!" Neecy squealed, her voice full of more disbelief than joy or horror. She'd joined us at the rail while the wheelhouse door banged to and fro on its broken latch, and Merv started yammering in time to the rhythm, a wordless, frightful chant. Neecy took it up, and I heard other small voices joining in from the helm.

"*I said*, permission granted," I bawled at the dinghy.

"We're trying," Murty shouted back.

"Permission revoked!" Hilda shouted.

"Permission granted!" I countered.

"Way hay and up she rises,
Way hay and up she rises—"

"I overrule you!" Hilda yelled at me.

"I overrule you back!" I bawled.

"I'm the captain!"

"Ship's cat!"

"I *outrank* you!" She had both hands on her hips, and she bent down so she could shout at me from a closer range.

"I'm a *cat!* You can't!"

"Who says?"

"I mean, *everyone. Permission granted!*"

"Revoked!"

Gertrude, meanwhile, had run down to the party deck. She grabbed the line we'd used earlier and hurled one end in a smooth, arcing toss to the struggling dinghy. Murty grabbed it and hauled, almost pulling the reaper over the railing, but she braced herself as Hilda and I ran down to join her.

"*No mermaids*," the pirate shouted. She shook her stick threateningly at the singers in the dinghy. They ignored her. They were both trying to pull on the line at once, and beneath the surface, indistinct in the murky water, was movement, suggestions of vast and muscular bodies. A little further out the first of the fins broke the water.

"*Way hay and up she rises, ear-ly in the morning!*"

"Let them up," I snarled at Hilda.

"Callum can come up. *He* can't." She pointed at Murty.

Water swirled by the dinghy, more disturbed than the waves already were, or *differently* disturbed. Turbulence knocked the rickety vessel angrily and sent water slopping over the gunwales. It was already settling lower into the water as the singing faltered, and now Callum stopped altogether.

"Murty, get up," he said, nodding at the ladder as the dinghy banged into the hull. Fragments of rotting wood crumbled from the gunwales into the water.

"*No,*" Hilda said, hefting her stick warningly.

"Murty, permission granted," Callum said.

"*Revoked.* Callum, get up here. He can *swim,* for the Deep Ones' sakes!"

"Permission granted," I said, because there was no way Callum was leaving the damn mermaid in there with the orcas circling about, so there was no point arguing. It was just slowing things down. So as Hilda opened her mouth to revoke permission again, I bit her in her good leg.

I admit it was tempting to try the other, just to see if it was a peg leg after all, but there wasn't time for research. Instead I launched myself at her good leg, wrapping my paws around it and biting her hard, just above the knee where I was sure her boots wouldn't reach. She yelped, more in surprise than hurt, and grabbed for me, but Green Snake came hurtling off the aft deck and landed on her shoulder with a furious hiss. She tried to brush him away, swearing, and while she was distracted Murty scrambled up the ladder with effortless speed for such a big creature. He flung himself over the rail and turned back to help Callum, and I let go of Hilda's leg, dancing away. She finally got a grip on Green Snake and threw him off, sending him flying toward the railings.

"Oh, hang the jib," she hissed, lunging after him, but Polly swooped in and snatched him up before he could go over the side. "Sorry," she said, then turned around and slammed her stick into the deck where I'd been a moment earlier. We glared at each other, then I went in for a second attack, avoiding the stick as she swung it at me.

"Rabid, useless excuse for a ship's cat," she yelled. "I'll bite *you!* See how you like it!"

I decided I'd made my point and ducked behind Gertrude, just in case the pirate decided to make good on her threat to bite me back. She sounded angry enough. I peered over the side to see Callum clambering up the ladder while the dinghy wallowed behind him. It was awash, the oars floating and the gunwales already almost level with the surface. He reached the rail and Murty grabbed the back of his fleece, all but lifting him over, and the dinghy started to sink into the green wash. As it did, long shadowy cables snaked over it, like sea serpents or creeping eels, pulling it abruptly out of sight.

"What was that?" Gertrude asked, and no one answered. The rats were still chanting in the wheelhouse, and the reaper turned to look at Hilda, who couldn't seem to decide whether to glare at me or Murty. Or possibly attack us with her stick. "Excuse me?" the reaper said. "Did anyone else see that? What was it?"

"The kraken," Murty said, his voice low, and the chanting of the rats went up a pitch.

No one else spoke for a moment, waiting for the sea to erupt in a frenzy of flailing limbs, but nothing happened. There was just the foam-torn sea and the wheeling gulls, and Callum and Murty both panting.

"Damn mermaids," Hilda said, and scowled at Murty. He grinned.

"I got your deckie back, didn't I?"

"What was with the whole sea shanty thing?" I demanded. "You were singing at the beach, too."

"Shanties were sung to keep crews together," Murty said. "To keep *boats* together. It still works, if you sing it with enough conviction." He glanced at Callum. "I mean, it's kind of a last resort for mermaids though, the whole boat thing. And for anyone else, if you just let a mermaid have their wicked way with you, you'll be fine. But some people play so hard to get."

Callum coughed wheezily, took Green Snake from Polly, and said, "We were in kind of a rush."

"Fair," Murty said, grinning. "Can't hurry these things."

Hilda glared at all of us, her purple eye taking the job of glaring at the sea at the same time. "Everyone happy then, are you? Can we get my damn boat home now?"

"What about Emma?" Gertrude asked, and we all looked at her. Her face was blooming painful-looking red blotches in the grey sunlight, and her voice had lost edges. "You can bring sunken dinghies up with *songs* but you don't know anything about Emma?"

"Well, like I say, I'm not the most popular in mermaid town," Murty said, putting his hands in his pockets. "No one tells me anything."

"Again, absolute bilge," Hilda said. "It's always on your terms, isn't it, Murty? What angle are you playing? You keep us out of the way? Mislead us? Tell us you'll help then do *nothing*? And what then – you get first pick of the treasure?" Her voice had lost its normal raging edges, replaced with something cool and hard and sure.

"Hilds—"

"Don't call me that. I haven't been Hilds for a long time. I've *never* been Hilds to you. I shouldn't have allowed you aboard back then, and I shouldn't have now." She moved, and I thought she was jabbing at him with the handle end of her stick, but the light caught and ran on the edges of a blade that had popped out of it as it touched his throat. Her stick had hidden surprises. "*Tell me what you're playing at.*"

Murty raised his hands. "I'm really not playing, Hilda. I can't help."

Hilda pressed forward just slightly, and blood bloomed on the mermaid's throat, thick and slow.

"Hilda," Callum said. "Stop. We'll figure this out."

"You don't know mermaids the way I do. You still think they're just nice little fish-tailed people, saving shipwrecked sailors and making necklaces from shells. They're predators. For everything. Ships and cargo and favours and people."

"The kraken rises!" Merv screeched from the wheelhouse, and Callum and I turned to look at him. The rat was standing in the doorway, ignoring the door swinging back and forth and threatening to wallop him. Hilda didn't look away from Murty, and Gertrude was staring at the sea again.

"Dude, give it a rest," I said to Merv. "Bigger mermaids to poach."

"The kraken!" he shrieked, and pointed at the sea.

"Oh," Callum said, and I wrinkled my snout, looking at the sky while Murty said, "This is going to be a problem."

"Maybe," Hilda said. "But I might feed you to it, so that's one less problem."

"I think the Sea Witch thing might not just be reaper legend," Gertrude said, and I finally turned and looked at the raging green sea, and saw the kraken rise.

ALL HAIL THE SEA WITCH

CALLUM FUMBLED IN HIS POCKETS, THEN REALISED HE'D dropped his jacket on the deck before he'd jumped in the water, and with it his cigarettes. And also our hours-old phone, but I doubted that was what he'd been looking for. He was hardly going to film this and put it on YouTube. He didn't bother looking for the coat, just made a small, frustrated noise, and shoved his hands in the pockets of his fleece instead, his eyes never leaving the water. For once I couldn't fault him for wanting a smoke. I personally wanted a box of Dreamies large enough to crawl inside and curl up in, and even more than that I wanted to be a very long way away from the nearest body of water bigger than a duck pond. But neither of those things seemed like happening in the near future.

This, however, is what *was* happening: the sea was boiling with the rise of something vast and ancient. Tentacles curled and twisted, sliding over one another like a pantomime villain rubbing his hands together. They slid underneath us, investigating *The Savage Squid*'s hull, or lifted clear of the water, tips pointing one way then the other as if to test the air or to get a better look at us. There was movement among them, indistinct and only half-seen, but the patches making it clear the panda fish hadn't given up hope of a snack just yet. The heavy muscular bodies of the beasts curved easily past the ever-shifting nest of tentacles, surfacing here and there to give their oddly human gasp for air, their tall fins smooth and indifferent. Murty muttered something to himself, stepping away from the rail as if he could stay hidden.

"*The kraken*," Merv cried. He'd emerged from the wheelhouse and come to join us at the railing, scrambling up to perch on the top despite the fact that the boat was still rolling violently. Hilda might have got control back, but without the autopilot on or someone at the helm *The Savage Squid* was wallowing, the waves pushing her toward shore.

"Come, my brethren!" Merv called, balancing precariously on his hind legs and spreading his front paws wide. Other rats started to slip out of the wheelhouse to cluster below him, more disciples of the kraken-king. Not just Neecy and Carlos, but a dozen others I'd never seen before, their ears flicking with the wind as they peered out into the wild water.

"Where the hell did you lot come from?" I asked the nearest, and he just sneered, showing long yellow teeth.

Hilda glared at me. "*Useless.*"

I couldn't really argue the point, although, in my defence, I was used to rats that just wanted a nice bit of cheese and a quiet life, not to sacrifice a ship to an ancient sea god.

"We offer this ship to the spirit of the sea!" Merv cried, and there was a chorus of "Aye!" from the assembled rats.

"You bloody do not," Hilda shouted at them. "This is *my* boat!"

"It belongs to the sea now," Merv said, and as if to underline the sentiment the whole boat lurched. It wasn't the sort of lurch that came from hitting a swell, or even from crossing the sharp wake of a fishing boat on a calm day. It was solid and muscular, as if the seabed itself had reached up to grab us. Gertrude stayed exactly where she was, still watching the sea, while Murty and Hilda leaned easily with the movement. Callum staggered a step away from the rail then back again, and we all turned to watch the kraken surface.

It rose like an island being born, lurching into volcanic life above the surface of a turbulent sea. Or, you know, how that looks on the sort of TV shows Callum watches on the phone. I've never seen it happen personally. Mostly what it looked like to me was a mound of sticky toffee pudding emerging out of a slick of custard, just saltier, colder, and much less appetising with its greens and greys. The swell of the creature's head was vast and bulbous, wider than *The Savage Squid* was at her fattest point, and its eyes were dark, depthless pools that glittered in the dull light. Its skin was slick and smooth, although barnacles and clams and clusters of seaweed and coral bloomed in patches here and there. Under the dome of its head, weirdly flabby and shapeless skirts led to tentacles which spread out around it in muscular rivers. Now I was thinking more of a melting ice cream scoop that had plopped off the cone, but you wouldn't want to lick it.

And standing on the creature's head, her arms crossed and her legs planted wide, was a woman with long coils of kelp-coloured hair, and eyes the same shade as the kraken's. She was curved and muscular and barefoot, and just as with Murty, I was having some trouble deciding if I was seeing some sort of smooth, glistening pelt or a set of suspiciously velour-like leisurewear.

"All hail the Sea Witch," Murty said, his voice flat.

Gertrude looked at him, then back at the woman. "Oh," she said, a careful sound that didn't give very much away.

"Yeah," I said. "I was expecting a throne made from the skulls of her enemies at least."

"It can be arranged," the Sea Witch said, even though we'd been talking quietly and she was a good boat's length from us. "Reaper. What are you doing on my waters? *In* them, too?"

"I'm looking for someone," Gertrude said.

"Oh? A little lost human, by any chance?"

"Yes," Gertrude leaned forward, gripping the railing. "Emma. Have you seen her?"

The Sea Witch grinned, and for a moment her teeth were more than big enough to make up for the lack of enemy skulls for decor. "Maybe. What will you give me if I have?"

"*Favours,*" Hilda snapped. "It's all favours and deals with you lot, isn't it?"

The Sea Witch's smile faded as she looked at the pirate. "Hilda," she said. "How's the leg?"

Hilda growled. "Still missing."

"Knew it was a peg leg," I said quietly, and Callum nudged me with his foot.

"And how's life on land?" the Sea Witch asked. "You're keeping bad company." Her gaze shifted to Murty, who looked at the deck rather than at the witch.

"Not by choice," Hilda said. "Bloody cat invited him on board."

"A cat? *Terrible* company," the Witch said, and Hilda snorted.

"*Excuse me,*" I said. "Rude."

"The kraken!" Merv shouted, waving his little paws. "We bow before you!" And he did exactly that, while the rest of the rats looked at each other a little uncertainly, despite their excited *ayes* a moment before. The Sea Witch seemed to have put them off. Some bowed hesitantly, but Neecy and a few others just watched as if waiting to see what way things were going to go. Green Snake poked his head out of the pocket of Callum's fleece, looked at the kraken, then looked at me, his head tipping. I twitched my ears at him.

"I don't think the kraken's going to pluck the sun out, Merv," Neecy said, and the Sea Witch chuckled.

"That old clamshell," she said. "The kraken's not going to end the world, little rats. Change it, perhaps. But not end it."

"But I saw it," Merv said. "It is foretold."

"By who?" Hilda demanded. "Because I'm going to cleave them to the bloody brisket. Stealing my boat!"

"*Arr*," the parrot said, in encouraging tones.

"If we will live on, the kraken must have its sacrifice," Merv said.

"The kraken's name is Keith, and he likes a nice tuna now and then," the Sea Witch said. "As a change from the haddock, you know. And of course the occasional drunken sailor as a treat."

We all looked at each other, then at Hilda. She scowled at us. "I haven't had anything since breakfast. I'm not *drunk*."

"Oh, I wouldn't let Keith have you, anyway," the Sea Witch said. "Drunk or not."

"I'm not drunk, Enid."

"I didn't say you were." The Sea Witch tipped her head to one side. "Are you sleeping better these days?"

I scrambled up to Callum's shoulder and hissed, "The Sea Witch is called Enid. I'm suddenly less worried about all this."

"You should still be worried," Murty said. "Trust me."

"Excuse me," Gertrude said, giving the Sea Witch – Enid – a little wave. "Have you seen Emma or not?"

"Oh, *Emma*," Enid said. "Nice little thing. Smells of baking and strange hopes and bad dreams."

"That sounds very like her," Gertrude said, and I could see her knuckles creaking on the handle of the scythe. I had a feeling she was fighting very hard not to jump off the boat onto the kraken.

"Now why would I let a reaper have her? It's not her time."

"Why would you take her, then?"

"Perhaps she came willingly. Perhaps life with a reaper isn't as fun as a human might like. Perhaps moonlight dances on wild sands and surfing the waves of storms sound rather more appealing than mossy crypts and old bones." She looked at Hilda as she spoke, but Hilda just looked at the rats, using her stick to try and push a couple over the side. They hissed at her irritably, shuffling around but not leaving.

"Perhaps you're right," Gertrude said. "But I'd still like to make sure that's actually the case."

"How sweet. I do have such a soft spot for the odd couple." Enid regarded Gertrude for a moment, ignoring Hilda snorting rather loudly, then said, "Well then, Reaper. Give me your scythe, and I'll give you the human."

Gertrude looked back at the Sea Witch steadily, warm spots of colour high on her bony cheeks. "I can't give you my scythe. A reaper can never give up their scythe. We dream it into being ourselves. It's part of us, and we cannot replace it. Without it we're nothing but ghosts."

"Well, then. No scythe, no human."

We were silent for a moment, then Callum said, "Why would you want a reaper's scythe?"

Enid examined him. "Why do you want to know, little human?" Her eyes narrowed. "Mostly human."

"What happened to the other reapers?" Callum asked. "Reaper Scarborough? Marine Division? Did you take their scythes?"

The Sea Witch nodded thoughtfully, then looked at Gertrude. "I see. You think you have some sort of grand mystery here, do you?"

"We can't find Reaper Scarborough," Gertrude said. "And there are too many dead in the sea. Now you want my scythe. You almost had it – and me – the other night. Or the sea-dead did. Why?"

I thought the Sea Witch wouldn't answer. She looked at Hilda as if wanting to abandon the conversation, and go back to picking at whatever old history lay between them. But Hilda just folded her arms and said, "And now you're setting Keith on my boat. What's that all in aid of?"

"I don't much like Murty," Enid said, shrugging.

"Mutual," Murty said, mostly to the deck.

"Honestly, it was thirty years ago," Hilda said. "Forty, maybe. I couldn't *stay*."

"I saved you," Enid protested. "And one leg doesn't matter when you have a tail."

"I only had a tail when I was with you," Hilda said. "And I get by just fine with one leg. I couldn't spend all my time sitting about the place plotting shipwrecks. I'm a *sailor*. I'm sort of morally opposed to shipwrecks."

"So, not a wrecker, then," I whispered to Callum, and he shook his head at me.

Hilda glanced at Murty and continued, "I don't much like him either, but *I* asked *him* for help back then. It wasn't his fault."

I hissed in Callum's ear, "Is this some sort of mermaid drama? Do you think they'd notice if we made ourselves scarce?"

"And go where?" he whispered back.

"Gah. Bloody boats."

Enid glanced at us as if she'd heard every word, then looked at Hilda and said, "It doesn't matter whose fault it was. You're hardly the only human that's joined and had second thoughts, Hilds. Most that make it back ashore swear off the sea, though. It's safer."

"Safer never appealed that much."

"Evidently." A smile touched the corners of Enid's lips and crinkled her eyes for a moment, then faded. "But I was making a deal with the reaper, I believe."

Gertrude stood there with the harsh winds dragging at the edges of her robes and her face unreadable. The pale light splintered on the edge of her scythe. "Oh?" she said, and her voice was Gertrude-mild, but something in it reverberated in my chest, making my claws dig into the damp thickness of Callum's fleece. I felt him shiver, and Green Snake, who'd been hanging out of Callum's pocket staring at Keith, dived back into hiding.

Enid didn't seem to have felt what I did. "I have your human," she said. "You can have her back if you give me the scythe. But if you do not – you're in my element now. The sea is mine. And I will take you *and* your scythe, just as I took Reaper Scarborough. And your human will stay on to dance to the mermaid's song for as long as the tides will run. So what say you?"

Gertrude bowed her head, and I could see the tight lines of tension drawing her skull like an etching under her sunburnt skin. She looked sideways at us.

"Don't," Callum said, his voice soft. "You can't lose your scythe. We'll get Emma back."

"And how do you propose to do that, human?" Enid asked. "You going to pop some snorkel gear on and come paddle with the orcas?"

Callum looked at her. "I don't know," he said. "But I also don't know that you'll really let her go. Or if you even have her. Where is she? Shouldn't you at least show us she's unhurt before we can start negotiating?"

"You're asking the Sea Witch to prove herself?" Enid pressed a hand to her chest in mock outrage. Or maybe it wasn't mock – there were sharp edges to her words.

"I'm asking a kidnapper to prove their hostage is alive." His voice was flat, but he had his own angry corners in there somewhere.

Enid snorted. "You are a strange one, human."

"I've heard that before."

"On a regular basis," I added.

Enid crossed her arms. "No," she said. "I prove myself to no one. Let alone scruffy little humans with ideas above their station."

"But what's the deal?" I demanded. "Why're you so keen on collecting scythes and reapers? Who're you working with?"

"What are you even doing here, cat? This isn't a place for you."

"I'm a ship's cat," I said.

"I can see you're doing a great job," she said, nodding at the rats.

"That's what I said," Hilda agreed, and Enid grinned, wide and toothy.

"Let me see Emma," Gertrude said. "If I see you set her safely ashore, I'll give you my scythe."

"Gertrude," Callum started.

"No," she said. "This is my fault. Emma would be safe if not for me and my scythe. So I will give it up and pass on, but only if I know she's safe."

"I'll put her ashore as soon as I have the scythe," Enid countered.

The reaper and the Sea Witch stared at each other, the collector of souls and the drowner of ships, and the moment stretched long and thin and delicate.

And into it, faintly, through the clash of the waves on the hull and the gloop of the kraken and the snarl of the wind, came the sound of singing.

"Well, heave her up and away we'll go, a-wayyy Santiana!"

I looked around, puzzled, my ears twitching. No one else seemed to have heard. I glanced at the Sea Witch, but she and Gertrude were still watching each other, and I had the sense that there was some struggle going on that wasn't being articulated, each of them as sunk into their own thoughts as chess players looking for the killing move.

"Heave her up and away we'll go, along the plains of Mex-i-co!"

Callum tipped his head slightly, frowning as if something had caught his attention, and I patted his ear with one paw. When he craned his neck to peer at me, I pointed my nose in the direction I thought the singing was coming from. Murty glanced at us, the corner of his mouth twitching, and followed our gaze, looking across to the far side of the boat and the wind-torn sea beyond. Hilda gave us a look that suggested she'd heard it too, but she stayed where she was, next to Gertrude.

"She's a fast clipper ship and a bully good crew, a-wayyy Santiana!"

And with that burst of song, the singers came into view.

Half swamped by the sea, the fat barrel-body of an old-fashioned, open fishing boat rolled its way toward shore. It only had half a mast left, and the whole thing was festooned with seaweed and caked with barnacles. There was also a massive chunk out of the gunwale, as if something had bitten it, but it hardly mattered. Physics wasn't what was keeping it afloat.

"And a Yorkshire lass for a captain too, along the seas of Whit-by-o!"

I was pretty sure they weren't the original lyrics, but they fitted the drenched form of Emma, rowing furiously with a plank of wood in the bows. Behind her, three other figures paddled just as enthusiastically with bits of driftwood and broken planks, their skin gleaming and their sodden clothes stuck to their bodies. None of them looked around, their eyes fixed on the beach, and I looked at Callum, then at Murty, then leaped from Callum's shoulder to the rail, teetering there for a moment.

"Hey, fish-face!' I shouted at Enid. "We do *not* accept your deal!"

"Gobbelino," Gertrude started, her tone bewildered.

"We don't even care if you *do* show us Emma. You're ... we don't make deals with *fish!*"

Enid gave a startled half-laugh. "Cat, you know whose realm you're in here, don't you?"

"I'm a *cat.* The whole world is my realm."

"Gobs, you might be over-egging it," Callum muttered.

"What? I haven't said anything about eggs. Why would I mention eggs?"

"Get your furry little bag of bones under control, human," Enid said. "Otherwise I'll sink the ship and take your skulls for that throne you mentioned."

"I will take—" Gertrude started, and Callum shouted over her.

"I've got a name, you know! You can't just keep calling me *human*, like it's an insult or something."

"Well, it kind of is," Enid said, and Hilda slammed her fist down on the railing. Merv very nearly went head first into the sea, which would've been such a shame.

"Bloody mermaids! Think you're so superior because you've got *tails?* Fish have tails! You're not special!"

"Excuse me, I was talking," Gertrude said.

"Listen to you two!" Enid shouted at Hilda and Callum. "What is *wrong* with you?" She waved at herself and the world in general. "Sea Witch, see? And a *kraken?* Can't you see you're outclassed?"

"I mean, out-*armed*," I said. "I'll give you that. You can't outclass a cat."

"Excuse me," Gertrude said.

"*Enough! I need that scythe!*" Enid pointed a threatening finger at Gertrude, her face all teeth and eyes. "*Give it to me!*"

I sneaked a peek over my shoulder. The half-ruined fishing boat was still wallowing toward shore, but it was a long way from safe.

"Why?" Callum demanded. "What does a Sea Witch need a scythe for?" His voice was hard and furious. "Why are there so many *dead*? Are you working for them? Are you?" The Sea Witch had stopped mid-shout, her eyes narrowing, and Callum shouted again. "*Are you?*"

"I don't know who you mean," she said.

"The necromancers. Those who'd raise the Old Ones. Those who want to make sure the reapers can't put the dead down."

In the wind-torn pause that followed I heard, dimly, "*Heave her up and away we'll go, along the plains of Mex-i-co!*"

Finally Enid said, "I don't work for anyone. I'm the Sea Witch."

"Yeah, we kind of got that," I said, and Murty snorted.

"So you're *with* them, then," Callum said, ignoring us. "You're trying to raise the Old Ones too."

Enid was silent again, examining him. "You're the North," she said. "They mentioned you."

"He's just a human," Hilda said.

"I'm *a* North," Callum said. "Not that it matters. You are with them, aren't you?"

Enid folded her arms. "I just want the humans to leave my seas alone. Is that too much to ask? That they stop poisoning them and scraping them bare? Emptying them of everything beautiful? Staining them with their greed?"

Callum shook his head. "It's not. But this isn't the way to do it. What the necromancers bring will be worse."

"They'll rein the humans in."

"They'll tear the world to pieces. The sea too. There'll be nothing left but the dead and those they serve."

They stared at each other for a long moment, then Enid shrugged and said, "The deal is done. And a mermaid's deal can never be broken." She looked at Gertrude. "The scythe."

"No," Callum said, and elbowed Gertrude.

She gave him a confused look, but said, "Um. No?"

Enid shifted her gaze to Hilda. "Sorry about your boat, Hilds," she said, then tapped her bare foot on the kraken. "Ay-up Keith. *Sic 'em.*"

"*The kraken rises!*" Merv shrieked.

"Sink me," I said. Because this time the rat was right.

FIRE IN THE HOLE

THE KRAKEN ROSE FROM THE SEA TO ENGULF US.

Well, *Keith* did, but that kind of downplays the fact that Keith was an ancient sea beast with a head that would have comfortably filled *The Savage Squid*'s party deck, never mind the swirling tangle of his legs, of which there were far, far too many. No creature needs that many legs. Humans don't have enough, and kraken have an entirely excessive amount. Cats are in the sweet spot with that, as they are with most things.

But back to Keith and his legs, which were curling hungrily toward us, creating vortices and surging swells and a couple of whirlpools, one of which an orca teetered on the edge of for a moment before bolting away again. Fat, squishy-looking suckers armed with nasty toothy bits lined the undersides of his tentacles, but more alarming were the two extra-long, thin legs that shot toward us with diamond-shaped pads as big as our lost dinghy on the ends of them. They thwacked into the boat, and I heard a toothy rasp as they latched onto the hull.

"What in the mucky realms is *that?*" I demanded, staring over the side.

"Tentacular clubs," Callum said, leaning over me. Green Snake was hanging dangerously far out of his pocket, watching Keith again, and Callum pushed him back to safety and zipped the pocket up.

"*What?*" I asked.

"The bits on the end. The long arms are feeding tentacles—"

"And the short ones are smash-them-to-bits-acles? Or squish-them-to-mush-acles?"

"They're just arms."

"They're not *just* anything," Murty said, proving that even mermaids are smarter than humans. "They're attached to a kraken who's about to smash this boat apart and pluck our bodies out of the ruins, so I suggest we come up with a plan, *very quickly.*"

The boat lurched, as if to illustrate his point, and the starboard side, the one furthest from the kraken, dipped toward the sea as he pushed the boat nearly all the way over and reeled us toward him hull-first. The two-legged among us grabbed onto the railing to stop themselves sliding toward it, and I jumped from the Callum's shoulder to the deck, slipping in the direction of the wheelhouse until I could brace myself against the lean. The rats were all hanging over the edge of the hull still, peering at Keith with varying degrees of enthusiasm. Funny how a kraken cult is all well and good until the kraken actually turns up.

"Excuse me," Gertrude said. "I seem to have missed something. I was going to give the Sea Witch the scythe and get Emma back."

"She doesn't have Emma," I said, and Gertrude stared at me.

"Where is she, then?"

"Halfway to the beach," Callum said. "Probably more by now. But we need to keep the Sea Witch's attention here until she's safely ashore."

"I think we're succeeding so far," I said, as a couple of enormous tentacles loomed over *The Savage Squid*. They flopped down almost lazily, one just forward of where we clung to the aft deck railing by the wheelhouse, the other just aft of the forepeak.

"You *witch!*" Hilda roared, rather accurately, and grabbed her stick in both hands. It evidently had more surprises than just the short knife in the handle, because when she pulled, the whole thing came apart, a much longer blade emerging out of the leg of the stick. Callum and I gave an appreciative *oooh* as she flung the sheath bit away, grabbed the handle in both hands, and started hacking enthusiastically at Keith's tentacle. He gave a squiddy groan of protest that reverberated through the water like whale song, and sent another couple of tentacles up to join the fight.

"*Give me the reaper and the scythe!*" Enid shouted, and I peered down the hull at her. She was still balanced on Keith's flabby head, crouching like a surfer on a tricky wave.

"*I'm not giving you anything!*" Hilda shouted back before Gertrude could answer, still hacking doggedly at Keith's arm. Or leg. I'm not sure if they were differentiated. Arm-legs? Args? That sounded about right.

"Why not?" Enid yelled. "I gave you *everything!*"

I looked at Callum. "Ever get the feeling you're intruding on something?"

"Probably." He looked at Murty. "Can you get us all a ride ashore? Like with the dinghy?"

"Not quickly enough. We're better off saving this boat if we can."

The rails on the starboard side dipped underwater as we tipped further, and Gertrude and Callum grabbed the rails on our side to anchor themselves in place. Heavy old wood splintered with a sound like gunshots, and Hilda slid down to brace herself against the wheelhouse. She didn't seem to have done much damage to the tentacle – it just had a few scores scraped across it.

Callum clambered across to the stairs and swung down onto the steeply sloping party deck, scrambled forward to the forepeak cabin and climbed in. Murty followed him, and I looked at Gertrude.

"Can't you use the scythe?" I asked.

"It's a living creature," she said, looking at Keith.

"You used it on the orcas."

"I just scraped them. And that was an emergency."

We lurched again, and I scooted over to the reaper, tangling my claws into her robes to stop myself sliding straight off the deck. The starboard side was rapidly becoming the *down* side. "I'm sorry, what's this, then?"

"Yes. I see your point."

But she still just clung to the rail with one arm and her scythe with the other, looking at the kraken with a worried expression.

There was a roar from below, and Murty bounded out, armed with a couple of saucepans. He slid straight down the deck and into the foaming water beyond, banging his saucepans as he went. As he vanished under the surface the sound was swallowed, but judging by the twitching going on in the tentacles, Keith was still hearing it. The kraken grumbled, and squeezed *The Savage Squid* a little tighter, setting off a new chorus of cracking wood.

Callum emerged from the cabin a little more circumspectly, but also promptly slid down to the starboard side rail. Rather than going over, though, he braced his feet on it and waved an axe at the sea in general, since only Keith's tentacles were visible on that side of the boat. "I'll use it!" he yelled.

"Use what?" Enid shouted back. With Keith pulling the boat bottom-first toward them, she couldn't see what was happening on deck. "Keith, for the Deep Ones' sakes – roll it *toward* us. *Toward.* No – the other toward. Masts to us. We've gone over this."

The Savage Squid creaked and bounced as Keith fumbled about, and Hilda shouted from the wheelhouse, "Hold on, mateys! We're going over!"

For one horrifying moment I thought Keith was going to keep rolling us in the same direction we'd started in, so that the deck would submerge and the keel go up on the way around to his side, and we'd all end up in the water, but after a threatening dip that way, accompanied by a shout from Enid, we surged back in the opposite direction. We were lying on our port side now, the deck near-vertical again, and the rail that Gertrude had been clinging to high above the waves was suddenly waist-deep in foaming water. I'd have been swept away if my claws hadn't been so firmly tangled into her robes. As it was, I went over the rail in a wash of sodden cloth, and tried desperately to both swim and hang on. I had time to think that extra legs weren't such a bad idea after all, then Gertrude grabbed me and flung me at the top of the wheelhouse. There were handholds there, in case of rough weather or drunken pirates, and I snagged one with my front paws, scrambling up to perch on it with my side pressed into the cabin top as if it were a wall.

Below me, Enid glared at Gertrude, who was standing on the uprights of the rail with her back pressed to the deck, hugging her scythe protectively. Water swirled around her legs, threatening to pull her off her perch, but she just braced herself harder. *The Savage Squid*'s masts were almost parallel to the water, and Keith had snatched Hilda up in one tentacle. She'd lost her stick and her arms were pinned to her sides, but she evidently still had full use of her lungs. She was employing an impressive torrent of curses and promises of violence, but I was more interested in Callum, who had snagged the railing on the starboard side (which was now very much *up*) as we rolled. He hung there from one arm with the axe in the other hand, his feet dangling free. *The Savage Squid* wasn't exactly built with an eye for sleek lines, and with her potbelly Callum had a good few body-lengths to fall. The fall also looked pretty unappealing – Keith had angled himself around to show us the underside of his head, where the tentacles joined, and there was a horrifying thing in there that looked a lot like Polly's beak, if Polly had been the size of a few London buses.

"There we are," Enid said. "Give me the scythe."

"I really can't," Gertrude said, sounding almost apologetic. "The souls need it."

"The souls will have other work soon enough."

"They will not," Gertrude said, and her sunburnt cheeks flushed a deeper red. "A soul's work is entirely done. That's why they need releasing." She scowled. "And where's Marine Division, anyway?"

Enid petted Keith. "They ran into some complications."

Gertrude gasped. It was an actual gasp, like the heroines in some of the tatty paperbacks Callum picked up in charity shop bargain bins, and if the reaper hadn't had both hands busy I was certain she'd have pressed one to her chest.

"*Did you sink them?*" she demanded.

"I just needed them out of the way for a bit."

Gertrude looked around at me. "She sank Marine Division! And did who-knows-what with Reaper Scarborough!"

"Bad times," I said.

"So you see what I can do," Enid said. "You've no chance. Now give me the scythe, and I'll let you go. I'll ensure the boat makes it back to harbour. Save your companions, Reaper."

"Not until I know Emma's safe," Gertrude said.

"Your Emma," Enid started, then stopped and frowned. She looked around, as if she'd misplaced Emma the way someone might misplace their keys. "Hang about. What's ... something's happened."

"*Polly!*" Hilda shouted. "Polly, get your feathered bum out here and help me!"

Enid didn't even look at the pirate. "What's going on?" she demanded, but she wasn't talking to any of us. She was peering into a suddenly still patch of water, rendered sheer as glass and just as clear, plunging down into the depths. I could see seaweed, and sand, and even starfish at the bottom of it, like a rockpool on a still day. "Where's that bloody human?"

Murty surfaced straight into the middle of her looking pool, still clanging the pots together cheerily.

"*We will, we will, rock you!*" he shouted, keeping time with the clashing pots. "*We will, we will, rock you!*"

"You absolute waste of a tail," Enid hissed. "What the hell are you playing at? You think the human's going to fall in love with you if you help him? How well did that work with Hilda?"

"Don't you mention my name, you bottom-feeder!" Hilda yelled. "*Polly!*"

"Hope springs eternal," Murty said to Enid, and banged the pans a little harder. "I can't help being a romantic."

"You're a copepod on the back of an ailing gummy shark," she said. "And that's not even a shanty!"

"Doesn't matter," Murty said, grinning. "It's *loud*." He banged the pans enthusiastically. "*You got shrimp on your face, fishy disgrace—*" Enid lunged for the pans and Murty vanished underwater, dropping away before she could grab him. The

Sea Witch teetered for a moment, as if unsure whether to follow the mermaid, figure out what was happening with Emma, or continue her assault on *The Savage Squid*.

Before she should decide, Callum yelled, "*Incoming!*" and let go of the rail. He slid feet-first straight down the near-vertical deck on his side, the axe raised over one shoulder as his fleece bunched about him.

"*Callum!*" I yelled, as Keith chattered his giant parrot's beak. "Someone stop him!"

Callum gave a yelp as he slid into the water and had a very near-miss with the railing before managing to get both feet on it.

"What're you *doing?*" I yowled at him from my perch.

"Crossing my fingers," he shouted back, teetering about as he tried to get his balance.

"*Polly!*" Hilda roared, and the parrot swooped over her, dropping a bottle of cheap rum perilously close to her head.

Hilda jerked her head away and the bottle splashed into the water. "What good's that going to do, you son of a scurvy biscuit-eater? Come and bite him!"

"*Child,*" Polly said reprovingly, as they tucked their wings and dropped in pursuit of the bottle.

"*Child of a scurvy sea-damned biscuit-eater!*"

Callum had managed to get himself into a relatively secure position, and now he braced himself as he brought the axe up. He swung at the nearest tentacle, putting everything into it, and the axe rebounded so hard it just about caught him between the eyes, barely leaving a mark on the over-grown calamari. Callum yelped and fell back against the deck, almost dropping the axe.

"Oi! Enough of that!" Enid shouted. "He's just doing his job!"

"He's destroying my *boat!*" Hilda shouted back. "Callum, hit him again!"

"Don't!"

"Do it!"

Callum readied himself for another shot, but it wasn't going to do anything. The one person who might be able to do something was the reaper, and she seemed more inclined to hand her scythe over, turn to a ghost herself, and bring on the undead apocalypse than use the scythe on a living creature to really inflict damage. She'd barely tapped the orcas and she'd been paler than even a reaper should be over it.

"Polly needs someone to use their head," Polly called, but the pirate captain and the mermaid were still yelling at each other, Callum was tapping his axe against a tentacle experimentally, looking for a weak point, and Gertrude was peering at the shore, looking for Emma.

The parrot skimmed the water, the tips of their wings precariously close to the sea, and hauled for the sky again, carting the rum with them. *"Polly at sea on a dead man's chest,"* they shouted. *"Yo ho ho and a bottle of rum!"*

"No one needs a bottle of rum," I yelled at the overwrought chicken.

"Yes they do," they yelled back. *"Devil and the drink will do the rest!"*

"What?"

"Fire in the hole!" Polly shrieked. *"Fire in the hole!"*

And then I got it. "Talk *English,* you feathered loon," I shouted at them, but at the same time I launched myself off the cabin top in a flying leap. I hit the rail that surrounded the aft deck and leaped again, landing on a roving tentacle and sliding down it until I could jump clear and crash into Callum, hooking my claws into his fleece.

"Ow," he complained, but I ignored him and yelled, "Polly! Yo ho ho, matey!"

"Avast, me hearties," the parrot said. They'd landed on the deck above us, trapping the bottle in place, and now they shifted, letting it go. No one was paying any attention. Hilda was still firmly trapped in one of Keith's tentacles, shouting abuse at him, Enid, and Polly, while Enid shouted at Gertrude to hand over the scythe if she knew what was good for her.

"Grab it," I said to Callum, and he snatched the bottle up before it could vanish into the sea.

"What," he started, then realisation hit him, and he scrabbled in his pockets. He came out with Green Snake, who hissed at him. "My lighter's gone."

"What's going on there?" Enid asked, looking at us.

"*Serpent!*" Polly shrieked, flinging their wings about wildly.

"Mighty serpent," I added.

"*Serpent!*" A chorus came from the wheelhouse, and I craned around to see the rats lining the railing peering down at us.

"It's just the snake," Neecy shouted, but some of the new rats didn't seem convinced.

"*Serpent! Get it!*"

Callum hurriedly shoved Green Snake back in his pocket and yelled at Hilda, "*Light!*"

"What?" she called back.

"*Lighter!*"

"Give it!" Polly yelled, bombing toward her, then added, "Argh, serpent! Eek!"

"*Serpent!*" the new rats chorused helpfully, and Neecy shook her head.

Enid gave us an irritated look, then turned back to Gertrude. "Final chance," the Sea Witch said to the reaper. "Otherwise we're sinking the ship and taking the scythe, and the rest of you can drown."

"Well, I can't," Gertrude said. "Drown, I mean."

"So you'll moulder down here with the rest of the reapers. *Honestly.* Do you have to be so literal?"

Polly had crashed down to Hilda's side, clinging to her with their claws and shoving their head in her pocket, and now they zipped back to Callum with a heavy silver lighter in their beak. Callum grabbed it and flicked it a couple of times, then rubbed the top of it against his arm frantically.

"I do, and you can't do that," Gertrude said, glaring at Enid. "These are innocent people!"

"I mean, not really," Enid said. "And anyway, the sea has its own rules. By the time you find your way back to shore you'll be more barnacle than bone."

"Sorry, *we?*" Hilda shouted, while Callum shoved a hastily torn strip of T-shirt into the neck of the rum bottle. "Who's this *we* that's going to sink my ship, Enid? You and Keith? Because I don't see anyone else. Where's your mermaid court? They not so keen on the whole capturing reapers thing?"

"Hilda, if you don't keep your mouth shut I'll *feed* you to the mermaid court."

"Big talk for a Sea Witch without even one hanger-on."

"Alright, I am *done!*" Enid roared, her hands in fists. She straightened up, standing on the uneven surface of Keith's head, shifting with his movement. He rolled an eye up to look at her, and Callum finally got the lighter to work. He held it to the makeshift wick, and there was a horrible moment when I thought it wasn't going to catch, that even the gut-rot rum wasn't strong enough to conquer the dampness of the fabric, then it flared into life.

"Keith!" Enid said, and her face was cold and hard. "Send them six fathoms deep."

"It's not even that deep here," Hilda shouted, wriggling wildly in the grip of the tentacle.

"That is *not* the point!"

The boat groaned as Keith tightened his grip. He dropped Hilda and she splashed into the water with a yelp, the waves swallowing her. The kraken reached out to envelop the hull, and Callum hefted the bottle.

"*Fire in the hole!*" Polly shrieked.

Callum threw the bottle in a perfect arc, and Enid shouted, "*No!*" as it drove straight into the parrot beak at the centre of Keith's tentacles. The glass shattered, and flame licked across the kraken's slick, slimy skin. He gave a grumble of discontent, and ripped one of the masts out of its footing, flinging it away petulantly. The flames guttered out.

"Oh," I said.

"Well, sink me," Polly said.

Hilda had surfaced not far from the railing where Callum and I were crouched, and she scowled at us. "This is what I get for trying to help out," she said. "Sodding *mermaids* and a *Keith*." She pushed off the hull, swimming hard for the kraken's head.

"Abandon ship?" I suggested.

"Looks like," Callum said, and there was an awful crunching sound from above us as *The Savage Squid* started to splinter under the weight of the kraken's tentacles.

"Swim, me hearties!" a small voice screeched, and the rats flew past us, hitting the water like tiny, furry cannonballs.

"*I can't!*" Gertrude shouted, and finally swung her scythe. It cleaved through a tentacle as if it were the cheapest sort of processed sausage, and Keith screamed. Dark blue blood splattered the decks and flew into the sea, and he flung himself away from us, submerging with his remaining limbs flailing wildly, churning the sea into a bubbling frenzy.

"*Hold on!*" Callum yelled, clutching the railing as *The Savage Squid* bobbed upright in a surge of white water, rolling so far in the opposite direction that we almost turned over entirely. We teetered on the edge of balance for a moment, while Callum hung from the rail and I hung from him, then surged back the other way, whipping about like a spinning top. A length of tentacle still lay on the deck, twisting itself in panicked circles and splashing kraken blood over everything. A glob of it hit me and I yelped.

"I'm so sorry!" Gertrude shouted as the boat righted herself. "I didn't want to! I didn't! But she can't keep taking reapers!"

"It's okay," Callum called, straightening up. "It's okay, we'll be fine, you had to do it!"

"Thar she blows!" Polly shrieked, and Callum and I both spun to the rail. Keith rose out of the water with his dark eyes glittering with fury, a slick of swirling blood surrounding him like a storm cloud. Enid was still on his head, with Hilda trapped in a headlock next to her, and she looked at us with almost as much rage as Keith did.

"Give no quarter, my love," she hissed, and Keith surged forward.

I tried out one of Hilda's curses, but Callum beat me to it.

SON OF A SEA BISCUIT

KEITH BOILED TOWARD US, AND GERTRUDE RAISED HER SCYTHE. Callum hefted his axe, and I wondered if drowning or crushing was going to be the easiest way to end this life. It looked like it could be a combination of the two, which seemed like the worst of both worlds. The kraken's eyes were fixed on us, and I could see my reflection in the depths of the closest one, as if I'd already been swallowed. *The Savage Squid* bucked and wallowed as tentacles swept underneath her, and a couple curled over the top of us too, concentrating on the foredeck. Keith wasn't getting any closer to Gertrude than he had to. The poor old boat groaned, and started to twist out of true as the kraken tightened his grip. A plank on the deck shattered violently, and others started to join in as a fault line appeared across the midships. Keith was folding the bow to meet the stern, trussing us up like a pirate sandwich.

I looked at that enormous, furious eye, then at Callum. "You better stay alive until my next life," I told him. "You only need to manage on your own for a couple of months and I should be old enough to find you again. Think you can handle it?"

"I kept myself alive just fine before I met you."

"You've really let things slip, then, haven't you?"

"It could be argued that you've just been a bad influence on me."

"I'm not the one insists on hanging around with mermaids. And dodgy magicians. And weres. And—"

"And mouthy cats?"

"I'm not mouthy. I merely express myself clearly." *The Savage Squid* gave a terrible cry, like a living thing, and more planks on the deck shattered. The bow and the stern were both rising, and she was settling lower and lower into the water. The Sea Witch already had Hilda, Murty had vanished, and even the rats had abandoned ship. There was just us and Gertrude, who was clinging to the railing with one hand and waving her scythe at Keith in a vaguely threatening manner with the other. "Just keep yourself alive," I said.

"Gobs, what—"

I was already airborne. I jumped from the half-submerged railing to his shoulder, and from there to the slick surface of one tentacle, then another, working my way toward the kraken's maw. Enid saw me coming and moved to intercept me, but she was still trying to keep Hilda trapped in a headlock. The Sea Witch's grip slipped, and Hilda bucked wildly, tearing herself free. She promptly tackled Enid into the water, both of them screaming insults at each other, and I leaped past them unobstructed while Callum shouted behind me. I landed on the kraken's head and dived at his eye with every claw out.

Keith grumbled with surprise, and simply submerged. I squawked as I crashed into the sea instead of an eyeball, and paddled wildly until the kraken surfaced again. He'd turned so his other eye was clear of the water, and Polly came plummeting in toward it.

"*Scurvy dog!*" they shrieked, descending claws first.

Keith ducked, and *The Savage Squid* bobbed as he eased his grip on her. He grumbled again, a reverberating bass sound that I felt in my chest. The waves were coming in all directions, washing me one way and then the other, and when they swept me onto the kraken I scrambled to the top of his head and crouched there, panting. The kraken's skin was softly smooth, mottled with deep greys and greens beneath my paws.

"Gobs!" Callum shouted. "Get back here!"

"Because that seems so much safer?" I yelled back, and Keith shook himself, a shudder that rippled through his skin and sent me sliding across his head, scrabbling for grip. Enid and Hilda almost rolled over me, Hilda with her hands in the Sea Witch's kelpy hair and Enid gripping Hilda's jacket at the neck. They splashed into the water again, and Keith lifted a tentacle, tipping them back onto his mantle. They didn't even notice.

"It's a *bit* safer," Callum called.

I skated up to the top of Keith's head and shouted, "Just think of something to get us out of here!"

"I mean, I've been trying."

There was a sudden crashing of heavy bodies at the stern, and three orca burst to the surface then came slicing toward us. Keith put a tentacle out to hold them back, and Murty surged out of the water to land next to Gertrude on the foundering boat. He was panting, his hair dishevelled, and he'd lost one pan. The other was half-crushed, and he looked at it, threw it back toward the orcas with a grunt, then turned to the reaper.

"Give it to me," he said, pointing at the scythe.

"Absolutely not," she said, holding it away from him.

Keith popped an eye above the surface and I lunged at it. He ducked again, and Polly screamed, "Polly want calamari!"

"Give me the scythe," Murty insisted. "I can put it straight into his brain. Or hers." He pointed at Enid.

"No," Gertrude said firmly, and Murty grabbed for her, which made me rethink where I'd put mermaids on the intelligence scale.

"*Hey!*" Callum shouted, and scrambled along the half-submerged deck toward them. Murty was trying to tear the scythe away from Gertrude, his bulk dwarfing her, but he apparently hadn't accounted for the fact that she was a *reaper*, and she wasn't letting go.

"Murty!" Callum shouted. "Stop it!"

"It's our only chance!"

"It's my *scythe!*" Gertrude snapped. She jabbed an elbow into the mermaid's nose, and he yelped, but didn't stop. He had one hand on the scythe now, and the other on her shoulder, pushing as if he thought he might be able to pop her arm right out of its socket. Callum reached the aft stairs and scrambled up them, but he wasn't fast enough. The mermaid glanced at him, then stopped trying to get the scythe. Instead he wrapped Gertrude in a bear hug and threw himself backward into the water.

The reaper had been concentrating on holding onto her scythe, not the boat, and Murty's weight tore her free before she could recover. They plunged into the water together, the mermaid losing that suggestion of leisurewear as he went, turning sleek and sinuous as the surface closed over them. They didn't leave behind so much as a swirl of bubbles. They were simply *gone*.

Callum hesitated, still clutching the stairs, and I yelled, "*Don't!*"

He looked at me, and I'd like to think he was actually listening, but then Keith, who'd evidently decided he'd had enough of Polly and my joint feline and avian attack, submerged entirely. I floated free with a yelp, and Polly skimmed the surface of the water with their claws, barely avoiding a crash-landing. *The Savage Squid* juddered, then folded in half so fast it seemed to be happening at twice normal speed. Her remaining mast toppled sideways, barely missing me, and the wheelhouse met the forepeak with a sickening crunch. Callum threw himself clear, swimming hard in the swirling sea while it tried to pull him back, and Hilda let go of Enid, twisting in the water to watch. She gave a mourning howl.

"*My boat!*"

"The reaper!" Enid shouted. "Where's the damn reaper?"

"Like we'd tell you," I yelled back.

Enid glanced around, then snapped, "*Murty*. That—" She didn't finish the thought, just vanished below the surface. *The Savage Squid* was rapidly following her, belching air and oil and a slick of paper cups and bobbing juice bottles and cheap rum. Hilda grabbed one as it went past and opened it, taking a massive swig.

"My boat," she said again, more quietly.

"Where's the bloody kraken?" I asked, and got a wave in the face for my efforts. I spluttered.

"Gone with it, maybe," Callum said, breaststroking up to me. I scrambled onto his shoulder, shivering.

"Polly thinks not," the parrot called, swinging above us.

I looked down from my slight vantage point, and saw a shadow rising toward us, dark and vast.

"Oh, you scurvy lice-ridden bilge rat," I managed.

Callum said something worse, and then I was flung free of him as Keith breached, his massive head driving up high above us and the tangle of his legs calling whirlpools into being all around. I hit his mantle and slid down it onto the slick surface of his limbs, all my claws out as I tried to stop before I either ended up as a snack in that nasty beak, or back in the water and gobbled down by a whirlpool.

It was a near thing. I was almost washed away before my claws hooked into a clump of seaweed on his skirts. He didn't seem bothered by my being there, but that might've been because he was more concerned with Gertrude. She was standing on his head with the tip of her scythe resting in the corner of his eye. She had one bare foot on Murty's chest, there was seaweed caught around her neck, and she looked as furious as I imagined it was possible for a reaper to look.

"This is *quite* enough," she snapped. "Take us ashore at once, Keith."

Keith looked like he was inclined to do as he was told, but Enid exploded out of the water and tackled Gertrude, taking her straight off the kraken's back and into the sea again. Keith turned the eye on me, and I stared at my own reflection for a moment before he started to sink.

"Gobs, let go," Callum called, splashing toward me, then called, "Bloody hell – Green Snake!"

I looked around to see Green Snake swimming toward Keith, the brightness of the snake's body against the sea an exclamation mark in the grey day. Keith paused, swivelling an eye toward him.

"*Serpent!*" Polly screamed, at no one in particular, and Murty sat up. There was a large red mark on his face roughly the size of a reaper's fist.

"Where?" he demanded.

"Sea serpent," Polly called again.

"That's just Green Snake," Callum said, paddling after him, but Green Snake was a surprisingly quick swimmer. He scooted forward until he was eye to eye with the kraken, and there was an odd, trembling pause. Then the kraken sank, I let go and paddled free, and Green Snake swam back to Callum.

"That was helpful," I said, following him, and the snake looked back at me, giving me a little head tilt. I looked at the shore, lost behind the swells and the thick haze of sea spray, and wondered if Emma had made it. She'd been going well. Better than we were, at any rate. There was no sign of *The Savage Squid*, and I was already shivering so hard I could barely make it onto Callum's shoulder. I could feel tremors running through him, too. "Hey, Murty," I managed. "Can you sing us up a boat?"

"No," he said. He was bobbing around comfortably, his shoulders out of the water like a seal. "*The Savage Squid*'s too big for us to manage, and the dinghy's long gone. I can try to find something else, but there aren't any handy wrecks. It's going to take a bit."

"Not sure we have a bit," Callum said around chattering teeth. "We'll have to swim for it."

"Great," I said, and looked at Hilda, but she was just drinking her rum moodily. "How's your distance swimming, Callum?"

"Probably not distance enough," he said, but he hooked an arm through Hilda's, turning her onto her back. "Come on. Just float. I'll tow you."

"I don't care," she said. "Leave me out here with my ship."

"Yeah, I won't do that." He started swimming, pulling the pirate with him, and Murty drifted after us.

"You could help," I said to him. "Being a mermaid and all."

"Scurvy sodden mermaids," Hilda said to the sky.

"I *could*," Murty said. "But then you'd owe me more favours, and you haven't paid the last one yet."

"You hardly fulfilled your side of things," Callum said.

"I did," he protested. "How d'you think Emma knew how to sing a boat to the surface? Or when it was safe to?"

"Sure," I said. "What about her buddies? They could've told her."

"No, they couldn't," he said. "That's mermaid magic. I told her how to do it, and I showed her a boat she could use. I couldn't bring her up myself. You can only go against the Sea Witch so much before you end up as sushi."

"Son of a sea biscuity scurvy-ridden Sea Witch," Hilda said, and Murty gave a grunt of agreement.

"*Now we are ready to head for the Horn ...*" A chorus of small voices drifted to us through the persistent snarl of the wind and surge of the sea. "*Way, hay, roll an' go!*"

I craned to see over the waves, and glimpsed a handful of rats on a plank of wood, balancing on it easily as they rode the waves toward the shore.

"*Our boots an' our clothes boys are all in the pawn, to be rollicking randy dandy-O!*"

"Nice for some," I muttered, and Polly dropped something next to us with a splash. I jerked backward, getting a snout full of water, but it was just a chunky, bright orange life jacket.

"Polly want a bonus," they said, and swooped off again. Callum persuaded Hilda into the life jacket, which she managed without letting go of the rum bottle. His shivering had got worse, and his lips were taking on an interesting purple shade. By the time he had Hilda strapped into the jacket, Polly had brought a second one back, and he struggled into it. His fingers weren't working well enough to fasten the clips.

"Oi, fish-boy," I said to Murty. "Help him out, can't you?"

"What will you give me?" he asked, and both Green Snake and I hissed at him. He laughed, then his face changed abruptly. "Oh, Deep Ones," he said, looking down.

"What?" I demanded. "*What now?*"

Murty didn't answer, just flipped into a dive and shot away as Keith surged out of the water, the force of his arrival sending Callum and Hilda bobbing away wildly, me clinging to Callum's life jacket. The kraken had Enid wrapped in one tentacle and Gertrude in another, and they were both shouting, a continuation of whatever they'd been saying underwater.

"*All I'm trying to do is save half the bloody planet – more than half—*"

"*I have never reaped a Sea Witch before but I am **more** than happy to try—*"

Keith gave them a little shake that made both reaper and Sea Witch yelp, then held them out toward us, his dark eyes intent. It was hard to tell, but he seemed to be looking at Callum. Probably a good choice, as Hilda had barely reacted to the kraken's reappearance. She was still watching the sky, swearing occasionally at nothing in particular.

"Um, yes?" Callum said.

Keith pushed them forward again.

"Thank you?" Callum tried. "Yes. We'd like Gertrude, please."

Keith released her, and she plummeted straight down, barely having time to give a little squeak of alarm before the surface closed over her.

"Catch her!" Callum and I shouted together, and Keith jerked forward. A moment later he lifted Gertrude to the surface, his tentacle wrapped delicately around her waist. She stared at us, her pale hair plastered over her face.

"Keith, what are you *doing?*" Enid demanded, pushing ineffectively at the tentacle gripping her. "Squash the damn reaper and hand me her scythe."

"No, don't do that," Callum said. Keith looked at him and tipped his head just slightly. I peered over the bulk of the life-jacket and spotted Green Snake curled on Callum's other shoulder, his head tipped to the same angle as the kraken's.

"Dude," I said. "Are you buddies with the sea monster?"

Green Snake looked at me, then back at Keith, and did a little head bop. Keith waved back with a free tentacle.

"*Keith!*" Enid shouted, and he lowered her below the surface, cutting her shout off.

"I take back everything bad I've ever said about you," I said to Green Snake.

He looked at me again, then at Keith.

"Also you, dude," I said to the kraken. "You were just doing your job, right?"

Keith made a weird surging movement, and Callum said, "Did he ... did the giant kraken just shrug?"

"I think so," I said.

"That was definitely not on the BBC," he said.

"How about the kraken-cult rats?"

"Yeah, those either."

"Poor reporting, that," I said, and looked at Keith. "Sorry about the eye thing." He gave another little shrug, and I peered at Green Snake. "So can your buddy take us ashore?"

Green Snake looked at Keith, and the kraken reached out to us. Hilda, Callum and I all yelled as tentacles curled out of the murky sea and wrapped around the humans, lifting them (and me, still clinging to Callum's life jacket) effortlessly clear of the water and depositing us on his head. Apparently Keith didn't trust Gertrude not to sink again, as he kept a firm grip on her. Somewhere beneath the surface huge limbs moved, and we started to slide toward the shore, a bow wave building below the kraken's eyes.

"My *boat*," Hilda mourned, swigging her rum. The level in the bottle was going down fast.

"Yes, but we're not dead," I said, huddling against Callum. "That seems like a real improvement on how things were going a few minutes ago."

"But what do I do now?" she asked us. "What's a captain without a boat?"

"You'll think of something," Callum said.

"Bloody Sea Witch. I'd give her an earful, I tell you!"

Keith lifted a tentacle, and Enid popped out of the water, still firmly trussed.

"*Keith!*" Enid bawled. "You let me go right now or so help me I'll tell your mum!"

"*You!*" Hilda shouted at her. "You're just some scavenging bloody mud skipper with—"

"Don't you talk to me like that, Hilda Green! You never even said goodbye—"

"Why would I say goodbye to my *captor*—"

"I was *never*—"

Keith swivelled an eye to Green Snake, who did an encouraging little head bop. The kraken submerged Enid again and kept swimming toward the shore. Hilda stopped mid-shout, looked at us, then took a swig of rum.

"*Arr,*" she said, and wiped her nose.

"Hey," Callum said to me. "Remember the kraken in the sink in Mrs Smith's flat? When Green Snake turned up?"

"Yeah, but that was tiny," I said. "Comparatively speaking, anyway."

"Do you know how quick they grow?"

"No," I admitted. Plus reality and dimensions had been a bit squiffy at the time, what with the sorcerer's book of power running a bit feral, so who knew how big the sink had been on the inside.

Callum lifted Green Snake off his shoulder and we both stared at him. Green Snake just stared back at us. I mean, reptiles have no expression whatsoever, but he looked smug. He *definitely* looked smug.

KEITH STOPPED at the edge of the surf, his tentacles trailing into the rough water while seaweed and sand washed over us with every wave. We'd passed the rats on the way in, and they'd done three cheers for the kraken. I couldn't quite work out what the aim of their kraken cult was. Apparently not to be eaten by one, anyway.

"Cheers, dude," I said, and rubbed my nose on Keith's back. It was slimy and gritty with sand, but he deserved at least that.

"Yeah, thanks," Callum said, and Keith wrapped a tentacle around him neatly. I leaped to Callum's shoulder, and the kraken extended his tentacle as far toward the beach as it'd go, then released us. He did the same for Hilda, who just bobbed disconsolately and somewhat drunkenly in the waves until Callum grabbed her and started to tow her toward the breakers that would carry us to shore. Gertrude vanished underwater as soon as Keith released her, but all we could hope was that she could walk in as she had the night before. I stayed on Callum's shoulder, staring back at the kraken. He raised a bunch of tentacles and waved enthusiastically, and Green Snake bobbed this head in response.

"Dude," I said, and then a wave surged up and hit us, tumbling us in its wake, Callum going one way and Hilda another. I was torn off my perch and ended up turning somersaults in the wave's wake, swearing and cursing and spluttering as I struggled to the surface. I wheezed once, then another wave caught me, sweeping me under again, and one moment my snout was being ground into the sand, and the next my hindlegs were pawing at the air, then I was tumbling again, and I wondered if I'd escaped a shipwreck and a kraken just to drown in the shallows of Whitby beach.

Then a hand curled under my belly and scooped me clear of the water, my legs sticking out stiffly in fright.

"Son of a sea biscuit," I wheezed, and squinted at my rescuer.

"You're more polite than I was," Emma said. She had a starfish stuck in her hair, and there was seaweed clinging to her sopping jumper. "I think I told half the sea what it could do with itself."

"Let me catch my breath and I'll put a better effort in," I said.

21

ENOUGH WATER FOR FIVE LIVES

THE BEACH WAS A WILDERNESS OF COLD SAND AND WINDBLOWN foam, seaweed and flotsam piled up where the surf had flung it, and other than Emma it was peopled by three sodden, unhappy-looking figures, one in a three-piece suit, another in a fluffy pink onesie, and the third in a fairly normal jeans and T-shirt combo. The T-shirt said *Beets me* and had a confused beetroot on it. Emma carried me out of the surf and handed me to Callum, who shed his lifejacket and tucked me inside his fleece. It was soaking and sandy, and he was so cold I could feel the chill of his skin through his sodden T-shirt, but it was out of the wind at least.

"Are you alright?" Callum asked Emma.

She nodded jerkily, her arms wrapped around herself. "Where's Gertrude?"

Callum turned to look out to sea, and for a moment there was nothing but the heavy pound of the surf. Then the trailing edge of a wave uncovered a pale dome. We watched as it resolved itself into a head, and the reaper slowly emerged from the water, her robes swirling around her and her scythe curving over her head. Green Snake glittered on her wrist like a particularly heavy bracelet, and the waves surged past without so much as shaking her steps. Emma splashed into the water to meet her, and they stood for a moment in the shallows, their arms tight around each other and Emma's head on the reaper's shoulder.

"Aw," I said.

Callum gave a sudden, jolting shudder and said, "We need to get warm." He went to Hilda, who was sitting among the seaweed with her life jacket still on, and grabbed her arm. "Come on. Let's go."

"My boat," she complained. "That *witch*—"

"Excuse me," a deep voice said, reverberating behind us, and I craned my head out of the fleece to see a tall, cadaverous man staring at us. "Are you in need of reaping?"

"*No!*" Callum and Hilda both yelped, and she scrambled to her feet, swaying as she stood.

The man blinked at us. He was wearing heavy black robes, and a glittering scythe sliced the wind above him, condensation sparkling on the blade. The handle was twisted wood that looked like it had grown out of some distant, molten earth. "Are you sure? You seem rather near that point."

"Scupper that," Hilda said, pointing at him unsteadily. "I'll reap *you*, you … you …" She took a swig of rum. "Something."

"That's not actually possible," the man – well, reaper, presumably – said, and looked past us. He blinked, frowned, and said with a very un-reaper-like tone of disbelief, "*Reaper Leeds?*"

"Oh dear," Gertrude said.

"Grim Yorkshire," Emma said, as brightly as she could around her chattering teeth. "Wonderful to see you again, sir."

Grim Yorkshire stared at her, then at the other three figures clustered on the beach. Now I looked at them properly, they all had the same *several centuries since the last good meal* look that Gertrude had. "Reaper Scarborough," Grim Yorkshire said.

"Grim Yorkshire," the woman in the three-piece suit said.

"East Yorkshire Marine Division?"

"Here," Onesie said.

"Sir," Jeans and T-shirt said.

Grim Yorkshire's face grew even tighter, which seemed impossible considering his scant skin. "Explain yourselves. I had reports of missed souls. DHL escalate to my office if they're missed repeatedly, you know."

Reaper Scarborough straightened her sleeves. A crab fell out of one, and her thin lips twisted slightly. "I was tempted into the sea by souls that needed reaping. My scythe was taken."

Grim Yorkshire frowned, the hollows of his cheeks deep. "Why should you enter the sea? Any souls there are the responsibility of the Marine Division."

"There were so many," she said. "And they were so lost."

"But how is this possible?" His gaze shifted to the other two reapers. "Why were they not reaped?"

"Because our scythes were also taken," Onesie said. He had dark, smooth skin, startling against the pink of the suit. "As were we."

"The dead led us in," Jeans and T-shirt said. She had some cockles in her thin hair, but no one seemed keen to tell her. "There were many, and they were so desperate, yet so insistent that they could not come to us. We had to go to them." She looked at Onesie.

"It was a trap," he said. "We went to release them, and they were just never quite within reach, always one step away, until we were deep beneath the waves. Until we were lost. And then the Sea Witch took our scythes."

"She just *took* them?" Grim Yorkshire said, that same note of disbelief in his voice.

Jeans and T-shirt nodded. "In the dark, with the dead, she took our scythes."

There was silence on the beach for a long moment, just the pound of surf and the insistent wind talking.

"You have all lost your scythes." Grim Yorkshire's voice was flat when he finally spoke. "This is unprecedented. And why—"

"We've been trying to find out," Gertrude said, and Grim Yorkshire turned to look at her, his eyebrows hiked as high as his tight skin would allow. I don't think he was used to being interrupted. "Necromancers, sir. There are necromancers behind this."

"That's impossible. Necromancers were wiped out."

"Not so much," I said, and Grim Yorkshire turned his pale gaze on me. "They seem to be coming back. That's why all the extra dead in the sea, and your lot getting dragged in. Not their fault."

Grim Yorkshire considered this, then turned back to the reapers. "And so it may be. But a reaper cannot reap without a scythe."

Reaper Scarborough nodded. "Understood," she said, and opened her hands out to the sides, her face lifted to the sky. "I will be reaped."

"No, *don't*," Callum started, but Grim Yorkshire's scythe moved quicker than even I could follow. Reaper Scarborough shattered to mist, the wind dispersing it in a breath.

"Aw, this sucks," Jeans and T-shirt said, and I blinked at her.

"Sir," Gertrude said, "this was a concerted attack—"

"A reaper is not a reaper without their scythe," Grim Yorkshire said, and then Onesie was gone.

"No, *stop*," Emma cried. "They helped me!" She tried to run forward, but Gertrude held her back.

The scythe swept again, soundless other than something that was more sense than sound, a high keening note on the edge of the universe. Jeans and T-shirt was slow to leave, her form lingering for just a moment, but not protesting. And then the only reaper left was Gertrude, and Grim Yorkshire turned to look at her.

"*No*," Emma said, and stepped in front of Gertrude. "You'll have to go through me. And I'm still alive." She looked momentarily uncertain, then added, "Apparently."

Grim Yorkshire looked at her blankly. "Reaper Leeds has not lost her scythe."

"Exactly," Emma said, shaking a trembling finger at him. "So you ... you don't go near her. You *don't*."

"Reaper Leeds," Grim Yorkshire said, and Gertrude peered around Emma. They were almost the same height, and Emma was apparently trying to block all view of the reaper from her boss. "Why are you in Whitby?"

"Ah. Mini-break, sir."

"I'm sorry?"

"A small holiday," she offered.

There was silence on the beach, filled only by the parrot shouting, "Polly want a hot toddy!"

"Reaper Leeds," Grim Yorkshire said finally. "You will return with me immediately."

"Of course," Gertrude said, trying to extricate herself from behind Emma.

"No, you can't," Emma said. "Gertrude—"

"I have to," the reaper said. "It'll be fine." She held Green Snake out to Callum, her pale eyes fixed on his. He took the snake and nodded jerkily.

"We need to get off the beach," he said. "Emma, come on, we're going to freeze."

"No! No, I'm not—"

"Reaper Leeds," Grim Yorkshire said. "Do hurry up. It's …" He waved a little distastefully, searching for words. "Salty," he settled on finally.

"Sir," she said, and turned to Emma, taking her face in both bony hands. I don't know what she said – Callum turned away as if he were checking on Hilda, and I didn't clamber out of the shelter of his fleece. I'd stopped shivering, but I didn't think that was good sign. Not at all.

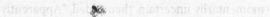

I THOUGHT the reapers would vanish off in some special reaper manner after that, but Grim Yorkshire just said, "I'm parked on the road up there," and pointed at the cliff.

We all looked in the direction of his bony finger, then Hilda said, "That's a path, not a road. Authorised vehicles only."

"I'm *Grim Reaper Yorkshire*."

"Still." She swigged rum and glared at him with her one good eye and one purple one, which was now aimed at her nose. The parrot swung down to perch on her shoulder.

"*Arr*," they said.

Grim Yorkshire looked from the pirate to the parrot, then at Gertrude. "Reaper Leeds?"

"We need to give them a lift to town," she said.

He stared at her. "What?"

"They're too cold," she said. "We can't leave them here. I'm coming, but they need to come too. Just into Whitby."

I wasn't sure what passed for swearing in reaper circles, but I'm pretty sure Grim Yorkshire indulged in some of it before he said, "Hurry up," and walked up the beach in long, smooth strides, his robes swirling around him in the hungry fingers of the fading storm.

I expected, in the absence of special reaper vanishing, Grim Yorkshire would have some sort of hearse, or at least a low-slung and fancy black car, but there was just a small, bright red, slightly squished-looking Mercedes parked where the path to the beach ended. It was a tight fit in the back for Hilda, Callum, Emma, the parrot, and me, but Gertrude immediately put the heater on high, and we sat there waiting to warm up. Grim Yorkshire *tsk*-ed.

"It's bad for the batteries, having that on so high," he said, turning the car in a tight circle that ended with our nose passing through the bank and our tail spinning neatly in thin air off the edge of the rocks. Reapers have a curious relationship to our reality, and it extends to whatever they're driving, as we'd found in a previous, rather terrifying drive with Gertrude.

"One of the new electric ones, is it, sir?" she asked.

"Yes. One does what one can for the environment," he said, and drove us straight up the face of the hill, Callum and Emma both yelping while Hilda drank more rum and muttered about scurvy scallywags.

He deposited everyone except Gertrude at the holiday cottage she and Emma had rented, and the little red car vanished off along the cobbled streets, a few people giving it doubtful looks when one side vanished into the wall of a pub and re-emerged again. We were left standing on the cobbles, dripping and salty and exhausted, and Emma gave us a wobbly smile.

"Do you want to come in? There's only one bath, but we can take turns."

Callum nodded, and looked at Hilda.

"Belay that," she said. "I'm going to the sodding pub." And she stumped off down the street, Polly wobbling on her shoulder as they tried to keep their balance. Hilda had lost both her woolly hat and her sea boots somewhere along the way, and—

"I was right," I said. "I *knew* it!"

"What?" Emma asked.

"Peg leg," I said.

"It's called a prothesis," Callum said. "Bit more advanced than a peg leg."

"Still," I said, and Callum scritched my head.

I'D HAD enough sea to last me my next five lives, but I still ended up lying in a kitchen sink full of warm water for the next half-hour. Green Snake swam in circles around me for a while, then draped himself over my back and put his head on mine, between my ears. I was too tired to bother shaking him off, so we just sat there like models for a really shoddy totem pole and watched Callum and Emma being polite at each other. There was a lot of, "no, after you" going on, until Emma clenched both fists and yelled, "For God's sake, Callum, just go and have a shower first, can't you? Then I can have a bath without knowing you're *waiting!*"

"Right," he said. "Got it." He vanished into the bathroom and re-emerged wrapped in about three towels not much later, still looking pale but at least no longer smelling of dead fish, although the same couldn't be said of the bundle of wet clothes he brought out with him.

Emma handed him a pale blue bathrobe with appliquéd kittens peeking out of the pockets, as well as a hot water bottle, and said, "Kettle's just boiled." Then she marched past him into the bathroom, closing the door a little more firmly than was probably required.

Callum shoved his clothes into a washing machine that

was tucked under the kitchen worktop and looked at me and Green Snake. "Warmer?" he asked me.

"Getting there," I said. "Be better with some chicken."

"Sure you would." He pulled the bathrobe on over his towels, filled the hot water bottle, then flicked the kettle on to boil again and went hunting through the cupboards to find a mug.

Emma was in the bathroom for a long time. Callum lit a dinky wood-burning stove that was tucked into the living area that took up half of the downstairs of the cottage, then shouted to her to throw her clothes out to him. She went into rather graphic detail of what he could do if he thought she was getting out of the bath, so he just put his own clothes on to wash and finished making his tea. I eventually climbed out of the sink and he wrapped me in a towel, setting me on the rug in front of the wood burner. The fire was framed by a small sofa and a couple of chairs, with a white-painted coffee table between them, and a round wooden table and four wooden chairs separated the living area from the kitchen. There was a lot of white paint and blue and red trim going on about the place, as well as driftwood and bits of rope in some sort of seaside theme that was entirely unlike my experience of the actual seaside.

But it was quiet, and dry, and by the time Emma emerged in a cloud of steam, looking very pink, the wood burner had got so carried away Callum and I were arguing about opening a window.

"My fur's still wet," I protested.

"You're probably sweating."

"I don't *sweat*."

"Gobs, it's like a sauna in here."

"Maybe I like saunas."

Emma looked at both of us, shook her head, and went up a little set of stairs that switchbacked up to the next floor, presumably to the bedroom. The cottage was a compact little place, all uneven floors and low ceilings, tucked into the rumpled fabric of Whitby's old streets, and it smelled of sweetshop fudge and sunblock and slow mornings. The only window on this floor was the one we were arguing about, behind the sofa Callum was currently sprawled on in his fetching blue bathrobe. Over my protests, he opened it a crack, then went to put the kettle on again.

By the time Emma came back downstairs in leggings and a heavy woollen jumper, Callum had two mugs of tea on the coffee table, along with a packet of biscuits he'd found in one of the cupboards.

"I gave Gobs some of the ham from the fridge," he said. "He was being a pain."

"*Hey!*"

"I'll replace it," Callum added.

Emma shook her head and sat down in one of the chairs, tucking her feet under her. She was either wearing very big socks, or three pairs of them. "It's fine. I'm going as soon as I pack anyway."

"Back to Leeds?" Callum asked.

She nodded. "I need to make sure Gertrude's alright."

"Do you know where Grim Yorkshire's taken her, then?" I asked.

She shook her head. "I don't even know where he has his … offices." She frowned. "Or crypt, or whatever he uses. But if I'm home then Gertrude will come back there. Or she'll call, or whatever, but I need to be there for when she does."

"Of course," Callum said. "And I'm sure she'll be fine."

"*She* didn't lose her scythe," I agreed.

"I hope that's enough," Emma said. "I don't think Grim Yorkshire is very open to mini-breaks."

Callum made some mumbled protest about being sure

that wasn't a problem, then we fell into an uneasy silence that wasn't helping anyone. I shifted a little closer to the fire and said, "So, what happened to you, then? In the sea?"

Emma took a biscuit and nibbled on it. Her hair was drying frizzy and a bit wild, and her eyes were red and puffy-looking. "I thought I was going to drown," she said, matter-of-factly.

"I'm so sorry," Callum started, and she waved at him.

"*I'm* sorry. I never should have insisted we go along the beach in the middle of the perfect bloody storm. If I'd just waited, Gertrude would have probably come back, and none of us would've got into this situation."

"Well," Callum started, and I spoke over him before he could insist on taking responsibility for the Black Dogs, the swim, and likely the storm besides.

"Was it the Sea Witch who grabbed you?" I asked.

Emma frowned. "Her name was Enid."

"That's the one," I said. "Hangs about with a big squid."

"I don't know about that. But when I was with her I could breathe, and it wasn't cold, and I had a *tail*." She looked at us with wide eyes. "A mermaid one, I mean, not like a little rat tail or something."

"Handy," I said.

"Well, yeah. If it was that or drowning, the tail seemed pretty good. But she wouldn't let me go back to the beach. I mean, she said I could later, if I really wanted to – she seemed to think I'd end up preferring to stay down there with her rather than come back to Gertrude." Emma shook her head. "Anyhow, she put me in this cavern, way down deep somewhere. There was an air pocket in it, so I could breathe when she wasn't around, and those other poor reapers were just sitting on the sand outside it playing with starfish and moping. She told me I couldn't get out on my own, and when I managed to get the reapers to come in and at least not let the crabs nibble on them so much—"

"Ew," Callum and I both said.

"I don't think they really feel it," Emma said, taking a sip of tea. "Anyhow, they said the same – that they didn't even know *where* the shore was, or how deep we really were, and I'd never make it if I tried to escape. The cavern wasn't cold, and there was fresh water, and Enid brought me food and so on, so I suppose I could've just stayed there indefinitely." She frowned. "There was even furniture."

"Furniture?" Callum asked.

"I think from a boat or something. It was a bit damp, but it was fine. And there were all these glowing fish swimming about the place, and luminous algae or something on the walls, so it wasn't dark."

"I suppose that's not so bad," I said.

"No," she agreed. "But I didn't want to *stay*. I tried to get the reapers to help me figure out how to escape, but all they were worried about were their scythes, and I didn't see anyone else until this other mermaid turned up. Or merman, I suppose."

"Murty?" Callum asked.

"That was him. He showed me this little fishing boat not far from the cavern, and gave me a song to sing it up with. He said the singing would stop me drowning if I did it right, but that I had to wait until he came back and told me it was the right time. So I taught the reapers the song, so that we could all get out, and when he came back that's what we did." She took another biscuit and looked at it thoughtfully. "It was all very odd."

And considering she lived with a reaper, that was saying a lot.

ONCE HIS CLOTHES had gone through the dryer, Callum helped Emma pack up the cottage and carry everything to a little white half-size van parked in the street. Green Snake and I stayed wrapped in our towel in front of the wood burner until Callum tipped us out unceremoniously.

"Unfair," I said.

"Lazy," he countered.

"Cat."

Emma checked the fridge then looked at us. "What are you doing, then? Are you coming back to Leeds?"

Callum scratched his chin, stubble rasping under his fingertips, then said, "Yes. I think we have to."

"Deep Ones know it's no bloody safer here," I said. "Between the mermaids and the cats and the bloody gulls."

"Gulls?" she asked.

"Vicious, bloodthirsty—"

"We're going to check on Hilda first," Callum said. "Make sure she's okay, then yes. We'll head back to Leeds."

"Do you need a lift?" she asked.

"No, our car seems to be running at the moment." He hesitated, examining her. "Are you alright to drive back?"

"Of course," she said, lifting her chin. "Come on, then." She led the way out into the street and locked the door behind us, then dropped the key back into the letterbox. I could smell the worry on her, burnt like scars into her skin, and she bent to scratch me between the ears. "Come and see me when you get there?"

"First stop," Callum said, and she patted his arm and headed off to the van, walking with her back very straight and her hair blowing even wilder in the wind as it snaked in off the sea. Callum looked at me.

"I suppose we have to talk to the pirate now," I said.

"If she *can* talk. That was a lot of rum."

"Especially for someone with one leg." I accepted a lift

from him, since everything was hurting. My scratched sides, my weary legs, my poor abused tail, and my snout, which I was certain still had sand in it.

The life of a PI was seeming rather easier than that of a pirate, I had to say.

22

SOMEWHERE LESS MERMAID-Y

WE MADE A STOP FOR MORE CIGARETTES AND SOME DRIED-OUT, packaged chicken, then found Hilda sitting by the fire in the faun's pub, a puddle drying slowly on the floor beneath her chair and a collection of empty glasses of varying sizes expanding across the table in front of her. The faun jabbed a finger at us as we came in.

"Are you here to collect her? Because she bloody well needs it."

"We can try," Callum said.

"*You* can try," I said, and the faun glared at me.

"I see you, troublemaker. I've got my eye on you."

"Alright, don't get your trotters in a twist."

"You—"

"Sorry," Callum said. "It's been a rough day."

"A rough day? What d'you think running a pub in this sinkhole's like, then? I could tell you stories, I could." The faun slammed a glass down on the bar and scowled at Callum. "I could!"

"I can see that," Callum said, and tried for the dimples, but either he was too tired or fauns are immune to dimples, because the bar-faun just grumbled and went to collect glasses from a table in the corner, where three dryads were doing shots of something luminously green.

Hilda looked up at us as Callum sat down opposite her. "Alright, Swab," she said, and took a mouthful of beer. "D'you have any rum? Shep's cut me off on the good stuff."

"Sorry," Callum said.

"Probably for the best," Hilda said with a sigh, and leaned back in her chair. Polly had been perched on a shelf over the fire, and now they fluttered down to join us.

"Polly says this place is a mess," they observed, moving a couple of glasses with their beak.

There was silence for a moment, then I said, "Well, if no one else is saying anything – care to clear up the whole Black Dog thing? How have *you* got Black Dogs?"

Hilda took another swig of beer and wiped her mouth with the back of her hand. "You do enough trades with people, you can get most anything."

I wondered what exactly you'd have to trade to end up with *one* huge scary beast that looked like it had been cut from the void, let alone four of the things, and Callum said, "So why did you set them to keep us in town?"

"Someone asked me to."

"Who?"

"Same person who told me to slip old Bob a few quid to let me take you off his hands."

"Excuse me," I said. "Did you *buy* us?"

She shrugged. "Couldn't very well pressgang you when old gangly here doesn't even drink." She thought about it. "Also, it's illegal, but whatever."

"What—" Callum started, and she raised a hand, heavy rings glinting in the light of the fire.

"Your troll mate from Leeds got Bob to give you a safe

place, right. But Bob's not exactly making his millions off the boarding house, so when he's got anyone able-bodied, he gets them working for him. Brings in a few quid, and when people are short of rent it's a good arrangement all round, right?"

"Right," Callum said, frowning.

"But you two … you two." She shook her head. "Tall skinny human with a heavy side of Folk, and some smart-mouthed black cat? You're not subtle, you know. And people talk." She considered it. "Bob was getting jumpy. He was worried it might bring his boarding house into disrepute if there ended up being a *situation.*"

"He was worried about the reputation of his *boarding house?*" I demanded. "It needs cleansing with fire, and that's coming from someone who used to live in a building that had holes in dimensions beneath the stairs."

Hilda coughed phlegmily and took a pipe from her pocket. She tapped sand out of it onto the table, and Callum offered her a cigarette instead. "No," she said. "Those things'll kill you."

Polly and I exchanged glances across the table, and Green Snake investigated a shot glass, flicking his tongue at the dregs. Callum pulled him back out and put the cigarettes away again, finding Hilda's silver lighter. He slid it across the table to her.

"Keep it. Call it a souvenir." She slid it back, then pointed the pipe stem at me. "Bob's house is a safe place. It's *unnoticed,* and it offers a certain protection to those who need it. But you were too high profile, and kept wandering about the place like you didn't even care about being seen. Bloody risky to the other residents. He didn't want to just kick you out, since that troll of yours is a mate from way back apparently, but we were having a wee tipple one night and he mentioned he was worried."

"On the boat," I said, thinking of Merv and his eaves-dropping.

Hilda sighed. "On my boat."

"Who asked you to take us on, then?" Callum asked.

"Or paid you to?" I put in.

"Asked, paid." She shrugged. "Same difference, really."

"Not really," I said.

"Polly watched you," the parrot said. "Polly saw *others* watching you."

"Who?" Callum asked.

The parrot shrugged. "Cats. Folk. Even humans. You're *noticeable.*"

"And noticeable means valuable," Hilda said. "So I asked some questions from some contacts in Leeds, and heard someone other than your troll mate was very interested in keeping track of you. More than one someone, actually, so I went with who I thought could pay the most."

"Oh, crusty bilge rats," I said.

Hilda shrugged. "Worked for Bob. Worked for me. Worked for you. All they wanted was you kept safe. So I set the Dogs to watch you, and offered you a place on board so you weren't roaming the streets and making things awkward for everyone." She sighed. "I'd've charged more if I'd realised you were going to lose me my sodding boat, though."

"I'm really sorry," Callum started, and I cuffed his hand. "*Ow.*" He poked me in the side, and I shuffled further around the table, glaring at Hilda.

"Who was it paid you? Was it the damn magician?"

"I respect my clients' privacy," she said, getting up. "Come on, Pol. Let's go and see if Bob's got some whisky in, since *someone won't serve me.*" She shouted the last few words, and the faun made a rude gesture in her direction. She growled.

"We'll come too," Callum said.

"We will?" I asked.

"We've got to sleep somewhere," he said, getting up. "Or get the car. One of the two."

"Yeah, if we can leave town without falling into a sinkhole or having our tails nipped," I said, and glared at Hilda as she led the way to the door. "How about that? Are you calling off the Dogs now?"

"If you want. Been a bit useful, though, haven't they?"

I couldn't really argue that.

We went back out into the last weary throes of the storm, the afternoon light fading and early lights coming on in the shops and pubs and homes, everyone turning inward and away from the relentless, endless sea.

BOB HAD RENTED our attic room out, but he offered us the cellar, which was, in his words, in need of a little airing. Callum opened the door and we took one look over the threshold into the dry, nerve-itching dark below, filled with little whispers and scrapings, and asked for the car keys back instead. Bob didn't seem surprised, and along with the keys he gave Callum a pair of old seaboots to wear, since Callum had lost his second set of footwear in twenty-four hours, and it wasn't exactly the weather for bare feet.

We left our ex-landlord and ex-pirate captain sitting at the kitchen table, swapping a bottle between them and singing snatches of shanties here and there. Bob was showing Hilda his ship in a bottle collection and promising to make a model of *The Savage Squid*, which I wasn't sure was particularly comforting, but the thought was there. The door to the front room cracked open as we went to leave, and a small green eye looked at us.

"You've a message," its owner said.

"We do?" Callum asked, and I tried to catch a whiff of

whoever lurked beyond the door. All I could smell was salt and dust and small quiet places.

"Wait," they said, and closed the door. Callum and I looked at each other.

"Gerry?" I suggested. "Since we lost the new phone, too. Maybe he tried to text you back."

"Maybe," Callum agreed, then the door cracked open again. A small hairy hand appeared, clutching a neatly folded sheet of pink paper. "Thanks," Callum said, taking it.

"Are you leaving?" the message-taker asked.

"Seems like time," Callum said. He had the paper pinched in his fingers, not opening it.

"Wait." The door was pushed to for a moment, then opened just far enough to allow the hand back through, clutching something. "Here."

Callum held his own hand out hesitantly, and a piece of Whitby jet, polished as dark and glossy as the Black Dogs themselves, dropped into his palm. I craned my head up to look at it, and he said, "Thank you?"

"*Bon voyage*. Nice meeting you. Come back soon," the room's occupant said, and the door clicked closed again. Callum looked at me, and I shrugged.

"Whitby," I said.

"Whitby," he agreed, and we headed back out into the last of the day.

The Rover was still parked where we'd left it earlier, and started first time again. The pink ribbon was gone, but a small pink shell had been left in its place, and Callum put it in his pocket along with the piece of Whitby jet. He turned the heater up a bit (it seemed to be feeding less exhaust fumes into the car than it usually did), and looked at me.

"What's the message?" I asked, and he took the slip of pink paper from his pocket and unfolded it. I put my paws on the handbrake so I could see it, catching the small, cosy whiff of the paws that had smoothed the paper down. There were pink hearts printed on one corner, and the message had been written in pencil, in careful block capitals.

Strawberry goes away and I thinks someone steals him. I hires you.

There was no mobile number written under it, no email address, no name, but I only knew one Strawberry.

"SharkDog?" I said. "Poppy thinks someone's stolen SharkDog and she wants us to find the bloody thing? What's she playing at?"

Callum just kept staring at the note.

"Callum?" I said, and he finally looked at me. His pale face looked even paler than usual, lines drawn tight around his jaw. I looked from him back to the paper, then at Green Snake, who had wriggled out of the pocket of Callum's fleece to investigate the note. Even he looked anxious. "It's not SharkDog at all, is it?"

"I don't think so," Callum said.

"Is this another one of your codes?"

"No," he said. "And Gerry didn't want Poppy or William knowing where we were. Too risky."

I looked back at the note and its careful printing. "Hairy Maclary back there seemed to have a pretty good grasp of the English language."

"They did," Callum said.

"Not that likely they'd carelessly be popping esses around the place. Unlike our Poppy."

"No." Callum ran both hands back through his hair, rubbing at his scalp as if to get his brain moving again, but it wasn't like we had much to think about.

We were both silent for a little while anyway, then I said, "All being here seems to have got me is sand in my ears and a run-in with the Watch. Nothing's changed, has it? We've not escaped anything. Nothing's died down."

"Not by the sound of things," he said. "Every message I got from Gerry was that things were getting more dangerous, and you know what he was like last time we saw him."

"Yeah. I've never seen a stressed troll before."

"Exactly. And now we know the necromancers are still about, and still working on whatever they're doing, and Ms Jones is still ... well, whatever she is. Not able to help, anyway. Then that weird call from Gerry, and now this? If anything's changed, it's for the worse."

My stomach gave a slow, sickening twist at the thought of the void clutching at my back in our old flat, but all I said was, "About bloody time we went back, anyway. If I have to eat another herring I'm going to start sprouting scales."

Callum scritched me between my ears. "Are you sure?"

"Are *you* sure? It's North stuff too, you know."

He shrugged. "Staying away seems to be making things worse."

I sighed. "Do we get another phone first?"

Callum took his wallet out of his jeans and checked inside. "Not if we want petrol," he said, peeling some seaweed out of it.

"So we're going back blind?"

"Pretty much," he said, and we both sat there for a little longer, looking out past the mini golf on the top of the cliff to the white-streaked sea beyond. The clouds were thinning along the horizon, and people were venturing out to walk along the hilltop paths, dogs bouncing in the wind.

Finally Callum put the car in gear and we puttered down into town, turning to follow the one-lane road that ran down the wharf toward the pier. A farewell lap, I suppose, or it would've been if Callum hadn't suddenly pulled us up onto the kerb and jammed the brakes on.

"Don't play with the mermaids!" I yelled at him, but he was already jogging around the car to where Murty was tying a

line off on a bollard. "Hairy squid rings," I muttered. He'd left his door ajar, so I squeezed out the gap and trotted after him, wincing as the scratches in my sides set up a chorus of stinging.

Murty straightened up as Callum reached him. "You made it," he said.

Callum didn't answer. He was staring past the mermaid, down at the water.

"Not many thanks to you," I said to Murty. "You were good as useless."

He pressed a hand to his chest. "Cats are so *harsh*."

"Mermaids are so wet."

"That's …" Callum said, then apparently ran out of words, and just pointed. I padded to the edge of the dock and looked down. Below us was a boat. It was a ragged boat, with broken bits on the decks and no masts, and one of the deck lockers was missing, but it was very much a floating boat. Enid stepped out of the ruins of the wheelhouse and scowled at us.

"Thought you lot would be gone already."

"We're going," I said, and hooked my claws into Callum's jeans, giving them a tug. "Aren't we?"

"Um," he said, and looked from the boat to Enid.

"What?" she asked. "Never seen a boat re-floated before?"

"But that's …" Callum looked at Murty. "It's only been a few hours!"

Enid shrugged. "Keith's holding it up, to be fair. But it'll do till we can get some repairs done."

"The Sea Witch has a soft spot for the pirate captain," Murty said in a stage whisper, and Enid scowled at him.

"Move your tail, Murt. There's some herrings in the bilge we need to get out before we can patch her, and Keith can't hold her up forever. He gets bored, and we don't want him wandering off before she can float on her own."

Murty laughed. "Sure, sure."

"You lost me my prisoners. You *owe* me."

"I know," he said cheerfully, and looked at Callum. "Hang about. I've got something for you." He jumped to the deck lightly and ran for the forward cabin, while Callum and I looked at each other.

"Do we run?" I suggested.

"Probably should," he said, taking the fresh pack of cigarettes from his pocket. "But let's see what it is first."

"We're not having a baby kraken. We don't even have a sink."

"Hey," Enid said, and we both looked at her. "It wasn't anything personal, you know. With the reaper. It's just ... no one looks out for the sea."

"You can't end the world over it," Callum said.

"What if the world ends anyway? What's a world when its sea dies?"

Callum lit his cigarette, looking at Hilda's silver lighter. "I don't know. Maybe that's the way it does end. But you don't call down an apocalypse of old gods on the off chance."

"*Apocalypse*," Enid said. "Why are humans so dramatic?" She scratched her neck, then said, "Did Hilda mention me?"

"There was a lot of swearing," I said. "Your name might've been in there."

"Right," she said. "Yeah." She turned as Murty ambled back on deck with something bundled in one hand. "Would you get a move on? You'll be telling me you're not working nights next."

"I'm not," he said, and stood on his tiptoes to pass Callum the bundle. Callum crouched to grab it. "There you go," the mermaid said. "Good luck and all."

"Cheers," Callum said, staying crouched as he looked at Enid. "Do you still have the scythes?"

"No," she said. "The dead took them. My part was to allow the reapers passage, and to confuse the currents so that they couldn't get out. Then once they gave up hope, to take their scythes."

"How do you get a scythe off a reaper?" I asked. "How is that even possible?"

She shrugged. "With hope, we can believe anything is possible. But when it's lost, we believe the same – just about the wrong things."

I didn't have an answer to that.

Callum blew smoke over his lip and said, "And then?"

"And then the dead took the scythes to wherever they wanted, and I kept the reapers." She frowned. "I didn't really want them, to be honest. Give me a human any day. Far more fun. The reapers just sat around complaining that the fish were nibbling on them."

"Ew," I said.

"Where are the dead now, then?" Callum asked.

"I don't know. That bit wasn't my business."

They stared at each other for a long moment, then he nodded. "Right." He looked at me. "I think we best head off, then."

I stared at the bundle in his hands. "Is that your coat?"

Callum looked at it and grinned. "It is, yeah."

"Oh for the Deep Ones' sakes – you *had* to save that?" I said to Murty.

"He likes it," Murty said with a shrug.

"I hope hermit crabs nest in your toes."

"I'll miss you too," he said, grinning, and winked at Callum. "I won't forget you owe me that favour, though." He didn't wait for an answer, just grabbed a piece of wood in one hand and a hammer in the other, and jumped into the water on the far side of the boat.

"Oh, that's just great," I said. "*Just great.*"

"It'll be fine," Callum said.

"Working-on-a-pirate-boat fine? Whitby fine? Or, I don't know, being-stalked-by-a-magician fine?"

"One of those."

Enid looked at us. "You're an odd lot, you are."

"Says the squid-whisperer," I snapped.

"That was your snake," she said, pointing at Green Snake, who was peering out of the sleeve of Callum's fleece.

"Don't help the necromancers again," Callum said to her. "If nothing else, there's no room in their world for Hildas."

Enid nodded, looking back at the boat. "I've got stuff to do. Look out for yourselves. Bloody humans. Bloody cats." She vanished into the forward cabin, still muttering. We stayed where we were for a moment longer, and Callum shook his coat out, checking the pockets. He came up with a folded bundle of notes and looked at me.

"Fine," I said. "But I bet he'll charge you a favour for that, too."

"But at least we've got enough for petrol to get to Leeds," he said, straightening up and heading back to the car.

"How much have we actually got?" I asked, following him. "Can we get to, I don't know – Spain? Greece? Somewhere less mermaid-y?"

"Leeds isn't mermaid-y."

"It's very magician-y, though," I said, jumping over him to the passenger side. "That's no better."

Not that we had much choice. Not with Gerry missing. Not with Poppy asking for help. Some things are bigger than worrying about your own skin.

The one-way street took us past the fake medium's trailer, past the fish'n'chip shops and the amusement arcades chattering with lights and music, past the gulls perched on the streetlamps with their beaks pointed at the wind, and on to the pub at the end of the street with its strange little collection of kiddies' rides and its weather-torn picnic tables.

Callum stopped at the head of the slipway that ran down to the beach, and I put my paws on the dashboard so I could see out the windscreen. Ahead, the harbour walls and the long piers held back the endless, yearning sea, and the stern, sturdy forms of the lighthouses and the stocky beacons called their warnings into the oncoming night, marking both the safe passage home and the raging, dangerous shore. The green sea rolled on to the distant horizon, holding secrets deep in its belly, and behind us the last of the sun broke through the low cloud, shattering gold onto the white caps of the waves and burnishing the beacons and the old walls of the town, painting magic across the world.

Callum put one hand on my back and said, "You really want to try for Spain?"

"Eh," I said. "Bet they don't have Dreamies."

Callum laughed, and as that moment of gilded light faded, stolen behind the clouds, we turned our backs to the sea and left Whitby, left its mermaids and pirates and Black Dogs to their wild beaches and strange waters. Ahead were familiar streets and familiar dangers, but some things you can't run from. And maybe, when the time comes to stop running, you find that you're just where you're meant to be, with just who you're meant to be with. Because they were the ones who always had your back, no matter where you ran. They were, in fact, the ones you were running *to*, without even realising it. And with them, you could face anything.

I turned my snout to catch the last of the sun, and Green Snake flopped out of Callum's sleeve and landed on my back. He tried to wrap around me again, like my own personal scaly scarf, and I hissed and flicked him into the footwell. He lunged at me, trying to nip my tail, and I yowled, "*Callum!*"

"Gods," Callum said, and jabbed the long-broken radio. "Please have fixed this."

They hadn't.

THANK YOU

Lovely people, thank you so much for joining me in this romp across the cold waters of the North Sea. Or Whitby, at least. Whether this is your first outing with Leeds' most dubious PI team or your sixth, I hope so much that you enjoyed it.

There's one more book in this series to go, and it's coming out very soon indeed (northern summer 2023). If you haven't read the previous instalments, I recommend heading back and starting with the very first one before book seven arrives, as all things are leading back to Dimly ...

And in the meantime, if you did enjoy this swashbuckling tale of Keiths, mermaids, and ferocious parrots, I'd very much appreciate you taking the time to pop a review up at your favourite retailer or Goodreads.

Reviews are like the best sort of pirate treasure to writers. We not only hoard them greedily (*arrr*), they also fuel our next voyage. More reviews mean more people see our books in online stores, meaning more people buy them, so giving us the ability to write more stories and send them back out to you, lovely people. A most excellent sort of treasure indeed.

And if you'd like to send me a copy of your review, a list of favourite pirate curses, cat photos, or anything else, drop me a message at kim@kmwatt.com. I'd love to hear from you!

Until next time,

Read on!

Kim

(And head over the page for more adventures, plus to discover just who's going to win the battle of *The Savage Squid* ...)

STRANGE STORIES FOR A
STRANGE WORLD

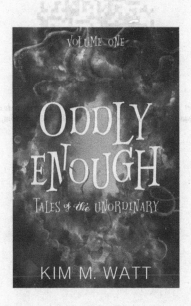

Old gods rise. A jewel thief falls. A late night wish is tragically granted ...

And somewhere, on the edge of the dark or in the belly of an unknown machine, stories are born. Stories of heroic chickens and lost demons, dangerous golf games and pies full of fury. Stories of magic and uncertainty. Stories of the unordinary.

Come on in and discover them. Don't worry, it's perfectly safe. This world is just like yours.

Well, almost. But there's nothing to fear here.

Except maybe the sheep. I'd watch the sheep ...

Get your copy of Oddly Enough by scanning the code or heading to: https://readerlinks.com/l/3356468/g6bmpg

NO ONE PIRATES A PIRATE

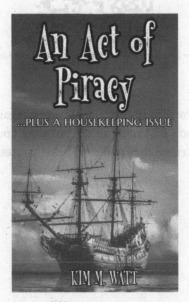

Hilda gives no quarter ...

What's a captain without her ship?

Really, really displeased, mostly. And highly motivated. Hilda's getting her boat back, even though there's not a soul in Whitby who dares risk angering the Sea Witch by helping her.

But it's not as if that's going to stop her. She has a parrot, a stolen dinghy, and some inside knowledge regarding kraken...

Scan the code to grab your copy, or head to the link below:
https://readerlinks.com/l/3355959/g6pg

(I've also thrown in an extra short story regarding Callum and Gobbelino's first night in the boarding house. Let's just say, there's a reason they preferred being pirates.)

ACKNOWLEDGMENTS

Firstly, I feel I should apologise to Whitby for both tweaking the town layout and casting aspersions on their boarding houses and pirate cruises. I adore Whitby, and not a single visit has resulted in my being abducted by mermaids, threatened by a kraken cult, or stalked by Black Dogs. It is, in fact, a completely beautiful, atmospheric, and interesting town, and you should go there if you get the chance.

And then I need to say thank *you*, lovely reader. My writing schedule has been erratic and less than predictable, so thank you so much for sticking with me. Thank you for being so invested in snarky cats and scruffy PIs and mysterious Green Snakes. Without you, none of these stories would exist, because they may start in my head, but they finish in yours.

As always, to my beta readers, who are never afraid to poke my early drafts and point out the leaky bits, but who are also so quick to tell me the parts that made them laugh. Thank you. Writing can be weird and lonely, but you make it weird in a good way, and much less lonely.

To my wonderful editor Lynda Dietz, of Easy Reader Editing, who is funny, talented, and a genuinely wonderful friend. I can't imagine going thorough the publishing process without your support. As always, all good grammar praise goes to Lynda, while all mistakes are mine. Find her at www.

easyreaderediting.com for fantastic blogs on editing, grammar, and other writer-y stuff.

Thank you to Monika from Ampersand Cover Design, who takes the concept of pirates and mermaids in the North Sea and somehow creates a cover that makes sense. Find her at www.ampersandbookcovers.com

And maybe last here, but never anywhere else, thank you to my wonderful friends, online and off, who have listened to me complain about misbehaving characters and U-turning plots and the problems of herding cats, and have never once said, *maybe you should write something a little more ... sensible.* That takes discipline.

Thank you all for coming on this strange adventure with me.

Arr.

Kim x

ABOUT THE AUTHOR

Hello lovely person. I'm Kim, and in addition to the Gobbelino London tales I also write other funny, magical books that offer a little escape from the serious stuff in the world and hopefully leave you a wee bit happier than you were when you started. Because happiness, like friendship, matters.

I write about baking-obsessed reapers setting up baby ghoul petting cafes, and ladies of a certain age joining the Apocalypse on their Vespas. I write about friendship, and loyalty, and lifting each other up, and the importance of tea and cake.

But mostly I write about how wonderful people (of all species) can really be.

If you'd like to find out the latest on new books in *The Gobbelino London* series, as well as discover other books and series, giveaways, extra reading, and more, jump on over to www.kmwatt.com and check everything out there.

Read on!

🅰 amazon.com/Kim-M-Watt/e/B07JMHRBMC
🅕 facebook.com/KimMWatt
🅞 instagram.com/kimmwatt
🅨 twitter.com/kimmwatt
▶ youtube.com/@KimMWatt-yd1qb
🆑 bookbub.com/profile/kim-m-watt
🅖 goodreads.com/kimmwatt

ALSO BY KIM M. WATT

The Gobbelino London, PI series

"This series is a wonderful combination of humor and suspense that won't let you stop until you've finished the book. Fair warning, don't plan on doing anything else until you're done ..."

– Goodreads reviewer

The Beaufort Scales Series (cozy mysteries with dragons)

"The addition of covert dragons to a cozy mystery is perfect ... and the dragons are as quirky and entertaining as the rest of the slightly eccentric residents of Toot Hansell."

– Goodreads reviewer

What Happened in London (a DI Adams prequel)

"This book will grip you within its story and not let go so be prepared going in with snacks and caffeine because you won't want to put it down."

– Goodreads reviewer

Short Story Collections

Oddly Enough: Tales of the Unordinary, Volume One

"The stories are quirky, charming, hilarious, and some are all of the above without a dud amongst the bunch ..."

– Goodreads reviewer

More free stories!

The Cat Did It

Of course the cat did it. Sneaky, snarky, and up to no good – that's the cats in this feline collection, which you can grab free by signing up to the newsletter. Just remember – if the cat winks, always wink back ...

The Tales of Beaufort Scales

A collection of dragonish tales from the world of Toot Hansell, as an extra welcome gift for joining the newsletter. Just mind the abominable snow porcupine ...

CPSIA information can be obtained
at www.ICGtesting.com
Printed in the USA
BVHW081026120523
664078BV00012B/241

9 781738 585434